PRAISE FOR DAVE

'gritty with well-realised characters and a taut
plot ... outstanding' *Canberra Weekly*
'fast-paced and intriguing ... Aussie noir at its best' *Better Reading*
'superbly plotted crime fiction' *The Burgeoning Bookshelf*
'Australian crime writing at its apex' *Australian Book Review*
'a pitch-perfect crime thriller' *Jim Skiathitis, The Atlantics*
'like riding the perfect wave' *Michael Robotham*
'a real page turner' *Fremantle Shipping News*
'keeps things moving at a lickety-split' *Sydney Morning Herald*
'dense with colourful vernacular and Aussie humour' *Sun-Herald*
'nail-biting' *Have-a-Go News*
'sophisticated crime fiction with a WA flavour' *Sunday Times*
'as Australian as a Tim Tam' *Adelaide Advertiser*
'as snappy as a nutcracker' *Books+Publishing*
'a great read!' *Launceston Examiner*
'gripping' *Herald Sun*
'a witty, enjoyable tale' *Murder, Mayhem and Long Dogs*
'an enjoyable, clever mystery ... terrific fun' *Canberra Weekly*
'a fun, entertaining story ... great supporting characters' *AustCrime*

Ned Kelly Award for Best Crime Fiction
(Longlisted 2018, Shortlisted 2020)

International Dublin Literary Award 2019
(Longlisted 2018)

Ned Kelly Award for Best Fiction (Winner 2016)

Western Australian State Living Treasure (2016)

Western Australian Premier's Book Award (Co-winner 1996)

DAVE WARNER SUMMER OF BLOOD

 FREMANTLE PRESS

This book is dedicated to my teenage garage-band mates Michael O'Rourke and the late Alan Howard, and to all those artists who made 1967 the greatest music summer of them all.

CONTENTS

1 TALES OF BRAVE ULYSSES

A Chippendale terrace. The street narrow as John's tie. Number 18 a bullied child permanently in the shade of the factory opposite. Fifty yards either end, a typical Sydney day for May; short or long sleeves a balancing act, a light breeze. The call had come in: possible homicide in progress. John midway through a sausage roll, a vanilla slice waiting in its brown bag, the Coke bottle he was nursing between his knees glinting with windscreen sun. An instant prior Detective Sergeant John Gordon's only thought: Could the Bunnies make it seventeen premierships in '67. All changed in an instant by that barking despatch, skolling the Coke, tossing the bottle in the back, gunning the Falcon here quick. Pure luck they were in the area. A visit to Sydney Uni for a dental professor to examine teeth of a skull unearthed by a curious fido in Botany.

Barker, his partner, mouth full of pie, sputtering back, 'On our way.'

Now here at 18, grimy bricks, sunshine starved, some unidentifiable smell from the factory over the road. Already workers in hairnets gathered under its roller door, curious. A uniform standing outside, neighbours pulling cardigans tighter. No ambulance, but a siren was closing. The constable could have been John himself, two years back when he found Sally Prescott, prostitute, butchered. Back before he made detective sergeant. John doubted the uniform was legal drinking age, white as the tablecloths in the kind of restaurant Denise's old man still took them for dinner most weekends.

'She's inside with O'Neil,' the kid stammering.

♦♦♦

The interior lighter than a cave's but not by much even with a standard lamp glowing. O'Neil, presumably the senior constable, standing in the gloom of the lounge room. John steeling himself. The first knife murder he'd had since he and Denise had been prepared for ritualistic slaughter themselves. Already he could feel his veins tightening.

'Jesus Christ,' Barker catching sight of the sprawled victim on the carpet behind the couch. Colour leached in the gloom, just black and grey, but you knew what the dark splotches were, and the stink of death was vivid.

'Gordon and Barker, Homicide,' said John. 'You check her?'

'Dead as a doornail.'

'What happened?' John knelt beside the body, a deep pool of blood. He felt for a pulse anyway. Nothing. The body still warm.

The siren was howling now right outside the house.

'Constable Everett was in Broadway when a woman came racing down the street screaming "He's killing her."'

Everett, presumably the young pasty cop out front.

'He got the address and called it in. I was up at the park on a break. We both raced here. Door was open. We found her like that. No sign of anybody else.'

'The knife?'

'Didn't see one. I checked upstairs. No-one here. Told Everett to speak to the witness while I held the fort. From what Everett caught on the way from the neighbour, the husband killed her.'

'Names?'

Head shake.

'And I didn't want to touch anything.' O'Neil righteous, and smarter than John had been that first time violent death had shoved its face in his. Maybe O'Neil would get lucky, maybe his life wouldn't be defined like John's had been by what he'd found in that Kings Cross bedroom. Innocent and guilty alike carried along in a whirlpool of blood, until you crawled out knowing you could never identify yourself again as one of the pure.

'Electricity bill for Mr and Mrs Rentich.' Barker hovering at the kitchen doorway fanning an envelope.

The ambulance crew bustling in.

John said, 'Mike, upstairs. Look for the knife.' Barker moved. John already heading outside. The knot of bodies out front had expanded. 'Is the neighbour here?' John to Everett who had improved from white to cream. A nod at a stocky woman, forties, a frizz of black hair, in conversation with two other women and a man, all sucking Rothmans.

'Excuse me,' John crooked his finger at her.

'How is she?' the woman's lip trembling.

John ignored that, looked for privacy. 'Which is your place?' The woman signalled. Bugger, right where the crowd was. John led her to the car, the doors still open how they'd left it astride the footpath.

'You are?'

'Liz Hawkley.'

'What did you see?'

'First I heard them. Rowing. A bad one this time, I could tell. Then there was a scream. I ran out the front. He rushed past me—'

'He?'

'Alan, the husband. He was carrying a bread knife. He headed that way.'

She pointed south. The radio crackled: a man armed with a knife had just entered the brewery. Two hundred yards from here. No coincidence. Easier on foot. John ran.

◆◆◆

It wasn't till he got there that the terror gripped him, a Killer Kowalski claw-hold in his gut. Workers were leaking out of a side entrance.

'Anybody see him?' John fighting panic by yelling.

'Looked like he was heading for the barrel room.'

John got directions, stepped into darkness, a few stragglers passing him the opposite way, running. His ears humming now.

He fought it, crossed through the first room, just an open space storeroom with crates and metal machinery. His hand went to his revolver. That should've helped but it didn't. All he could think of was the last time he tried to play hero, winding up bound, naked, a madman's plaything.

He took a right down the corridor, then cut left, didn't pass anybody this time. The sounds of fellow humans grew distant. The corridor ended, the keg room to his right. Cavernous and dark, just one big overhead fluoro mid-room that didn't lick the darkest reaches. Concrete floor, wooden beams, the smell of hops and mouldy timber and stacks of steel kegs like the bared teeth of an Alsatian. Rows of them. The gun was in John's shaky hand. More than a year but he still wasn't ready for this, edging ahead.

'Rentich! Police.' Pleased his voice sounded stronger than he would have guessed. No idea if there was a way out of the room besides the way he'd entered. 'Come out now with your hands up. I am armed and ready to use my gun if necessary. Just come on out, throw down your weapon and we can sort this out.' Inching forward, steel kegs on his right floor to ceiling, to his left pallets and forklifts. That side, enough light to show as clear. He crept towards the blackest pools near the wall opposite where he had entered. He stopped. Listened.

'Alan, come on.' Nothing. Moving deeper now so the only light was on his back. His eyes growing more accustomed. A metallic sound somewhere to his right behind this first row of kegs. He moved fast to the end of the line, stopped, tensed, took a breath and swung round the end barrel, revolver pointing the way. Another row of barrels on his left, a narrow valley path between the two walls of metal kegs now. Very dark.

'Come out, Al, come on.' Slowly advancing. One step, two …

Movement to his left, a shape. His finger started to pull the trigger … Stopped.

'Did I kill her?'

Too dark to see anything but a darker mass at the heart of the darkness. He hadn't expected that reaction, almost timid.

'No, mate. You cut her up bad, but she can make it. The ambos got there quick.'

He could see just enough to make out the knife. He was getting dizzy now. Shit.

'Throw it down, Al.' Real dizzy, sweating. He was going to have to shoot, he couldn't face a knife again.

A clang, steel on concrete. He breathed easier.

'Arms high, now.'

He could smell fear, not sure it wasn't his own.

◆◆◆

Geary's office. Louvre windows, streaked in grime, a sill of pigeon poop and discarded butts. From here, the only vista available for entrapped damsels desperate for a glimpse of their rescuer was slate tiles and a wedge of an adjacent park's green grass.

Geary's back was to him as the Homicide chief fiddled in the second filing cabinet. Swinging around with a bottle of something the colour of tea and two beer glasses, the kind with a frosted band around the outside. Very thin glass snapped easy but kept the beer cool.

'Rum's my poison. It's in the blood of this force.'

Traces of John's old social studies still embedded in memory. The original soldiers, the police in the colony paid in rum shots. Geary poured a generous amount in each glass, didn't ask his permission. Handed him one. They clinked then sipped.

'Good work, Sergeant. You had every right to shoot the bastard, but then we'd have had those Surry Hills pricks up our backside.'

Geary's reference to the press, quartered nearby. The older cops like Geary hadn't quite got around to considering television relevant. Newsprint was the battleground that had to be won. John wasn't sure Geary even had a TV at home.

'You'll go a long way, son.' Geary took another sip. 'Now I didn't call you here just to piss in your pocket—' Breaking off suddenly. Cocking an ear to what was drifting in through the window. What John at first thought was a two-way from the vans in the compound below but he now identified as a megaphone. He moved alongside

Geary and looked out. In the narrow keyhole formed by rooflines, buildings' corners, heavy tree boughs, the eye focused on the park. A parade of coloured scarves, beards, skivvies, a lopsided banner at the mercy of students who'd never done a day's work. A few letters only visible but enough: NAM. The megaphone words indecipherable up in this eyrie and likely no better on the ground.

'Uni students and draft dodgers.' Geary pulled the window in, twisted the clasp, said, 'You missed out?'

'I did, yes.' At the time he would have been happy to do national service. A lottery barrel, marbles representing birthdates. Your marble got pulled, it was dungarees, rifle drills and short back and sides for a couple of years. Vietnam had raised the stakes though. Now it might be real bullets coming your way.

'You were in the war, sir?' Of course, John knew he had been. You always knew stuff about your superior officers.

'Air force. I was colourblind, shouldn't have been allowed to fly but my mates told me the sequences on the lights test and I got through.' Casting one last glance outside. It might have been equally rueful as wistful. 'Bit of military service is a good thing. I'm not saying I'd send them to war, mind you. But a couple of years away from the television, not a bad thing.' Sitting down behind his desk, indicating John sit opposite. 'You've been going fifteen months solid. How would you like a break?'

Panic shooting through him, thinking he'd covered his tracks, hidden that he was strung taut as a guitar string. Just coming down now a week on since the Rentich arrest. He'd told nobody. Except Denise. Shivering in her arms that night.

He started to stammer something, didn't know what.

Geary smiled. 'How about some time stateside.'

That clean bowled him. 'I don't follow—'

Geary leaning forward on his elbows breaching the space between them. He always spoke quietly but right now more so.

'The Commissioner is obviously thick with the minister who is best friends with the Minister of Transport.'

John racking his brains as to who that might be. Clueless on the state cabinet outside of the Premier, the Police Minister and the Attorney-General.

Geary coughed. Too many Turf fags. 'Eric Davis …'

The name ringing bells: Minister of Transport, right.

'… has a son, Martin. Smart kid. Got into Berkeley, San Francisco, doing maths. Five weeks ago, the kid disappeared, only his parents didn't know until a fortnight ago. The San Francisco PD did your standard piss-poor bullshit look-see and wrote it off as a kid bailing out of college. The Commissioner got a request from our Police Minister to have a word to San Fran PD. They've done a second investigation and listed Martin Davis as a missing person, but they have hit a brick wall. Apparently, Berkeley is a hotbed of this shit …' gesturing at the window. 'The kids hate cops. Call them pigs. Out of their mind on LSD. My day, LSD was pounds shillings and pence.' A crooked grin. 'Still can't get my head around this dollars-and-cents business. So …' the rolling mall of words came to a stop. 'Long and the short of it is the Commissioner wants one of our own there doing our own investigation. Got to be a smart young cop. If this goes bad, and it might, we need somebody who has been there.' Not meaning the US. A meaningful look. Death, blood, spilled guts was what he was saying. Yes, John had been there.

'I said John Gordon is the best.' Shooting his cuffs. 'The job is yours if you want.'

John trying to stumble through smoke. 'When?' he managed.

'Yesterday. Soon as you can. There's a new flight to San Fran direct with a couple of stops in the Pacific. We'll organise that for you, passports and so on.'

John gulped rum. Shit. The US. San Francisco. A dream. But common sense regrouping.

'When you say "our investigation" …'

'Unofficially sanctioned by the heads of San Francisco and Los Angeles police departments. Davis had met a girl. She disappeared. His roommates said he wouldn't believe she'd just dumped him and lit out. He reported her missing. The San Francisco PD told him they had better things to do. He decided to look for her himself. He cleared out from his student house, and nobody has heard from him since. There's a big chance the kid is in LA. So, we need LAPD in too.' Geary rocking back in closer. 'The key word is "unofficial". That applies to both sides of the Pacific. The taxpayers can't know we're looking for a minister's missing kid using their money.' Miming zipping his mouth. 'You'll have no police status in the US. They will issue you with a private investigator's licence. You can carry a gun.'

John trying to process. 'And I would be on normal pay?'

'Plus expenses. Three-star hotels, car, petrol, food and a small slush fund. You can't threaten anybody with arrest so you might have to buy favours. If you need more money, request it through me. No official paperwork. Davis has promised a hundred quid – sorry dollars – of his own. More if necessary.'

'Will the American cops cooperate?'

'They'll be ordered to.'

That didn't mean they would. John wasn't green. An overseas cop poking his nose in would not go down well. Geary finished his rum.

'Verdict?'

John sat back. 'Does the Commissioner know you are approaching me about this?'

Geary nodded. They both knew that meant John's balls were in a vice. If he refused, he could forget advancement.

'Sorry, Sergeant, but I had to pick someone, and I reckon you can do this on your ear. You'll be Inspector within two years.' He tapped a file by his hand. 'Sounds like the kid is chasing this wild sheila but the cops have more to do than run after stray students. They've got Black Power, drugs, Vietnam. It's the chance of a lifetime.'

Sounding like a hire-purchase salesman now. But he was right. Problem, if John didn't find Davis or the kid was dead …

'I know what you're thinking. You do a solid job I will back you to the hilt. So will the Commissioner.'

He would have to tell Denise. No way out of it.

'I'll have to speak to my wife.'

'Of course.'

To these blokes, speaking to a wife meant telling them how it was going to be. They weren't used to women as strong-willed as Denise.

'These expenses. They are for two, right?'

Geary cracked the crooked smile again. 'They were thinking one cop could work with one of theirs.'

'You know that's not going to play.'

A grin. Of course, he did. 'I told them. I'm not sending one of my men on his own. Two-man team. One hotel room though. You want Barker?'

John said, 'I have somebody else in mind.'

2 CALIFORNIA DREAMIN'

The turf at 5.00 a.m. silver as if gelatine crystals lay on top. The image coming to Ray's mind because toddler Cassandra loved sprinkling them all over the sparkling lino Marie had just mopped and polished. The domesticated Ray Shearer. Who'd have thought it? Not Ray. Two years back he was sure he was destined to see out his days in front bars with other single men. He'd blown his chance already, thought there could be no reprise. Yet here he was, folding highchairs and strapping tiny feet into tiny shoes. Two horses thundered by close to the rail, Ray forced back as clods flew. The big man, Granite didn't flinch. Mind you, his suit was cheaper. Granite had insisted Ray come here before breakfast. Ray couldn't refuse, he needed his help. Hell, even if didn't, he would have turned up. He'd always enjoyed Granite's company. The two strong-arm lieutenants for the late George Shaloub's empire: the cop and the crim.

Ray wondered if Granite had really forgiven him for putting a gun to his head that time. More than a year ago now but a different ice-age since George's passing.

'Isn't she pretty?' Granite nodding at disappearing hindquarters.

'The bay or the chestnut?'

'The chestnut.'

'Yeah, she's got a cuter rump than Marie has these days.'

The big man grinned. 'She's mine.'

'As in you've backed her?'

'As in I own her. Two-year old filly. Georgie Moore helped me pick her out.'

Moore, the greatest rider Ray had seen but Ray's take: hoops were no great judges of horseflesh. Then again, what did he know?

His on-the-side job for Shaloub had been collecting from reluctant gamblers and that had quashed his appetite for chance. He was saying nothing anyway. Keep Granite happy.

'You can afford it? I thought you were out of the game.'

'I am.' Granite had run Shaloub's prostitutes and helped on the illegal gambling joints. 'But I put away money for a rainy day. And George left me almost as much as he did you.'

Ray hadn't wanted the money, but with a kid on the way he wasn't tossing it away. Now they owned a nice little place in Paddington. Nothing flash but his inspector salary at Arson meant Marie didn't have to go back to dancing. He wanted Cassie to have her parents with her, knew firsthand how sharp the world's teeth were on orphans. Granite started ambling away towards the stalls.

'I'll just say goodbye to Shiloh. Then you can buy me breakfast.' Trudging over sludgy ground. 'You like the name? Shiloh? It's a combination – Shaloub after George and Hi-Lo after the hi-lo game 'cause George cut me in for ten percent of the casino take.'

'You sly cock. I never knew that.'

Granite smirked.

'Course, he gave me ten percent of the roulette.'

Granite stopped, stunned. Then smiled. 'Bullshit. George would never give anybody anything of the cards or the wheel.'

Ray laughed. 'No, he would not.'

◆◆◆

Instant coffee, bacon and eggs, laminex chairs in the greeny pattern, the sweep of Bondi Beach across the road, the sky stubbornly steel. Winter heading in slow like a punter with a winning ticket wanting to savour his triumph over summer its old enemy. Surfers filleted slices of the Pacific.

'You like Arson?'

Yes, he did. Easiest fucking job in the whole force. The firies did all the hard work.

'I do.'

'You seem a lot more relaxed now, Ray, if you don't mind me saying.' Granite disappeared a whole slice of bacon and toast. His throat didn't even seem to move as it slid down. The guy was like that big fucking Indonesian lizard Ray had seen pictures of. 'You still looking for the shit who killed your mum and dad?'

No. But I'm not telling you that. Instead, Ray said, 'I think he's probably dead by now. But you know, I never forgive and never forget.' That was after all why he was here. 'What about you, Granite? You forgive me?'

'It's old news, Ray. You got a little kid now. A top sheila. I can imagine if somebody burned my parents alive how I'd feel – well, actually, I'd happily burn my father alive if he hadn't walked in front of a diesel. But I'm saying, comes a time …'

'We'll see.'

'You are looking relaxed, though.' He poked another slice of toast at Ray before that vanished. 'So, you said you needed my help.'

'Matt Dempsey.'

Granite looked skywards like one of those saints on a holy card, thinking, said, 'Ex-cop. Stakeout specialist.'

'That's the guy. I can't find him.'

'You're a fucking superintendent or whatever.'

'Chief inspector. I think he's hiding from the ex-wife. No driver's licence, no electoral roll.'

'And you think I can find him?'

'I know you can find him. Nobody ever hid from George when you were on the case. Well, not for long.'

He could tell Granite enjoyed the flattery.

'You're not going to knock him? 'Cause I don't want any part of that. Unless you're paying a shitload of money but given the tight-arse you are—'

'I don't want to kill him. I want to use his services. I have a target and I absolutely need the best.'

'Your guys aren't good enough?'

It's too close to home, thought Ray, but didn't say that.

'It suits me to have somebody who has been out of circulation for a while.'

Granite seemed to accept that. 'How much?'

'A hundred.'

'Quid or dollars?'

'Quid.'

'Two hundred dollars.'

'Yes.'

'That's my fee? Not his.' Clarifying.

'All for you. You're going to need it if you've got a horse.'

Granite daintily dabbed his mouth with his serviette. 'Because we're like brothers. Okay. If I come up with nix, you don't have to pay a zack except what I might have to lay out for information. And as a special favour because you're shouting breakfast, I'm telling you: Georgie Moore is heading back to England. He's riding Royal Palace in the Epsom next month and it's a stone bonker.'

◆◆◆

Feet up on his desk, Shearer jotting a reminder in his diary for June: *Royal Palace*. The diary empty except for Marie's birthday and mates' weddings. He sensed someone enter, sighted over the toes of his Windsor Smiths.

'Bloody hell. I am graced with a visit by the prodigy.'

Not much trace of the nervous young cop John Gordon had been a couple of years back. No need to shake hands, they knew one another too well, though lately their meetings had been sparse as outback petrol stations.

'How's Denise?'

'Doing her second year at art school. Loving it.'

Shearer gestured at his neck with his finger. 'Your hair's longer than Ringo's. They let you get away with that?'

Gordon sat down opposite, shrugged. 'Long as I do the job.'

The Windsor Smiths came down. 'Geary must love you.'

'How's Cassandra?'

'Cute as a button.'

'We should get together. You and Marie, Denise and me.'

'You tried the new place? The Bourbon and Beefsteak? It's terrific. As long as you don't mind the Yanks. They're everywhere.

GIs, sailors. Poor old George would be kicking himself. He'd be making money hand over fist. Not that he ever went short.' Ray trying to read Gordon. It wasn't a social call.

Gordon leaned back. 'So, you like American stuff? Bourbon, steaks ...'

'Mate, sometimes I even like Americans. I prefer them to fucking banana-benders that's for sure.'

'What about that song, "California Dreamin'"?'

Shearer knew the one he meant. It's winter and somebody's dropping into a church. Soft and a little mournful. Ray liked to jive. Little Richard, Johnny O'Keefe, Chuck Berry more his style. Or cool stuff, a soft piano tinkling background, smoky-voiced chicks in dark sequins. Ray wondering why the kid was smiling, all teeth on display.

'God, they're not going to know what to make of you.'

'Who?'

'The hippies, mate. You're coming to San Francisco with me.'

Ray knew the kid wasn't bullshitting. 'When?'

'Day after tomorrow.'

'How long?'

'Till the job's done I guess.'

Ray didn't ask what the job was. He already knew it would be for somebody important.

◆◆◆

John had never heard Anything Fucking Like It. The guitar this groaning, yawning, wailing monster. Drums tumbling. Was that fucking waltz time? You couldn't *think* the rhythm, but it throbbed in your balls. Urgent as death-row prisoners on the run. Denise naked astride him. Too long without this. So much stolen from them. Denise a vampire. Her wailing matching the guitar's. He was about to come, rolled her till he was on top. What did the Yanks call it? Balling. He came with a gush, a flash of the Rentich Chippendale lounge room, life spilled over the floor. Denise's mouth found his. Life flowed back into him.

'Jimi Hendrix,' he was reading the album cover now under a sputtering candle. A slow blues dawdling. Something about a red house.

'Stephanie, this new chick from London, just started at the school. It came out a week ago. She said The Beatles, Stones, everybody there digs him.'

Stretched out on the floor, a rug on dark boards, the old man's money getting them into this Dover Heights two-bedroom.

'Maybe you'll get to see him in San Francisco.'

'You sure you don't mind?'

'Why would I? Wish I was going. Haight-Ashbury, that's going to be a trip.'

'Don't know if we'll get to hear much music.'

'You won't be able to avoid it.' She started laughing.

'What's so funny?'

'I'm just thinking about what the hippies are going to make of Ray.'

That made him smile too.

'Be careful, hun.' She stroked his hair.

'It's a simple job. I just find the kid. Hopefully alive.'

She pressed her lips to his. He had no idea how strong he might be without her. Or her without him. Supposed they would find out.

3 SAN FRANCISCO

Seemed to John his world was still vibrating. Thirty hours give or take, BOAC out of Sydney. Nandi a blur. No real sleep. Champagne, glam stewardesses heavy on Gossamer, passengers stamping their 'international passport to smoking pleasure' puffing the whole way. Shearer loving the leigh ceremony on the Honolulu tarmac. And now San Francisco; warm, skirts short and legs bare. A cab to downtown, asking the driver, a Chinese guy who sounded like Dick Van Dyke, to swing via Haight-Ashbury. He took them through slow, though the traffic was choked anyway. Paisley shirts, floppy hats, fringe suede jackets, bull-cops in dark helmets scanning streets like John Wayne looking for Injuns across a treacherous open plain.

'It's quiet for now,' the cabby gesturing loosely. 'Hour or two it will be packed. There was a big concert in the park yesterday. Right now they're still tripping or sleeping it off. Come alive tonight.'

The driver looked late twenties. Short-sleeve white shirt, grey pants.

'What do you think of the hippies?' Shearer lighting up.

'Not so bad except they fuck up the traffic with these walk-ins, the protest marches. It's shit driving these last few months. I wouldn't care if they used cabs, but they don't. They use the trolley car, the bus. The cops beat up on them. I mean I don't like that, but they do fuck the traffic flow. So, Australia, huh?'

Shearer said. 'Yeah.'

'I hear you got these kangaroos in the main street.'

'That's right, just like your hippies. They slow down the traffic and they don't use cabs.'

The driver showed teeth. 'What are you guys doing here? You on holiday?'

'I'm his manager,' Shearer nodding at John.

The cabby looking in the rear-vision, found John's eyes. 'What do you do?'

'Don't answer that. You gotta ask me or he'll start to wonder why he needs a manager.' Shearer enjoying his role. Then, 'He's a surfer.'

The closest John had been to surf was the washing powder of that name.

'I wish I could surf,' the driver hitting a right turn. 'The chicks are freaking outtasight.' Then, nailing Shearer. 'I thought you were a cop.'

'Really?'

'Yeah, you got that look.'

Strip malls. A shopfront raced by, The Psychedelic Shop. A cluster of young people on a street corner around a bongo player. Chicks with flowers in their hair. A weird mix, pawn shops and cheap liquor stores alongside a candle store. Record shops. A bit like George Street, south end. Some streets tall houses with high windows, weatherboard. Others three-storey plus, terraced, stone step walk-ups. Nice architecture made you think of parasols, penny-farthing bikes, fob watches.

'We want a hotel. Close to here but clean. Not too exxy. You know a place like that?' Shearer doing all the running. John almost nodding off.

'No crabs, right?' the driver smiling.

'Right.'

'I know a good place. Close but not too close to the Panhandle.'

◆◆◆

The Hotel Clarence looked like some of the hotels in Bondi, only bigger. Four storeys on a corner. They pulled in behind a VW van painted in flowers. Long-haired guys, pulling guitars and amplifiers out the back.

'They stay here not play here,' explained the cabbie. 'The Fillmore is only three blocks west. You heard of that?'

John recalled some vague party chat with Denise's crew.

'All the psychedelic bands play there. I don't know if somebody's playing tonight, but you want to see hippies, that's the place.'

Shearer dubiously scanned his fellow hotel guests milling around their truck.

The cabbie reading him. 'Don't worry. The bands that stay here have a record company, mainly from Los Angeles. The place is clean. No rats. And the soundproofing is good.'

They climbed out and grabbed their suitcases. Denise had told John you were expected to tip everybody. John peeled off an extra couple of bucks for the driver who seemed to expect more.

◆◆◆

One step into the hotel out of the wafting marihuana and Ray knew the driver had done well by them. The Clarence at least one generation, more likely two since its glory days, but the faded burgundy carpet with the gold coat of arms was freshly vacuumed, the short reception desk a dull wooden mirror. The lobby was compact but the bank of six elevators off to the left, roomy. A businessman's hotel back before stockbrokers leapt from windows. Suited Ray. He copped a look at the baggage captain. Like the carpet, his uniform worn but neat, cuffs white, no missing buttons. Early fifties, Ray figuring he'd had this job since the war, maybe before the war. Something said navy. Proud of his work, in it for life, a big tick.

Best of all was the clerk. A little rectangular badge said 'Kitty', a hairstyle from the Dusty Springfield school, hairspray but not too much, little blonde horns under the ears, a great smile, smoker's lines but not many. Just three years too old to want to tune in and drop out, say thirty-one, perfect age for Ray, old enough to know who Tony Bennett was but young enough to own a few Beatles records, and definitely she would rock to Elvis. He let John enquire about the room, waited for Kitty to shoot a glance his way, which she did as she was asking if they would want a twin or two separate rooms.

'Twin.'

That they were cheapskates didn't put her off. Yes, they had a room available. Gordon said the price was fine.

'So where are you gentlemen from?'

'Australia,' Ray muscling in, elbows on the polished wood lowering his chin to her level.

'Oh my. You're the first Australians we've had stay here.'

Ray felt no compunction to stay faithful to Marie while away from Sydney. He'd not be unfaithful to her there, ever. He'd provide for her and Cassandra. He'd lay down his life for them. But he knew life could be short. It was a foolish man turned his back on new experiences. Besides, he was Catholic and there was always confession.

'Are you on duty most days?' asked Ray.

'Except for Sunday.'

'Good.' Ray enjoyed the blush on her cheeks.

♦♦♦

'Can't help yourself,' whispered Gordon, the lift rising. Newish, not one of those with the collapsible cage. A silent bellhop facing the doors, his back to them.

'God helps he who helps himself. Besides, unlike you, I'm not married.'

'I don't recall that stopping you when you were.'

'You requested me.' That shut him up. He liked poking Gordon's certainty.

The elevator jerked to a stop. The 4 button glowing. The bellboy's heels leading the way, a bit scuffed. A Hilton bellboy's would have gleamed, but no complaints. The corridor, as with the lobby, tidy and well tended. Big brass key, tall door. The bellboy showed them into a wide, high-ceilinged room. A still life of fruit in a balsa frame hanging on flock wallpaper. Aqua and gold colour theme. A large bay-window, views of a street and sky. A bathroom boasting old faucets, deep tub and large green tiles.

Gordon swapped the bellboy a tip for their room key before he pulled the door shut.

'I'm bushed,' Gordon flopping on a bed beside folded towels and a miniature bar of soap.

Ray said, 'Change your shirt and let's get to police HQ. You sleep now, you'll wake at three in the morning.'

A big old building downtown, huge arched windows like a library's, long bannisters, a solid staircase, worn but, like the Clarence, still with dignity despite the inevitable chips off the rubber-lino mats. More museum than cop station. Put that down to the legal traffic here. Attorneys, secretaries and assistants looking like Debbie Reynolds. The deeper they headed into the second-floor jungle, the cops' lair, the more it became like every other police HQ Ray had ever known. It didn't matter where you put a police headquarters, its innate properties never altered: the smell of hair and gun-oil, overused corridor toilets, pencil shavings, the clatter of typewriters and jarring crash of a filing cabinet followed by a curse. 'Who took my ...' Didn't matter what it was, some prick always swiped it and you never learned who.

The lino dirtier here too. Rows of offices, doors shut with glass rectangles opaque as cloudy Osrams. Names stencilled in gold letters, standard fans. Their guide, a short-back-and-sides uniform knocked on a door that said *Deputy Chief of Police*.

A voice: 'Come in.'

The uniform opened the door, showed them in then closed it leaving himself outside. The man standing in the office in uniform was lean, about fifty with a crop of black hair Frankie Avalon would have been proud of.

'I'm not the Deputy Chief,' he said, 'I'm Captain Frank Spinetti, his assistant. Welcome to San Francisco, gentlemen.'

They shook hands. Gordon introduced them. Spinetti indicated they take a seat facing the desk, slid into his boss' chair. There was a flag behind him, a bear, with words: *California Republic*.

'The Deputy Chief apologises he's not here in person, but we've got kind of a lot on right now.' Smarmy smile. 'Black Panthers, hippies, you name it. But we are here to help our Australian brothers in whatever way we can.'

Clearly word had come from on high just like Geary had promised. Spinetti put his hand on a manila folder sitting on the desk. It was thick but not that thick.

'What we have here is the case file worked by our Missing Persons and also the original investigation done by Berkeley. Don't be too hard on them. We have hundreds of kids everyday disappearing then turning up, then disappearing.' Picking up a sealed envelope, placing it on top. 'Your California driver licences and private-detective licences.'

'Can we carry weapons?' asked Gordon.

Spinetti laughed. 'Everybody here carries a weapon, but these permits give you the right to carry a concealed weapon. You brought weapons with you?'

Ray confirmed they had. 'Smith and Wesson, snub-nose.'

'Fine. You can buy ammo for them anywhere. You have a car accident, you get into any problem with law enforcement, you get the officers who attend to call me direct.' Cards appeared magically in his fingers, one for each. 'If you wind up in LA, you better go through the same process. You get in the shit, they won't give a rat's ass about our blessing. Your PI licences are good for anywhere in California, but you cross the state border you are on your own. Where are you staying?'

'The Clarence,' said Ray.

Spinetti nodded like it was a good choice.

Ray asked if they would have access to the investigating officers.

'Of course, but please go through me, not direct.'

'And Berkeley? Will they be pissed off?'

'I'll see they cooperate fully. Gentlemen, is there anything else you need?'

Gordon said, 'I think we're good.'

Spinetti stood. 'In that case, let me wish you good luck.' He handed over the file and licences and they shook hands. 'Chances are the kid took a bad acid trip and is curled up in a ball somewhere. Sometimes they come out of it but not always.' He opened the door for them. The uniform was waiting. 'The officer will show you out. Remember, you need anything, don't hesitate to call.'

◆◆◆

The tiredness had left, hunger moving in. Shearer was for eating then and there but it was too early for John and the clothes felt wrong now they'd had their meeting.

'Let's go back to the hotel, get changed.'

'You're the boss.'

The hot bath had John nodding off. He fought it, dragged himself from the tub, threw on a dark turtleneck and maroon pants, found Shearer unchanged on his bed reading the case file. He looked up, said, 'You can catch up over dinner.'

'You're not going to change?'

'What's the point? Two hours out there we'll smell like a hippie ashtray.'

'At least take off the tie,' said John. Ray obliged.

John said, 'Tomorrow we should hire a car first thing.'

◆◆◆

Steak with mashed potatoes and beans. A quiet restaurant, dim Tiffany lamps, hiss of soda siphons and the rattle of a martini flask. An occasional guffaw off a shared joke between men in suits in some distant booth. The file was standard police form, with the same crappy typing as a New South Wales one. Had to jam the pages right under the lamp to read.

Author of the report a *Sergeant A. Groenwald SFPD*.
Subject: *Martin William Davis born March 1945, Australian. Student at UC Berkeley.*
   The last confirmed sighting of Davis was in the Tenderloin district, San Francisco on the evening of Thursday April 6. He'd turned up at a house looking for a girl named 'Spring'.

Paperclipped to the file, a standard matt colour print from a cheap camera, probably an instamatic. It showed a pretty blonde with the ubiquitous dreamy-stoned Mona Lisa smile of young hippie women. Mostly just her face and neck, so it was hard to see the top she was wearing. Something blue and flowing maybe. No more than twenty.

John read on.

The residents in the house reported Davis was highly distressed. He told the Tenderloin crew he was worried Spring had been abducted because she'd not been in touch for days. She'd vanished. He'd tried to report it to the police, but they weren't interested.

Here there was a note in the margin:

Subsequent investigation established that a young man had arrived at the Berkeley Police Department claiming his girlfriend had disappeared. When told it had been less than forty-eight hours since she'd been in touch, and as the young man was unable to provide a full name of the missing person, he had been told there was nothing the police could do at that time. From descriptions given by attending officers, it was likely this was Martin Davis. However, no official report had ever been lodged so it could not be completely verified.

Back to the report on April 6.

Residents at the house at 1148 Chalmers in the Tenderloin said Davis claimed that a man had been asking around after Spring. They were unable to say whether this was prior to or after her disappearance as Davis had been 'babbling' and not 'totally coherent'. He appeared to be under the influence of narcotics. The house residents told the police that they did not know Spring before she had turned up at their house on the night of Tuesday April 4. She had called at their door about 5.00 p.m., mentioned a friend of a friend and asked if she could crash there the night. They had said fine. They were in the habit of having numerous transients come and go. She had seemed anxious and had mentioned she needed to avoid 'somebody'. She left next morning. They had no idea to where but speculated she might have hitchhiked to Los Angeles as a number of their circle had been heading south to attend a be-in there.

When Davis called two days later, the residents had told Davis the girl, Spring, was no longer with them and may have left town. They did not know if he was the person Spring was trying to avoid, or if that was, as Davis claimed, some other man. Spring had kept to herself the identity of whoever it was she was hiding from. They described Davis as agitated but not aggressive. The friend of a friend Spring had mentioned when asking to stay the night was one 'Kansas Annie'.

The steak excellent. John kept reading. Groenwald's enquiries had revealed there was a young woman known in the Haight-Ashbury district going by 'Kansas Annie' but that, 'to this point in time we have been unable to locate her'. It was assumed that on Wednesday April 7 after his visit to the Tenderloin house Davis had then returned to his residence, a share house at 114 Washington in Berkeley. He was not seen there by the three housemates, but they heard noises in his room at approximately two a.m. and they noted the next morning, April 8, that some of his clothes and shoes were missing as well as a holdall and toiletries.

In their interview they said that Davis' behaviour had become erratic since he had met Spring about three weeks earlier. They believed he was drug taking: definitely marihuana and likely LSD. He had stopped attending classes. They had not heard from Davis since that early morning. They possessed one photo of Spring. That was the one in the file. They did not know her real name.

Following was a list of the campus places the police had attended seeking to get a lead on Davis' current whereabouts but without success. They had checked hospitals and police stations and the morgue but found no trace of Davis. They also canvassed bus and train stations. Davis did not own a vehicle. They tried various known popular nightspots. No luck. Given his last sighting may have led him to believe that Spring had headed to Los Angeles, they concluded that most likely he had headed there, probably by hitchhiking. They had telephoned their LAPD counterparts and asked them to check hospitals and morgues. They had sent photos of Davis to LAPD. LAPD had got back to them two days later. There was no sign of Davis ever having been hospitalised and he did not match any morgue John Does.

Davis had a Berkeley bank account and on April 6 had drawn down the sum of two hundred and twenty-five dollars. That had left eighty dollars remaining in the account but no more had been drawn down since. There was a note jotted in pen that the balance as of 'yesterday' had still been eighty dollars. The assumption was that Davis had set out in pursuit of Spring, possibly to Los Angeles. He had drawn down sufficient funds to last at least a month, however, the possibility that he had met with foul play could not be ruled out.

John closed the file, finished his beans.

Shearer drained his beer, said, 'What do you reckon?'

'Sounds like he lost the plot. Spring took off.'

'You think he was the one she was running from?'

John did. 'Otherwise why wouldn't she stay in Berkeley with him? And he never mentioned this guy to the cops. There's nothing specific in what he told the cops, like some man was asking around for her. We can assume the SFPD didn't miss him in a hospital or morgue. He could spin that money out for two months so we can't assume foul play.'

Shearer played with his coaster. 'Maybe the housemates and this other lot know more than they're letting on. We need to find Spring and we've got one lead.'

'Kansas Annie.'

Shearer nodded. 'Didn't our cabby say there was a dance on somewhere near here tonight?'

John couldn't help smiling; 'dance', Shearer really was a relic.

'I don't know that it's actually a dance.'

'Well, a musical show, what the fuck. Let's go and meet some hippies firsthand.'

'No. You need an invitation.' The doorman a black slab, square cut as a Rothmans pack, hair a nylon dust-buster. Shearer opening his palms.

'Come on, mate. We've come all the way from Australia to see these blokes.'

'I don't care if you've come from the moon, man. Tonight is invite only. You even know whose album launch it is?'

Shearer's palm a cheat sheet. He'd jotted from the poster moments before. A sly peek.

'Jeffer's Airplane.'

The big guy cracking a huge grin, turning to his bald white associate, Killer Karl Kox in a jacket. Then back to Shearer.

'Shit, man. That's tomorrow. And it's Jefferson, like the president. Bye now.' Holding up fingers in the peace sign to stir.

John saw Ray's hackles rising, got in quick with a hand on Shearer's arm.

'We'll come back tomorrow.' Dragging him away through a phalanx of arriving jeans, tie-dyed tees and headbands.

Pungent dope smoke turning the air blue. No regulation look: cavalry jackets, boots, moccasins, most girls with hair parted in the middle hanging straight but short cuts too, and afros, paisley smocks, minis, crossed laces over white plastic boots, a small guy in deep conversation with a spade … Eric Burdon? John swivelled but all he saw now was the back of a Hells Angels jacket.

They figured the hotel direction, shuffled that way. Ray pointed at yellow neon that read *Liquor*.

'Let's get ourselves some supplies.'

Off the sidewalk into the store. Decidedly low-rent. Bottles on shelves behind the counter, coloured paper specials scrawled in texta on chopped card. The big store clerk arguing with a chunky unkempt hippie chick, her beads clacking as she threw her arms about. Waiting his turn behind her, a moustache in a watchman's hat growing impatient.

'What's this bullshit?' The chick's voice like a rasp on a hoof.

'Don't swear at me, miss. You gave me a five. There's your liquor and that's your change.'

The guy looked like Hoss from *Bonanza*, big and balding and like he sweated easily.

'I gave you a ten.' The chick turning to Moustache. 'You saw, I gave him a ten.'

'Pretty sure I saw a five.'

The chick's hands to her hips. 'What is this, the Moe and Curly show?'

'The witness says a five.' The storeman getting righteous. 'Now, git.'

Moustache with a grin. 'Yea, get back out there hooking. Mug like that, you're going to have to work awful hard to earn a five-spot.'

'That's no way to talk to a woman, mate.' Shearer in close on Moustache before John had a chance to stop him.

'I'll talk how I like in my country, Limey. And the woman part is up for debate anyways.'

'I think you should apologise.' Shearer's gaze a steel blade.

'I think you should get f—'

Shearer's left snapped the guy's chin before Moustache had managed to even halfway draw back his right hand. Moustache dropped like a dead fly. John reading the clerk's eyes: Should he reach for whatever he had had under the counter.

John shook his head at him. 'Come on, the customer is always right.'

The store clerk flipped out a five. The girl took it, stuffed it in her jeans, gathered her bottle off the counter.

'Thanks,' to Shearer and John in turn. She walked out. Shearer smiled at the clerk. Moustache was moaning now.

'We'll have a quart of Scotch whiskey. Your best cheap one.'

The clerk turned to the shelf and pulled out a flask, stuck it in a paper bag, twisted it like that was how he would have liked to wring Shearer's neck. 'A dollar and a dime.'

Shearer shelled out, saluted the clerk with his whiskey on the way out.

She was standing just up the street, waiting.

'I wanted to thank you, boys. Just didn't want to spend another minute in there.'

John said, 'You okay?'

'You get used to that shit. Just don't expect it here in San Fran. Where are you guys from?'

Shearer said, 'South and across the Pacific. Australia.'

She nodded. 'Vietnam. You're there too. You soldiers?'

John sensed she was going to put the hard word on them now, thinking boys on R'n'R, easy money.

'No.'

She pointed at Shearer. 'You look like a cop.'

'Lot of people say that.'

'Punch like Cassius Clay.' Her eyes twinkled. 'What are you doing tonight?'

Yep, there it was. John decided to get in quick.

'Heading back to our hotel. It's been a long day.'

'You want to go to the Fillmore?'

'We tried that,' said Shearer. 'A grand piano on the door didn't want to let us in.'

She smiled. 'I might be able to help. I got a bit of pull. Come on.'

John about to decline but Shearer gave him no chance, following her back along the street. The air was still but carried a dampness. Hippies drifted past mixed in with normal people clutching shopping bags. They cut up an alley. John tensed. His gun was back at the hotel.

'This is the back entrance,' the girl said.

John looked at Shearer who seemed unconcerned. The alley gave onto another wider alley, parked trucks, a few guys lounging about with vests, muscles. Some big Harleys in a cluster. Another large dude at the narrow door.

'They're with me,' she said, and the guy stepped back. Maybe she was sleeping with the head man?

A narrow passage, a fog of marihuana smoke. Another passage ran off halfway. A hint of music being pumped the other direction.

'I gotta go, get ready. You guys head straight up there.' She pointed to the end of the corridor they were already on. 'Thank you, Aussies. I appreciate a gentleman. I'm Janis by the way.'

'John, Ray.'

'You have a good time, boys. Maybe I'll see you around.'

'You know a Kansas Annie?' asked Ray. John realised he should have thought of that. Janis, lips pursing, the name pinballing in her brain from the looks.

'Not right off. I know an Idaho Irene and a Nebraska Nellie. The boys might know her though, if you know what I mean.' She winked, vanished into smoke.

The end of the corridor a thick velvet curtain. John pushed through. His mind popped. He was in a movie theatre, and he was its screen. Darkness, lights swirling through a smoke haze, dancing over a sea of long hair, sex indecipherable. Two-thirds full. Bodies too dark for features. Instead, a spirit world. Recorded music from somewhere, drifting guitar and tambourine, Ray beside him suddenly tattooed in purple, green and red. Incense and dope.

John swung around, saw a high stage, guys fiddling with drums, speaker boxes. Girls floated past his eyes, smiled at him. Shearer drawing suspicion-heavy glances as they pushed through towards the centre of the room.

'Kind of like the Ghost Train at the show,' Shearer muttered.

They found a patch in the middle of the floor, a little magic circle of clear space around them, still outcasts, not kosher hippies. Ray shuffled towards the nearest group, two guys, two women. John didn't hear what he asked them, guessed it was whether they knew Kansas Annie. Curls shaking in the negative. Ray edged back. The guitar sound was ethereal.

'I should have changed,' Ray said. 'You try.'

John shouldered his way west, found a huddle of young people. Somebody flashed him a peace sign. He smiled.

'I wonder if you guys would know a Kansas Annie?'

A low-word-count conference spinning around the circle.

'What do you need her for?' The guy asking tall, skinny, coffee-coloured.

'A friend mentioned her.' John thinking, stay vague.

'You need weed?'

Something he hadn't expected. Tapping his pockets, translation 'empty' either side of the Pacific. 'Just flew in from Australia today.'

Mention of Australia raised eyebrows. The skinny guy turning to a headband, pointing at the marihuana joint Headband was puffing on, then back at John. Headband took one last hit, handed over the joint.

Now what? Declining would kill the cause stone dead. John took it, sucked. His lungs screamed. He went to hand it back. His new friend waving him off.

'This is San Francisco, man. We share.'

John nodded, his head fuzzing.

He started back to Shearer, the joint like a spaniel's nose leading the way.

'Jesus Christ,' Ray laughed. 'You're really living the part.'

Handing Ray the joint. Ray dragged. A few surrounding sly eyes noted. Good, not the fuzz.

'Ladies and gentlemen.' The metallic clang of a PA voice. 'One of our favourite bands, Big Brother and The Holding Company.'

Hippies applauding hard, whooping. John turned. The stage now filled with musicians. Drums starting an urgent rhythm. Then guitar exploding, distorted, twisting and ... Shit! On stage at the microphone was that ... the chick from the liquor store?

John nudged Shearer. 'Is that Janis?'

Shearer's face split, teeth showing pie-shape like a happy cartoon-cat. Ray aimed for California patois.

'Hey, we're cool, man, we know the singer.'

John turned his eyes back to the stage, couldn't believe this was the same woman. Waves of almost visible energy flowing out of her. Even though she didn't do much except holler backing vocals, she drew your focus, connected. You were the fish, she had the reel.

Later on, the song got this rhythmic soul feeling. Bodies around him were throbbing in time and she took over the mike, her voice too big for her, arcing through the thick blue smoke like a jet doing loop the loops. The end of the song came quickly, the rhythm laying itself down to rest, the voices ash when the last of the log has burned through. Over way too soon.

John's palms smashed into each other, all around him the same. Even Ray, whistling loud. A low buzz working its way into John's bloodstream. This couldn't be the 'high' they talked about. One puff couldn't do that, surely? But the air in here now was choked with the smell of pot, and it was hot and humid, John feeling his clothes were on fire from the lights burning and swirling in this petri dish. Janis took a step to the mike. The noise tapered.

'Thank y'all. We're real excited to be celebrating with our friends Country Joe and the Fish on the occasion of their album release.' More whistles and cheers. 'It's just a shame that not everybody out there tonight wants to share our message of peace and love. Why only a little while ago I went to a liquor store minding my business to get me a fifth of Comfort to see me through this show and these very uncool guys started putting me down.' A low moan of disapproval spanning the air. 'Thankfully two very fine gentlemen from the deep south – I'm not talking Mississippi but Australia – came to my rescue. This is for them. Song called "Ball and Chain".'

If he hadn't heard Hendrix just a few days back, the sound would have blown John's mind. But that Hendrix guitar jab made him prepared, so he got it now, the buzz-saw guitar ripping the air, high-squealing electronic harpies hovering, beauty out of chaos. The psychedelic lights soaked up your individual identity, carried you around the room, a platelet in a communal bloodstream.

And then her voice. Whoa. It was like a powerful locomotive when it first starts to roll, a rumble mixed with steel. He'd never heard anything like this, wished Denise was here to share. He spun, caught Shearer in some hippie's ear, offering the last of the joint. Shearer looked his way, gestured: come. John forcing himself to move. Giving less than one hundred percent attention to Janis, a travesty.

Shearer squeezed his shoulder, leaned in. 'That bloke says he saw Kansas Annie in here, tonight. Over there. Says she has a peace symbol drawn on her forehead.'

Shearer pointing in the direction of a thinner crowd near the back right of the room.

Pushing between vests, fringed leather, Levi's, exiting the dense heart of humanity and landing in a twilight space where a few even had their backs to the band while they smoked and nodded. Talking politics, John's gut feeling. Shearer had latched onto a young woman in a floppy felt hat, eyes hidden behind rose-coloured glasses. John trying to keep one ear on Janis, squeezing in beside Shearer who was already rolling.

'... Kansas Annie?' John caught him ask.

The girl can't have been much over five foot. 'I don't know her. I know most people in the scene, Diggers, Panthers, the Dead. What do you want with her?'

John jumping in before Shearer blew it.

'We heard she could play bongos. Don't know if that's true. We're looking at maybe cutting some tracks.'

'I can play bongos,' the girl, smiling. Janis finishing, John couldn't help but look, feeling like he was being brushed by some magic, ushered into history, Columbus, the shore of the New World all that.

'Well, great. How do we find you?'

'The Dead know me. Lulu. Ask at their house.'

'Lulu the bongo player?'

'You got it.'

'We'd still like to talk to Annie. About your height with a peace symbol on her forehead. Maybe she could play tambourine?'

The crowd stomping now.

'Oh, I saw a girl like that. Ten minutes ago. She went that way.' Pointing to a corridor, a staircase off it.

'Thanks, Lulu.'

Ray the prow slicing through a tide of pot-soaked denim, up the stairs. A narrow gallery, longhairs with cameras slung around their shoulders. A small wiry guy appeared, blocked them.

'This is a private area.'

Ray said, 'We're looking for Kansas Annie.'

'She ain't here. 'Cause like I said, this is private.'

'Small with a peace sign on a forehead.'

'Downstairs. She's wearing pink glasses.'

Shit. The hair and hat must have hidden the peace sign. A quick look to the maw below, just catching a floppy hat pushing through towards the exit at the back of the room.

'There!' John pointing, Ray already moving. Barrelling back down. Another song cranking out from the stage. They hit the boards and swung, tried to slide through the pressing crowd. Pushing against human sludge, finally out the other side across the foyer and onto the sidewalk.

Traffic, simple clear light, just in time to see her turning the corner one block up. John faster, taking the lead. Black leather and striped top stepping in front, palming him to a stop.

'You don't want to run here, man, you could get hurt.' A dirty headband around a bald skull, stubble, the vest screamed biker. John tried to sidestep. A side of ham blocked him.

Blood rushing to his head, ready to storm the battlements, Shearer's restraining hand on his shoulder. A quick look at the chrome parked just behind their human barrier. Two more bikers ready and waiting.

'Do I hear a thank you?' The biker staring into his eyes.

'Much obliged.' Shearer from behind.

The biker's eyes swinging that way. Nodding slowly.

'That's better. Be careful now, easy to slip and crack your skull.'

John felt his legs moving again, the two back-up bikers watching close. A knife blade glinting through a fist.

They walked fast to the corner. There was no sign of the girl in the hat.

4 THE GOLDEN ROAD
(TO UNLIMITED DEVOTION)

They settled on a Buick Skylark because it was cheapest. And Ray liked the colour, turquoise. He had a Holden Premier back home but fawn. Being prepared was something Ray had learned in scouts, and so he'd brought with him not just his gun, but a bunch of other things that might come in handy. Placed these in a leather satchel, slid it under the seat.

'What's that?' Gordon indicating the satchel.

'The stuff you're not sure you need till you need it.'

Gordon raised his eyebrows and settled into the passenger seat.

Ray liked to feel the wheel in his hands. Gordon making it clear he didn't mind Ray driving so long has he could ride the radio. The car was automatic. That was different, Ray always used to a stick. Gordon hot for chasing down Kansas Annie but Ray convinced him to wait. He knew girls like that. All Marie's friends fitting that bag. Somebody you don't know is asking questions about you, you get the hell out of their sights because you're a girl and chances are somewhere back there you burned somebody, or somebody you know, burned somebody. She'd be lying low for a day or two just in case. Meantime they had plenty on their plate.

The traffic thick getting out of downtown but by the long bridge heading east, thinning. They had no idea if any of Martin Davis' housemates would be home. Better not to call. Gordon's twiddling scored soul music, made Ray think of Marie who loved all those black groups with names ending in 'ions'. Ray partial too but after hearing Janis last night it sounded tame.

Berkeley: cars combover sparse. Judging from the map, the house was maybe a mile or two from campus. 114 Washington turned out to be a single-level weatherboard, not spic and span but for a rental not too shabby. Ray parked, the big car easy to handle. A narrow path led over thin lawn to low wooden steps. A woman's bicycle by the front door, bubble glass and a small leadlight feature. Ray rapped on the wood.

Footsteps to the door. It opened. A black bob, eyeshadow, slim in a dress with tiny flowers patterned, boots. Her eyes sliding one to the other. Ray put her early twenties. He took the lead.

'Good morning, Miss. Ray Shearer and John Gordon. We're private detectives from Australia looking into the disappearance of Martin Davis. Might you be able to spare a few minutes to talk with us?'

Her mouth part-opened and that gave her a little sexy something. Before that her face had been one of those you scan in a blur, like the features of a sewing pattern cover, just a vague sense of femininity.

'I have to leave for my lecture in about twenty minutes.'

'That should be plenty.'

She stepped back and allowed them in. Worn carpet and wallpaper, no dope fug.

'Are you Miss Donahue or Schier?' asked Gordon. 'The police gave us their report.'

'Mary Schier.' Throwing it over her shoulder like a bride's garter, correcting Gordon's pronunciation. He'd used the one that made her sound like a district, hers rhymed with beer.

The first room on the right a sitting room. They kept going, passed a closed door on the left, landed in a kitchen. Study books open on a formica table, pop from a transistor atop a fridge. Canisters neatly labelled *Rice, Flour, Sugar* arranged by height on a shelf, dishes drying in a rack, a tea towel hung square on an oven door. She clicked off the radio.

'Would you like coffee?'

'No thanks.' Ray taking the chair opposite where she'd sat. Gordon took the one to her right.

'He still hasn't turned up?' Her eyes tracing the textbook one last time before closing it.

'No,' Gordon this time. 'And he hasn't been back?'

Shaking her head. 'His room is down the back.'

'What are you studying?' Ray wanting to dilute any residue cop concerns.

'Medicine.'

Ray wondered how he'd go seeing a female doctor. Well, he never bothered with his male GP, so maybe better.

'We don't know anything much about Martin as a person,' Gordon coming in. 'Can you tell us what you thought of him, how he fitted in? What kind of person he is?'

'I can tell you what kind of person he *was before Spring*.'

She'd go well as a doctor, thought Ray.

Three months ago, when he joined the house, Martin Davis was a 'nice young bloke'. Using the Australian expression, showing, Ray guessed, they'd all sat around drinking cheap red wine and politely giving each other their backgrounds. Schier explained that Davis and Kate Donahue were the newer housemates.

'Patrick has been here three years, he's the veteran. John's a sophomore like me.'

Davis specialised in math. He was shy, not very worldly.

Ray picked her up. 'What do you mean by that?'

'He'd never lived on his own before. I'm not sure he'd ever had a girlfriend.'

'Politics?' asked Gordon.

'He didn't seem to have any when he arrived. He wasn't even anti the war. I'm not saying he was pro it, just it didn't feature.'

Davis was a good housemate. They spent a fair bit of time together but were all studying different courses. Davis got more interested in politics, but he was no radical. Everything changed around mid-March.

'There were some rallies on campus. Anti-war stuff. Some bands played. Moby Grape, I think. A lot of people from off-campus came.

Next thing Marty is growing this silly moustache and starting to use all the cliches in the book, like "What's your trip, man?" and all this stuff that sounded just so fake on him. Then she starts to turn up.'

'She' being Spring. Davis never introduced her as anything else. Very pretty, blonde, and if she was over eighteen, Schier would be flabbergasted. Spring reeked of pot and while she didn't smoke it in the common areas, the housemates were all sure she and Marty were getting stoned in his room where they pretty much stayed. Schier bumped into one of Marty's male classmates who had visited here a few times and he told her Marty had lost it and wasn't even coming to lectures.

'He told me Marty had experimented with LSD and had a bad trip.'

They got the friend's name: Harvey. Ray scanned the SFPD list of interviews, noted a Harvey Reynolds.

'It lasted about three weeks with Spring. I don't know if she broke up with Marty or what, but I came home one night, and Marty was in here at this table crying his heart out. He said she'd vanished. He had no idea where to. I made some comment about he had to expect that from girls like her and he jumped down my throat.'

'Can you tell us exactly what night that would have been.'

She checked the calendar on the wall, declared Wednesday April 5.

'I asked him how long since he'd seen her. He said she'd slept over two nights before.'

The Monday.

'He said he hadn't seen her since Tuesday morning. She'd gone out and hadn't come back.'

Davis had gone searching for her Tuesday night. He'd been unable to find her and told Schier he'd stayed up all night waiting for her. Then he'd spent all Wednesday searching for her. It had been about 8.00 p.m. on Wednesday when Schier had found him in tears.

'After you made that comment about Spring, did Martin get violent?' Drugs and booze could run some people that way, Ray wondering if Davis was one of these.

'No. He snapped at me, like, he was angry but not violent. He said something must have happened to her. I don't know if that was just wishful thinking on his part. My read was she'd moved on from him. I haven't seen him since that night.'

He'd gone out again but apparently returned. Thursday when the others left for lectures in the morning, his door was closed so they had no idea if he'd found Spring or not. The rest of Thursday nobody saw him. Schier heard him come in the back Friday morning in the early hours, go through to his room and then leave the house shortly after. That was that. Nothing from him since, no phone call, no letter. His rent was paid for another two weeks.

Twenty minutes had passed, she needed to hit her lecture. Schier doubted the other housemates could tell them any more than her.

'You have any photos of Spring?'

'We had one. We gave that to the police.'

'Spring always come here by herself?'

'I think so. I don't remember her bringing anybody else, but she might have when we were out.'

'Could we see his room before you go?' Gordon turning on the charm. She had no qualms about showing them in.

A single bed, the room dark even with the light on until Ray pulled back curtains. Dust motes floated over rumpled bedclothes; the blanket pulled up but only partly tucked. The room spacious, high ceilinged, the wallpaper holding its breath but bursting to let go. A faint smell of dope lingering even now. The dresser old but in good nick. Dark wood, three drawers on the left, two on the right, Bakelite handles mostly intact, an oval mirror with flaky backing its centre piece. Between the drawers in front of the mirror, a flat rectangle glass top where women could place lipsticks and hairbrushes. Gordon checked the drawers, Ray training his guns on the wardrobe. Ray had shared a hundred hangovers in upstairs rooms in country pubs with brothers of this very wardrobe.

Similar vintage to the dresser. A couple of dress jackets, trousers, all good quality. A few plain shirts. A pair of brown leather shoes at the base.

'Ties and underwear,' Gordon holding up samples from the dresser.

What Ray guessed was a study table squatting in the corner. Textbooks, seemed to be maths, strewn across it, pencils, a couple of biros. No diary. A notepad, jottings. A quick flip suggested lecture notes, a doodle of a girl's face, not very well done. Could have been Spring or just a generic girl image, impossible to tell. Davis might be a maths genius, but he drew like a bad golf green. On the floor was a record player, LPs and singles scattered. Ray recognised The Beatles. A cursory flip through before he began to trawl the metal wastepaper basket. Schier came back, said she had to go. They took the hint. Ray scooped up half a dozen LPs.

'We'll take these.'

Gordon handed Schier a piece of hotel stationery with their names and room number.

'If he should call or return …'

Ray wouldn't be holding his breath.

◆◆◆

Lunch, a burger and Coca Cola downtown, close to 3.00 p.m. A long time since John had patrolled the Cross, his feet aching after two long hours. The Berkeley campus a bust: longhairs on megaphones, placards: *Yankee Go Home, Make Love Not War*. Earnest young men in glasses, hair about the same length as his own, turtlenecks, talking ten to the dozen through bullhorns. Other students scurrying past, head down, not prepared to shelve their career yet.

Harvey Reynolds had been surprisingly easy to find. Ray spinning bullshit to the perm in admin with horned eyeglasses about how the nice young guy had helped his mother after a fall and he would like to personally give him a small reward. The woman had a photo. Reynolds looking all My Three Sons, short curly hair, clear eyes, clean shaven if he even needed to yet. She told them to hurry, Reynolds' physics class was ending nigh. They checked a campus plan on the wall, ran.

The exiting class, all male, could have been one family except for two black kids. Snapping on Reynolds hustling out with another of the look-alikes. Reynolds was happy to talk. They stood outside, sun bouncing up a sweat.

Davis and Reynolds had hit it off from day one.

'He was a good guy. Conscientious. Smarter than me but not the top in the class.'

Reynolds came from Texas, the long distance to home a bond. Also, they were squares.

'We didn't try drugs. People were always offering.'

They'd catch a movie, have a few illegal beers, hit on campus girls with zero success.

'They don't want anything to do with us guys over this part of the campus.'

Things changed a couple of months back.

'Moby Grape was playing a concert here and everybody was going. Martin and me like music. We're not that square. This girl comes up to Martin and asks if she can have a sip of his Coke. And she's gorgeous. Like Jeannie in *I Dream of Jeannie* except younger.'

From then on Martin Davis changed. He started hanging out with Spring all the time. Reynolds estimated Davis attended only two or three more classes. Those in the days immediately after he met Spring. It went downhill from there.

'Marty started skipping classes. I went around to the house he was sharing to check he was okay. He had that thing that acid casualties get, you know, you think you're talking to them, and they understand but then you see there is this blank wall, like nothing is really registering.'

Reynolds pretty much gave up after that, but he did bump into Davis a couple of weeks later.

'I went to see Sopwith Camel. Martin was there.'

This time Davis had been more coherent, like whatever bad trip he'd had had worn off. 'But he was uptight.'

'What's that mean?' Shearer knocking a cigarette from the packet he'd brought.

'Anxious. He was raving that Spring had been taken, that if she wasn't dead already, her life might be in danger.' Reynolds was worried at first, but the more he quizzed Davis the less convinced he became that anything bad had happened to Spring. 'I think she probably left him for somebody else. She's that kind of girl, you know, interested in the bands and stuff, Martin didn't fit. He was pussy struck, plain and simple. At least that's what I think.'

John said, 'Do you know what day this was?'

Reynolds pulled out a tiny diary, checked.

'Thursday April sixth.'

Ray said, 'And this was at night?'

'About nine p.m.'

John said, 'Why did Martin believe something bad had happened to Spring? Was it just because she wasn't in touch?'

'No. He said some guy had been asking around after her. I think it was easier for Martin to believe she'd been killed than that she'd broken up with him.'

Reynolds gave them the names of another couple of male students that Davis had been close to at some time.

They went looking. Lecture halls, coffee shops, a track meet. It took time but they located them. Neither had more to offer than Reynolds.

◆◆◆

John rating the burger a six: no beetroot, the bun soft, the cheese weird, but the meat was tasty. Shearer was studying the vinyl records in what light struggled through the diner's grimy window.

'You a Mamas and Papas fan?' John angling his head at studious Ray, the idea of pickle in a burger growing on him.

Shearer deadpanning, 'You know what ignorant people do? Especially young people? Especially stoned young people?'

'Tell me.'

Brandishing the vinyl in John's face. 'They pull records off the player with their greasy fingers.'

Shit. Gordon saw it now, why he'd taken the records.

'Fingerprints.'

Shearer pointed. 'These surfaces are perfect, and I'd say there are two different sets.'

'Davis' and Spring's.'

'Yeah. We might get an ID on her. Just have to print them up.'

'I don't suppose you happened to bring a fingerprint kit.'

Shearer grinned. 'In the bag in the car.'

The things you don't know you need till you do. John had to hand it to the bastard.

The prints were clear as day. At least two sets on most of the albums, on some three or more. Shearer had laid the albums out on the floor of their hotel room.

'I'm guessing these other prints might be J. Burnley's.'

'Who is J. Burnley?'

Shearer handing up an album cover. In small, neat printing in biro on the back top corner, J. Burnley. John walked to the small desk pulled out the phone directory, A–M.

One only Burnley, J. Sometimes you got lucky. John dialled. The phone burred. Sometimes your luck was short-lived.

'No answer.'

'What's the address?'

'Four nine eight Hemlock.'

Shearer flicking through a street directory. 'It's not all that far from Chalmers where Spring stayed that night.'

Two birds, one stone. Worth a shot. Shearer said they should try the share house first.

John drove. Weird heading to the other side of the road, traffic thicker than Sydney. A crawl to the Tenderloin. The neighbourhood grimier than where they'd been. Nude Bar signs sleeping till showtime, hippies in clumps, old black women walking with a shuffle and rope grocery bags hanging off their arms, metho drinkers limbering up for the evening. Chalmers wasn't such a bad street, out of the action. The address was a large house with those typical bay windows. John parked twenty yards away. They walked back, the evening pleasant like that first beer of a Saturday, easing its way into your blood. Steps led to a narrow porch and a mangy-dog sofa. The door was open.

Ray nodded: You make the running.

John called, 'Hello?'

No answer but the sound of an acoustic guitar somewhere back there. John leading the way into gloom, no lights burning yet, the smell of entrenched damp, the hallway narrow and long. Ragged carpet spat them out into a central lounge room. A staircase headed up, but they didn't need it, the guitar player was in here, male, long black hair, bare-chested except for a vest, loose harem or circus pants on narrow hips. The smell of past marihuana strong but nothing was burning right now. The guitarist looked up, a goatee, olive skin from what John could tell. A standard lamp, its shade a wire hoop with a paisley dress slung over the top.

John said, 'Hello. We're looking for anyone who might have been here when Spring stayed over.' John could see his new friend thinking, 'Are they fuzz?', saved him the trouble.

'We're private detectives from Australia looking for Spring's boyfriend.'

'Like we told the cops, she came here alone.' The guy's voice was anaemic.

'Did you speak to her?' Ray this time.

Guitarman shook his head.

'The only one she really spoke to was Suzie.'

'Suzie here now?'

'I don't know.' Pointing upstairs. 'First on the right.'

The staircase wobbled. They reached the landing turned back towards the front of the house. Door on the left was open, the bedroom empty. First on the right was closed. Shearer knocked. No answer. He opened it anyway. A vacant mattress, bedclothes tangled, no human. John wondering what their next move was when they heard boots below, voices. Next, the boots climbing their way. A mop of tight black curls rising slowly into frame. She topped the landing, a narrow face, pretty. She wore striped tights, some kind of brocade jacket.

'Looking for me?' A deep voice for a skinny thing, deeper than Guitarman's.

John said, 'Suzie? We're private …'

'Jake told me. Room's a mess, better out here.'

She dropped, sat cross-legged on the floor. John and Ray followed her lead, like cowpokes in a powwow with Geronimo.

'None of us knew her but she knew a mutual friend.'

'Kansas Annie.' John getting in ahead of Shearer.

'Yeah. You should speak to her.'

Ray said, 'It would be easier getting to Jackie Kennedy.'

'She can be hard to find if she wants to be.' A smile camping on the bank of thin lips.

'Can you tell us anything about Spring?' John hoping she caught his sincerity.

'I didn't know her beforehand, and we only talked that one night. She was looking for a place to crash and we try and let anyone stay here if they need. She mentioned a festival that a few people I knew were going to in Los Angeles. I had the feeling she was planning to hitch to LA the next day. She said she knew people there.'

'Did she mention Martin Davis, the guy we're looking for? She'd been his girlfriend for a few weeks … well, it seems Davis thought that.'

'Not directly. She said she had people, or a person, she was trying to avoid.'

'People or just one person?' Ray pressing.

'I think one. I'm not certain.'

But was it Davis who Spring was hiding from? John asked Suzie straight.

'She never said.'

'Was she scared?'

Suzie thinking. 'I don't know. She wanted to avoid whoever it was, that's for sure. Maybe she was scared before she got here.

I wouldn't say scared exactly when she was here. Here you don't ask, you listen. Annie could tell you more.'

Shearer asking the best place to find Annie.

'Four o'clock in the park when The Diggers hand out food. But if she doesn't want you to find her, you probably won't.'

John queried how Martin Davis presented when he came around.

'He was high. He said he was scared for Spring, anxious.'

'You're sure he wasn't just angry?' Shearer stretched out his legs. John's cramping too.

'Like faking?' She shook her head. 'I don't think so. He was almost paranoid. He was raving that he was worried somebody might have attacked Spring. We told him she was fine when she left here.'

John piecing it. 'You tell him you thought she'd gone to LA?'

'No. We just said she mentioned getting out of town. I didn't feel like he wanted to harm her, more the opposite. I didn't feel threatened by him. I couldn't imagine Spring would have been either, not from what I saw of her. But I was cautious. Acid can screw with your head. A few weeks back a girl got stabbed to death not far from here.'

Shearer said, 'Where exactly?'

Suzie flung out a finger. 'A dozen blocks that way. Hemlock Street.'

Zap.

'You remember the girl's name?' John wondering if it could be J. Burnley.

'No. Sorry.'

John fed her 'Burnley'. It rang no bells.

They lingered another twenty but neither Suzie nor Jake could remember the name of the murdered girl. It was too late to call Spinetti. Simplest way to find out if Burnley was the victim was to go see for themselves.

Talking on the drive over, Ray said, 'Maybe Martin Davis wasn't so paranoid after all? Davis had Burnley's albums, so he likely knew him or her.'

John thinking: Burnley could be the victim. Or killer for that matter.

It was a quiet nook of the Tenderloin but plenty of people about. A low sun, the streetscape muted. They parked, stepped out, night rushing over, nuzzling them. Shearer reached down the floor and unzipped his bag, extracted a large ring with at least fifty keys hitched to it.

'In Arson we need quick access. This is a whole lot easier than breaking down a door.'

'You planning to break in if Burnley's not home?'

'That's the thing, it's not a break-in.'

Shearer grinned. John knew, no point arguing.

◆◆◆

Burnley's apartment block a Weeties box: four-storey, walk up, four apartments per floor judging by the mailboxes in the small reception hall doused in weak lemon electric light. Burnley, he or she, top floor, number 14. John checked his gun. Ray followed suit.

John had the two LPs bearing Burnley's name tucked under his arm, *The Mamas & Papas Deliver* and *Highway 61 Revisited*.

The staircase more substantial than the last they'd ascended. The door brown, a bad paint job, not stripped just painted over, no bell visible. Shearer knocked then moved back, his hand resting inside his jacket on the Smith & Wesson. John felt exposed, clutched the albums as a shield. Wondered if they were calling on a dead girl.

A lock twisted, the door opened: male, twenty-seven to thirty-two, tall, slim, jeans and a shirt, better groomed than Jake the guitarist.

John took a stab. 'Mr Burnley?'

'Yes. Jay Burnley.'

At first John thought the guy was taking the piss, like "You only know my initial, right?" then he got that Jay was the guy's name. He'd never met a Jay before.

'I have a feeling these might be yours.' Displaying the albums.

Burnley taking them and examining.

'Yes.' Surprise billowing. 'Where did you find them?'

'Bit of a story. Sorry, I am John Gordon and this my colleague Ray Shearer. We're from Sydney, Australia. We're private detectives working a missing persons case and we came across these and … would you have ten spare minutes?

Standing there with the albums in his hand, on the spot. He could still close the door in their face.

'Sure, come in.' Stepping back, letting them inside.

The apartment roomy, smelling of cigarette smoke but not pot. A large sofa by the window, too late to scoop sun. Big armchairs.

Ray said, 'The family of a young man named Martin Davis hired us to try and find him. Would you know him?'

'The name is not familiar. I might know him by sight.'

Ray brandished the photo they had of Martin Davis. John watched Burnley. It looked like he studied it close.

Burnley shook his head. 'Don't know him.'

John said, 'He's a student at Berkeley. We found your albums in his room at the share house, thought there might be a chance you'd had contact with him. He went missing about four weeks ago.'

'How about her?' John this time with the one and only photo they had of Spring.

'Oh, yeah. What's her name again?'

'Spring.'

'That's right.'

Burnley sat on the sofa, gestured they join him. He leaned over, slotting the albums into an accordion of LPs extending from the wall. Ray taking the armchair.

Burnley said, 'She was at a party I had here, month or so ago. If your guy was here, I don't remember. But I remember her. Like a young Grace Kelly.'

'Did you give her the albums?'

'I think she asked if she could borrow them. I said yes.'

'You trusted her to bring them back?' John would never loan his to Denise's crowd.

'I hoped she would.' Smiling easily.

'Did you know her well?' John trying to get a read on Burnley.

'Never met her before that night.' Burnley's arm back along the sofa, relaxed. 'I told her to drop in any time, but figured she'd passed on that invitation.'

Ray said, 'Sorry to press you but if you could remember when exactly the party was?'

Burnley had them regularly, recalled it was a Thursday, four or five weeks back.

'I do stuff with The Diggers. You know about them?'

John recalling Susie's info. 'They hand food out?'

'And other stuff. Anarcho avant-garde cultural theory as expression. But don't quote me.'

John guessing Ray was in as deep a fog as him on that.

'I know that it was the week after Brautigan did a read.' Burnley shuffled around among a mountain of handbills stacked next to the sofa, found the one he wanted. 'This is the Brautigan night. So, yesterday it would have been ...' calculating, '... six Thursdays back.'

'You didn't know Spring till she came here?' John pushing.

'I'd seen her around. I invited a bunch of people. They invite others. We talk, play music.'

'What did you talk with Spring about, you recall?' Ray this time.

'Not politics, mainly music, Quicksilver versus the Dead. Big Brother versus Moby Grape.'

'Janis is a friend of ours,' said Ray. Burnley seemed impressed. 'We met her our first night here. She was going to introduce us to a woman named Kansas Annie. You know her by any chance?'

'I know the name.'

'She wasn't here with Spring?' asked John, then described her.

'I don't think so.'

John asked how Spring seemed. Was she anxious?

'No. She was fun, enjoying herself.'

'She didn't mention someone was after her?'

'No.'

John said, 'Martin Davis was rambling to people that she might have been killed. Did she strike you as in danger?'

Burnley a slow shake. Then, 'But a few days after that party, a girl on the floor below was murdered. Stabbed to death. So maybe that was on his mind.'

'That was in this building?' After Burnley had answered the door, John had banished the killing from his thoughts. Now it circled back on him.

'Yes. It affected everyone. I didn't know the dead girl, but I'd see her now and again on the stairs.'

'What was her name?' Shearer.

'Judy. Ilkin or Ikin. I saw her surname in the papers. I think we introduced ourselves once by our first names. We had cops all over the place here.'

'They interviewed you?' John wondering if he was being too cop.

'Yes. She was killed sometime on the weekend and the body wasn't found for about three days. I was in Marin with friends when it happened. I came back on the Thursday and there was a note under my door to call the police. A detective came around right away.'

That Thursday would have been around the time Spring had left for LA. John wondering if Spring had known about the murder. He asked if Burnley could be specific but all he knew was it was sometime after the weekend they found the body.

'They get who did it?' Ray again.

'No so far as I know.'

John asked if Spring might have known Judy.

'It's possible. I mean, the community is pretty tight, but Judy never came up here, so if Spring knew her it wasn't through me, and like I say, Spring never came back. Maybe she would have been spooked coming back up here.'

At least they had something more to track down.

'You got any idea where we might find Kansas Annie?'

'There's a guy named Theo does the design on a lot of these.' He held up the Brautigan handbill. 'He's working on an exhibition at the Glide Church. Taylor and Ellis, near Union Square. He knows everyone.'

'Anyone else who was at your party that night who knew Spring?'

'I don't know who specifically gave her the invite. I saw her hanging around with some people who are close to the Dead. You could try their house.'

Ray asked if Burnley could give them contacts on any people he remembered being at the party. He came up with four phone numbers.

'The others I know don't have phones. These people might know her.'

'What apartment was the dead girl in?'

'Two floors down, number eight.'

They thanked him for his time, slipped him the Clarence number. Ray said, 'If Spring should turn up would you mind calling us? We'd love to find our bloke.'

Two floors down. Dark at the end of the corridor, John felt goose-bumps. There was a bell. Ray pressed, nobody answered. They tried 7 but got nothing. A TV sounded behind the door to 6. John knocked. And again. The door opened on a chain, suspicious eyes, elderly, the hair creeping out from behind the door suggested female.

John said, 'Hello, Madam. We're private detectives working Judy's case. We wondered if we could ask you a couple of questions.'

'I'm watching TV.' A larynx through which the smoke of ten thousand cigarettes had journeyed.

Shearer opened his wallet, the door-slit eyes following like they are supposed to do in a good painting. Ray peeled two dollars, held them out. A lizard hand snatching.

John said, 'Did you know Judy well?'

'We talked sometimes. When we did laundry. Couple of times

she came in to borrow flour. Young people never buy enough flour.'

'Just wondering if you ever saw this young woman with her?'

Filmy eyes squinting on Spring.

'I can't say. I saw her with girls like that.'

'How about this man?'

Davis' turn.

'I don't think so. She had a boyfriend in the navy, she told me.'

'She have many visitors or parties?' Ray leaned against the wall.

'No parties. She was quiet. Like I said, she had girls she saw. Sometimes men visited. She went to a couple of the protests in the park. Worried about her boyfriend. I told her, 'He'll be fine.' That was a lie. I lost my brother in the Philippines in the war. Nineteen years old. But I didn't tell her that. Now she's dead and the boyfriend's the one left crying. It's a dumb world.'

'Were you here when it happened?'

'The police say she was likely killed on the Sunday night. I was in bed then asleep.'

'When was the body discovered?'

'That was the Wednesday. One of her friends from work came around to check she was okay and got the super to open the door. They said it was like an abattoir.'

◆◆◆

A dark bar, golden liquor on ice. Staccato laughter to a dirty-joke punchline from some suits on stools. Ray enjoying kicking back. Kansas Annie and her whacko avant-garde Digger mates could wait. Gordon had asked what his read was on Burnley. Ray was thinking and savouring simultaneously.

'If his alibi holds up, and unless the SFPD are incompetent, I guess it does, then it's like he says. He loaned some records to Spring.'

John with a biro jotting a timeline, speaking his thoughts aloud. 'Phyllis Diller says the body wasn't found till Wednesday. If she's right, then the murder is coincidence because Spring is already at the Tenderloin house by Tuesday. So that wasn't spooking her.'

Ray kicked that tyre. 'Unless she met some psycho at the party.

Maybe somebody from the building who knew Judy, who gave off bad vibes. A long shot, granted.'

Note: see if Spinetti had anything to go on. Sometimes you made things more complicated than they needed to be, Ray reminded himself.

Ray said, 'Most likely scenario. Davis is tripping on acid. Spring has vanished, he's already freaking. Then he hears about a girl getting stabbed where Spring was, that's enough to send him out of his tree. See, when he fronts the police to ask them to look for her, he doesn't mention that a bloke is after her. Wouldn't he mention that if he wanted to be taken seriously?'

John nodding. Ray running with it.

'Davis doesn't want to face up to the fact she's dumped him, he'd rather think she was murdered.'

John said, 'You're thinking if Spring was avoiding anybody, it was Martin Davis.'

That was exactly what he was thinking.

'If she was genuinely in fear of her life, Susie would have picked up on it.'

'But Susie didn't think Martin Davis was threatening.'

Ray shrugged. Plenty of killers you'd think butter wouldn't melt in their mouth. 'I'm asking myself, why wasn't Davis at the party?' Raising his eyebrows, inviting Gordon's best guess.

'Because she didn't invite him.'

'Exactly. I mean maybe he was there, and Burnley didn't notice him, but if you're going to chat up a girl, you check that stuff out first. So, I don't think he was there. He wasn't studying. So, either she didn't want him to come or he was doing something else, but from what we hear there was nothing he'd rather do than be with Spring.'

'Maybe he was out of his tree on acid.'

'Possibly.'

Ray pulled from his pocket the note paper with the phone numbers Burnley had given them.

'We need to start dialling, see if we can be sure he really wasn't there.'

A civilised bar, phone booths where you could place your drink on a napkin on polished mahogany while you chatted. Ray's calls drew two males. Both remembered Spring, neither recalled Martin Davis. Gordon pulling two females in the Burnley lottery. One remembered Spring being there and 'dancing extravagantly'. Neither recalled Martin Davis, or any Australian or Englishman for that matter.

By the time they left the bar, it was after 9.00 p.m. Ray hungry now. Gordon insisting they try Chinese. Ray would have preferred opium. He'd had Chinese food. Twice. Fried rice he could stomach, that was it. But Gordon was determined, going on about the trendy art-student crowd Denise knocked about with, and their Asian fetish.

Chinatown was narrow, all sudsy drains.

They found a place that spoke English and sold beer. Gordon had something in 'black bean sauce'. No thanks, not for young Ray Shearer, but the dumplings Gordon forced on him were tasty, he had to admit. Ray thinking, get back to the hotel, canoodle with Kitty. This morning when they'd left, her eye had strayed after him, they'd locked gazes and she'd smiled. But it was too late tonight, her shift was long over. He was wondering if Janis might be playing somewhere.

Gordon said, 'What do you want to do?'

Ray said, 'I think we should leave Annie for tonight. If we find her and she runs, I can't be fucked chasing her.'

'Let's head to the park. Maybe there's a show on.'

Images of Kitty fading. Ray knowing where he'd like to be, but this was work. Gordon was right. They weren't finding Davis without hippies and drugs first.

◆◆◆

They parked at Haight-Ashbury, left the car, joined the moving sidewalk. John buzzing. There was a spirit about this place, this time, real as the heat of your bonnet after a long drive. Sure, every other street corner there were fakes, self-conscious marionettes thumping bongo drums and flashing cheesy peace signs but for the most part, people were just ambling along sidewalks, arms around shoulders, part of the same night. Like they knew this whole thing was bigger than them, like even if they were no more than fleas along for the ride, they were special for it. The closest John could tag it was a grand final he'd been to, St George and Souths, where every fan knew they were part of history. But this was bigger than that too. Bigger than this city even, you could feel it.

Cops watched on from squad cars, or in small groups in dark uniforms, itching for trouble. There was going to be plenty of that sometime, John feeling that in his bones. But right now, he was electric. People high on love, gave off a charge even if it was illusion cranking the handle.

Tonight, the action seemed to be more on the borders than in the park itself. A small stream of longhairs was heading up an alley, coagulating twenty yards along, talking, smoking. Ray tilted his head, 'Let's check it out.'

The attraction was a cellar, a handpainted sign outside: *Poetry.* Descending, the staircase iron and narrow. Incense-heavy darkness lit by a string of low-watt party bulbs giving onto a wider, lighter space. Barrels and crates, a few kitchen chairs, a small stage with a microphone. A balding, bearded, fat guy, mouthing into it, articulate and bitter, a torrent of words, some hooking John in passing: 'Castro', 'castrate', 'castanet', 'CIA', 'MIA'.

John studying nodding heads, shining hornrims. Ray more interested in the fishnets on a girl in a beret and mini.

The poem rushing to its climax: 'I'm on the Polaris, ascending your womb, my tomb, the shuddering beauty that only comes with the silence of self-destruction and the certainty that we are own most effective assassins.'

Loud applause, a royal wave by the vanishing poet, a middle-aged man in tee-shirt and jungle fatigues taking the stage, gesturing to the disappearing arse of the poet.

'Let's hear it for The Man.'

Wolf-whistles, more applause, the wave of admiration slowly calming. The MC back on air.

'Thank you thank you. It's great to see every week more people down here. We're multiplying.' Comradely whoops.

'You know there are many lies perpetrated in the name of war but one of the greatest is that we need more war to protect what we won in previous wars, like there is some unending cycle where peace can't survive by itself and needs to be fed by blood, but that is something that I, and my brothers in the Vets Against War don't subscribe to.' A hand-point to three bellies and beards standing to the side. Cheers from the faithful.

'I put my life on the line in the Pacific, saw things you wouldn't credit humans could do to one another. I came back but I never quite came back. And every night on my news I see young men dead and torn apart just like before, only then I got it, but not this time. This thing doesn't stop. Not until we say "enough". And Vietnam … we should not be there.' More applause.

'LBJ would have you believe that we're defending freedom but me and my buddies have been down that road and I'm telling you it solves nothing. But that's enough from me, now welcome Ernst Deiger and his sitar.'

Ernst in a shiny emerald-green satin Cossack shirt, purple trousers and leather belt began fingering the sitar. John looked to Shearer, wondering how long he'd last. One minute and a little in, Ray motioned drinking. John approved. Ray had obviously already scoped the place far better than John. Heading around a pillar to a quiet back corner. Bottles of wine on a trestle-table, a biscuit tin, a third full of cash beside them. John looked for guidance, spied the MC and one of the other vets sitting at a long table.

'Is there a cost?'

'What you can afford.' The MC clearly deciding Ernst didn't need him either.

John stuck in a dollar bill, they helped themselves to styrofoam cups, filled with red wine. Ray pulled up a chair at the long table the other end to the vets. Here the sitar no more than a mosquito buzz. Fatigue was sapping John now, like the grapevine wrestling hold was supposed to.

Shearer said, 'I should have gone back to the hotel early, snuggled up with Kitty.' He pulled the photos out of his pocket and slid them along to the table to the two vets.

'You seen either of these two kids around recently?'

The MC said without warmth, 'You cops?'

'Private,' said Ray.

The vets checked the photos out, shook their heads. Long shot. They slid them back.

A man's finger stabbed, pinned them to the table. John looked. A longhair, thirty, sinewy.

'You were the guys looking for Annie.'

John's eyes meeting his partner's. Ray's hand snaking to his pocket for his gun.

John said, easy as silk, 'That's right. Who are you?'

'Nitro. Friend of Janis. She says you guys are cool.'

''Ken oath, we're cool.'

Nitro unsure what to make of Shearer. 'Wait here.'

Ray met John's eyes again, said, 'Search me,' belted his wine. John following suit.

A woman stepped through the crowd, heading their way.

Kansas Annie.

5 WHITE RABBIT

'Sorry about last night. You understand, couple of strangers looking like pigs asking around … gets a girl …'

'Uptight?' Shearer with the lingo now, impressed with himself.

Annie smiling. Shearer hauling the bottle from the bench, grabbing a cup, pouring, sliding it across to their guest.

'You're the guys helped Janis?' Annie twirling the cup.

John gestured Shearer's way. 'He did the hard yards.'

The sitar jangling, reverent attention elsewhere.

'So, you want to know about Spring?' For a small woman, Annie could slug her liquor quick. The cup already rattling when she sat it down.

John said, 'We've been hired to find Martin Davis. We understand he was her boyfriend.'

Her eyebrows rising. 'An exaggeration.'

'He was playing hide the salami.' Ray filling her up again.

'They were balling, yeah. But he was not long for her world. Spring was already casting around for someone more interesting.'

The Jay Burnley party, Spring going solo. Fitted. John asked if Annie had met Martin Davis.

'Once or twice. I like him, you know. But he was trying to find me to learn where Spring was, so I stayed out of it.'

Ray said, 'We heard Spring was avoiding somebody. Was that Martin?'

Shaking her head. 'Some other guy from her past. She had to get out of there quick.'

John asked if this other man was a past lover.

'Might have been. She didn't elaborate. That's cool. But she was scared. She didn't want to go back to Berkeley. I think that's where this guy busted her. She said something about her hometown, bad history.'

John said, 'You get his name?'

'No. Spring told me she needed a place to stay for a night, then she was getting out of town. I think to LA but I don't know for sure.'

Shearer asked if she knew Jay Burnley. 'Lives in an apartment on Hemlock.'

'Name is familiar but I can't place him. Why?'

John took it up. 'Spring went to a party there a week before she disappeared. As far as we can see, she didn't take Martin.'

A shrug. 'Like I said, she was ready to move on.'

'That weekend a girl in the building was stabbed to death.'

'I remember that. I think Spring was gone before that even broke. What was freaking her out was this guy from Squaresville, Illinois – that was her home state – who she had a history with. She had her biker pals looking out for her though.'

'You got any photos of her?' John wanting whatever he could get.

She didn't. John asked what Spring was like as a person.

'Happy-go-lucky. She'd give you the shirt off her back. She never has much money, but she always shares. See these ...' she pulled at what he was sure were dog tags around her neck. 'She found these. Knew I was into weird shit like this and gave it to me. What's hers is yours.'

Shearer said, 'Is she trusting? Cynical?'

Annie's face screwed. 'Don't let her looks fool you. She's worldly but there's a sweetheart in there. She really wanted to help Martin, you know, be there on his first trip, give him great sex. Even though she's a rolling stone. She didn't want to break his heart but time's up on that. I hope he doesn't find her. For his sake.'

From the sound of Spring, John would be surprised if she had a job but asked anyway.

'Not that I know. I think for a little while she might have worked washing cars at some auto place.'

'She have a room somewhere?'

'Wherever she puts her head. Martin's for the last few weeks. A few days with me. Just wherever.'

Suddenly easier to hear, the sitar finally curling up and dying. Annie pulled out a joint, stuck it between her lips.

'Got a light?'

Ray reached for his hotel matchbook, too late, a butane flame was already burning paper on the tip of the joint in Annie's mouth. The MC leaning in, playing Sir Galahad.

'Zippo. Never out of style,' he said.

Annie chuckled. 'Thanks, Murph.'

Murph the vet looked over at Ray and John. 'No more of that oing and boing music. Got a folky up next. Stick around.'

Annie offering Murph the joint. The vet taking a deep hit. 'If those boys in Nam aren't doing this right now, they will be soon.'

Murph saluting, going up to back-announce Ernst. John couldn't imagine the diggers at The ANZAC march sucking on joints. Different worlds.

Ray said, 'If Spring is in LA, do you have any idea where she might be?'

'She's mentioned friends up in the Hills, but I don't know any more than that.'

John knew the hills around Hollywood were the apex of cool: musicians, movie stars. He got Annie's phone number.

'It's the tattoo place underneath my apartment. They'll run up and get me, slip a note under my door.'

John palmed her the Clarence number. 'Please, if you hear from Spring, or anybody who knows where she or Martin is, call us.'

She said she would.

Ray held up a finger, wait. 'You said you never told Martin where Spring was.'

'That's right.'

'But he turned up at the Tenderloin house later. How did he know?'

A Dylan song started in the background. John couldn't remember the name of it.

'Only thing I can think of, is when I told her I had some friends who'd let her stay the night we were at the markets getting this fixed.' She touched the dog-tag necklace. 'There's a girl who deals cheap, Peggy. Peggy and she were talking while I was looking at bangles and rings and Josephine was doing the clasp. She's an amazing jeweller. I'd say Spring must have told Peggy 'cause we went straight from there to Chalmers.'

John said, 'Would Martin Davis know Peggy?'

'Hell yes. He would have been buying his pot from her.'

'Where would we find Peggy?'

'Probably partying with the Mothers.' Reading their void. 'A group: The Mothers of Invention. They are so weird. In a good way.' A beat. 'I think they're back in LA. Last I heard, Peggy was balling the bass player … or drummer … or, shit, maybe both. She hauled out of here with them and said she'd be back in a week or two.'

Annie said she had to go. John reminded her to call with any news. Then she was gone back the way she came, through a curtain of denim and hair.

'What now?' John yawned.

'Bed,' said Ray.

◆◆◆

A breakfast of orange juice and toast. Ray spied Kitty behind polished wood tending pigeonholes, waited till she turned and smiled.

'Mr Shearer!'

'"Ray", please, Kitty.'

She asked what he'd been up to, leaning in so he caught a whiff of her perfume. She smelled good.

'Hippie poets, hamburgers and bourbon.'

'Sounds like a full card.'

'Except there's a huge hole … in my heart.'

'You might need surgery.'

Dancing eyes. My Lord, she was gorgeous. 'I'm scared. I'd need someone to hold my hand.'

'I could do that.'

Gordon emerged from the lift. Ray blew Kitty a kiss and met Gordon halfway to the door.

It being Saturday, Gordon had taken the precaution of calling Spinetti's number to check if he was at work. Turned out he was, but only till midday. He told them to haul their arses down there. Obvious they'd used up their one official SFPD greeting. This time no big desk, no flag. Spinetti's room stunted, paperwork a landslide, plaster pitted. The cop listening as they ran through progress. John Gordon taking the lead. 'We don't think there is a connection between Spring's disappearance and the murder, but we want to be thorough.'

Ray said, 'They had LPs from a Jay Burnley who has an apartment in the same building. We returned those, ran our eyes over him. But these LPs were almost certainly handled by Spring and Martin Davis. They were on the floor of his bedroom.'

Gordon handing over more albums. 'Inspector Shearer took a set of prints.'

Ray reached into his pocket pulled out the sample he'd lifted, now in a plastic bag. Spinetti reaching.

'You brought your own powder?'

Ray nodding.

'You're shitting me. I should hire you two now.'

Spinetti lifted his phone, pushed buttons mouthed to the receiver. 'Tell Schmidt to come see me. And to bring the crime book on Ikin. Now.' Dropping the receiver, rattling the cradle. Ray figured it was safe to resume.

'We heard that Spring was originally from Illinois. Maybe she has a criminal record there. You might be able to pull some strings?'

'We can *try.*' Ray caught the tone: Spinetti's optimism blunted by a thousand 'no's' over the course of his police history. A knock on the door.

'Come in.'

A broad-shouldered detective, late thirties, file in his hands, had to be the crime book.

'Gentlemen, this is Detective Jeffrey Schmidt. He's got the Ikin case with Detectives Corser and Nadle.'

Introductions. Schmidt pulled up a chair. Spinetti gave the lie of the land, asked Schmidt to assist 'the Aussies'.

Schmidt spoke, deep and clipped. 'We've got nothing. A month in, I don't like our chances. Nobody saw or heard anything. So far as the ME could tell, she was stabbed to death the Sunday night late. I say "stabbed", but she was just about bisected.' Opening the book, gory crime-scene photos, Ikin's bloodied and eviscerated, body in the bathtub. 'No sign of sexual assault but we found tissues in the bin, and stains on the tub suggested he masturbated after. Either somebody she knew, or somebody who tricked her into opening the door. We think she had her throat cut in the living room then was dragged to the bath and butchered. It's as bad as I've seen. No bloody prints though. Nothing.' Schmidt's big right hand did a magician's disappearing gesture. 'This asshole knew what he was doing. Must have brought a change of clothes with him and the weapons. Body was not found till the Wednesday, late morning, when a work colleague called.'

Ray said, 'You questioned Jay Burnley, two floors above.'

'Wasn't him. He was in Marin County from the Saturday, and we have three witnesses who swear he never left.'

John Gordon asked if there was anybody else from the building who rang bells.

'Mechanic on the third floor had a conviction for assault going back three years but he was alibied too.'

'Any connection between Judy and Berkeley campus or hippies?'

Spinetti said, 'This town these days, everybody has a connection with Berkeley or hippies.'

Schmidt took it up. 'Nothing stands out. She was a quiet girl, knew hippies but was only on the fringe. Serviceman boyfriend who she respected. Her friend where she worked at the library said she had attended a pro-servicemen gathering where there was some friction with the freaks. Nothing major, no threats, didn't know of any enemies.'

Schmidt spilled more, nothing snagging for Ray. Neither Spring nor Martin Davis' name had come up in the investigation.

They told Schmidt about the Burnley party the Thursday before. He wasn't hopeful.

'There would have been a dozen parties between Thursday and Sunday in that building. If Judy met her killer in the days before she died, it's a fluke. We went over the residents with a fine-tooth comb.'

They thanked him for his time. Mutual promises to help if they could. Schmidt left, already another homicide hotter than Judy Ikin's calling him. Ray glad this wasn't his turf.

'Need anything more?' Spinetti checking his watch. Ray taking the hint, thanking him for his time. They shook hands. Spinetti said he'd try to get action on the fingerprints.

'Maybe I can get Chicago to take a look. I've got some friends there, but Illinois is a big state. If you get the hometown, we can put in an official request.'

Ray saying he understood.

Stepping out onto a warming pavement. Ray said, 'I think we're going to have to go Los Angeles.'

Gordon was the colour of chalk, ever since Spinetti had pulled out the crime book. Ray pretended he didn't notice.

You think you can banish the screaming fear. You can't. You think time will heal that wound. It doesn't. John's insides all seaweed. Stepping into the house in Chippendale had brought back the terror. Him and Denise ready to be slaughtered by a madman. Denise dangling over a pit of knives, John straining to hold the rope, praying, out of his mind. Death kissed you, enveloped you, left its scent on you. Shame, inadequacy, guilt swam in your blood.

You were hollow, like you were watching somebody else, but it wasn't anybody else, it was you, and you knew that was the real lie, that you had to create this phantom identity watching yourself in the third person. But it was you alright, you just couldn't face it. He hadn't dealt with Chippendale properly. Now here it was again. Judy Ikin almost sawn in two. Black-and-white photos but in a way that was worse than colour, made your imagination jump. The pools of ink you knew were blood. Ray spoke to him, and he talked back, but deep down in the bottom of the well, down here where the moss grew and the water was rank with the sopping flesh of dead goat, here there was nobody to help.

A café somewhere, instant coffee, some kind of pie. Shearer looking at him over his fork like he could tell John's ghosts were in his heart.

John avoiding. 'I think we can rule out any connection between Judy Ikin and Spring.'

Ray pointing with his small fork. 'Davis gets dumped. Spring doesn't tell him why, doesn't tell him there's a man from her past in town. Either she doesn't want to involve him for his sake or ...'

John accepting the challenge. '... his part of town, his circle, is too hot. Or both.'

Ray nodding. 'Let's call the guy from her past Nick Beal.'

'Why Nick Beal?'

'You don't know that film *Alias Nick Beal*! It's a beauty. Ray Milland is the devil, Nick Beal.'

John thinking, 'Nick as in Old Nick?'

'I suppose. I hadn't thought about it.'

'You're the Catholic. Beal, short for Beelzebub.'

John had thought plenty about the devil since he'd met him in person.

'Who knows?' Shearer ploughed on. 'So, Spring formerly of Mouseville, Illinois, is going about her business when she encounters Nick Beal and skedaddles.'

John working the logic. 'We assume she encounters Nick Beal at or near Berkeley or in some circle of friends that Martin might be part of. She needs to vanish.'

Shearer finished his pie. 'What would you do if you were Nick?'

'I'd go to wherever I saw her, and I'd start asking around.'

'Right. So, stick with me here. We don't know Spring's name, but Nick Beal almost certainly does. If we could find out if somebody besides Martin and the cops was asking about Spring, we might get a lead on Spring's real name.'

And once they had that, she would be a whole lot easier to find.

John said, 'The police report never mentions the cops hearing somebody was asking for Spring. So maybe we can rule out all the places in Berkeley they tried. Let's go back to the place on Washington and ask them what the cops might have missed.'

◆◆◆

A perky blonde greeted them. Kate Donahue was the only one home, grabbing a break between classes. She knew about them from Mary Schier. Still no contact from Davis, and there'd been no sign of Spring either. Donahue confirmed Schier's report re Davis: a quiet young guy, did the dishes, no parties. Then he'd gone off the rails.

'Personally, I'm glad he's gone. I don't want to be mean. I liked the old Marty a lot, but I don't want stoned hippies in my house when we're not here. And I don't want them when we're here either.'

John handed the list of places the cops had visited, asked what they'd missed. She grabbed a biro and wrote a dozen more names.

'They got all the main ones, but these are more underground.'

John thanked her.

'You staying in town long?' Bright eyes twinkling.

'Not sure. We might have to check out LA.'

'Drop by if you're in the area.'

John feeling himself blush.

On the way to the car, Ray leaned in, 'Double date: me and Kitty ...'

John said, 'Don't even think about it.'

Stabbing flashes in his brain, the Ikin crime scene: dark blood, gashed flesh. He pushed it away, told himself, the past can't be changed, only how you deal with it. Wishing he had Denise beside him to hold.

Two hours of walk, drive, park. Berkeley crisscrossed. Finally, a break. A record store, posters and handbills pasted over walls, a couple of acoustic booths with headphones, racks of recordings by groups with weird names Ray had never heard of. Not an Elvis record in sight. The long-haired blond guy with a thin moustache serving at the counter listened.

Ray knew right off he recognised the Spring and Martin Davis photos, even though he acted vague and pretended otherwise.

'I don't think so, no.'

Ray said, 'We're not cops.' Best to set him straight. Ray gave their private D spiel: Australians hired by a concerned family. Saw the guy's attitude shift. Ray floated the notion there could be money in it for a lead. 'Was there anybody here looking for the girl, other than cops?' Ray held a dollar bill between his fingers. Snaffled.

'Yeah, there was a guy in here asking about Spring.'

Thank you, Efrem Zimbalist Junior for making a dubious profession cool.

'How did he do it?' Ray getting in tight.

'Like you, showed a photo of her.'

'And then did he say, "You seen this girl around?" or "You know a girl, Betty Smith?" and then show you the photo?'

'He said something like, "I'm trying to find a friend of mine from back home. I heard she was living near here."'

'Then he showed the photo?' Gordon making sure.

'That's right.'

'How do you know Spring?' Ray momentarily distracted by the Big Brother gig poster behind Blondy.

'She's a regular. And she's kind of memorable.' Unsaid, she was a dish.

John Gordon weighed in. When was it the guy showed up?

Blondy recalled it was around the last week of March.

'What did he look like?' Gordon pushing.

'Twenty-three, six-foot, square shoulders, square everything. Short hair, one of those Pat Boone two-tone shirts ...' Ray felt the guy judging him, assessing his unseen wardrobe, '... Goldwater type, slacks and leather shoes, Midwest voice. Said he was an old friend from her hometown visiting and heard she was living in Berkeley.'

Ray said, 'What did you tell him?'

'I said she was through here every so often. Hung out with a student type. That guy.' Pointing at the Davis photo.

Ray wondered if the guy gave a name.

'Said his name was Clint and he wanted to surprise her so next time she came in to call him but not say anything to her. Paid me a buck for my trouble, said there was five in it for me when I called.'

Ray said, 'And did she come in again?'

Blondy smirked. 'She did.'

'But you didn't call Clint. Instead, you told her.'

'That's right. For all I know the guy is some narc from Kansas City.'

John Gordon said, 'And her reaction when you told her?'

'Like I'd said, King Kong was looking for her. She asked me for a description and then all there was was dust where she'd been standing.'

'Could you give me an exact date when this was?' Ray peeling another buck out.

Record man thinking.

'We just got our first batch of *Surrealistic Pillow* in and I'd already sold like five when she turned up. The order should have arrived Monday, but they were so busy we never got it till the next day. It was Tuesday April fourth.'

He'd not seen Spring, Clint or Davis since.

'You still got Clint's number?' Ray itching.

Blondy reached under the counter and found a card with a phone number scrawled on it. Ray copied it, handed Blondy the Clarence card and told him that if Clint, Spring, or the kid in the photo came in he was to call.

'There's ten bucks in it for you.'

◆◆◆

John making the call. A rooming house in Western Addition. Clint Adams had checked out Sunday April 9. He'd paid cash and left no forwarding address.

'You think it's a false name?' John asking as they sipped weak beers in a waterfront bar, oysters the special.

'I'm guessing so. But he might keep using it.'

'You think he found her?'

'If he did, then he must have found her after Thursday night.'

John wondering why, if he hadn't found her, he wouldn't check back with the record store.

'Well, remember he likely knows her real name. If she bought a bus ticket say, he might have been able to track where she's heading next.'

Either way it was a bust. Shearer insisted on getting back to the hotel before Kitty knocked off. They made it with twelve minutes to spare.

'Got a message for you.'

John impressed how fast she could bat those eyelashes at Ray. Kansas Annie had called, a one-word message, 'News'.

John phoned from the lobby. The phone picked up, the rattle of the tattoo gun background to a voice conjuring a mouthful of broken teeth and beer.

'Yeah?'

John asked to speak to Annie, said it was the Aussie PI.

'Hold on.'

Three minutes occupied watching Ray and Kitty getting cheek to cheek over the counter.

Then, 'Yeah.' Annie's voice.

'It's John Gordon. I got your message.'

Annie said, 'A friend of mine just hitched back from LA. She says she saw Davis at a Buffalo Springfield concert there, couple of weeks ago. He was still looking for Spring.'

'He say where he was staying?'

'She thinks she might have written it down. She's going to call me back. But look, if she hasn't got it, just find the Mothers. You find the Mothers, you find Peggy. You find Peggy, you likely find Spring. Also, there's been some guy asking around about me. Not Martin Davis. Looks like one of the Four Freshmen.'

Clint Adams, bet on it.

John said, 'Sounds like the guy who was chasing Spring.'

'That's what I figured. I was thinking, if he is from back home, he'll know her real name. That would help you guys.'

It would for sure. But—

'You need to be careful, Annie.'

'I have Angels on my side, and not the kind with halos. Don't worry about me. If I learn anything, I'll let you know. Hey, you going to the Fillmore tonight? The Airplane are playing.'

John flashing on street posters and the album cover of *Surrealistic Pillow*.

'I don't know,' Looking over at Shearer getting touchy-feely with Kitty.

'It'll be a sellout, but you'll be fine. Just say you're Janis' Australian friend. You gotta see the Airplane. It's like saying you were in San Fran and never checked out the Golden Gate. I'll catch you there. Might have Marty's address for you by then.'

As the receiver clunked, Shearer sauntered over. John told him they had a confirmed sighting of Davis in LA a couple of weeks back.

Shearer grinned, 'Perfect.'

'We're leaving for LA tomorrow morning.' John looking over at Kitty as he spoke.

Shearer whispered, 'You might need to take a long sightsee tonight then.' Kitty smiling Shearer's way. Shearer in John's ear pre-emptive, 'No sermons, please. I doubt I'll ever get out of Australia again. I know I'll never see Kitty again.'

What the hell, it was Shearer's life. He had already screwed himself over bad, but John wasn't his keeper.

John said, 'I'll be in at two. Either she's gone by then or you book yourself another room. We leave at eight, whatever happens.'

'Aye, aye, Captain.'

Shearer saluted, walked back to where Kitty was waiting demurely, her handbag lowered to her dress hem. Shearer took her by the arm and escorted her out into the warm San Francisco evening.

John reflecting on Annie's call: Davis alive and well in LA as of two weeks ago. John tried to call home, a decent morning hour in Sydney. The operator did her best. The phone rang out. Denise likely at college. John abandoned, headed to the desk, grabbed a telegram form, put down Geary's name as the recipient and wrote, *Davis sighted LA. Leave for there tom A.M.*

He handed it to the concierge to take care of, felt less anxious. His tree not yet dropping fruit but there was a bud. The Ikin bloodbath still giving him concussion. Denise would be at one of her art classes, nothing to worry about. Reassuring himself because he wasn't certain he would ever be normal again and prayed she would be.

◆◆◆

Annie proved right. The grand piano manning the door remembered John, allowing him in. The vibe different this time. With Janis and Country Joe it had been let's get stoned and jig and holler. A good time feel, whacky tobacky, peace signs. This was something else. Acid?

John didn't know enough to make that call but the atmosphere made you feel like you were at the bottom of the ocean among some weird marine life. It was darker, the hues colder, the music more tidal, the human kelp thicker than before. He pushed through, scanned for Annie; tough in the dark. She wasn't near where he'd found her last time. It was a little lighter here, his eyes growing accustomed too, so he was pretty sure she wasn't there yet. A girl slid past, stopped, turned and fastened her mouth to his. John responded instinctively, felt something in his mouth other than her tongue and she was moving on, blowing him a kiss. He should have spat out the pill, didn't. Because he'd faced death, and something worse, the threat of killing the one you loved. After that nothing scared you, and everything scared you. He swallowed. He did a lap of the room one way, then the other, poked around a corner near the entrance, no Annie. He found himself drifting back to the heart of the room.

Like the soft footfall of a leather moccasin missed by a sleeping cavalry man, he hadn't registered the shift in the room's nuance. The girl's vocals hit him like a tomahawk, lights seeming to explode in his cranium, then settling. On stage a girl with black hair. The beat martial, the words almost a chant. The lead guitar gently nuzzled a snake-charm melody.

Then drums and guitars crashed and the singers on stage shouted and so did everybody around him. Like he'd walked into a religious service where everybody was baptised and schooled and knew the right words, and he was nothing but a heathen. They were chanting about wanting, needing someone to love. Expecting him to join in.

Sure, we all want someone to love, he felt like shouting back. But love is dangerous. Love exposes you. Love makes you dependent.

But the singer persisted, like she could see directly through his skull, telling him that his mind was full of red.

Yes. YES. How did she know that? Red. Blood. That was what he saw when he closed his eyes. Judy Ikin, the Rentich woman, Sally Prescott, Michael Foley …

And now he was chanting too.

Colours. Shapes, shifting. Was it the lights? The ceiling seemed so far above him. The world's tallest cathedral. Another song already, time untrustworthy, a muted tom-tom, jangly guitars bathing him. But there was no him. No John Gordon. Not here in this church.

He felt his soul sucked into a universal gulf stream, bathing in warmth. A common womb. Is this what you felt, Martin? Yes, it was, wasn't it? A rebirth. Something floated by, through the muddy waters in his brain. He sensed it. Something about Martin and Spring and albums, and violent death. But reason could not survive long in here and it was flushed away before taking root, and him with it in his cradle of bulrushes.

The girl on stage whispering now, shining green like a witch. Casting a spell about chasing rabbits down rabbit holes. Exactly. He understood. He understood it all. Everything, himself, the universe, everything.

It all made sense.

◆◆◆

Somewhere between two and three in the a.m., John sitting in the cold cabin of the Buick out front of the now silent tattoo shop, the trip he'd taken at the Fillmore had become barely a ripple but occasionally a wave breaking. Annie hadn't shown. John staying right till the end, asking around, nobody had seen Annie. Directions freely given for him. He was certain this was Annie's street. This had to be her place, like she'd described above the tattoo parlour. Staying clear of the hotel as long as he could for Shearer's sake, but resenting feeling like an accomplice. John left the car, scanned. A light on in the room above, dim, maybe a desk lamp. Faint music too. Chipped concrete steps. A rusted iron railing. John climbed, taking a lungful of San Fran air. Damp tonight. He reached the narrow landing. No bell. He knocked. No answer, but for sure a radio.

'Annie, you there?'

He turned, retraced to the car, sat behind the wheel. His eyes fell on Ray's toolkit. Why not? Maybe Annie was stoned, sleeping it off. If they could get Martin Davis' Los Angeles address, they were almost done. He opened the bag, pulled out the big ring of keys, climbed back up, knocked one last time. The lock seemed standard Lockwood but John with no clue if the US versions would match the Australian. Locating a master key of the typical size for door keys, tried it. The door opening.

John stepped in. 'Annie?'

A sparsely furnished living room doubling as a kitchen. An old sofa, a TV, a small table. The light coming from an adjoining room, presumably the bedroom. Its door part open.

Annie was lying on the floor beside her bed, fully clothed, the lamp's light showing the glassy stare of death in her eyes. A drug tie trapped beneath her left arm. The needle had spilled from her right hand. Shit. John knelt, felt her neck, but any pulse had long fled, her body already cold. Shit, shit.

An anguished ache began drumming softly on the inside of his gut. An unspoken cry of 'No.' He'd seen too much of death. While it was one thing to have your life snatched by a killer, it was another entirely to give it up for nothing but a narcotic buzz. What a waste.

He gave the body a cursory check. Maybe slight bruising on the left side of her head from where she'd nodded off and slipped from the bed. No saving you, girl. Had she got that Davis address for him before this? Practicalities. A silent apology.

He began to look through her things. Yeah, it was a shitty thing to do with her body right here on the floor, but it had to be done. She had a tote bag on a small dressing table. Her purse was still inside, a few dollars, old notes, a half-smoked joint, cigarettes, a couple of biros. No notepad there or on the dressing table, just a spoon and a lighter. Shit, shit, shit.

He should have got the name of the friend who had seen Davis in LA. Now they'd only find whoever she was with a shitload of work and truckful of luck. John chiding himself for thinking this way. Annie was dead. A few hours ago, she'd been full of life, excited to help.

What now? To call police and ambulance he'd have to leave the apartment, find a call box. It complicated things. Leaving everything as was; the radio still playing the light on; he slipped the lock back on and slid quietly out.

He drove half a dozen blocks, found a payphone, put on his best American accent and called it in as a drug OD.

Then he slunk into the night like a tomcat on the wrong end of a fight.

6 BROWN SHOES DON'T MAKE IT

'You did the right thing.' What else could Ray offer his partner. He'd woken refreshed, a glorious night with Kitty; intermittent images still flashing; her astride him, gasps and screams, her head side to side like a go-go dancer. He'd walked her out to a taxi around 2.00 a.m. and fallen quickly to sleep. Woken an hour ago to find Gordon grey and uptight. A word Ray was growing to like. Gordon had told him about finding Annie, saw the man was torturing himself.

'What else could you do? You don't want to get stuck in red tape for hours. A day or two maybe.' Gordon as still as a founding father's statue with pigeons perched. 'No sign of a struggle or anything?'

'No.'

From the description Gordon had laid down, Ray reckoned the storyline was nursery-rhyme simple.

'No forced entry. She was looking forward to her night out, she scored and sampled, and died.'

Even before Ray had left Liquor and Gaming for Arson, he'd seen a smattering of these deaths in working girls in the Cross. From what he'd heard it was growing all the time. US servicemen bringing bad Vietnam habits with them.

'I feel like … I abandoned her.'

'She abandoned herself, mate. I don't think she'd blame you.' The best thing to shake his partner out of the mood was to get moving. 'We need to get a wriggle on.'

Gordon silent, nodding.

Good, that was a start. Now for something he'd conjured the last day or two, tossing and catching it like a shiny apple.

'What's say we swap the Buick for something more spunky? I'm thinking convertible.'

A six-hour run, blue Mustang, tar and breeze just like TV detectives. Ray's shirt print, pineapples and sunglasses. Normally saved it for summer barbecues with the likes of Granite skolling chocolate soldiers. Gordon, no fuss over the car idea, still troubled, but the lines on his face shallowing the further south they went. Stopping for fuel, hot dogs and a piss, just twice. Minimal conversation, Gordon saying he was 'Okay'.

Like bush flies thickening the nearer you got to dead meat, cars coagulating with every click nearer the city's heart. By the time Ray swung into Sunset Boulevard, they were hemmed in by a moving wall of chrome and rubber. Ray had never seen so many cars. You had to be there to get it: Los Angeles wasn't a city so much as a cathedral to the auto.

No motel booking yet, playing it by ear. Ray headed towards the just setting sun. A row of motels catching his eye. Well, actually it was the big signs that caught his eye. They nearly all said 'pool', 'television' and 'cheap'.

Gordon said he didn't care so long as the cheap part was true. It was.

They parked in the lot of one of the motels, the Paradise. Double-storey, concrete verandas in a U shape. Took a twin room. Sunday, and too late to drop in on LAPD even on spec. Gordon desiring to shower and rest. Ray scoring a beer with the help of the desk clerk, stretching outside.

The sun had bite. A faded umbrella blunted it some. The beer tasted like a shandy without the lemon. Not that Ray gave a damn. He stretched out his legs, his shoes all wrong but his shirt a good fit. A steady stream of bikini babes finding their way to the pool. Half his age, but they all smiled at him and said 'Hi.' Ray thinking this was as good as life got.

A song floating out of the transistor radio one of the bikini babes had hung off the umbrella's butterfly nut. A lilting, soft song, not Ray's style at all but the words got him smiling all the same.

'If You're Going to San Francisco …'

He was thinking of Kitty. Hell, she wasn't wearing flowers in her hair last night, she was wearing nothing of anything anywhere. He flashed on Marie.

'Sorry, love.'

He'd buy her something really nice before they left the States, something that would last.

◆◆◆

John showered, dressed fresh, dabbed Old Spice. Every now and then his being splitting, schizo. Maybe the tab he'd popped, maybe the whole Annie thing. The finality of death, its unexpectedness, wrapping him in mud. Annie dead on the floor, merging with the Rentich woman, fading, zooming. He felt his heart beating, wondered how long before the line was written that marked the end of his story and the book slammed shut.

He'd felt drained, couldn't be stuffed arguing with Shearer about the car so just went along with it. The Mustang run fun despite everything, the motel okay. He felt tired but too restless to lie down. For an instant last night, he felt like he was close to some truth, but it was a drug-induced mirage, and the feel of Annie's cold body on the floor of her apartment mocked him.

The Fillmore's god had deserted him. Instead of an airy vault of music and light he was in a mundane motel room: twin singles, blond wood, varnished shelving and a small bathroom with a lopsided sliding shower panel and a paper band that showed your toilet hadn't been used in the interim.

The room phone went via the switch anyway, so he walked down to the office to grab a Coke and call from there. Postcards on a spin rack: Hollywood sign, beaches featuring hairspray and 1964 two-piece bikinis way bulkier than the slimline the girls in the pool were in. Time passed us in a fizz. Three years and the world had changed forever.

The motel guy in the Hawaiian shirt a decade older than John directed him to the desk phone and gave him a line. John rang the Clarence just in case anybody had left a message, hoped he didn't score Kitty wanting to goo-goo with Shearer. He didn't. The nightshift had started. The new girl had no messages for him. So, Martin Davis still hadn't contacted his family or that would have been passed on. Flashed on Geary. The boss would be waiting for this updated contact address. No rush. A telegram tomorrow.

John headed outside. Heat from paving slabs roasted his soles. Shearer poolside with a beer, grinning.

'You gotta hear this song, "San Francisco".'

A voice screeched, 'I love it!'

She must have been eighteen tops. All the youthful energy Denise had back then. Eyes still bright and carefree. She was lying on the lounge beside Shearer's.

'Stacey, this is my friend, John.'

'Pleased to meet you. You're a private eye!' Every sentence ending with an exclamation.

John confirmed he was. Stacey, he figured, might be useful.

'Stacey, do you know a band called The Mothers of Invention?'

'Oh yeah, they are sooo foul. My friend Annabel thinks they're the best. I can't stand them. I like Mark Lindsay, The Monkees. Fun stuff you can sing along with.'

Stacey had gestured with her head of long brown hair to another girl in the pool who was canoodling with a quarter-back type.

'Hey, Annabel,' John called, and she turned his way. 'Where would I find The Mothers of Invention?'

Leather, Castrol-stained jeans, greasy hair, laughter, girls bouncing on biker knees, a jukebox pounding Chuck Berry. First look Ray grabbed of Barney's Beanery from the street got him thinking tea houses like you'd sometimes find up the coast. But this no tea house. Cheek to jowl flesh. Spearing barwards the second time, pert bums poking his loins.

The barman had already informed him he hadn't seen any Mothers tonight, adding 'Maybe later.' As for the Spring and Davis photos, might as well have shown playing cards. The barman's default position, a head shake. But he added he wasn't the regular bartender, Kostas would be in tomorrow.

Gordon was persevering though, edging his way around the perimeter where there was a little space. Ray returning bearing beers, Gordon still drawing blanks. They forced their way outside, the dope smoke giving Ray a headache.

'No hits?'

'Even if they know them, they aren't saying.'

'We'll call into LAPD tomorrow, get the ball rolling.'

A female voice crackled behind them. 'The things you see when you don't have your gun.'

Ray turning. 'Janis!' The upward LA exclamation catchy. Now he was doing it.

'What the fuck, you following me?' Grinning through greasy hair.

Ray handed her his beer. She slugged. Guys in the shadows behind her. Ray told her what brought them to LA.

'Shucks, and I thought it was me.'

'We would have come for you.' Hell, of course Ray was flirting. There was an energy about her, took him back to his first FJ. Each time you started up, you expected adventure.

Gordon said, 'You were brilliant the other night. We loved you.'

'Why thank you, gentlemen.'

Ray asked if she had shows on.

'Doing a little studio work on some songs. But if you see us playing anywhere, you just tell them I said to let you in.'

Gordon said, 'Any chance you would know where we'd find the Mothers? There's a girl with them might know where we can find Spring.'

Janis called into the shadows. 'Where's Zappa and the boys staying?'

A voice called back, 'Somewhere in the fucking prairie, Reseda.'

'On Willow,' said another voice.

Janis translated. 'Willow in Reseda. Look for vans. I gotta go get drunk now. My man just dumped me.'

The 'San Francisco' song played twice before they made Reseda, which could have been Parramatta. Bungalow, low-level houses, family sedans. Uniformity a good thing, the vans standing out. A low-slung ranch style place, more modern than most in the street. Ray parked right out front. Lights on, music playing but not loud. They rang the bell. Nothing. They knocked. The door opened on a sleepy longhair.

Ray said, 'You with the Mothers?'

The guy's gaze a scalpel.

'We're mates of Janis.' John Gordon getting that in quick.

The guy silent.

Ray said, 'We're looking for Peggy.'

The guy said, 'They're bowling.'

Ray asked where.

'About five blocks south. Look for the big fucking bowling ball in the sky.'

◆◆◆

She had to be the one with the wild red hair, the silver jewellery, the rose-pink John Lennon glasses and tired jeans. Every other female in a twin-set or a dress, and most under sixteen with chubby brothers, fathers in slacks that screamed accountant, and moms who'd snuck in home-baked cookies in wide handbags rather than pay the alley mark-up.

It wasn't just the three long-haired, bearded blokes with her. Or that she was incessantly gabbing through the cloud of smoke she was puffing up. She was stoned. After a few days in San Francisco, Ray clocked that quick.

'Peggy?' Ray leading off. Gordon swigging on a Coke, more a prop than that he was thirsty. Red eyes turned their way. Curiosity a nose in front of hostility. Gordon opened proceedings.

'We're friends of Kansas Annie.'

They'd decided en route not to mention Annie's death unless it was necessary.

Peggy drawing on a Camel, eyes narrowing. 'Really? I never seen you.'

Ray said, 'And we are so much poorer for that.'

She smiled, liking the bullshit.

'I'm Ray, that's John.' A quick look towards the guys, 'We ran into Janis at Barney's, and she gave us the tip. We're looking for Martin Davis. Was dating your friend Spring for a while.'

Good enough for the entourage. One grabbed a ball, loped in, slung it down the lane.

'I saw him a few weeks back at the Hollywood Bowl.'

A clatter in the background. Ray guessing six pins.

John Gordon said, 'Buffalo Springfield?'

'Yeah. We only drove down the day before and there he was, hanging around where the bands are. He looked like shit. Fraught, that's the word.'

Ray said, 'Was he on his own?'

'Totally. Seized on me like I was a lifeboat: "Have you seen Spring?", "I'm worried. I think something's happened to her." The guy is fully paranoid. Bad acid.'

'This was how long ago?' John getting specific.

Peggy turning to her pals. 'When did Springfield do the Bowl?'

Two weeks back, a Saturday. That made it April 29, three weeks after Davis split from San Francisco.

'So he's still looking for Spring?' Ray piecing it.

'Yeah, but he's even worse than he was in Frisco.'

'How so?'

The girl distracted, watching another of her pals pick up a spare. 'He was rambling. Paranoid.'

'Saying what?'

'Total garbage non-stop. "Somebody's killing chicks. Chicks like Spring and you. Don't trust anybody. Especially not at these shows." That sort of shit.'

Ray wondering if Davis had learned about "Clint Adams". Would explain why he was freaking.

'He say where he was staying?' John Gordon.

'He might have. I don't remember.'

'Annie told me somebody, a girl I think, had seen Martin at that show and might know where he lived. I think whoever she is went back to San Francisco. Any idea who that was?'

'Could be this chick, Monica. I don't know her real well.'

Ray could see what Gordon was thinking, find Monica, get a lead on Davis. But Peggy didn't know where Monica had been living in LA, or was likely to be in Frisco. She thought that she was one of the 'Marin County bunch' but wasn't sure. Peggy was up. They waited while she bowled. A gutter ball. She thought it hilarious.

John Gordon said, 'Was it you told Martin about Spring staying on Chalmers?'

'I definitely told him. I don't know if anyone else did. About three weeks before the Hollywood Bowl he cornered me outside the Dead house. He was freaking out, saying he was sure something bad had happened to Spring because she'd just vanished. I felt sorry for him. I said I heard she was in the Tenderloin. I knew she'd be gone by then, she was heading down here, but I didn't want him worrying. Lot of good it did. Like I said, he was much worse last time.'

Ray said, 'Annie told us that Spring was worried about some guy from her old town tracking her down.'

First Peggy had heard of that. Gordon trawled the name Clint Adams. Nothing.

Ray said, 'Do you know Spring's real name?'

'Spring. That's how I know her.'

Gordon said, 'When you were in San Fran, did you and Spring speak about catching up down here?'

'Sort of. We said, you know we'll probably catch up at a Mothers gig or Barney's. I thought I would have seen her, but I haven't.'

She wasn't worried. Spring, she said, was the kind of girl who would go anywhere at the drop of a hat. They waited for Peggy to have one more bowl. Two pins this time. Ray asked if she'd seen Martin Davis with a vehicle. She hadn't. She had no idea where to find him except 'concerts and Barney's'.

Gordon gave her the number of the motel, asked her to call if she saw either Spring or Davis.

Peggy picked up her bowl, said, 'Guys, don't get your hopes up. I know lots of acid casualties. Most don't get back.'

7 SUMMER IN THE CITY

Captain Maurice Schubert the LAPD equivalent of Spinetti, but less warm. Not that John had thought of Spinetti as warm until Schubert. The captain John's height, a few minutes past forty, his shirt and torso both ironed flat, his nose too. And his voice. As welcoming as a concrete wall.

'Just came in this morning after you called me.' Sliding a typed page across a sparse desk.

John still deciphering as Schubert explained. 'Your boy, Davis, pulled sixty bucks out of his account last Monday. We'd been monitoring as much as we are able.'

John pointed at a number that made no sense to him.

'That's the branch number, North Highland. It's a big branch.'

'You only got this today?' Shearer sounding critical.

Schubert laced his fingers, no expression.

'We only get the information after this branch passes it on to your boy's branch in San Francisco. They tell SFPD. Spinetti called me as soon as he heard. I'm telling you within the hour. We had already checked morgues, hospitals, jails and there was no sign of him. Looks like he's another spoiled rich kid taking drugs and wasting everybody's time, especially ours. I can send my officers there if you want. Ask at the bank who served him, do they remember him. But I figured you might save me the trouble.'

John told him they would.

'We appreciate the help. I wonder if I might send a telegram to my chief in Sydney.'

'Of course.' Schubert stood. His shake was an ore-crusher. He called-ed in an aide, ordered him to help these 'gentlemen' send a telegram.

Still early but already scorching. Kind of day as a kid you'd give up on park cricket, ride your bike to the beach and jump in. Bank of America on North Highland was busy. Four tellers working nonstop and at least some vague air conditioning, thank God. A slim brunette, a helmet of lacquered hair, shapely calves on their way into the 'Staff Only' door, John stopped her. Asked for the manager, said it was a police matter.

She listened, entered, closed the door. They waited. A balding man in a suit opened up, ushered them into to a small office where the air-con didn't reach. He had a desk fan on full. A nameplate sat on the desk announcing 'John Webster.'

'You're police?'

'Australian police,' said John, 'working in conjunction with LAPD and the San Francisco Police Department.'

Webster sat, indicated two chairs. A squeeze, filing cabinets at their back.

John said, 'We're looking for an Australian man, Martin Davis. We believe he was here a week ago and we'd like to speak to whoever may have served him.' Handing over the typed sheet from Schubert. Webster pulled glasses from his coat pocket, read.

'Ah, yes. I remember sending the San Francisco branch this information. I'll get the teller, Henry Lake.'

It took about three minutes. John studied a calendar that showed cows in a meadow. Wondered if somewhere a farmer had a calendar on his wall of the Hollywood sign. There was no extra chair for Lake so, when he entered, they all stood. He didn't take up much room. Skinny with a Herman's Hermit part and fringe, and glasses. John imagined he got picked on at school in his athletic singlet. Lake remembered Davis.

'The accent. And he wanted at least forty singles.'

Shearer said, 'Did he seem jumpy? High?'

Lake shook his head. 'He was polite.'

John showed the pic to make sure. Lake confirmed. Davis didn't mention where he might be staying, was on his own from what Lake could see. That was it.

They asked Webster if they could xerox the photo for copies for the tellers so if Davis turned up again, they could be contacted right away. No problem. The brunette did the copying. Not much use, Davis looked like a charcoal smudge. They hand wrote the Paradise Motel phone number on the copies and printed 'LAPD Captain Schubert' as back-up.

Back outside, the sun torching them. Much hotter here than San Francisco. Hotter than Sydney usually was. John guessing at least ninety.

'I'm Davis. I just left the bank. I've got sixty bucks in my pocket, what am I doing now?' Shearer glancing around him, stopping on a diner across the street. Their eyes met.

'Worth a shot,' said John.

The people at the diner didn't remember Davis. Nor did anybody from the other places nearby: a bookstand, restaurant, bar, drycleaners.

Martin Davis might be alive and kicking in Los Angeles, but he was still in the wind. And this was a fucking big city.

Too big for two guys, John was thinking. Tuesday almost spent and it had brought a big fat nothing on Davis or Spring. Their legs were stiff and sore after a day and a half of pounding scorching pavement. Last night they'd sat by the pool with their bikini friends, sipped beers and then tried to find any clubs open but a Monday night even West Hollywood was a quiet canyon. With no better lead than Davis' bank visit they had picked up where they left off yesterday, back in North Hollywood again right after breakfast, expanding the radius of their search. Maybe their premise that he lived near the bank was wrong. Maybe it was just handy that day.

John feeling like he'd sweated half his body weight. They'd tried likely places: diners, record stores, bars. Not a whiff. The heat searing. Back at the motel for a breather before the clubs and

Barney's. Shearer bobbing in the pool. The sunset was golden, the mood ugly. The clerk's radio informed John it was LA's hottest May day ever. John wished he wasn't part of that history, wished he was able to put the cue in the rack, park the investigation but he couldn't stop.

He put himself in Martin Davis' place: You're looking for Spring. You still haven't found her, what do you do? Surely, he has to call back to San Fran and see if anybody has heard anything.

And who would he likely call? Annie. But if he did, any info on where he was staying died with her.

Back beside the faded postcards and car-rental flyers John cashed notes for a stack of coins with the sunglassed reception clerk. He pumped coins, managed to get Kitty at the Clarence, asked if there were any messages, hoping Spinetti may have left something. Nothing.

'How's Ray, doing?'

John looked through the dirty glass window, saw Ray diving into the pool.

'Working his bum off. He told me to tell you he missed you.'

'That's sweet. Tell him I miss him. Both of you.' That last bit added hastily.

◆◆◆

Sunset and twilight grinding on like an England partnership with Barrington involved. The Mustang threaded its way to Santa Monica. At least now they could put the top down without their scalps burning. They'd decided to start at the coast and work back.

'You told her I missed her?' Ray grinning.

'Somebody had to.'

'I'll ring her tomorrow.'

Sure he would.

They parked a few streets back from the pier, walked inland following the sound: jangly guitars and flower-power harmonies. It stopped at a place not much more than a coffee shop. Inside, young people, nodding with serious intent, blowing smoke.

A small poster in the window: *The Beau Brummels*. A band on a tiny stage. John and Ray scanned, waited for a break.

John liked the music a lot, especially because he could imagine Denise here, digging it. At the break they got to work. Nobody there had seen either Davis or Spring. They club-hopped back to Hollywood, striking out every time, finished at Barney's. Kostas the bartender offered liquor but no succour.

'You know it's the hottest day in May ever?'

John did. The air-con in the motel room rumbled but didn't cool. They had to open windows. John slept badly.

◆◆◆

Next morning, arriving back from ham and eggs breakfast to find Shearer sitting out front of the motel office. He'd been asleep when John headed out.

Shearer said, 'I called Kitty.'

'Good for you.'

'She said Spinetti called first thing and left a message for you to call him.'

John hustled in quick. The phone was free, and he had coins aplenty. Maybe Spinetti had turned up Spring's real name. Or better, maybe he'd turned up Davis. He got put through quick smart, told Spinetti he'd got his message.

Spinetti said, 'Davis turned up yet?'

'Not so far.' Now he was thinking it must be a lead on Spring, why Spinetti had called.

Spinetti said, 'That girl we got a tip on while we were chasing down Spring, Kansas Annie, you located her, right?'

Anxiety bubbling. Had Spinetti somehow figured out it was John who made the call? Play dumb.

'Yes, I did. She was keeping her eyes open for me.'

'Not any more she's not. She was found dead in her apartment night two nights back. Heroin overdose. Long-time junkie went to the well once too often, but the attending officers found your card and my name, so it came straight to me.'

Spinetti had thought John would want to know.

'Thanks,' said John, feeling weird to be thanking the cop for letting him know Annie was dead. They talked a few minutes. Spinetti asked if he would mind making an official statement when he got back. John said of course not. He hung up, drenched again in guilt.

Shearer was going to drive. They would start further south today around Melrose, focus on record stores and hippie places. John's heart wasn't in it. All he could think was what a waste Annie's death was. Ray was doing his bit to cheer him up.

'Hey, they're kids but it's their choice. They think they're living the dream but they're dying in it too.'

John said, 'I really didn't think she would go that way.'

Ray popped open the door of the Mustang. 'Once you start on that junk, brains go out the window. They can't help themselves. Let's hope Davis isn't on the same path.'

The exact same thought was crossing John's mind.

The day bringing nothing. The only thing the night delivered was bad dreams. Annie and Denise trapped in a cave. John stranded outside unable to help.

◆◆◆

Thursday passed in a blur. John felt he was running a marathon with his feet in concrete. That night when they walked into Barney's after already striking out, first at the Troubadour and then the Whisky, Kostas didn't wait for the question. He just shook his head. John's drive anaemic. He'd given up hope of ever getting a lead.

He pushed the photos on yet another couple of young guys.

'Shit, yeah. I remember him.'

The Australian accent hitting John like a shovel. The two young guys in the booth in tees, tanned dark brown.

'You're from Australia?' First Aussie accent John had heard in the US, apart from Shearer.

'Sydney.' Ross and Mick from Newtown and Harbord respectively. Following the surf. 'He was here. About two weeks ago. We got talking.'

Shearer wanting the exact date. A conference, mutual decision. It had been Thursday, May 4. Ross was sure because Thursday was their Barney's night.

'You'll never guess where I'm working.'

Ray tried Disneyland. Ross and Mick laughed through beer.

'LAPD. In the motor garage. Back home, I was a car detailer. We convert the standard Dodge sedans into cop cars. You take out the console put in a shotgun rack.'

Davis had been going all around the room showing photos of his girlfriend, asking if anybody had seen her. He got to them, and they recognised the accent and shared a beer.

Ray flipping out the Spring photo, showing them.

Yes, that was her. Neither Mick nor Ross had seen her in the flesh though.

'Would like to have,' said Mick sucking on a cigarette. The guys got talking with Davis who was worried something had happened to his girl. She'd disappeared from San Francisco.

Ross and Mick were pragmatic.

'I think she dumped him. Too good-looking for him.'

Davis, they said, didn't seem stoned or psycho. Just worried.

Had he said where he was staying?

Ross nodded. 'Yeah, Silver Lake. Said he was renting a room above a house garage. We're in Eagle Rock. Too far for a catch-up but we told him we come here Thursdays and we'd have a beer again if he was here.' But last week he hadn't showed.

'We had to leave early,' said Ross. 'Maybe he came late.'

They drank, talked, checked out the chicks. The surfers had been away five months, the last three in LA.

'We surfed all down the coast, crossed into Mexico. That's something else down there.'

Two hours in, the surfers bailed. John and Ray hung around. Some Hells Angels came in, the mood went edgy. No Spring, no Mothers, no Janis, no Martin Davis. Too late for Silver Lake. They could start there, first thing.

◆◆◆

Ray was an Australian because his great-grandfather had been an optimist. One of the six thousand who arrived every week into Australia after gold was discovered in Ballarat. They grabbed their picks and pans and went digging and fossicking for nuggets. They believed if you worked long and hard enough there would be a reward.

Ray working on the same theory: you put in the hours, sooner or later you struck gold. They drove to where signs indicated Silver Lake, found a shopping hub. Lots of Mexican-looking people and restaurants. Citizens who didn't speak English or pretended they didn't. A slog. Two hours into their Silver Lake canvass, they struck paydirt at Highway 61, a record shop in a secondary street strip. The young owner, Chad, was all hair and jeans.

'Yeah, I know Marty. He was coming in most days but not so much lately.'

Chad had noticed Davis 'mooching' around. 'At first, I thought he was trying to steal. We get a lot of that. But he explained he was only here temporary, renting and didn't have a record player. I'd let him grab headphones and listen. He loved the psychedelic bands.'

'You know where exactly he lived?'

Chad didn't. They'd never talked about that more than that it was above someone's garage. What he had talked about was Spring.

'He told me he was looking for his girlfriend. I saw him one day he was in tears. This girl was found murdered up in the Hollywood Hills and the cops couldn't ID her and he was bawling his eyes out telling me he was sure it was his girl, cause the description was so close.'

'When was this?' Gordon.

'Around two weeks ago.'

Ray asked if he had seen Davis since.

'Yeah, he came in a few days later. Said he'd gone to see the detectives. The cops had been asking for help on the ID. He said when he got there the cops had already identified her, but it wasn't his girl. You'd think that would calm him down, right? Wrong. He was sure something bad had happened to his girl too. He told me there were other people there, like him, worried it had been their kid or friend. He said two of the three missing girls had last been seen at love-ins. And the girl up in the Hills, same thing. He was sure there was some kind of link.'

Ray asked if he'd been on drugs.

'No. he was stone-cold sober, man.'

Gordon questioned if that was the last time he'd seen Davis.

'No. I saw him about four or five days back.' Davis had told him he was gathering information to take to the cops 'to make them take notice'. He was spending time at the library. This, he'd said, was bigger than he'd ever thought.

'I wished him well. He said he was sorry he hadn't been in the shop much, but he was working from some place over on North Western.'

They thanked Chad, gave him their number, asked him to call if Davis turned up.

Ray said 'We need to make Highway 61 our centre and draw a circle of say three miles. If he lives in that radius, we'll eventually find him.' Ray pulled out his map, stuck a pencil on their location and drew a crude circle. 'That should be a radius of about three miles.'

More footwork. A half-mile east of Chad's store they got a couple of hits: a laundromat and a rare Asian restaurant among the Mexican ones: the guy looked 'familiar'. No hint yet of his residence but you had to guess he lived somewhere around here. Breaking for a late lunch of noodles at the Asian restaurant. Different again to what they had eaten in San Francisco, but Ray liked it. They ate quickly, got back to work.

'If You're Going to San Francisco' was playing out of every second car radio and transistor. The rest, Latin rhythms. Kids were out of school. Kids noticed things. They questioned them. One boy was definite. He'd seen the guy waiting at a bus stop regularly.

'Which stop?'

The kid racked his brains. He thought it was two east of here. They asked at the next stop east just in case. No hits. They tried the next. Nothing right off.

Then another schoolkid on a bike said, 'Yes. I've seen him waiting at the stop in the morning.'

They split, working opposite sides of the residential streets, keeping an eye out for a flat above a garage. There were a few. They rang the bells and asked owners. They struck out.

A little after 6.00 p.m., Ray's feet were tired, the noodles fading.

'It's Friday night,' he said. 'One of us should head to Barney's, just in case.'

John Gordon thought it a good idea, said, 'I don't like the traffic. You go to Barney's. I'll keep working here.' They saw a diner named *Ray's*, laughed, made that their meet-up point.

The traffic was a pig. Ray didn't care. He needed to rest his feet, ate the last of the rays tumbling out of the Los Angeles sky. Wished he could take the convertible back home. Be fun cruising Bondi.

The Beanery packed already, forced to park in a distant block. Twilight had finally vamoosed by the time he stepped inside. No sign of Kostas tending bar, some other newcomer. Ray about to pull the photos and start in but glimpsed a shape at the end of the bar, that was immediately obscured by long hair, sheep wool vests and cowboy boots. He pushed through.

She was sitting hunched, leaning forward staring at a tumbler of honey-brown liquid.

'Janis?'

Phrasing it like that 'cause he wasn't sure from this angle. The fingers of her left hand ran along the part in her hair. Bleary eyes turned his way, like a parrot's, spied him in the triangle of space between her forearm and bicep. A smile struggled to its feet. She was drunk or pinned, or more likely both.

'Hey, Ray.'

Ray pulled himself onto the stool beside her. 'You remembered my name,' he said.

'Girls always remember assholes,' she laughed with cigarette throat. The barman approached. She said, 'What're you having?'

'I wasn't drinking.'

'Fuck that for a plan.'

'Whatever you're on.'

Janis looked at the barman pointed with her finger at her drink and jerked a thumb Ray's way. Economical.

'You on something?' Ray trying to sound casual.

'My own. I'm on my own, Ray, in Barney's Beanery on a fucking Friday night.'

'Not any longer,' said Ray. His drink arriving space-ship quick. He asked the barman where Kostas was.

'We ran out of some of the spirits. He'll be back soon.'

Ray and Janis clinked glasses.

'You're not in the studio.' Ray hit a tone midway between statement and question.

'Naaah. The "guys" are working out guitar shit and all kinds of other stuff that a girl isn't qualified to fucking hold an opinion on.' She rolled her eyes.

'So it's gotta be romance trouble.' Ray took a slug. The honeyed liquor burned good.

Janis gave him a thumbs up.

'I was in love, Ray. Genuine twenty-four carat. Shit, I still am.'

'And?'

'And he booted me, straight-up. No niceties about how great I am but, because he's a musician too, we're always going to be apart blah blah. Nothing to help me even *pretend* that horseshit might be real. Delivered like a communist manifesto. He said, "We're over. I want to still be friends but I'm going with Mary fuck-face here."'

Ray took another slug. 'You're better off without him. You're what, twenty-six, your whole life is ahead of you.'

'Twenty-four.'

Ray had already shaved two years off what he thought. Christ, the world was coming down hard on this girl.

'The guy wrote songs about me. He told me I was Cleopatra and

Billie Holiday and fucking Ginger from *Gilligan's Island* all rolled into one. Then he cut me like a butcher splitting ribs on a block. You're a man. Why would a man say that? And then do that?'

She was crying now. When he and his wife split, he'd felt how Janis looked right now.

'Tell me, Ray. Come on.'

He put his arm around her. 'Well, the way I'd explain it, baby, all men want to get as close to the volcano as they can. It's exciting, dangerous. But they sure as hell don't want to be there when it explodes.'

She buried her head into his shoulder. She said, 'You want to ball? Right now?'

The barman saved him. 'Another?'

'Yeah.' Ray didn't expect anything, but he pulled out the Davis photo, as much to keep Janis at bay.

'Don't suppose you've seen this guy?'

The guy studied it, lips pursed. 'Matter of fact. I do fill-ins. Bars are short-staffed, they call me. The Rimshot in North Hollywood, about three nights ago. That kid comes in and asks if I've seen some girl.'

Ray fought the urge to swear.

'Her?' Laying down the Spring photo.

'That's the one. I hadn't. I told him he should try Marsha who I was filling in for.'

Ray genuinely excited. He paid for the drinks turned to Janis, found her head on the bar.

Ray handed ten to the barman, said, 'Get her a cab home when she wakes.'

◆◆◆

The fill-in barman's directions were good. The Rimshot was on Cahuenga, Burbank way. The ride took about twenty minutes. A knot of Harleys covered the back entrance from the lot. The bar small, the lighting minimal, the music the kind Ray was getting used to hearing but mostly wished he wasn't, psychedelic, wafting-clouds-shit. Inside voices were lower than the lights.

Custom was solid but a slower pace than Barney's. There was a pool table jammed down the side, barely enough cue room. An exotic girl who looked like Cher tended bar in transparent cheesecloth. Silver snake bangles up her arm, rings on every finger, shimmering like the rim of a tambourine.

'What's your poison?' she asked as Ray eased between leather and suspicion.

'Marsha?' asked Ray.

'That would be me.'

Ray asked for a beer though he didn't need one. He laid out the photos while she poured.

'I saw your relief barman at Barney's. I'm looking for this kid. He's looking for her.'

'You fuzz?'

'Private. Australian.'

'Near Switzerland, right?'

'More or less.'

Ray felt she was about to spill. Then, mood change. The chill.

'Nope, sorry.'

Ray's eyes slid sideways. A bearded biker, prison-workout biceps, staring over.

Ray holding the line, hoping. 'Sure? Take a close look.'

She placed his beer right on the photo. 'Definitely not.'

John doing the blocks of Silver Lake. Once again, kids the biggest help. Two boys about twelve playing twilight catch on a narrow strip out front of their house.

'I've seen him. I think he lives somewhere up that street.' The kid pointed. These blocks the cars had less dents, the houses better, working-class to middle.

John started ringing bells, knocking on doors. Husbands unhappy to be pulled away from their dinner, a few teenage girls smiling with shy eyes, the *Gomer Pyle* laugh-track pissing itself at him with each successive 'No'.

He hit the next street, saw *Star Trek* in colour through half-drawn curtains. Kept moving, more bells. An occasional housewife in rubber gloves with suds puffing into the warm night. He walked back out along another fruitless path stopped. His attention grabbed by an older house across the road.

Cracked concrete driveway, thin plants with spikey pom-poms on top that looked like they did okay without water. The house in darkness. Grabbing his attention, the garage and louvre windows on the structure above it. He crossed the road.

Didn't look like anybody was home now, but it was well-tended, so maybe just out. No bell visible. A feature bevelled glass rectangle in the door. He rapped beside it with his knuckle. Nothing. He looked back up at what seemed to be a flat above the garage. He stepped off the low porch, walked past the closed garage door, following a narrow path that ran to the back of the house. A wire fence to his left marked the boundary with the neighbours. Ivy and trees covering.

At the back of the garage rickety wood steps. He climbed the weathered wood, reckoned he'd leave a note. As he hit the landing, he saw a small gap where the door should have been shut. He edged closer, listened. Couldn't hear any sounds from inside. No proof this was even Davis' place, hamstrung.

'Hello? Is anybody in?'

Silence.

He pushed the door with his fingers. A little moonlight glowed behind the louvres, but the room was still dark. Looked like one room. He took a step inside. Stuff littered the floor, clothes, a pair of—

Something hard cracked into the back of his head.

Lights out.

8 ELECTRICITY

Gordon taking another slug of undrinkable coffee, still dazed. Ray finding him in the booth of Ray's Diner, 9.30 p.m. as pre-arranged. An egg-sized lump on the back of the kid's head growing by the second. Ten minutes so far, all he'd got out of Gordon: he thought he'd found where Davis was staying and had been jumped in the dark. Estimated he'd been out to it for a minute. Came to, heard a car engine fire up, tyres squealing off. The skin on his scalp only a little broken. Ray thinking, not a gun doing the damage, more likely a sap or even just a hard punch.

'You think it was Davis?' Ray giving up on the coffee, glad now for the bourbon Janis had bought him.

Gordon shook his head. Then winced. 'The place was turned over. I didn't mention that?'

'No.'

'When I came to, I had a proper look. The flat is just a bed and a kid's desk. Everything was strewn over the floor, clothes and shoes that likely came from the wardrobe that had nothing in it but a couple of coathangers. Some pencils and pens, and exercise pads scattered like somebody had swept them off the desk, all the drawers emptied.'

'The bed slept in?'

'Couldn't tell. Whoever it was had ripped the bedclothes off too, chucked the pillow, hauled up the mattress and just left it.'

'This was how long ago?'

'Half-an-hour or so. Thirty-one Carmino. It's about fifteen minutes' walk, but I was slow. When I walked in here, I think they thought I was drunk.'

'You want to go to a hospital, get checked out?'

'I'll be okay. I'm going to need some aspirin though. How'd you go?'

Ray sketching him in: Davis, the Rimshot.

Gordon said, 'Would have been nice to have had that lead three days ago.'

Ray shrugged. It was what it was. He'd thought Marsha would have been worth another crack but now that was unnecessary. A pity, she was foxy.

'Did the house look vacant?'

Gordon tried to shake his head. Looked like that pained him. 'No. I think whoever lives there was maybe just out and about.'

Ray asked if he wanted to wait here while he went back to the house.

Gordon said, 'Another crack on the head will do less damage than this coffee.'

◆◆◆

An old pick-up truck in the driveway, low light inside the house proper. Still dark upstairs.

Ray said, 'Let's check the flat first.'

They climbed. The door open. Ray clicked on the single light switch. A bulb dangling off a cord in the middle of a single room igniting under a cheap, dusty green shade. Nobody had tidied up, the floor a junk heap. Ray could see the door been jemmied.

'He waited for you here.' Ray pointing where the attacker must have flattened himself against the wall. There was a handbasin on the far wall, no toilet or shower but a toothbrush propped beside a tube of Ipana.

John Gordon scooping the pads from the floor, flicking through. Copious handwritten notes, what looked like frenzied scrawl. Ray couldn't read it easily. Initials instead of names, arrows on a kind of diagram. *ATTENDS BE-INS* written large. Tempted to take them but resisted, placed them on the table.

'Check the wastepaper basket,' he told Gordon. Ray rifling the pockets of the trousers and shirts. Gordon finding a candy-bar wrapper, nothing else. Ray not even a wrapper.

They turned the light off, retraced their steps to the ground, then had to climb the low porch to the front door. The air still warm with a hint of insects Ray sensed but couldn't see. The low sound of what he thought was a radio from inside. They rang the bell. Movement. Eventually the door opening on an old bloke – white hair and whiskers, singlet, trousers. The top of his head reaching Ray's chest.

Ray said he was sorry to bother him at this time of night and introduced himself and Gordon.

'We're looking for this man. We think he might rent upstairs.'

The old man studied the photo.

'Martin.' Saying it with an accent. South of the border as specific as Ray could manage, all Mexican to him. Ray explaining they were private detectives, giving the story shorthand: Martin's family in Australia was worried about him.

'John here came earlier. The door of the flat was open, and somebody was in there.'

'I called out, nobody answered,' said Gordon.

'Soon as he stepped in, they hit him over the head.'

'You might want to take a look,' said John. 'Whoever it was trashed the place.'

The old fellow had a bad limp. He gripped the rail, hauled himself up the steps. When he saw the mess, he swore in Spanish. He checked the door and muttered at the splintered wood.

Gordon said, 'We'll help.'

They put the thin mattress back on the bed, relocated the pillows and the sheets. The old fellow tidied up the clothes, said, 'Kids, they rob you as soon as look at you.'

Ray wondering why a burglar would start with a near empty flat if the house owner was out?

'You going to call the police?'

A bitter half-laugh. Ray interpreted: a waste of time, no way would this be a priority.

Ray said, 'I've got some beers in the car. I could swap you for an aspirin for my friend.'

Beers, uncomfortable garden chairs. They sat on a low back porch, the door to the kitchen at the rear of the house open now to help it cool. Their host who had introduced himself as Hector Jiminez explained he only had a small fan, and the house was 'very hot'.

'It gets more like my homeland every year. I move here in nineteen fifty-one.' He spoke with the precision of a person with limited words in his new language but determined to get them all right.

Ray never rushed anybody doing him a favour. Savoured his beer, heard how Hector's wife had shuffled off the mortal coil four years earlier. 'Right after President Kennedy. She loved that man. You couldn't say a bad word against him.'

Ray making the running. 'Did you see Martin before you left for your sister's?' Hector had explained that's where he'd been earlier.

'No. I hear him walking around early this morning. About eight. Hear the door close. Then I hear the car starting.'

'He's got a car?' Gordon instantly alert despite his skull being tapped.

'My car. Old Chevy Bel Air. It sits here. He ask can he rent. Sure, why not. His rent here paid up a week. He pay me three days advance for the car. I got my truck.'

Ray said, 'How long has he had it?

'Two days.'

Gordon asking if Hector knew the registration. He said of course he did, the car was sitting in the garage the last five years. Hector took Gordon's pencil and pad and made a note. John asked what colour the car was.

'Blue with white roof.'

John Gordon said they had heard that Marty was working out of some place on Western.

'He said he had some space over that way, needed the extra room.'

Jiminez had no idea exactly what work Marty was doing there.

'He only tell me "research". I don't push him.'

Ray wondered if he had mentioned an address.

'I don't remember. He might have.'

Ray said, 'What time does Marty normally get back?'

'All times. I get up some night for a pee, maybe three o'clock. He just getting in.'

'So he's gone most of the day?'

'Si.'

'What does he do for a bathroom?'

Hector jerked a thumb at a closed door to their right where the concrete patio ended.

'Toilet in there. If he want to shower, he use mine.'

John Gordon asked if Davis had any visitors.

'No. I never see nobody.'

Ray offered the photo of Spring. 'Her?'

Jiminez shook his head. 'Not once. Martin by himself.'

'How did he find this place?' Gordon.

'I put notes up on boards. Cheap rent. He ring, ask if the room is available. I say yes. He come over.'

It looked like Davis had lobbed here Saturday April 8, pretty much right after arriving from San Francisco. Ray described the man who called himself Clint Adams, asked if Hector had noticed him around. Sadly, he had not.

'But I see a motorcycle one night across the street when I put out my trash. Like he's watching the house.'

Hector hadn't got a look at the guy. He was out of the streetlight. Ray thinking: could have been Adams.

They finished their beer. Ray said he would slip a note under the door for Martin.

'We'll call you tomorrow morning, see if he's turned up.'

As they walked to the car Hector called, 'You guys welcome any time. I have tequila. The good stuff.'

◆◆◆

Ray drove back to the motel. Gordon said, 'What if he comes back and Hector's asleep? We should stake it out.'

Ray said, 'That's exactly what I'm going to do after I drop you.

You never know. Hector seems straight-up, but he might be on the phone first thing to Davis.'

If Davis didn't want to be found, he'd likely return to grab his stuff before splitting.

Gordon said, 'What do you think this research is?'

Ray had no idea. 'The kid's brain might be fried from drugs. You saw those notes. I've seen schizos like that. Speaking of which, you need to rest, mate. This ain't TV. A hit to the head like that actually hurts.'

Gordon protesting how he was the boss of this thing.

Ray said, 'You want the glory, fine. I don't want anything. I'm just being practical.'

'I'm not after glory. I want to be there.'

Ray got it. 'You took one for the team, and you made the breakthrough. Be happy with that. Besides, maybe he won't come tonight. Then I sleep and you'll be the one on the spot.'

Staying long enough to brush his teeth and take a piss. Told Gordon to get some sleep, left him on the bed, turned out the light.

Heading back Silver Lake way, the streets never deserted but the constant hum gone. Alone despite the immensity of the city, thinking of Kitty in San Francisco wondering if she was thinking of him, then Janis down and out in Barney's. We never know who our lives will brush, whose will touch us. Sealed up for now, an astronaut in his capsule quarantined from the rest of humanity. Thinking: we need one another; I get it, Martin, you need Spring, and maybe I shouldn't be here to fuck it up for you.

Apologising in advance. Not just to Davis but to all of them, coming to mind a phrase his brother Patrick, the priest, had been fond of bandying around: for what I have done and what I have failed to do. So many mistakes, omissions. Michael Foley especially. Well, Sue Foley really, that was how Ray first met Foley. George Shaloub's lover, never realised she was a he till Granite told him. Sweet on John Gordon. The kid might have felt the same way about Sue. Ray had thought Foley was Prescott's killer, got that wrong along with most everything else in his life. But Gordon and

Foley were the ones who had paid. Nothing he could do about it. Not yet.

◆◆◆

Hector's house dark again, so too the flat above the garage. No sign of a Chevy, the street sleeping. It could have been the back of Balmain. Ray stretched out, found a beer under the seat, popped it, sank it slowly. This was an interlude, still unfinished business in Sydney. He wondered how Granite was doing.

Sometimes two years seemed like an eternity and an eternity seemed like two years. Same with a stake-out. It could pass like a lifetime in prison or a fifty-five-yard dash between the jetties. Trouble was, you never knew in advance.

The night still warm even with the top down. You couldn't see the stars like you could lying on your back around the cemetery in Clovelly, but they still twinkled. Even if they were dimmer. Enjoy this, they were telling him. The good times never last as long as you wish.

John's head thumping. No. Wrong. Not his head. The door. Blinking awake, squinting at his watch. After nine. Shit. A glance. Shearer's bed not slept in. Last night tumbling back, reassembling like Sandman, reminding him Shearer was on stake-out at Hector's. He opened the door. Bright and sunny but mostly blocked by a patrol cop.

'You Shearer or Gordon.'

'John Gordon,' it came out in a croak.

'Captain Schubert sent me over. You might want to get ready fast.'

A hundred questions fighting to get through a slim doorway.

'Schubert?' His brain slow to warm.

'Said your man might have turned up.'

John said, 'We found his place in Silver Lake.'

The cop said, 'This is Venice Beach. You can ride with me.'

John said, 'We've got our own wheels, just give us the address. Shearer's in Silver Lake staking out the house.'

The cop said, 'I'll be quicker. Besides, without me, you don't get in. It's a homicide scene.'

John climbing into the black-and-white in a daze, concussed all over again. He'd called Hector's from the lobby. Ray had been with him, enjoying coffee.

'No sign of Martin,' said Ray.

The beat in John's chest sounded like a funeral drum. 'You need to get to Venice Beach.'

The cop's name was O'Connor. He turned the key, pumped gas and screamed out of the motel lot, slamming west at speed and hitting the siren. John's stomach lurched, cars smeared over the outside of his window, a blur.

John cordial to his driver. 'What do your friends call you, O'Connor?'

'Irish or Murphy or Mick.'

'So, Mick, what can you tell me?'

'Next to zero. I'm cruising, get a call on my radio from my Lieutenant telling me he has a request from Captain Schubert to collect two guys in my area and take them to a homicide scene in Venice. I am to get you there like my ass was on fire because the ME might not be there much longer.'

John shut his eyes. The siren did the screaming for him, a ball of dread wound tight in his gut. The trip could have been three minutes or thirty, logic said halfway between.

O'Connor killed the siren, John opening his eyes: a back parking lot, a collection of cars parked akimbo like the drivers didn't give a fuck. Which they didn't, because they were all cops or functionaries of the LAPD. Rubberneckers had been shooed on. O'Connor cruised in and shut down. They climbed out. John's gaze fell on the coroner's 'meat wagon'. He wished Ray was there, wondered how far off he might be.

O'Connor said, 'Wait here,' and pushed through a loose cordon of suits and uniforms to two guys in white shirts and striped ties, John guessed, the homicide D's. Both white guys, one maybe forty, the other low thirties. Busy talking to one of the forensic or coroner people. O'Connor had to wait. The knot in John's gut expanding. He wished he had water. The D's finally finished their discussion, chatted a moment with each other then looked at O'Connor. He pointed John's way. They didn't look overly pleased. A reluctant nod. O'Connor beckoned him through.

One side of the alley still in heavy shade, but the sun was bouncing hard off the concrete by its entrance, some kind of area for rubbish. Flies buzzing loud, a smell of rotting food.

The older cop said, 'I'm Lieutenant Ted Lackowitz, Lieutenant Joe Burns.'

John introduced himself.

Lackowitz said, 'You're just in time. They're about to load him. The Captain says you have an interest. Want to take a look?'

John's eyes fell on the white sheet on the ground covering a body jammed between a fence and a dumpster. The flies dividing their time between it and the pool of congealed blood around the sheet. John nodded. Out the corner of his eye, he saw the Mustang pull in. Ray must have tramped it.

Burns pulled back the sheet.

Disappointment stabbing John like an icepick. The face matched the photos. He had found Martin Davis. Too late.

9 INCENSE AND PEPPERMINTS

Lackowitz and Burns resting backsides on the hood of their Dodge. The body of Martin Davis already on its way to the morgue, Ray managing a quick look before the wagon sped off. The detectives treating them like any worker treats guests of the boss: like they'd love to tell you to fuck off but preferred to stay employed. Ray would have felt exactly the same.

Burns said, 'He had ID on him that identified him, name and student of Berkeley.'

Ray said, 'In a wallet?'

Lackowitz went to punch out a smoke from his pack, restrained himself. 'Yeah, but apart from that it was mainly empty. No cash.'

John Gordon said he believed Davis would have been carrying at least some cash.

'Then it's a likely robbery-homicide.' Burns scuffed his soles on the loose bitumen. 'He was stabbed twice through the heart. No weapon here. We got patrolmen looking for any sign.'

'Time of death?' Ray wondering if the killer was the same person hit Gordon on the head.

Burns said, 'You know what it's like. They won't give us anything definite right off, but he thinks about two a.m. Didn't find the body till nearly eight this morning when the owner of the lighting store went to empty trash.'

Lackowitz took it up. 'Three doors up that's the backdoor to a bar. Rough place, bikers, drugs. Big chance whatever finished here, started there.'

Ray said, 'You find keys on the body?'

Burns checked a manifest. 'Yes. One house key. One car key.'

Gordon said, 'You're looking for a nineteen fifty-seven Chevy

Bel Air.' He passed over the registration number of Hector's car.

'I spied one up the far corner of the lot.' Burns jerking a thumb that direction.

Lackowitz said, 'What else can you tell us?'

Ray let his partner fill them in, watched their eyes light up when they heard about Davis going off the rails, indulging in drugs. He could see them piecing it: doped-out student winds up out of his depth.

'What time did you get jumped last night?' Lackowitz offered his cigarette pack around. No takers. He stuck one between his lips and lit up.

Gordon said it was near 9.00 p.m. The two American cops exchanged a glance.

Ray said, 'We got a lead on Davis being in a bar, the Rimshot, over in North Hollywood, about three days ago. The bartender froze me out. Had a feeling she knew something.'

Burns made a note. 'You say there were bikers there?'

'Yeah. I don't know if there's any bikies who don't look like they would slit your throat. If there are, this wasn't them.'

Burns said, 'The bikers, patched? Vagos or Angels.'

'A few patched, Hells Angels. Vagos are the green ones, right? I didn't see any of them.'

Lackowitz said, 'This bar is mainly Angels too. They deal a lot of speed and grass.' He shot Burns a look. 'What are you thinking?'

Burns said, 'Way it could have gone down. Our killer knows Davis through drugs. Maybe Davis scores off him and owes money. Or vice versa is possible. Killer goes to Silver Lake, busts in, looks for cash or drugs, nothing. Waits for him. Realises he's been sprung when you walk in ...' a nod to Gordon, '... knocks you out, gets the hell out of there. They meet up here later, bam.'

Ray couldn't argue with the logic.

The cops straightened up off the car bonnet. Time was up.

Lackowitz said, 'We gotta move on this now. Officially we'll feed everything back through the captain but give me a call tomorrow and I'll tell you what we have.'

He passed a card across to each of them. As Gordon went to take it, Lackowitz's fingers gripped it tight.

'Let's get one thing clear though, cop to cop. You don't muddy our water. You don't pee in our stream.'

Burns chimed in. 'This is over for you now, right?'

'I guess so,' said Gordon.

'Enjoy Disneyland, take in the Dodgers.' Lackowitz was already moving to the driver seat. 'You got a ride back?'

Ray said, 'We're fine, thanks. Catch the bastard. His family will be grateful.'

◆◆◆

Venice Beach. Sand school-pant grey, ocean flat as a stick of Wrigley's, passing breasts perky in the new season's bikinis. Ray couldn't place a Sydney beach like it. Buildings up to its flank, supposed Bondi at a pinch with the Easter Show transplanted. John and Ray sipping Cokes under a corn dog sign, transistor radios everywhere, most playing 'San Francisco'. An occasional kid passing balanced on a small landboard, a few rollerskates but most teen strollers. Nobody ever seemed to work in California.

Ray coveted a lime green tee-shirt on a long-haired surfer, psychedelic flowers. A neat souvenir he'd wear as a barbecue party trick; the apron of the bull roasting the bloke in thongs and shorts was tired now. Speaking of tired, Gordon looked hollowed out.

Ray doing his best. 'It's not our fault.'

'We were so fucking close.'

They had been. But the reality was, 'close' might as well be a million fucking miles. Sometimes fate smiled. More often from Ray's experience, it swiped your arse with a razor blade.

He tried again. 'You want to go to Disneyland?'

'No.'

'Of course you do. Everyone wants to go to Disneyland.' Down on the beach a guy was doing sand sprints. Ray hated those.

Gordon said, 'Even Ray Shearer?'

'Yes. Annette Funicello might be hanging about.'

'I thought she'd be too young for you.'

'She's twenty-five.'

For the first time Gordon looked his way. 'How do you know that?'

'Fantails. I took Marie to *Bikini Beach* at the drives.'

Gordon, looking like Ray had just said he'd seen a flying saucer. 'You really want to go to Disneyland?'

'What losers would we be if we came all the way to Los Angeles and never went to Disneyland. I'll buy a set of mouse-ears for Marie and get her to parade around me in nothing else. Some toys for Cassie. And I want to go to Frontierland. I like bowie knives and Indians and shit. You?'

'I'm more Adventureland.'

Ray crushed his empty Coke can, wondered what caused the satisfaction that made people do that. They'd fought a good fight. It just hadn't been good enough.

He said, 'Bags Annette if we see her.'

◆◆◆

Heading south, Beach Boys on the radio. The air clearer down here. Shearer was right, they had to go to Disneyland. But for him this was a delay, an escape. He should have already sent a telegram to Geary.

'What do you think of their theory?' John dealing a look to Shearer. Ray in his bright short-sleeve Hawaiian and square chin, he could be a fucking private eye here. He'd fit right in.

Shearer, yelling over the breeze and road noise, 'It works. If Davis was still a crazy dope fiend.' Hitting the 'if'. John pleased Shearer thinking the same way as him.

'Hector and Chad didn't reckon he was a stoner. There was no smell of dope in his room at Hector's. Seems to me he got jolted out of that shit.'

Shearer said, 'He was obsessed with finding Spring. Maybe she's taken up with this bikie guy.'

'Or Davis thought the guy at least knew who she was with and fronted him.'

'Either way,' said Shearer, 'it's over, and no matter how rotten we feel, we can't bring him back.'

That was true. Same as Michael Foley would never be brought back. Death was the only finality life offered in its whole swag. Kansas Annie spiked in his memory. Now Martin Davis, stabbed and left to bleed out by a rubbish bin in an alley. A few weeks, ago they had been breathing Peace, Love, and We-Can-Stop-A-War, drinking cheap red, smoking dope. Now they were as inert as the morgue slab their bodies rested on. He wished none of it was true.

He'd told Shearer he wanted to go to Adventureland. Fact was, he craved Fantasyland, the happiest kingdom of them all.

◆◆◆

A little after nine that night they were back at Barney's, their local now, John figured. They'd done all the 'lands' at Walt Disney's complex. No Annette Funicello, but Mickey Mouse was there. Loads of kids. John never thought about having kids. Didn't suppose Denise had either. But seeing those families there having fun together made you wonder. Then again, kids grew up.

Back in Sydney, Martin Davis' parents still held hope. That was about to be quashed, John had sent his telegram to Geary, an admission of failure. His brain skimmed over love, infatuation, need. If Davis had never met Spring, he'd still be alive. The girl had consumed him. But what was his alternative? A degree, a lifetime of loneliness?

He nursed his beer, scoped the bar. Busy, people his age. Feeling their power. But it wasn't the same vibe as San Francisco. Up there he'd felt a sense of being part of something, like heat haze or road shimmer, a conviction the illusion was real. It was different here. Change, yeah, you felt that. The men in suits with bald patches weren't calling all the shots. Electric guitar and dope and sex without frenchies because young women were on the pill and balling to their heart's content, and bikini girls cruising in convertibles looking for Fun Fun Fun were like a fucking tidal wave sweeping dowdy dresses, and pens with nibs, and men's ties, and Sunday church, into the ocean. *My Three Sons* was out, *Star Trek* was in.

Yet he didn't feel he was part of anything much. And he didn't think the people here felt they were either. Like Dylan sang, something was going down, but John had no idea what.

Shearer yakking with Janis and a couple of her musicians at the bar. He had that look in his eye again. He'd signalled John to join but John wasn't up for it. He sipped his beer, soaked in the music, recognised Paul Butterfield, something he would not have known four days back. He thought of Spring, where she was now, wondered how she'd take Martin's death. Shearer swaggering over, tumblers a third-full of clear fluid, lemon twist on the rim.

'You ever had tequila?'

'Nope.'

'Me either till just now. Try it.'

John did. It tasted like gin.

'You bite the lemon. You're supposed to put salt on your hand, but I couldn't be fucked. Janis and the guys have invited us to the Whisky to see The Byrds and some other band.'

John said, 'I might go back to the motel. Try and get some sleep.'

Shearer said, 'You need company, not sleep. You're coming.'

The 'other' band playing. Right up to this second, walking into that crowded club, John thinking 'blow your mind' was the worst hippie bullshit phrase. Jimi Hendrix had electrified him. Janis was fucking phenomenal. They put a charge in you. But these guys on stage … this was something else again, a fist reaching into that darkest part of your soul.

The music not so much sounded as glowed. Kryptonite buried on the ocean floor. Organ and guitar riffs subterranean currents. The rhythm predatory. No bass player. The organist pumping pedals. But the singer … a voice that had come down through the ages. King Agamemnon bellowing through a sandstone tomb exhorting them all to break on through to whatever lay beyond.

John felt it, that desire. To touch death, God, the unknown. He felt Martin Davis, here beside him, rocking to the pounding rhythm. The music transported you to another dimension, the terrifying tightrope between life and eternity. A place John knew as well as his mum knew a Hills hoist. He'd been there before, the plaything of a madman. And even now he could not escape its grasp on his soul. Break on through. That's what you had to do. Somehow.

The coals of that song still hot when another ignited. It seemed to be called 'Light My Fire'. The singer, writhing leather, a tempest of hair, a cobra.

Women creaming themselves, orgasmic, in a voodoo thrall. It wouldn't surprise John if more than a few conceived, right there. Immaculate conception seemed possible. Everything seemed possible. He was paddling the Amazon, the Nile, pulling on an oar on a longboat under a Norse sky in a lightning storm.

White light spun off a mirror ball, cut the dark like scissors. In that instant, across the far side of the room, a face illuminated. The face he'd seen every day for the last two weeks, the face he'd laid out before a hundred strangers: Spring. The tomb closed again. Darkness. He spun. Caught Ray in low light at the bar in tight conversation with Janis, yelled his name, his cry muted under the band magic. He turned back, tried to pinpoint where he thought he had seen Spring, pushed towards that way.

'Spring? You sure?' Ray trying to read his partner. Gordon's eyes the texture of mist on a lake. Maybe that whack on the scone still affecting him. Gordon shook his head.

'I'm not sure of anything.'

They'd found a nook by the cigarette machine in high demand, Marlboro leading a half-length to Lucky Strike.

'You looked?'

'Best as I could.'

Ray casting around. No easy task to locate anybody, the Byrds into their second song.

'I tried to find you.'

Ray apologised. Janis had taken him backstage. Some bloke tying up to shoot Horse. Not Ray's idea of a good time. Janis had greeted the junkie like he was making himself a coffee. That didn't augur well for her future. But Ray was too old to lecture, and she was too old to be lectured to. He'd left her laughing with the singer who'd just come off stage.

'I'll take another look now. You go that way.' Ray pointing Gordon clockwise. The photos still in his pocket. Starting with the door girl.

Perched on a stool, one fishnet crossed over the other. She was to eyeshadow what Tarzan was to bodybuilders.

'Maybe. I'm not sure.' Sucking on a Salem.

They were running about sixth behind Marlboro.

◆◆◆

Thirty minutes brought nothing. Ray still waiting for 'Mr Tambourine Man'. That first group just weird. Gordon had even checked the back entrance, no sign of her. Ray frustrated at JG. He had to let go. Davis was dead. The chase had to stop.

'What if it is her? What are you going to say?'

Gordon scratched the top of his head, thinking about that. 'I don't know. I suppose I just want to see if she cared about him. Maybe she'd want to see his body. I'm not ruling out she was involved somehow.'

'See,' said Ray, 'that's where you're going wrong. That's over now. We let Lackowitz and Burns do their thing.'

Ray bullshitting himself, knowing it. Of course, it wasn't over for him any more than it was for Gordon. He wanted answers too. Had Spring taken up with some biker who'd nailed Davis because he kept pestering him? Or was Spring just the trigger for a lonely kid to get out of his depth – drugs, bikies, shit with a capital S. But no matter how curious they were it wouldn't bring Davis back. You had to pick your battles, and you didn't pick ones you'd already lost.

Janis pushed through towards them. Ray went to her eyes straight away. Still clear.

She said, 'The studio's got a test pressing of Zappa's album. We're all going down to listen. You coming?'

◆◆◆

Ray had lost track of time. Standing on the flat roof of the studio looking out over broad streets, a few headlights glowing like cigarettes in some dark lovers' lane. Not much moon. Got him thinking of that Julie London track he loved. He'd never been in a recording studio before. Downstairs all wood panels and gold records hanging.

Ray and John had driven Janis and a couple of her roadies, Nitro and Gunner here. Nitro they'd met before with Kansas Annie.

Probably ten of them altogether in the studio. They'd sprawled over sofas, the floor. Thick smoke, marihuana mainly. A guy named Doug, who seemed to be in charge, had taken this LP that had just a white label with pencil writing that said *Absolutely Free*, carefully placed it on a turntable, dropped the needle. The music, if you could call it that, was the weirdest shit Ray had heard in his life.

His eyes travelled back to sky. If a bartender served a lemon wedge that thin, you'd want your money back. Found himself singing, 'No moon at all it's so dark ...'

'... even Fido is afraid to bark.'

Turning. Janis there, cigarette in one hand, flask in the other, laugh lines.

Ray leaning back on the parapet facing her. 'You know that song?'

Janis easing over. 'You sound surprised.'

'I am a little.'

'I'm surprised, Raymond, that you can sing.'

'Nobody ever calls me Raymond.'

She draped an arm over him. 'Not even your mom?'

'She used to call me "Scamp".'

'I like that name.' She was wearing perfume. Ray liked it.

She said, 'What did you think of the album?'

'Weirdest shit I've ever heard. Funny, but. You?'

'I have admiration for it. But I like blues.'

Her fingers playing with his hair. Their mouths close. Ray couldn't help it. They kissed. Not a long kiss just ... inevitable.

'Why do you like me?' he asked.

''Cause you're sad. Like I said. Blues.'

Ray shifted, felt Los Angeles below him. He was Zeus. 'You think I'm sad?'

'Aren't you?' she sucked on her cigarette, drilled smoke to the vault.

'I was. Now I've got a woman. A baby daughter.'

'But it's still there, right? Like original sin. That stain you can't fake away.'

He said nothing. She reached over, stroked his forehead with the back of her fingertips.

'Tell me. Tell me about yourself, Scamp.'

And for no reason he could understand, her pressing into him, perfume swimming over a lonely rooftop thousands of miles away from where it all happened, he did.

Told her about the day his life changed, the family holiday, pre-teen. Patrick and him in the river. Smoke suddenly in their nostrils. Terror. Running out as best they could, the water tugging at them. The caravan ablaze. The screams. Orphan years, adopted by a tough uncle, separated from his brother, Pat. She listened with tears on the threshold.

'The fire was deliberate. I spent half my life trying to find out why somebody killed my parents.'

'And did you?'

He nodded. 'A mistake. The guy fucked up. I think that's why … that record, Zappa or whatever his name is. I liked it. It's saying: Life is bullshit. Our lives are stupid. Shining your shoes, getting a job. All of it. it's a con job. You never marry the girl in the song. Or if you do, it doesn't work. For years I smelled that smoke every night I went to bed.'

'Things change us,' she said, and ground out her cigarette in the pot of a small cactus. 'And we can never get back to what we were.'

She came in close. They kissed again.

'What about you?' he whispered.

'Me? Well, I'm always the wrong person. For everybody.'

'Not when you're on stage.'

Tilting her head, giving him that. 'But sooner or later, the gig ends.'

They stood there, silent. Then she said. 'So you found the guy who killed your folks?'

'I did.'

'And what?'

He shrugged. 'I settled it.'

She knew what he meant, was still curious, 'And it's over now?'

'I don't smell the smoke any more. But there's still a loose end or two.'

She said, 'My life, that's all there is, loose ends.' She offered him her flask. He took a slug of sweet rye. They stared at one another.

'We're imperfect, you and me,' she said.

No point denying it.

He said, 'We're the ones the Pied Piper would have left behind.'

Janis pulling out a cigarette, pointing the butt at him like saying 'Bloody oath.'

She said, 'So your boy you were chasing wound up dead.'

He hadn't told her that, figured Gordon must have.

'Yeah.'

'No wonder you're blue.'

'I'm a cop back home. I'm surrounded by death. Used to it. But it still punches you in the gut.'

'But it's not your fault.'

Him thinking, sometimes it is. Remembering how he and Gordon raced through the streets to get to Michael Foley, trying to save a life before psycho Foley butchered his victim. The glint on the knife still spiked in his brain. The loud boom of Gordon's shotgun. Only Foley had been innocent. Gordon the one bearing that weight, but Ray knowing it was him who led him there.

Meeting her eyes. 'You got to watch that needle shit.'

'I can handle it. No needle's going to take me. We're Texans, tough as Davy Crockett.'

'But he died at the Alamo.'

She kissed him, real hard this time. His body was charging up, breathing shallow. She whispered hot breath in his ear.

'You and me could work.'

'No we couldn't,' he managed to whisper back.

'But we could have fun trying.'

She pulled him down, her body pressing into his chest. She reached between his legs, said, 'I feel the need to explore Australia with you right now, Scamp, and so the fuck do you.'

10 STRANGE DAYS

Saturday morning Bondi, the smell of bacon and eggs, *Two-Way Turf Talk* on the radio. Granite's favourite time. Of course, he had found Dempsey just as Shearer had wanted, and Dempsey had got a result. First, they'd had to set the cat among the pigeons, but Shearer had sorted all that before he left: a solicitor's letter, 'You may be entitled to an inheritance … please have your solicitor verify by signature that you are indeed …' blah blah blah. Then Dempsey did his thing, followed the target like bad luck. Now it was time for act two.

The café door opened, small bloke with a beard. Looking around, clocking Granite, heading over.

'You eaten?'

'Nah, I'm right. Cup of tea though.'

Granite hollered to the waitress.

'Been a while, Westy.'

Last time Granite had seen him was Long Bay, nearly three years back. Granite with Shaloub money for the warden to keep Westy in good health. It had been a bad time, Melbourne painters and dockers trying to muscle in. Granite thought it had been good of Shaloub to step in. Shaloub didn't owe Westy. Not for the job he got busted on; that was all down to Westy throwing in with some young dickheads and Maoris. Shit, you wanted to keep a bank job quiet, don't get them involved.

'I'm curious,' Westy angling his head like a parrot as his tea arrived.

'Why's that?'

'Not a peep out of you for three years.'

Granite said, 'I'm retired. Semi, anyway. Ever since George, not much point. You?'

'More or less, depending on the circumstance.' Cagey, sipping his tea.

'House in Rose Bay, one old Labrador that will lick you to death.'

'Where's the safe?'

Granite knowing Westy was sharp like that. Nobody was going to request him for a simple B and E. He was the safe specialist.

Granite said, 'That's your job to find out. There's a den, ground floor. I'm guessing there.'

'You don't even know if there is a safe?' Westy shaking his head.

'Pretty sure has to be in the den.'

'How much you offering?'

'Eighty quid. Not dollars.'

'A hundred.'

'No. Eighty tops. You're not to open the safe. Just locate and tell me for a later date how best to do it. The important thing, the critical bit: don't get tempted. I will put you down myself. Understand?' Granite tapped his coat. There was a revolver in there.

Westy didn't need convincing. He said, 'When?'

◆◆◆

John woke up in his motel bed with a jackhammer right in the middle of his head. Last night a blank page after they hit the studio. One of the musos had given him a big slice of cake, mumbled, 'Hash.' Too much alcohol on top. Shearer lying back on his bed, dressed, reading a newspaper.

'What happened?' John's voice a croak.

'You were back at Disneyland.'

'What time did we get in?'

'Moon had been replaced by sun.'

John throwing a glance at the clock. Shit. 11.20. Shearer looked okay. Chipper even.

'How come you look healthy?'

Shearer shot the paper like cuffs. It crackled. 'I didn't partake of anything.'

John struggling to get his head off the pillow, said, 'I better check about getting a flight back home.'

Ray said, 'It's Sunday, remember.'

Damn. Schubert wouldn't be in at work. Lackowitz and Burns were likely on the case hunting down leads and might not appreciate a call right now.

Ray was the one said, 'We should let Hector know.'

◆◆◆

They each had glasses with little coloured motifs on the side. Beach balls for him, kittens on Ray's. Must have been a set of kids' glasses Hector had kept or picked up cheap. Shearer sampling the tequila but John steering way clear, lemonade only. Hector hadn't mentioned any children but there was a family photo on the mantelpiece. Boy and girl about twelve, the fading suggested it had been sitting there at least a decade.

Hector had shrunk since he got the news about Martin, looking now like the boy in the photo had jumped into his father's chair. One of those old comfy types, wide flat armrests for your glass and cigarettes. The lounge room was a small box, dusty. A bowl of plastic fruit occupied the middle of a dining table that hadn't hosted a dinner since Sinatra outsold Elvis. Looked like it would glow with one wipe of a rag. Hector had been right about the old chrome fan that sat on the floor tilting up. It put out as much wind as a pensioner fanning herself with a playing card.

'They send people in first with gloves and camera, check out the room above the garage. The main detectives come around for a little while after that. They ask me questions like you: Does he bring anybody here? Do I see anybody? I tell them "No". They tell me they keeping my car for a bit.' Hector sipped, seemed to scan memories. 'He was a good kid.'

John pointed at the photo of the kids.

'Yours?'

Hector nodded, sad. 'The boy got himself in a heap of trouble. I never see him. Broke his mother's heart. My daughter has two kids. She live in Florida. You got kids?' Scattering it over both of them. John shook his head, Shearer nodded.

'They the best thing that ever gonna happen to you. But like love, my friends, the other side of the best thing is the worst. I feel for Marty's parents.' Tapping his singlet about where the sacred heart of Jesus was located in the shiny photo on the wall. 'They got a lot of grief coming.' He swallowed his drink, reached for the bottle poured himself a slug, offered the bottle. John covered his glass. Shearer went another half-measure.

'So, they think maybe drugs.' Hector stating, not asking. 'I see a lot of kids …' imitating a Boris Karloff wide-eyed stare '… Marty not like that. But …' he tapped his head.

'Troubled,' John venturing.

'Si.'

Shearer said, 'He was worried about his girlfriend. She probably dumped him, but he believed something bad had happened to her.'

'But you not find her?'

No, John admitted, they had not.

'So, maybe Marty right after all.' A shrug, another sip. 'You want to take his clothes and things? I box them up after cops come through.'

John thinking Mrs Davis might want her boy's effects, figured he could drop this stuff off with what was left at the house in Berkeley.

'I suppose.'

Hector pulling himself up, waddling into some rear section of the house. Returning with a taped box and a short-sleeve shirt over his shoulder.

'He must have put this in the basket. I tell him, put dirty clothes in there, I wash with mine.' He indicated the box. 'I already taped up the box before I find it.'

Hector handed over the shirt, Gloweave green geometric patterns. The small human things are what hit you. John felt himself choking up.

They spent another hour with Hector talking shit. A touching front-lawn farewell with Hector, solemn.

'You send me a postcard from Sydney,' said Hector, now with a shine on.

They promised, thanked him for the drink.

'You ever come back to Los Angeles. You come say hello.'

Clapping him on the back and vice versa. Hector still out front of his house, swigging from the bottle, waving as the Mustang pulled away.

◆◆◆

Waiting for them at the motel, a message to call Lackowitz. John rang. Burns answered, said they were heading out to lunch, join if they wanted a progress report. Destination a sandwich joint near the heart of downtown. The traffic only Sunday strength, finding a park easy. Lackowitz and Burns munching Reubens. John went plain old egg. Shearer a Reuben, 'When in Rome.' John wished he had followed the adage, too much mayo on the egg.

'It's been the usual shit,' Burns wiping his fingertips with a serviette after each bite. 'We got two witnesses, one the bartender, who remembers Davis in the Dolphin on the night.'

Shearer clarified that was the bar that led onto the alley where the body had been found.

'Correct. Most of the clientele were Hells Angels and lowlifes. The bartender says there was no altercation or dispute that night in the bar. He says he's damn sure because it was one of the few nights there wasn't one.'

Lackowitz swallowed. 'The bikers are mainly from a clubhouse on Pico close to the bar. We paid them a visit and surprise, surprise, none of them remember your guy or any fight.'

Burns said, 'The employee leaving the realtor office late says she's sure she heard an argument around two a.m.'

Shearer said, 'What was she doing there that late?'

'Fucking the boss. He admitted it but asked us to keep it from the wife. He didn't hear the argument.'

'So you've got nothing?' John seeing no point sugar-coating.

Lackowitz said, 'Oh no, we've got plenty. Like a double homicide in Wilshire. Wealthy businessman and wife who donated to the mayor's favourite funds. You can imagine the heat on that case.'

Shearer came at them straight, 'Ours is on the backburner.'

Burn said, 'No, we're looking but it's going to take one of these assholes to get themselves in trouble. Then they're going to look to get themselves out of trouble telling us who cut your boy up.'

'Meantime,' Lackowitz finishing the sandwich, 'we have a lot of shiny shoes up our asses asking what the fuck happened to Mr and Mrs Theodore Belling.'

Paying the cheque, John's eyes lit on a handbill advertising Big Brother, stuck on the wall. A good souvenir, about all he was going to get out of the trip from here on in.

◆◆◆

'We could take our time. Wind our way up the coast,' Shearer heading to take the wheel. John not really caring how they spun the days out. The sun had grown brighter, or maybe it was his eyes adjusting after being indoors. John opened the glovebox for his sunglasses, dormant since yesterday. They were lying on top of Davis' stray shirt that Shearer must have shoved in there after Hector's.

As John picked up his sunnies, he felt something in the shirt pocket. Pulled out two receipts. One larger, handwritten and torn from a small receipt pad, the kind that used carbon paper to make a copy. It read *Unit 6. Rent paid to 5/21*. The other was a cash register docket for a Coke and burger. There was no business name on it. The smaller one had been folded inside the larger one.

Shearer looking over said, 'What you got?'

John showed him.

'Well, odds-on that rental receipt's not Hector's. He took cash and I'm sure he doesn't want the taxman to know.'

John agreeing. Besides, the writing looked too neat and English for Hector.

Shearer said, 'That's likely from wherever Davis was renting space.'

'That room at Hector's was pretty crummy. If he did turn up any important stuff with his research, it's probably here.' Flicking the receipt, annoyed there was no address.

'There might be something there to help Lackowitz and Burns nail the killer.'

Shearer scoffed. 'You weren't listening. This case is no longer a priority. They'll wait for a tip, which could come never. Then they'll find a scapegoat or bury it.'

John thinking aloud. 'Davis was renting somewhere on Western.' He reached into his trouser pocket, pulled out the handbill he'd just taken off the diner wall, opened it to reveal the luncheon cash register receipt wrapped inside. 'When we get two receipts close together, we wrap one inside the other, right?'

Shearer said, 'Done it a million times.'

John said, 'My guess is Davis ate somewhere then paid his rent and wrapped the two receipts together when he stuck them in his pocket. Wherever he ate is most likely near where he's renting. Why don't we drive over that way, stop at all the diners and ask if they've seen a guy could be Davis driving the Chevy?'

Shearer said, 'I don't mind. It's not like we have anything else to do.'

◆◆◆

They drove to the southern end of North Western and scanned. The first diner was a bust, the next closed for Sunday. At the third the cashier said the docket could be one of theirs. They waited while the waitress, a young Lucille Ball, filled a fat man's mug with rank percolated brew. Then she turned her attention back to the photo of Davis.

'Yes. I think so. Been in a couple of times around lunchtime.'

'By himself?'

She was pretty sure he had been alone. ''Cause you know when somebody takes a booth and there's no room for a family, it's … irritating.'

'Did he take a booth?'

'If it's the guy I'm thinking of, yes. He had all these notebooks with him and photos. He just made notes the whole time while he ate.'

The waitress went to do her thing with another customer.

'We're getting warmer,' said Shearer.

John supposed it was good to feel you were doing something. Even if Martin Davis was loony-tunes, he might have left something valuable, or some important clue to his killer's identity in the space he'd been renting. John needed to piss. Shearer didn't.

John came back out through the swing door to find Shearer mulling. Before John had said a word, Shearer tapped the corkboard above the payphone.

Lots of handwritten notices there: people looking for flatmates, a guitar for sale, a VW for sale, a couple of dogs missing. And another one offering 'Cheap spaces ideal for filmmakers, costume or clothes design'. There was a phone number and an address.

Shearer picked up the phone and dialled. It rang out. Shearer raised his brow and wrote the address on his forearm.

John drove, Shearer studying spiderweb streets in the atlas across his lap. John punched on the radio, caught The Supremes telling him he couldn't hurry love. If only Martin Davis had listened to that, he might still be around.

The sun still deafening, telling himself, 'You should have bought a hat,' rolling his sleeves up, envying Shearer in the kind of shirt you saw in Randwick public bars on summer race-days.

Less than ten minutes in, above a single-storey brick warehouse on a corner block, a sign, *SPACES TO RENT LARGE OR SMALL.*

Shearer pointed, 'That'd be the place.'

Parking no problem, a space right outside. They walked to the big front doors. Locked. No bell but a number to call, the same as what had been on the noticeboard.

Shearer said, 'Give me the car keys. You walk around the side and back, see if there's another door.'

There was no door on the other main street but then a service lane ran to the back of the building and gave onto a recessed doorway;

a single wooden door sporting an 'alarmed' sticker, standard lock. Shearer appeared, striding down the alley carrying his tool bag.

John said, 'It's alarmed.'

Shearer grunted, got in close. 'Sometimes they just put a sticker on. If we use a key to get in, we'll have thirty seconds at least before she rings.'

Shearer studying the lock. It looked more professional than any old Lockwood.

'This looks like a five,' said Shearer and selected a key, tried it. 'Wrong. Six.'

The key turned.

They stepped into gloom. Alarm box blinking green just inside the doorway. Disarmed already. Could mean company. Shearer a finger to his lips, shutting the door quietly. Their eyes adjusting. Started as quietly they could up the corridor. Locked doors to their right, successively numbers 12, 11, 10, 9. Another corridor breaking right, light spilling from it. They edged around.

Now there were units both sides: the left side facing the street and their car at the front of the building, to the right even numbers denoting units in a partition wall. Unit 6, second on the right, source of the light. John watched Shearer pull his gun and move in. John followed.

A room about the size of a large lounge room or one of those double garages. A small, cheap desk, hunched over it a guy with a crew cut flicking through a diary or something. By the time he turned he was facing Ray's gun.

'Clint Adams, I guess,' said Ray.

11 I HEARD IT THROUGH THE GRAPEVINE

John patted Adams down. Wallet, breast pocket, driver's licence said James Perry. No gun. Shearer keeping his revolver where Perry could see it.

'I should fucking blow you away right now.'

With Shearer, you couldn't be sure he wouldn't do exactly that.

'What's your problem?' Perry indignant.

'I don't like murderers.'

'This some anti-war bullshit?' Perry sneering.

'You hit my friend here. Friday night.'

Perry's eyes slid over to John, but he stayed silent.

'And then you murdered the kid. Why? Because of Spring?'

'I don't know what the fuck you're talking about.'

'Martin Davis, the kid who rents this unit. You killed him.'

His eyes darting between them. Something dawning. 'He's dead?'

'Save the act.'

Agitated now. 'I didn't kill anyone. Where was he killed?'

John spoke. 'Like you don't know.'

Shearer said, 'Back of a bar in Venice. Around one Saturday morning. So where were you, James?'

Perry's eyes moving fast. 'I think I know who killed him.'

Ray cynical, 'Who is that?'

Perry pointing at a bunch of small photo prints littered across the desk.

'This guy. I think his name's Larry.'

❖❖❖

Ray glanced down. Lots of snaps, taken from various distances, surveillance style. Some maybe in the parking lot of the Rimshot.

The subject, a guy in his twenties, long hair, a white Triumph motorcycle.

Ray said, 'Larry?' Like he didn't believe a word. And so far he didn't. 'Who the fuck is Larry?'

Perry said, 'I don't fucking know. I only got here a bit before you guys. There.'

Perry pointing to left hand side of the room. Ray seeing it for the first time. The whole wall covered in butcher's paper, writing, arrows, photos, newspaper cuttings. They moved in for a closer look, Ray not letting his weapon stray. An improvised case board like they might use themselves. The paper sheet had been divided into half-a-dozen panels by hand-drawn vertical lines. On the left-most was a list of names, dates, locations.

Francine Leach 19 – Jan 14 Human Be-In Golden Gate Park.

Jenny Wallace 18 – Feb 19 Airplane-Big Brother, Fillmore. Hitchhiking from San Fran to L.A. for concert.

Pauline Gerschaff 21 – Mar 26 Elysian Park Love-In.

Sherry Linden 20 – April 7 San Francisco Buffalo Springfield and Jefferson Airplane concert St Ignatius High School. Body found Hollywood Hills April 11.

Mary Gannon 20 – April 11 Long Beach, Scherer Park. Local bands.

Spring – April 5, hitchhiking to L.A.

The succeeding panels filled with smaller notes, cuttings, photos.

At a glance, one panel for each of the women named. The right-most panel headed *Larry*. A photo: same guy as in the smaller photos Perry had been rummaging through. John connecting dots quick: Martin Davis tracking Larry, linking him to missing girls. The last of those, Spring. Knowing Shearer would have got there ahead of him.

'Who the fuck are you guys anyway? You're not cops.'

The barrel of Ray's snub nose making an o on Perry's forehead. 'We're the ones who decide if you live or die. Spring is your ex?'

A crooked smile playing on Perry's lips. 'That bitch? Not in a million fucking years.'

John said, 'So what are you doing here? What were you doing Friday at Davis' flat. That's where you got the key, right?'

'I could ask you the same question.'

Shearer wiggled the gun and said, 'Except I have this.'

Perry spat, 'Why do you think I'm here. I want to find that little bitch.'

'So you can reminisce with Spring over old times in Bumfuck, Illinois?'

'I never knew her by that bullshit name. Only learned that's what she's calling herself in San Francisco. Mary-Anne Weddeker, that's her real name.'

'Why was she scared of you?' John not buying anything yet.

'Because she knows I will rip her fucking heart out when I catch up with her. You're Australian, right?'

How the hell ...?

'I've drunk beers with a few Aussies in Hong Kong. On leave.'

A picture slowly developing. John said, 'You're a soldier?'

'Twenty-fifth infantry.' He looked up at John. 'That was you I hit? Sorry about that. I thought she might have been hiding out there.'

Shearer said, 'What'd she do to you?'

'Not to me, my kid brother. She drove his car into a tree and put him in a wheelchair for life. But best of all, she left him dying in the car while she got her ass out of Dodge.'

'Maybe she panicked.'

'She was thinking pretty clear when she went back to his place and took all the money he had in the world, before she lit up out of there.'

From what he'd learned so far about Spring, John reckoned the story rang true. He could see why Mary-Anne would have been worried having this angry GI on her tail.

Shearer said, 'Let's wind it back. Take it from the beginning. Mary-Anne fucked over your brother. You came looking for her.'

Perry told them. He's fresh back on leave from Vietnam, sitting in his hometown looking at news reports of the hippies in San Fran when he spies Spring on TV. Drives there fast. Starts asking questions, tracks her to Berkeley.

'She was shacked up with this guy Marty. That's what I learned first. Then she split. I heard to LA. I heard Marty had gone after her, but I didn't know if he was with her or not.'

John said, 'How did you find Marty here?'

'Mary-Anne was always big on the stars. The Hollywood ones too but mainly the twinkling ones. Our old man had a telescope, and she would sit out on our porch and look up the stars and go on and on about planets and shit. Phil, my brother, he used to put up with it. Amazing what warm quim will do to a man. I figured that when Mary-Anne came to Los Angeles she'd be heading to the observatory up Griffith Park. So, I went up there and asked if anybody had seen my little sister and showed the photo. One of the ladies there said she hadn't seen her, but another young man had been in just the day before asking about her. Kindly, he had left his address in case she came in.'

John said, 'You went to the place in Silver Lake.'

'Yeah. I was watching the place, looking out for Mary-Anne. No sign. Then about six, Marty arrives home. He gets changed, comes back out. I follow him to some place over Santa Monica way and he slows down passing some biker house.'

'This on Pico?' Ray.

Perry thinking. 'Yeah, I think it was. Then he leads me to some biker bar in Venice Beach.'

John asked if Marty had gone into the bar.

'Yeah, he parked and went into the bar, then I went in.'

'Was this "Larry" there?'

'Sure was, talking bullshit with other bikers.'

Shearer asked if Marty had approached Larry.

'Not when I was there. He's keeping to himself, but he's got eyes on that guy. Pops a pill. I'm thinking this is some drug shit, I'm wasting my time, maybe she's back in Silver Lake, or there's some clue there about where she might be. So, I leave Venice, and I drive back to Silver Lake and turn the place inside out but there's nothing except a key. And I think, maybe that's to wherever she is holed up. That's when I hear somebody coming up the stairs and calling out …' He looked at John, 'I'm sorry. I hauled my ass out of there.'

Shearer checking the key Perry had brought with him. A cheap plastic tag with the address written on it attached. 'Why'd it take you so long to come here?'

John thinking: because Perry figured Sunday night this place would be deader than Boycott's bat. He could rummage in peace.

'I don't know who I've hit back at the flat. To be honest, I panic. I drive around wondering if I should up and quit LA. I go and have something to eat. I'm thinking, I don't fit in here, I am wasting my time. I decide to give up. I'm on my way back to my motel, and then I think, no fuck it. I drive back to the biker bar and poke my head in. There's no sign of Mary-Anne or Marty. And I'm heading back to my car when I see Biker-Boy Larry here, heading out in a hurry, so I jump in my car and follow him to a dump all the way out in San Bernadino. I'm low on gas and it's three in the morning so I sleep in my car. I came back to LA, decided to check this place out when it was quiet.'

John said, 'So it was about two when you left the biker bar?'
'About that.'

John thinking, that would match the time of the argument that was overheard, thinking Larry could have followed Davis out of the bar into the alley or vice versa. One of them kicks up. Only one way that is going to end, the way it did, Davis stabbed to death and left to die by garbage bins. Also thinking: this would be a good story for Perry to spin if he was the one killed Martin Davis. And he was still the best candidate.

Ray said, 'You get a number plate on Larry?'

'Nope. But like I said, I followed him to his place.'

Ray snorting. 'Your story doesn't stack up. You found Marty like you said. But you wanted Spring bad. You followed him to the Dolphin Lounge, probably true. She wasn't there. You drove back to Silver Lake, see if she was living there after all. You didn't find anything. You'd had enough. Why waste more time? You drove back to the Dolphin Lounge. You waited for Marty to leave, fronted him, told him that unless he told you where Spring was, you were going to kill him.'

'Bullshit.'

'Maybe he resisted or went to run or attacked you. Maybe you didn't mean to kill him.'

'Listen, cocksucker. I never saw him when I went back. I only saw the biker asshole and I followed him.'

'To San Bernadino?' Ray infecting that with doubt.

'Yeah. Anybody killed the kid, it was him.'

There was a payphone in the reception area by the front doors. John tried Lackowitz but it rang out. Shearer watching him, obviously what he'd expected.

'What do you reckon now?' asked John.

◆◆◆

Past eight by the time they reached San Bernadino. Perry in back, cuffed. From what John could see, hippiedom hadn't quite reached this far inland. The neon was all bowling, hamburgers and movie palaces. Back at the unit after that call, Shearer had said, 'How do you want to play it?'

John knew what he wanted. 'I want justice for Martin Davis.'

'We could drive to San Bernadino, take a look.'

'We have no jurisdiction,' John had replied.

'We have Smith and Wessons and we have him,' Shearer nodding at Perry.

They had all taken a piss before leaving the warehouse. Decided on Perry's roomier Chevy. No end of what Ray had brought with him in his bag. Handcuffs snapped on Perry, who had complained.

'You don't need to do that. I'm taking you to him.'

For all they knew he was leading them into a trap. Maybe Perry had help waiting the other end. After that, Perry grew sullen.

'Hey, you cracked my mate on the head, you're getting off light.' Then, Shearer trying to bond. 'What's it like in Nam?'

'When you're on base, it's as boring as this fucking car ride. When you're on patrol, there's a hundred little invisible gook fuckers trying to kill you.'

That was all he said the whole way.

They rolled through the main drag. A bunch of bikers outside a hamburger joint watched them carefully. No wearing flowers in your hair around here. John guessed the bikers down in Venice might have already rung through to their brothers, told them the pigs were after Larry.

'You remember the street?' John asked.

'Keep going.'

The buildings got lower and darker. They headed out of town. The suburban blocks got bigger and messier. A semi-rural feel now, weatherboards and fibro and rusting wire fences.

'Turn right.'

Ray did as he was told. John had his hand resting on his gun. No street lighting, the road narrow bitumen.

Perry's voice floated from the back. 'Couple of hundred yards on the right. I parked just here off to the side.'

To their left a paddock or maybe an orchard. Ray doing what Perry had. Pulling off to the opposite side of the road by the fence, killing headlights. They could see the outline of a house about one hundred and twenty yards up to the right. Pleasantly warm, the air clear and dry. Made John think of Parkes back home. Perry had told them he'd seen nobody at the house except for Larry. No other bikes or vehicles.

'For now, you're going in the trunk,' said Shearer.

'Fuck you. What if he kills you motherfuckers.'

'Better pray he doesn't.'

Perry complied. Before he slammed the trunk lid down, John offered hope.

'If Larry's in there, I'll come back and let you out.'

No traffic on the road. The glow of houses spread apart at intervals like rosary beads dotting snaking bitumen. They walked fifty yards up the road on its left-hand side then crossed to the same side as the house that was set back about forty feet, low yellow glow from a porch light, or window pooled around a parked motorcycle, mainly white, but with a dark colour, likely blue. The house built on a rise or small hill, so at first John thought it had a garage underneath but as he got closer, he saw the house was one level.

On the side facing them, mounds of head-high dirt afforded cover. John had no idea what the dirt was for. They edged forward to the weatherboard, windowless on this side. Backs to the building they crab-walked to the rear nearside corner of the house. A back patio of some sort visible, old iron chairs and table under a low shade roof. Music inside, modern stuff: guitars and drums. The back of the house all louvred windows, light from somewhere deep in the house flirting with the moonlight outside. Two steps leading to a flywire door. Shearer drew his gun pulled the door gently out, stepped inside. John following.

Finding themselves on an enclosed back verandah, bare iron camp stretchers each end. Access to the house proper, another dark doorway. Shearer went first. Started down a corridor, the old boards beneath his feet creaked but the music masking that. John followed. To the right a bathroom, next a kitchen. It was hot in the house, the desert night not far enough along to have cooled it yet.

A girl's laugh. Shearer looking his way too. Shit. Each of them now standing in the darkened hallway, Shearer on the left, John the right. John poking his head out of the safety of border shadows to get a better look at the living room. A glimpse of a mirror over a mantlepiece. In its reflection, a long-haired male, naked from waist up, maybe a glass of something in his hand, his body hiding the girl. The music ended. John held his breath. The guy moved. A flash of face in the mirror: Larry. Putting down his glass must have been moving to put on another record, his voice thin and nasal, floating.

'… they're called The Blues Project.'

Disappearing beyond John's vision. The girl was not Spring. She was topless, maybe wearing shorts. John's guess, no more than nineteen. She reached for a cigarette. John couldn't help thinking: if Martin Davis was right, her life is in danger. Right now, while she was bending over to light that cigarette, Larry could be reaching for a knife. Shearer caught John's eye, held up three fingers. John knew the drill. He would cover while Ray stepped in. Ray's fingers counted down: three, two …

The loud rumble of arriving motorcycles split the night.

12 BORN TO BE WILD

A headlight spearing in from the back. Fuck. And another. Double fuck. Shearer sliding backwards into the dark kitchen. John, no choice but to retreat into the bathroom on the opposite side of the hall. Stepping into the bath behind the shower curtain, nothing else to afford protection. The back door banged. Boots thumped up the hallway.

'Heyyyyy,' an exaggerated greeting: Larry by the sounds. 'What's doing, cats? This is my friend, Guinevere.'

A rougher voice. 'That's your fucking name?'

Larry, 'No, I just gave her that. You know Lancelot and Guinevere.'

The sound of a bottle clinking against glass.

'You want a joint?' Larry again, the perfect host.

John tortured, thinking, good time to retreat, call for back-up. Except what if Davis was right and Guinevere was about to become the latest victim? What if these guys were in on it too?

Decided for him.

'I need to piss.' Gruff voice. Boots now heading down the hall, turning into the bathroom. Not bothering with the light, door open, dark twilight. John peered out, could see the big shape, legs astride hunched over the toilet bowl. John stepping carefully over the rim of the tub, gun pointing at the biker.

'Hands in the air and kneel,' he whispered.

The scream came close behind him. The girl. Couldn't help it, he swung her way. Mistake. Biker boy pivoted and backhanded him. Hit by a bag of cement. John went backwards and down quick. The revolver jarred free as his elbow smashed the concrete floor. A beard on top of him and reaching for his boot, a knife in a blink. John caught a glint, the biker astride him, the dagger ready to plunge—

The gunshot rang loud in his ears. The biker hung for a fraction then toppled back with a howl. Chaos unleashed.

John on the floor, side on, slithering for his weapon. Boots thundering down the hallway. Shearer's shout, 'Out the fucking way!'; a tangle of bodies near the bathroom doorway, the rear flywire door banging. John's hand reached the revolver. Shearer swung in.

'You okay?'

Outside at the back patio, a bike roaring into life.

John yelling 'Thanks.' Still half-deaf, the girl wailing, the biker on the floor moaning.

Shearer reached for the girl. 'You alright?'

She bit him.

Shearer, 'You fucking b—'

The sound of the front door, yanked open, footsteps running out.

Fuck. Larry.

John scrambling, following Shearer, bursting through a tawdry lounge room reeking of dope, charging at the front door.

Shearer shouted back, 'Down!'

A bullet smashed into the top of the open door. The first bike already turning and roaring left back to town. Larry, gun in hand, onto his white Triumph, roaring off in the other direction towards darkness and distant hills. Shearer crouched, traced the path, squeezed a shot. The bike ploughed on.

They both ran for the car.

Ray's one thought. Get him. Jumping in powering up the Chevy. Larry somewhere ahead, no headlight, deliberately dark. Larry knew the road, Ray didn't.

Gordon said, 'Shit. What about Perry?'

'Can't be helped.'

The big car bouncing on the pitted road, high beam catching Larry's bike. He turned off sharp right. A dirt track, judging from the dust cloud. Ray, eight seconds back, following. The Chevy gaining. A big rut, the shock absorbers pounded. Rocky cliff and trees ahead, the motorcycle slowing. Ray hoping his shot did damage.

Close in now, some kind of picnic ground, tables and barbecue pits. Behind those a cliff. The cycle seemed headed straight into it, shimmied late and slipped into rock. Ray powered on, death looming. A narrow gap, just wide enough for the bike. Ray hoping for magic. No fucking magic. Thumping the brakes. Shit.

Gordon jumped out, popped the boot. Perry scrunched and angry. Clambering out.

'What the fuck?' Perry reading their mood. 'He got away, didn't he?'

Ray said, 'Shut the fuck up.' Uncuffed him. 'You're driving.'

They started back down the crappy road. Halfway along, saw a column of single headlights like the torches of angry villagers out for Frankenstein and his monster, on the main road coming from the direction of town.

John Gordon said, 'His biker pals?'

Ray checked his revolver. 'I reckon.' To Perry, 'GI, you with us on this?'

Perry said, 'Is that an apology.'

'Yes,' said Gordon.

'I'm asking him.' Perry's eyes in the rear-vision on Ray who had taken the back seat.

Ray said, 'Let's call it a truce.'

'Guess I'm with you for now then.'

'How many do you reckon?' asked Gordon.

Ray thought seven or eight. His guess: the bikers would wait for them at the turn-off, armed. They would either open straight up on them or make them stop.

Perry said, 'You better give me my gun from the glove compartment. I seen a lot more of this shit than you guys.'

Ray didn't have to think too long on that. Perry knew he couldn't buy a free pass from the bikers by claiming ignorance. His car, him driving, pissed-off bikies. Ray said, 'Give it to him.'

Gordon handed across the gun.

Two-thirds to the junction now. Like Ray expected, the cycles slowing and bunching there. The ground between their feeder road and the bigger road looked like low dirt and scrub. The Chevy should be able to handle that. If it couldn't then they were in all sorts of shit.

'When I say go, I want you to cut across that paddock and head left.'

If they cut to the right they'd be heading to nowhere. They had to get back to town.

Gordon said, 'I don't suppose you have extra bullets.'

'Just the four.' Deducting the shot in the bathroom and the Hail Mary after the fleeing Larry.

Gordon and Perry had likely twelve between them. Perry was steady behind the wheel.

The glow-worms growing fatter.

'Don't cut too early, we want them as far up to that junction as we can.'

The Chevy three-quarters of the way back to the intersection now. Just a little longer. 'You might want to get that window down now too.'

They wound their windows.

'Go!'

Perry pulled the wheel left, floored it. The big Chevy bumping across the dry field.

'They've seen us.' Gordon calling it.

The bikes that had stopped at the junction already wheeling to pursue. The Chevy moving fast now, the wind, a looter's hand reaching through the windows. It was going to be close. Thank God there was no drainage ditch, a flat run from dirt to bitumen. They were twenty yards off ... ten ...

The foremost bike accelerating faster than them. Ray calculating:

interception soon after they would hit road, aiming through the open window. The Chevy's front tyres stretching for bitumen, the Harley spearing in, forcing them to the left lane. The wrong lane for highway USA. The rider going all out, crouching over handlebars. A tactic that probably cowered a Beetle in the past, but Perry didn't flinch. No need. The Chevy no Beetle. Maybe the rider was on pills or mescaline or both. Or flunked geometry. Too late trying to flatten the angle. The bike thumped into the Chevy in the gap between driver and passenger door. The rider and bike going sideways and down in sparks.

Suddenly the Chevy cabin spotlit from behind. Crunch!

Glass showering Ray. Back window blown out. Ray fired blind through the gap, but the light already moving taking the right again, the Chevy straddling the middle of the narrow road. No oncoming, small mercy. Ray saw it then, a big bike, a driver, his pillion man going Buffalo Bill Cody, half-standing cranking a sawn-off shotgun at the driver window.

Perry reaching for his gun. John seeing the pillion guy rise. The shotgun blast would hit him or Perry or both. He yelled, 'Duck!'

Perry dropped his head. John firing across and through the driver window. The shotgun man flying backwards. The rider slowing. The other pursuing lights making no ground on them, status quo, then receding. The Chevy whizzed past the house where it all started.

John said, 'I don't like our chances of getting back to LA tonight. Nearest police station.'

13 YOU KEEP ME HANGING ON

'Citizen's arrest?' Schubert's tone flat and scornful. John flashed on Schubert's wife, blistered fingers from hours of ironing. The man's shirt was immaculate and defined as his chin.

A little before two in the afternoon back in car city. After they had given statements to the San Bernadino cops, John had caught a couple of hours sleep there in a spare cell. Perry the trump card. The San Berdoo cops bending over backwards to help the GI. No doubt where they all stood on the war.

Larry identified by them: Larry McKnight. Small drug busts and other bullshit on his San Bernadino CV. Not a member of the Hells Angels but an associate. Ray and John detained till Lackowitz and Burns had made it from LA. They weren't impressed.

'You pulled a gun on Perry and put him in the trunk? Jesus, you guys are lucky he's not pressing charges.' Burns' voice cranking higher the more pissed off he got. Lackowitz glared, pulled a cigarette from its packet.

Ray said, 'He hit my partner first.' Then, 'Look, we fucked up, we know that, but we tried you guys, no answer. We're thinking: we don't check this out, Larry is going to be in the wind.'

'And where is he?' Lackowitz finally speaking, leaning back and lighting his cigarette.

Shearer opened his palms, acknowledging.

'But come on. You have a name, address. And there's all this other shit too. Maybe he is responsible for missing girls.'

Burns glanced at his notes from the statement they'd already given. They'd mentioned the makeshift case board at the unit.

'This would be the well-planned methodical research you came across from your acid-freak junkie client?'

John about to pipe up, held it.

Ray asked if they had found anything in Hector's car that might doom McKnight.

'No blood,' said Burns, 'clean as a whistle.'

'Was there a camera?'

'No.'

'Or diary?'

'No.'

'Maybe McKnight stashed them at his place.'

Lackowitz said, 'Thanks for your advice. The techs will be finishing up out at McKnight's soon and we'll be sure to take a look. We'll get you dropped back to Parker where you will wait until Schubert's ready to talk to you.'

He jerked his chin. Burns followed him out.

◆◆◆

Two San Bernadino patrolmen had driven them and Perry back to LA. Three to the back seat. Nobody speaking much. Perry given the courtesy of being dropped at his motel. Looked just like theirs, a couple of blocks further east on Sunset. As he got out, he said, 'You guys want to meet up for a drink, I'm here, room twenty-one.' Funny how a shotgun blast in your direction can bond.

The cops delivered them to the Parker Center. Schubert had made them wait. Four hours, uncomfortable chairs. John would have to call Geary in Sydney, but it would be too early yet. He wished clocks would stop, dreaded the moment when he could no longer put it off.

Finally, a cop had materialised: Schubert was ready.

Riding the elevator to the big guy's floor with the kind of foreboding John remembered when you'd been told to go see the headmaster.

And now, sitting across from them he'd just said, 'Citizen's arrest!'

Letting them know it was bullshit, like they'd just told him man would soon be walking on the moon. 'You didn't even make an arrest.'

Shearer stayed silent. John knowing it was on him.

'We didn't feel we had a lot of choice in the matter. We called detectives Lackowitz and Burns. I made a note of the time.' John showed the captain his notebook. Schubert's eyes didn't bother, stayed on his face. 'The phone rang out. We knew from our discussions with the detectives that they had been unable to locate McKnight. When James Perry arrived on the scene with intelligence as to where McKnight might be, we felt it our obligation to check as soon as possible and relay that information. Regrettably, the situation escalated when we realised there was a young female with McKnight, who, quite possibly could be an abductor or killer of young women.'

'"Quite possibly".' The words being hung in front of John's eyes, sneering at him.

It stung. John feeling like an idiot, but he could handle scorn. Nothing compared to being readied for slaughter by a psycho. That gave you spine. No backing down.

'It would have likely worked out fine except for the other bikers turning up.'

'You know that how? From your crystal ball?'

Holding his tongue. What could he say? The captain grunting, sitting back ever so slightly. The first time John could remember him being less than ninety degrees vertical.

'I thought I had some cowboys on my watch but you two are better than Gene Autry and Tom Mix. You're lucky. None of the bikers have come forward. We don't think any died. The hospital said they had a motorcycle dump a badly injured man on their doorstep. Guy has a broken leg, shoulder, ribs and cranial fracture, but he's alive. Two gunshot victims who both claimed their firearms accidentally discharged. The girl has fucked off.'

A pause, then Schubert back to perpendicular. 'The bikers won't come forward. Have you spoken to your commanding officer back in Sydney?'

John said he was waiting for the right timing. Schubert managed a lopsided grin.

'I'll bet.' Then, 'You gentlemen are free to go.'

Which translated as 'Fuck-off, assholes.'

A cab back to North Western. The car was ticketed. Gordon swore, went to climb in. Ray said, 'Look what I have.' Dangling the key to the unit.

Gordon was bugged. 'Shit. You didn't give them that to them?'

'I'll say I forgot. Come on, aren't you curious what happened to Spring? Maybe the kid was off his tree, maybe not.'

Gordon followed him in, just like Ray knew he would.

Workday, the units mostly occupied. They let themselves back into Davis'.

Gordon said, 'We can't remove anything.'

Ray said, 'Unless it would hurt the parents, right?'

'Nothing pertaining to the investigation.'

'Of course not.'

A cursory look around the unit. Ray lured back to the makeshift board. Noting another large plain white sheet of paper at the far end wall from the doorway. At first thinking Davis simply hadn't got to that yet, then realising a home-movie projector was pointing at it.

'It's a screen,' he said as much to himself as Gordon who went up close to read the writing on the butcher's paper.

Ray joined him, taking his time to re-read it. The first panel, with six names in order of disappearance starting in January: *Francine Leach*. February, *Jenny Wallace*. March, *Pauline Gerschaff*. April, *Sherry Linden, Mary Gannon* and *Spring*.

The second panel was devoted to Francine Leach exclusively. Gordon studying a bunch of newspaper cuttings of the Human Be-In taped beneath a black-and-white newspaper photo of Francine. A big spread from some teen music magazine too. One pic focusing side-of-stage: Larry in a cowboy shirt watching the band. Somebody, likely Davis, had circled him in marker pen.

In one of the other photos, Ray did spy a familiar face. At first, he couldn't place it, then he remembered, the sitar player from the basement where they'd met Annie. A note had been written on an exercise book and taped to the paper.

Francine last seen 7.00 p.m. at the Be-In talking to biker types. Reported missing Jan 16. Lived Western Addition.

The next panel, devoted to the second potential victim, Jenny Wallace. Scant but a cryptic note:

L confirmed L.A. Feb 22.

Read L as Larry. And right after that:

Jenny confirmed Grateful Dead house, SF, Feb 17. L known visitor.

Another note read:

Friend said Jenny was going to hitch to L.A. after Airplane-Big Brother concert at Fillmore Feb 19.

L at concert, road crew?

Ray's eyes following the arrow drawn all the way over to the final panel headed:

Larry.

John Gordon taking a closer look at the bunch of instamatic-type photos that Perry had been studying when they'd disturbed him. Some taken in daylight, some at night. The night ones blurred: Larry exiting the rear door of the Rimshot. All were from a distance of maybe ten to twenty yards.

Conclusion: Davis had been following Larry.

Gordon said, 'He's obsessed with this idea that this guy Larry is killing these girls.'

Ray stated the obvious. 'He must have been trying to collect evidence, catch him out.'

There was no sign here of the camera that had taken the photos. Maybe it would be found at McKnight's house.

'So, Martin Davis is following Larry. Snooping, looking for Spring with him, trying to catch him out.' Ray thinking aloud.

Gordon said, 'Think he was on to something?'

Ray's attention grabbed by a small glass jar alongside the projector.

'More like on something.' Tipping up the jar. Pills rolled into his hand.

'What are they?'

Ray didn't know. 'I'm guessing speed.' He pocketed them. 'So much for the drug-free new Martin Davis.'

Gordon picking up a piece of folded paper that had fallen under the desk, reading aloud, 'Desmond Campbell, Monkey Bar five thirty p.m. Monday.' Handing it over. 'It must have fallen when Perry started rummaging through the photos.'

So, who is Desmond Campbell? Ray turning back to the board. The third name, Pauline Gerschaff.

An instamatic print of a young woman with long dark hair parted in the middle. Next to it a note.

Was dropping acid at Garden of Allah on Sunset, night before disappeared. Jill's description of guy with her sounds like L.

So, Davis had found somebody, probably this 'Jill', to give him the photo and talk about Pauline. Beneath the note: a bunch of black-and-white eight-by-ten photographer's prints. One clearly showed Gerschaff, bubble-blower to generous lips. Another showed Larry among a bunch of Hell's Angels beneath an anti-war banner. Again, he was circled. Ray pulled one of the prints off and checked the back. Sure enough, the photographer had stamped his name and address: *Ian Suffolk 12/46 Chamberlain, West Hollywood.*

'Marty?' A girl's voice. She stepped around and into the doorway, petite, brunette, surprised.

John Gordon said, 'Hi.'

She looked uncertain but not in any way scared. She said, 'Is Marty here?'

Ray said, 'I'm afraid not.'

◆◆◆

An army of ghouls and monsters, green, purple and black scowling at them, bodyguarding their creator. Ray lost in a forest of inanimate masks, the smell of glue and resin hung heavy. The girl's unit half as big again as Davis'; shelves of costumes, a long trestle table taking up one wall littered with glues, scissors and who-knew-what, beads, other costume shit. A big xerox photocopier at the back. They had one in police admin, but Ray had never been allowed to use it. The girl was trying to dry tears. Ray offered her a clean hanky. Her name was Carol.

Ten minutes since breaking the news. Her unit, across the way from Martin's had at least some kind of seating. An old armchair for her, crates for them. They'd not held back anything.

Gordon said, 'We thought we should come here and see if there was anything important his parents might want. It's a good thing we did. Those photos might help the cops here clear the case.'

'I hope so,' she managed, seemed to settle. 'I've only known him a few weeks, but we got on. He was a nice guy.'

Ray putting her early twenties. She'd explained she was a costume and prosthetics designer. 'Mainly B-grade horror movies. I didn't see him this weekend. He and I are sometimes the only ones here.'

'When did you last see him?' asked John Gordon.

'Friday about six. I was still working. I've got a movie starting next week. He asked if I could xerox his research for him.' Pointing to pile of paper sheets neatly stacked at the end of her table.

John Gordon asked if Davis had revealed what he was planning that night.

'Not exactly. But he'd hinted. You know about his girlfriend, right? Well, he was convinced there were girls being taken from love-ins and concerts and stuff. Being killed. He thought that's what had happened to her, and he said he was getting close to the guy who'd done it.'

'Larry?' said Gordon.

'Yes. That's the name he mentioned. I think he only knew his first name. I told him he should go to the police, it could be dangerous, but he said the cops wouldn't listen unless he had something strong.'

Ray wondering, was Davis foolish enough to confront McKnight? Or careless, asking around about McKnight, reports getting back to the bikie.

Ray said, 'Was Martin on drugs?'

She opened her hands, closed them, torn.

'Not really. I mean, when he first came here, he told me he'd been dropping a lot of acid, but he'd given that up. Pot too.'

Ray showed her the pills, 'We found these in his unit.'

Carol glanced at them.

'Uppers. I drop one or two sometimes when I have a deadline. But I'm not sure he was taking them.'

Ray cocked an eyebrow.

'He seemed straight. I mean, he was … troubled, with the acid, and his girl and everything. He could … overheat, stress out.'

'How much did he tell you about his theory?' Gordon.

'A little bit. What happened was, he told me, he came to LA to find Spring and then about the third or fourth day he's here he saw this report of a girl's body being found up in the Hills. He was convinced that was Spring.'

Ray picturing the board: Sherry Linden. Her body had been discovered in the Hills.

'He even went to the police.' Carol looking for a piece of material to blow her nose on. 'It wasn't her. But while he was waiting, he said he met these other people worried it might be their daughter, or sister. They got talking. Those girls were missing too. They'd just disappeared.'

Confirming what Chad at Highway 61 had said. Ray piecing it.

That would be how Davis got photos of Pauline Gerschaff, running into friends or family at the police station.

Gordon said, 'And he figured they'd been abducted?'

'Yes. That's when he started his research. He told me all the girls went missing after love-ins or concerts in Los Angeles or San Francisco. He said nobody bothered to look for them because they thought they had just "dropped-out".'

Ray said, 'What was his research?'

'Going to the library. Old newspapers, magazines. I helped him get some movie film of the Elysian Park concert and he found a photographer who was taking photos for magazines and newspapers. He said the cops weren't interested so he was going to have to present them with a whole heap of stuff and give them no choice.'

Explained why he'd need a unit. Too much stuff for the cramped bedroom at Hector's.

'The girl whose body they found, Sherry Linden, I think her name is. Do you know if they caught her killer?'

'They arrested some guy, but Marty was sure Larry killed her. I think he had a meeting with the lawyer tomorrow.'

Ding: Desmond Campbell, the Monkey Bar.

'The cops will likely turn up and may want to talk further with you,' advised Gordon.

She said she was going to pack up now, go back home. Threw her hands out gesturing at the props.

'This all seems a bit stupid now.'

They were about to go when John Gordon said, 'That copy you made of Martin's research. You think we could have it? I'd like his parents to know he was trying to do something good.'

◆◆◆

The drive back to the motel, John's insides floating away. That emptiness when someone dies. He'd failed Martin Davis. Should have found him sooner.

Ray, driving, said, 'I know why you took the copies of his notes.'

'Like I said, I want to show his mum and dad.'

Ray said, 'I think some part of you is wondering if he could have been right. And if Lackowitz and Burns are going to look into it hard enough.'

That was all true.

John said, 'We'll book a flight tomorrow and drive back to San Francisco.'

◆◆◆

The hostie on the poster held a globe of the world on her palm. Big letters said *I Can Take You Anywhere You Desire*. John's gaze drifting back to the man sitting in front of it. Cardigan and striped tie on a white shirt, hair a mix of steel grey and white, cut sharp at the sides, bouffant on top, Danny La Rue style. He lowered the receiver from his ear, covered it with his hand.

'Earliest they can get you on a flight is June ten.'

'What?' John wanting home now, needing to hold Denise tight.

'The route in in high demand. You don't take this flight, you could be another two weeks at least.'

John looked at Ray.

Ray shrugged. 'We can take our time cruise up the coast.'

John nodded to the agent. 'Okay.'

The traffic outside was Monday heavy, the relative quiet of Sunday excised quick. Shearer said. 'It's not that bad. We're on full pay.'

John said, 'We might not have a job after I call the boss.'

They drove to the Hilton which was close by and air-conditioned. John booked a long-distance call with Geary. Time to kill. Shearer happy enough indulging in the cocktail hour. John brooded. A redhead with a lot of expensive hair told him his call had come through and directed him to the booth. His palms sweating. After the telegram Geary said he had been expecting a call all yesterday. John said he and Shearer had been chasing the killer of Martin Davis and things had gone a little awry.

'How fucking awry?'

John playing it all down. They had almost managed to grab the suspect, but he had escaped. A couple of his biker associates had been shot in the chaos.

'Jesus Christ.'

John explaining there was not likely going to be blowback.

'LAPD is looking for the fugitive and the bikers won't come forward.'

'Thank God this is unofficial. When are you back?'

John hit him with it.

'Fuck me drunk! That's close to three weeks.'

Geary fiddling with a matchbox, striking. 'The family will have the body back before you're home.'

'What are they doing about that?'

'They are going to have the body flown to San Francisco, then on to Australia.'

John breathing a sigh of relief. Part of him had feared he'd be ordered to drive the body back to San Francisco.

'What was the story with the kid? Was he a junkie? Hippie?'

'I think that's how LAPD is looking at it. We're not so sure. He was worried his girlfriend had been abducted, maybe killed. We think he was trying to investigate that.'

'Be nice to give the family that to hold onto. He wasn't really a drug freak, he was a hero. They will likely want to speak with you when get back. Shit, this must be costing a bomb. Keep me informed.'

Shearer on his second martini. John told him the news.

'So we still have a job.'

'Geary was pleased we thought Martin might have been trying to solve these disappearances.'

John had decided Ray's plan was a good one, take a few days driving up the coast, then a fortnight around Northern California. There was one more thing he needed to do though.

'I'd like to see him,' said John.

◆◆◆

Death had long painted Martin Davis with cold whiteness. The boy looked so young, just how John himself had been two years back. Love did this to you. Without Spring in your life, you would be up in Berkeley, studying math, eating ham and cheese rolls in the cafeteria, and wondering if you'd ever have a woman love you. But whatever you may have done wrong in your short life, you'd lost it trying to do something good. John thanked the morgue attendant. Schubert had made sure they had clearance.

Outside the day was heading for the pension, the light soft and even.

Shearer said, 'We're in Hollywood. We should go and see a film tonight.'

John checked his watch.

Ray said, 'What are you thinking?'

John was thinking that this couldn't all be for nothing. That young guy back there dead. Trying to save his girl, to hunt down a killer. He was thinking the winds of fate had driven him here, that if Martin Davis in all his crazy acid haze was correct, that meant there was a psycho running free. He was thinking that wasn't right. He was thinking somebody had to care about this more than the LAPD cops could afford to, somebody had to bring down McKnight. But shit, they were just a couple of Aussie cops with no jurisdiction.

What John said was, 'I'm wondering if we should keep Martin's appointment with the lawyer.'

Ray with a lilt, 'Just in case?'

John said, 'Yeah.' Balancing. If Ray kyboshed the idea, he wouldn't insist.

Ray said, 'Fuck it, why not?'

◆◆◆

The Monkey Bar was downtown. A man cavern for professionals, dark suits, darker wood, black and white photos of old Los Angeles on panelled walls. There were thirty men and about three women all looking like the day was the one that broke the camel's back. Desmond Campbell could have been any of them, but the bartender in a neat red vest and bowtie that stood out against his black shirt pointed out a man in a side booth by himself. Glasses, fair hair with a part that looked just like Glen Campbell, John wondering if the hairstyle came with the surname. Narrow tie recently unknotted, a suit coat that looked like a dog after a long walk uphill. A pitcher of beer in front of him nearing its end.

'Mr Campbell?' asked John quietly.

'Last time I checked.'

John said, 'You have a meeting with Martin Davis.'

He was curious, 'Yes.'

Ray said, 'I'm afraid he won't be coming.'

John came right in tight, 'He was stabbed to death in the early hours of Saturday morning.'

Campbell sighed. 'I'm sorry to hear that.' He drained his pitcher, made a move to go.

John said, 'But if you have a moment, we'd like to talk with you. We're Australian police officers who were sent to find Martin. We didn't quite make it in time.'

Campbell signalled they were welcome to squeeze in opposite. He had his big briefcase beside him. 'I'm afraid I didn't know him well. We'd never even met. He called me Thursday. I have a case I'm defending, and he thought he might be able to help. I'm sorry.'

Ray said, 'That's the Sherry Linden murder?'

Campbell raised a brow. John explained that Martin Davis had made copious notes.

John said, 'Did he speak to you about a suspect he had for the killing?'

'He did. He didn't go into detail and frankly we get a lot of these. People telling us their uncle was the real killer. He said a guy named Larry. He didn't know his surname, but he insisted we meet.'

Shearer said, 'The guy is Larry McKnight, and he is the prime suspect in Martin's murder.'

A chunky waitress with curly blonde hair arrived. Ray ordered beers for John and him, Campbell put the pitcher on the tray and said he would have one too. John asked the lawyer if he could tell them about the Linden murder and suspect. Campbell obliging.

He was with the Public Defender's office. In Los Angeles, poor people had the right to a court defence. The Linden case fell into his lap because he was the next cab on the rank, as simple as that. The cops found the body dumped in the Hollywood Hills.

'Some of the detectives aren't bad but Hawkshaw and Fiorini are not top shelf. Sherry Linden was a twenty-year old Ohio girl who had travelled to California for sun and a good time. She'd been staying at a hostel for young women in San Francisco and had told other women there that she was planning on heading to LA to see Disneyland and then might go back home through Arizona. She was last seen at the hostel picking up her things after she'd been to a concert at Saint Ignatius High School. Hawkshaw and Fiorini's theory is that Linden hitchhiked here, arrived here safely and was killed by John Francis Patcher, a forty-three year old drifter camping in the Hills about a mile from where the body was found.'

The beers arrived, Shearer gulped. 'Surely, they had something more than proximity.'

They had. In Patcher's suitcase they found a bracelet that was identified as Linden's. Patcher claimed he had found it the day before when he went foraging through the brush, up higher than where the body was found, closer to the road.

John thinking it could be true. If somebody pulled the body down there, the bracelet could have snagged and broken. Unfortunately for Patcher, he had a history of violence and sexual assault.

'When he was nineteen, he grabbed a fifteen-year old girl at the local swimming hole in Austin, started fingering her. He claimed it was consensual, nobody believed him. He is an alcoholic too.'

John said, 'You think your client killed Linden?'

Campbell swallowed froth, put down his beer. 'I never consider whether my clients are innocent or guilty. I just defend them.'

'Bullshit.' Shearer taking a slug of beer. Campbell smiled.

'You speak like cops.' Campbell considered. 'Patcher had a knife but I don't think it could have done the damage. You seen the photos?'

They explained they had not. Campbell tapped his case.

'I'll show you if you've got a strong stomach. Nobody saw Linden in LA. Not alive at any rate. I think she was picked up in San Francisco, killed and dumped by whoever gave her a ride. Patcher has no vehicle. How did he get the body there? No witnesses to put Patcher with Linden, so no proof he met her. And we're going to believe she accompanied this tramp to the Hollywood Hills? Yeah, right. The time of death puts it at least a day before the body was found. The blood at the scene is less than might be expected. I think she was killed elsewhere, then dumped.'

Ray asked if Linden had been raped.

'Pathology couldn't say.'

'Patcher see anything? Hear anything?' Shearer playing with his glass like he needed another beer.

'Night before he found the bracelet, he was walking through brush. Said he saw some kind of van near there and a couple of convertibles at various times.'

'Motorcycle?' John noting Campbell studying him carefully, filing away that question.

'No. But he may remember one.' The lawyer made a note. 'You gentlemen know your chances of getting the LAPD to change their very tiny mind on this is about the same as the Astros winning the World Series. What did Davis have?'

John told him they were only just finding out, ran through the cases as he remembered them.

'So the only body is Sherry's?'

'Yes.'

Campbell sat back, grunted. 'I tell you now what the LAPD is going to say about this: there are thousands of young people all over the country, tuning in and dropping out; nobody knows where they are but they are not all dead, maybe brain-dead but that doesn't count. There is only one body so that's all they are going to focus on. No body, forget it.'

John fighting the negativity. 'What if Martin was onto something and McKnight killed him because of that?'

'If they catch McKnight and he confesses, fine. Otherwise, they'll say it was a dope fiend's dream.'

Ray asked if they could see the photos of Sherry Linden. The lawyer warned again.

'It's not pretty. She was cut up and then animals got to her.'

Campbell slid the photos across to John. 'The top one is how she looked before.' The photos were in a waxy paper sleeve. John tipped them out started looking. The first one showed a happy teen in a bob. Probably a high-school graduation photo. He peeled that away.

Bang. His head began throbbing. Bile welled up. Blood, a whole summer of blood. He was looking at the close-ups, the neck sliced through, the torso almost completely severed from the lower body.

Shearer must have seen his reaction. He said, 'What is it?'

Campbell said, 'Sorry. I warned you.'

John settled, moved the photos across to Ray. 'Look.'

He watched Ray's face, plain and simple like a beach before the wave struck, then, boom.

'San Francisco,' the words like an air compressor.

Campbell twigging something going down here.

'What is it?' he asked, a whisper now.

'Judy Ikin,' said John. 'A girl who was murdered in San Francisco and looked just like that. So, unless your drifter has a car or a helicopter, your guy is innocent.'

14 IT'S A HAPPENING THING

Xeroxed sheets of Martin Davis' butcher's paper spread over the floor. New base, the Marquis, a hotel up near the Whisky that Janis and crew had mentioned. Nearly new carpet, modern prints on the wall. More than the three-star the budget allowed but they'd saved on the motel. Ray laughing at himself. Could have been relaxing but instead he's kneeling on the floor, the familiar pump of adrenaline, a case lifting off like a jet airliner. Might have lied to himself, said he was doing it for Gordon, but knew better. He'd been to Disneyland and Barney's and now it was time to work.

McKnight was a killer. He was a cop. A bent cop, a cop who'd fucked up plenty of lives including his own. But they had time on their hands and as pretty as the Californian coast might be, Ray would be happy in the corner of a diner with shit coffee and a good lead. So, he was working like was in his blood, paying his way in this dumb stupid life where he had fuck all to contribute of any value. Except this. And it felt good. Davis' chart on the floor in front of him.

Francine Leach 19 – Jan 14 Human Be-In Golden Gate Park.

Jenny Wallace 18 – Feb 19 Airplane-Big Brother, Fillmore. Hitchhiking from San Fran to L.A. for concert.

Pauline Gerschaff 21 – Mar 26 Elysian Park Love-In.

Sherry Linden 20 – April 7 San Francisco Buffalo Springfield and Jefferson Airplane concert St Ignatius High School. Body found Hollywood Hills April 11.

Mary Gannon 20 – April 11 Long Beach, Scherer Park. Local bands.

Spring – April 5, hitchhiking to L.A.

It was Tuesday now, checked in, checked out the pool, the terrace, quick lunch and down to work. First thing he did was take a textacolour.

'Here, between Pauline Gerschaff, March twenty-sixth and Sherry Linden, April seventh, we add …' He wrote: *Judy Ikin, April 2, Tenderloin.* 'So, let's get our theory straight in our heads.'

Maybe it was already, but experience had taught him best to talk it through.

John Gordon ran it. 'Larry McKnight is a multiple murderer like the Boston Strangler.'

'Victims?'

'Young women.'

'More specific.'

'Young women in California who go between concerts and events. The advantage for him is that nobody takes too much notice, even their friends. Most of them are constantly moving, sleeping on a floor, heading off at the drop of a hat.'

Ray agreed. 'McKnight is in the perfect situation, works with the bands. The women all hang around the groups, he's there, offers them a lift or just gets an invitation over to their house.'

'Looking at this chart though, Judy Ikin. Why her? She's not like the others. She has a job and a flat and a boyfriend. You think we're right?'

'We better be, or the only body is Sherry Linden. But you saw those photos.'

'Same killer,' said Gordon.

'So we don't know why yet but every chance he knew her from somewhere. Okay, if – and it is a big if – all these women have been taken, then, according to this, Davis has a connection with Larry for all of them except Linden and Gannon. For Spring, he has written "seen with him day before disappearance". But the only body that has turned up is Linden's and he doesn't have a link to McKnight on that and LAPD has arrested Patcher.'

Gordon tapped where Davis had made a handwritten note on that. *Weak evidence. No. No. No.*

Ray looked at the graduation photo of Linden that Campbell had gifted them: a young girl, life ahead of her. That life snuffed, her body dumped for wild animals to ravage.

Davis hadn't liked the evidence against Patcher, that's why he contacted Campbell. Have to assume he had no idea of Ikin.

Davis had made a note that 'L' was in San Francisco April 7, the last time Linden had been seen. But after that he had written *April 8 where? SF? LA?*

Thinking aloud. 'So Davis knew McKnight was in San Francisco the last time Linden was seen and he was trying to establish whether he was in LA around the time her body was dumped here.'

John said, 'That was also around the last time Spring was seen.'

Ray wondering about that. Could he have killed both girls at the same time? Suppose one saw him with the other, might be a case of eliminating a witness. Ray put that aside for now.

'What's our first move?'

Gordon said, 'Establish that McKnight was in the right city when these girls went missing.'

'That's the second move. First, we need to make sure none of these women have turned up alive. Or that any more have turned up dead. And we need to confirm the Ikin case is still open. San Francisco might already have arrested somebody.'

Gordon said he would try Spinetti for the San Francisco end. That left LA to Ray. Jenny Wallace who was supposedly heading here to stay with her brother; Gerschaff, who sounded like a hippie; Gannon; and Spring. No phone numbers on any of the girls but according to the notes Gerschaff had been dropping acid at the Garden of Allah the night before she vanished.

Curious that Martin's address book had not been found in Hector's car or flat. He wished they knew what the cops had got at McKnight's. Would save a shitload of time.

Ray said, 'Carol back at the unit said Davis met some people who were looking for bodies too. He has information on Gerschaff and Wallace, so my guess is he got his intel from their family or friends. If they turned up to check a body, they must have officially reported those girls as missing persons. Maybe Gannon too, but there is not much on her.'

♦♦♦

It took some ringing around. By the time the sun was melting back to the sea, Ray had news via Missing Persons. It was mixed.

'Mary Gannon turned up safe and well four days ago. She'd run away with a boy, gone to Vegas and returned broken-hearted. Gerschaff and Wallace are still missing. Gannon turning up doesn't help our case. The cops will say it goes to show.'

John Gordon had called Spinetti, who had expressed his sympathy over the loss of Martin Davis.

'I told him we'd like to give the family something to cling to: find Spring if we could. I've given him the name Mary-Anne Weddeker, see if that helps. Francine Leach is still officially missing. The Ikin case is "cold as Nebraska in winter", to quote him. We need to know if LAPD got McKnight.'

He was right. A lot of this might be a time waste if McKnight was in custody and talking.

Ray reckoned by now Campbell would have been in touch with LAPD. He had suggested to the lawyer that it would be advisable to leave their names out of it, make out that he'd had the meeting with Davis last week and that's where the information about McKnight had come from.

'We might have a better chance if we don't put Lackowitz offside completely,' Ray had emphasised.

Campbell agreed, happy to take the heat. They hadn't heard from him since.

They rang. The lawyer's secretary said he was in court all day.

Ray laying it out for John Gordon. 'We can wait, or we can try LAPD ourselves.'

John said, 'They may not be happy to hear from us.'

Ray said, 'They won't be.'

Prescient. Burns answered the phone. He wasn't happy at all.

'Thanks to you assholes, he's disappeared. Probably in Mexico by now.'

'You didn't find an instamatic or address book at McKnight's?'

'No, and goodbye.'

Ray snuck a toe in before the door could slam shut. 'Davis' idea about the girls—'

'We've got a prime suspect for Davis, we're parked. And now Patcher's lawyer is kicking up on the Linden case.'

No mention of them, good, Campbell had played a straight bat.

'Right now we are knee-deep in the double-homicide in Wilshire.'

Ray said they were staying at the Sunset Marquis.

'We'd be very grateful if you notify us when McKnight is caught.'

'You'll be first on our list of course.'

The receiver thumped in his ear.

John Gordon smiled, said, 'I could hear.'

Ray said, 'Maybe they haven't been to the unit yet.'

He was thinking about the movie reel.

♦♦♦

A standard eight mil home movie was already teed up. On the phone, Carol had said no police had been in yet. She was gone and her unit locked by the time they got there. Ray still had the keys to Davis' unit. A small empty circular box on the stand beside the projector had written on its lid *Elysian, Easter*.

Shearer killed the lights. John started the projector, used to it, Denise's old man always making him the projectionist when they watched her family home movies: Denise in mouse ears, spinning, hula hoops.

The box said *8 mins*. Hippies, flutes, bongos, crazy dancing, bubble-blowers, mimes. The usual protest lot: Mothers Against

War, Vets Against War, Students Against War. Then the camera went to a band for a couple of minutes. John had no idea who they were. As the cameraman walked behind the stage for different shots, a profile flashed past. John had seen that face enough to know now, but Shearer beat him to it.

'Bingo.'

McKnight, no doubt about it. Hanging with a line of bikers and their rides.

They ran the whole film three times but couldn't spy Pauline Gerschaff. They put the lights back on and rechecked for any more notes, camera or address book. It would likely be the last chance they got. Came up empty-handed. Ray removed from the board the clearest snap of McKnight.

'Might come in useful.'

Near 8.00 p.m. now. Ray dropped the unit key in the box in the small reception hall. They hadn't achieved much but it still felt good to be working.

'Garden of Allah, or the photographer?' asked Ray. 'I'm thinking we try the bar first because I need a drink.'

John Gordon said, 'The Garden of Allah it is.'

◆◆◆

The Garden of Allah, a cocktail bar that had appropriated the name of a famous Hollywood hotel now developed into offices. Ray fronted the barman, slim, dark, possibly Latin, definite homo vibe.

'We're looking for a girl named Jill, might be a regular.'

The barman raising neat eyebrows, shaping his body like a ballet dancer at a barre. If Ray had been that way inclined, he might have been attracted to him.

'You might need a bit more mustard on that hotdog if I'm to help you.'

John Gordon said, 'She's a good friend of a girl who seems to have disappeared. They were drinking here Easter Saturday before the love-in.'

A smile playing on the lips now.

'I know who you mean. Yes, she came back a couple of times asking if we'd seen her friend. One time with another young man.'

Shearer pulled out a photo of Martin Davis.

'This guy?'

The barman twisted the photo around, so it faced him.

'Could be. It's pretty dark in here as you may have noticed.'

Ray said he had noticed that. He wondered if by chance they had been asking about another patron.

'This man.' Placing the photo of McKnight on the bar.

'They were, yes, but I didn't know him, or didn't remember him. Unlike you, for example.'

The guy is either flirting with me or putting shit on me, thought Ray. He preferred to think the former.

Gordon said, 'Can you give us any idea where we could find this Jill?'

'Just a minute.'

The barman broke away to serve a customer.

Ray said, 'This could be a slow process.'

'At least we have time on our hands.'

The barman was standing before them again. 'There are a bunch of them that come in now and again. I think they are in some commune. You know, hippies and all that. They are called Earth's Eden. That's all I can tell you. Another?'

Ray pulled out two one-dollar bills, laid them on the bar, jotted their room number on a cocktail napkin.

'That's our room at the Marquis. If they come in, we'd appreciate a call. That's not an invitation but I do think you make a mean cocktail.'

The barman smirked. The bills disappeared in his pocket. 'I like your style,' he said.

◆◆◆

Ian Suffolk's apartment block was surrounded by neat gardens. The photographer lived in West Hollywood not all that far from their hotel. Suffolk didn't answer his buzzer. They decided to return to the hotel and try again in the morning. Gordon said he was going to write to Denise. Ray knew he should be doing the same to Marie. He'd managed a postcard at Disneyland.

He said, 'I might call Marie. I'll use the lobby phone.'

Gordon said he could take a shower if Ray wanted privacy.

Ray said, 'No, I'll have a drink while they hook up the call.'

The hotel bar small, patrons sparse; longhairs, English. One commented on his accent.

'Where are from, sport?' he asked. He had bad teeth like most Poms.

'Sydney.'

They got talking. The guy managed bands. He reeled off names Ray didn't know. His drinking buddy worked for the BBC.

'He's been in San Francisco.'

Ray said, 'You wouldn't know how I could get any film on the be-in back in January?'

As a matter of fact, he did know somebody in San Francisco Ray could try. Ray pocketing the contact as the reception girl found him. His call to Sydney was booked.

Squeezing himself into the private booth. 'Hello,' he said. 'How's it going there?'

There was a long pause and he started in on his greeting again when a voice came back at the same time echoey and distant. 'Sorry,' he said. He'd never called overseas before. Fucking amazing that some cable stretched across the oceans. The world was changing fast.

'Everything is good,' came the voice, disembodied but the same old Granite. 'We found the bloke you wanted.'

15 ANDMOREAGAIN

'How was Marie?' John dressing. Apparently, he'd been asleep by the time Shearer had got back from the bar.

Shearer still in bed. 'You know, missing me, wanting me back, the TV screen is always snowy and so on. You spoken to Denise?'

He hadn't. He wasn't sure why he'd resisted. Thinking it was because he didn't want to have to go into detail about Martin Davis. And death.

'Not yet. I've been writing though.'

That was so much safer. First thing after Shearer woke, he told John he'd got a lead on some documentary filmmaker in San Fran who might have useful footage. You stuck Shearer in a bar for a couple of hours, he'd come up with something. The phone rang. John checked the clock. Just before 9.00 a.m.

Desmond Campbell. 'McKnight is still AWOL. The cops are taking a "patient" approach.'

Decode: slowly checking through McKnight's known associates, leaning on them. John knew the tactic well enough. Wait until a McKnight KA blew it, got themselves arrested for some shit. Offer a deal for information. Campbell apologised that he was due in court and couldn't talk.

Before ringing off, offering: 'The best thing you can do is to establish that McKnight was in the right place when all these girls went missing.'

Didn't they know it.

Twenty minutes on déjà vu at Suffolk's apartment building. No answer to the buzzer. Maybe the photographer was on holiday or assignment. Shearer buzzed a neighbour's bell, got a middle-aged woman.

'It's the police,' he lied. He asked if she knew where her neighbour Ian Suffolk might be.

'I barely know the man.'

'Do you know if he was in last night?'

'He keeps different hours to me.'

'Do you know where he might be now?' asked Ray.

'You're the police. You tell me.'

John fought an impulse to shoot down the door, throttle the woman.

They cruised out to Santa Monica, stopped at any hippie shop they could find, asking about Earth's Eden, the commune that missing girl number three, Pauline Gerschaff had been part of. People had heard the name but that was as far as they got. They cruised back to Hollywood, dusk a warm poncho, grabbed an early meal from a steakhouse up on Sunset.

Shearer said, 'We could try and find McKnight with a "less patient" approach.'

◆◆◆

The Rimshot empty apart from Marsha, and her balding manager swinging in and out of a door behind the bar in a shirt that he'd bought at a bargain store where all the other lonely divorcees shopped. Marsha remembered Shearer.

'Two detectives came here,' she replied when Shearer asked about LAPD.

'You were no help, right?'

She shrugged. 'Above my pay grade to play hero.'

John pulling out a photo of Martin Davis, likely the same one Ray had already shown her. 'You sure you didn't speak to him? We saw shots he'd taken from the parking lot.'

'I don't remember him. I don't remember all my customers.' She smiled. 'Beer?'

John felt obliged.

Shearer said, 'Larry McKnight knifed the kid. You know Larry? Tall, cowboy shirt. Hangs with the Angels.' Producing a snap taken from the parking lot.

172

'Yes. I recognise him.'

'Your relief barman said the kid we showed you came in asking about her.' Now Spring's photo hit the bar. 'You think you ever saw her in here.'

'She's pretty. Maybe.'

John said, 'With McKnight?'

'It's possible. He likes to hang with girls.'

John said, 'And the girls he hangs with have a habit of disappearing.'

'He seems like a nice guy.'

Ray tapped Spring's photo. 'Seen her recently?'

'No. If she ever was here, not in the last week or so. I would remember her.'

John pulled out the photo of Sherry Linden that Campbell had given them. 'How about her?'

She studied carefully. Shook her head. 'No.'

John said, 'Her body was dumped up in the Hills.'

Marsha said, 'I'm not lying. She might have been here, but I don't recall her.'

Ray asked what time Larry's crowd normally began to gather. Marsha's intel: they didn't come every night but when they did, from 9.00 p.m.

Shearer said, 'We'll come back and wait. When one of them comes in, we'd like you to give us a sign.' Laying down another couple of dollars.

Time to kill.

John suggested they see a movie. 'We're in Hollywood after all.'

Like everybody else they plumped for *Casino Royale*. It was a silly film. John liked David Niven and Bond films, but this one mainly irritated him.

'If it was supposed to be funny, I prefer *The Three Stooges*,' said Shearer.

◆◆◆

The Rimshot's carpark nearly full but the bar not yet crowded. Marsha still working. Long hours. On your feet too. She played her part well.

'What would you gentleman desire?'

John bought bourbons. She slid her eyes to a broad, swarthy guy in a leather vest. The kind who would be used to working in close with a knife.

'He the only one?' whispered John.

'At the moment.' Marsha moved off.

Shearer said to John, 'Watch him,' then took himself off to the gents. John used the mirror to keep an eye on McKnight's pal. A couple of minutes later, Shearer was back.

'There's no lock on the door. So, you'll have to stand guard.'

Who knew how long the guy's bladder could hold out or who else would be in the bathroom? John was hoping he might head outside, easier to take him there.

Twenty minutes in, things got worse. Another biker type arrived, sat at the table with the first guy, clearly pals.

Ray read John's mood, said, 'Hey, it doubles our chances one of them will go for a piss.'

John thinking, if another rolls up, pull the pin. On cue, the first guy up and heading down the short corridor to the gents. Ray sliding off his stool. John making sure the second guy was busy with his beer and fag, then following.

The gents small, two stalls and a cramped urinal, tiles cracked, a window somewhere for ventilation but not wide enough for the stink to crawl out. McKnight's pal at the urinal as John entered. They had it to themselves. John braced himself, back to the door. Ray walked up behind the swarthy guy, pulled out his revolver and pointed it at the back of the guy's head.

'Keep your hands on your prick or I'll blow your head off. Got it?'

The guy had tattoos on his hands. He spat into the urinal.

Ray pulled out the photo of Sherry Linden. 'Ever see your buddy Larry with this girl?'

'No.'

Ray slammed the guy's head hard into the top of the trough. The guy went to push back. Shearer pressed the muzzle of his gun into his spine.

'Look properly.'

The guy looking to the left. 'Still no.'

Ray pocketed the photo. Shoved Spring's photo in his face. 'Her?'

'You got one of her pussy, I might be able to tell.'

Shearer went to slam him again. The guy ready, throwing back his head. Smack, bone on cartilage like the snap of kindling. Swarthy spinning, shoulder-charging already stunned Ray back into the cubicle post.

John pulling his gun, but no shot with Ray in the mix. Replica move to what happened in San Bernadino, Swarthy's hand quicksilver to his boot, a blade in his fist, driving it down. Ray's left hand somehow seizing the powering bicep, stopping it in time for a shimmy, his right hand slamming the gun butt into Swarthy's crown. Ray's knee smashing up into Swarthy's chin, then a straight left sending Swarthy sliding back into the urinal. Ray drove his foot down on his attacker's wrist. A snap. The knife in Ray's hand now. Yanking Swarthy's legs towards him. Swarthy's back and shoulders still swimming in piss and naphthalene, his arse and hip on the urinal step, his legs on the floor.

Ray holding the knife over the thigh, his own nose smashed, blood pouring.

'Where's McKnight?'

Swarthy grunted, shook his head.

Ray said. 'One more chance, or this goes into your femoral artery, and you bleed out here. Where is he?'

'Last I heard, heading for Mexico. That's the truth, man.'

Ray said, 'I believe you.' Then he grabbed the urinal pipe lifted himself high and drove all his weight down on the guy's leg.

The crack even louder than when Ray's nose shattered. Ray tossing the knife in the dunny.

'Back door.'

They left quick, Ray holding his arm across his face. Into the car and out of the lot, John driving. No sign of pursuit, already a fast-moving fish in a gulf stream of traffic.

♦♦♦

They found a chemist. Bandages and aspirin. Back at the hotel, Ray cleaning his face up, laughing like he enjoyed it.

'At least we have good idea where McKnight might be.' Wadding cotton wool up a nostril.

John less optimistic. 'Won't do us much good if he's in Mexico.'

Ray laughed. 'Not Mexico. You saw that guy. You think he was going to give up his mate?'

John lost. 'The guy was lying?'

'Of course he was lying. He knew I wasn't going to shoot him there and he was hoping I wasn't going to stab him, but he was ready. If McKnight was in Mexico, where would be the easiest place for one of his mates to lie about him being? Not San Bernadino, too easy for us to check that.'

John guessing it would be San Francisco.

'Right, because that's where he goes all the time. So why not lie that he's in San Fran? That's where we should look first.' Shearer checked himself in the mirror, a big plaster across his nose, cotton wool, circles under his eyes. 'Not bad,' he laughed. Then he said, 'Let's check out the photographer.'

♦♦♦

Ian Suffolk was in. He told them to come on up, was waiting at the door. Tall, slender, hip guy with boots, jeans, collar-length hair and moustache. An American Terence Stamp. Surprise and curiosity tussled for the upper hand when they mentioned the photos they'd seen at Davis'.

'Yes, that's me,' he said.

Ray's nose still throbbing. His voice like Bluebottle in the Goons, letting Gordon run through the basics: Australian, private detectives, Martin Davis.

Recognition. 'He looked me up and I sold him some photos.'

John Gordon said, 'We'd like copies of those photos.'

Suffolk showed them in with a sideways glance at Ray.

The apartment looked two-bedroom; bamboo, paintings, prints and pot-plants, pot being the operative word, the smell was strong even with Ray's nostrils squished. Suffolk found them Cokes, explained he worked from his studio.

'But I stamp my photos with this address because I never know how long I'll keep a studio.'

He shifted an album cover off the coffee table, *Psychedelic Lollipop*. Photos everywhere, black-and-whites of bands and festivals.

Ray said, 'How did you meet Martin?' Hard keeping the whine out of his voice.

Suffolk said one of the magazines he freelanced for gave Davis his phone number.

'He rang me, told me he wanted to try and locate his girlfriend who had gone missing and wanted to check out my photos of some of the concerts and stuff I'd shot.'

'Like the love-in at Elysian Park?'

'Yes. And the be-in up in San Fran. I shot that too. I told him to come by my studio, he was free to browse my negatives and contact sheets and I could print up what he wanted. He was there nearly a whole day. Why?'

Ray said, 'Somebody stabbed him to death, likely a biker whose photo you might have taken.'

Suffolk shocked, reaching for a cigarette.

John Gordon said, 'What was Davis after in the photos?'

Suffolk coming back to a reality he'd rather not have to. 'Mainly his girl. But then he wanted pretty much any crowd stuff. He was thinking of getting in touch with the TV stations up in San Francisco who covered the Golden Gate concerts and the be-in. He thought she might be on their film footage. He also told me he was looking for anything on an Airplane concert in Frisco at some high school in April. April seven, I think it was, Springfield and Airplane. I told him I wasn't there but knew a couple of guys who'd shot that for the pop mags. I called and asked them to send me their contact sheets.'

Ray said, 'Did they?'

'They have, but I haven't received them yet. Must be in the mail. I thought they would have arrived today.'

John Gordon asked if he could print them out the same photos he did for Martin Davis.

'Sure. I'll have the contact sheets at my studio already marked.'

The studio was in the Wilshire district.

Suffolk said, 'It will take me a while. If you come by in tomorrow afternoon, they'll be ready.'

As they were leaving, Ray thought to ask him if he knew of a commune called Earth's Eden.

'No. I don't know the communes so well, but I know someone who does. Mushroom Mark. He lives above a purple panel shop on La Brea near Melrose. But don't bother trying now.'

Ray said, 'You know where he'll be?'

Suffolk lit a cigarette. 'He'll be in the pad above the purple panel shop, but he won't be home, if you get me. He's not called Mushroom Mark for nothing.'

Had Ray felt better, he might have given it a try but for now he was happy to return to the hotel and lick his wounds. All in all, it had been a good day.

◆◆◆

He didn't look like the kind to know hippies, let alone be their mushroom supplier. John thinking, more like the funny ensign in *McHale's Navy*. The apartment fitted though: a big psychedelic swirl on a black brick wall, rugs on the concrete floor, odd bits of furniture, a fluoro, a dunny, no sign of a proper bathroom.

A mattress lay on the floor, stereo speakers either side, sheets grey and swirled like a tidal pool, pillows but no slips, just the zebra under-skin. There was a bench with a toaster and small portable gas-stove. And a fridge. It was 11.30 a.m. but it seemed like Mushroom Mark's brain was only heating up now.

'Earth's Eden, sure I know them. They drop in at least once a week.'

'You know where they live?' Conversation was punctuated by hammering on metal from below. How the hell did the guy live here?

'They live up in the Hills. Laurel Canyon. I don't know an exact address, but I've been there. For a party.'

Throwing that in the way someone who doesn't get invited to many parties would.

'You know a girl, Jill?' asked John.

His eyes lit. 'Redhead. She's a honey.'

Okay, sounded like they were on the right track.

Shearer said, 'Take a ride with us, show us where they live.'

'I couldn't do that. I've got a business to run.'

John sensed Ray about to strong-arm him, jumped in. 'How about you draw us a map?'

Mushroom Mark had a street directory. They worked from it, got a close approximation.

It was good to get away from the noise and the fug on the apartment.

They were getting there, slowly. Next stop, Suffolk's studio.

◆◆◆

Ian Suffolk's studio was sandwiched between a draper and drycleaners, in a row of single-storey buildings, modern, glass and aluminium. His ashtray was heavy and full of butts. It sat in the middle of a big trestle table beside scalpels and photographic paper.

'I'm sorry guys, problem. I got a deadline brought forward to tomorrow.' Suffolk was almost eating his latest cigarette. 'I've been here since seven and haven't had time to scratch my ass.'

'What's tomorrow?' John scoping the place: cameras, a backdrop down the far end, lighting stands. A record playing.

'Tomorrow is D-day. Or B-day. The Beatles' new album, *Sergeant Pepper's*. They're rushing it out in England and we have to be ready for next week. The cover is insane.' Suffolk rifling papers, finding something shiny, sliding it their way.

Wow. The Beatles had gone psychedelic.

'I've got every fucking music magazine in California ringing asking if I have old photos of them live. And Zappa and the Mothers are out tomorrow as well. Fucking unbelievable.' Like he'd stage-managed it, his phone started ringing. He ignored it. 'I've had couriers coming and going all day.'

John said he couldn't believe the magazines weren't prepared.

'They never are. But now the album's going to be out in England they're shitting themselves. I'd printed up about ten photos, just in case. Now I've already done more than fifty. Tomorrow will be quieter. I'll do your photos first thing. I'm sorry.' The phone momentarily silent. But then it started back up. Suffolk reached for it.

John said, 'Okay, we'll be in by ten.'

Suffolk gave a thumbs up and answered as they quit.

◆◆◆

The plan was to try Laurel Canyon, but Shearer suggested seeing as they were in the area, they should drop into the old motel, see if there were any messages for them.

There were two. One from James Perry asking if they wanted to meet up. It was from two nights back and he still hadn't found Mary-Anne and was going to head back home soon. The other was from Peggy in the Valley.

The cryptic message said 'Friend said they saw Spring a few weeks back'.

There was a phone number. They tried it. A guy answered. There was loud weird music in the background.

'Is Peggy there?'

'Not right now.'

'When's she due back?'

'Maybe never. Maybe about two hours.'

John said, 'If she comes back, tell her the Australians are on their way.'

Laurel Canyon could wait till tomorrow, Spring couldn't.

♦♦♦

Party time in the Valley. The door open, carpet and wallpaper, sofas, prints on the wall, a large kitchen window to a backyard pool, music and bombies.

'The album comes out tomorrow. Frank and the guys are playing New York tonight.' Peggy snorting speed off the kitchen bench, biro tube up her nose.

'So who are these guys?' John pointing through the window, a dozen guys and dolls in bathers.

Peggy shrugging. 'Friends, girlfriends like me.'

Elevating herself maybe.

John said, 'You know Kansas Annie is dead?'

'What?' Eyes as big as a seal's.

He told her about the overdose. No point keeping it quiet any longer.

'But she was off that shit. She was clean.'

Ray said, 'Come on, Peggy, you know you're never off that stuff.'

A wobbling head, a concession. 'I thought she would be one of those who made it.'

John pointing out, 'But you're still dealing?'

'Pot, acid when I can get it, speed. That's all.'

Shearer met his gaze.

'What happened to you?' Peggy nodding at Shearer.

'I had a fight with a Hells Angel in a urinal.'

Peggy found that amusing. 'Frank would like that.'

John said, 'Tell us about Spring.'

'I ran into a chick I know from Frisco. She was balling one the guys from Moby Grape. She and me and Spring have hung out together before. She swore she saw Spring around three weeks ago at Bido Lito's.'

'Where can we find this girl?'

A squealing couple had run dripping wet into the kitchen playing chasey.

'Ruth. I have no idea, but I remembered to call you guys,' giving John a come-hither look.

Shearer flashed the McKnight photo. 'You know this guy?'

'Sure. Larry. He's a sweet guy.'

'You seen him with Spring?' Ray eager.

'Not that I remember.'

Shearer tried the Sherry Linden photo but got only a shrug.

'She looks familiar, but I can't be sure.'

'Where's Bido—' Shearer had to stop as the chasey couple started to use him as a post. He pulled his gun. 'Would you two fuck off outside for a minute?'

A gasp. Then nothing but wet footprints on lino.

Peggy said, 'That's not very nice.'

John took over. 'Where is Bido Lito's?'

'Hollywood, near Selma.' She draped her arms around John's neck. 'But you're welcome to stay here.'

From the outside, the place looked like a cross between a disused church and a foundry. It was packed. They sucked beers, tried Spring's photo.

Too loud and crowded to elicit more than a shake of a head. An overcoat of dope and incense draping them. John abandoned work, gave in to the music.

Multiple bands. The second last only played two songs, and their final, a Troggs-like riff, went for fifteen minutes. Nearly all drum solo with this hypnotic chant, 'Ina-gatta-da-vita'. The crowd lapping it. The last band, Love, was melodic, almost folky. Third song in, John looking barwards to see if it was a good time for a drink. Shape of a girl's head, her hair. Deadset look-alike for

Spring. He nudged Ray. Shearer's eyes tracers. No need to explain, moving fast, shoving past beers held in ringed knuckles. Ray reached her first, tapped her shoulder. She swung—

The face was all kinds of different.

Later, the drink oozing into his brain, swaying like underwater kelp to the hypnotic sound, John closing his eyes, listening. A song about some girl, Anne Moore. Mysterious, a sense of yearning. The singer assuring him if he sees Anne Moore again, then he will know her, for she could see him in her eyes. Certainty, inevitably, longing, all wrapped in one song, one name, one girl. Like Spring.

Wham! John's eyes flicking open catching the bar mirror. And there she was: Spring, fucking Spring! About to grab Ray before realising it was no more than wishful thinking and the strong sea of dope he was drowning in.

The singer was right, you could give all you had, and despite that, things still turn out bad. Love and desire guaranteed no road to happiness. You could empty yourself yet bring nothing but your own annihilation. Martin Davis was proof of that.

He closed his eyes again. So many secrets. Where is Spring? Did you take her McKnight? Where did you leave her? Deep in a cold grave? Or tossed in the scrub with nothing more than a blanket of leaves to keep her from the coyotes.

Thrum pum pum pum.

16 LUCY IN THE SKY WITH DIAMONDS

Friday morning traffic Ray cruising slow up Sunset. Something going down. Queues around the block. Mainly young longhairs, a few suits and housewives. Gordon clueless as him. Ray curb-crawled.

'What's going on?' To a college kid with a V-neck and wing-nut ears.

'The Beatles' new album. This shop got some from England.'

A girl running down the street from wherever the head of the worm was. Screaming, waving an LP over her head.

'I got it! I got it!'

Right about then the radio kicking in with Sgt. Pepper Day, the jock boasting they were the first with the best. Every track one after the other all the way to the Hills. Mushroom Mark's map not as accurate as it might have been. He had been 'fairly certain' Earth's Eden commune was located off Oakden Drive but ninety minutes of canyon-edge parking and doorknocking bringing nothing but sweat and frustration.

Every time they came back to the car, a different Beatles song. Ray had only just got acclimatised to the old Beatles. He liked 'Twist and Shout' and 'Hard Day's Night'. This new stuff convincing him the Fab Four had been hanging in the same places he had been this last couple of weeks.

They broke for lunch, cruised, hitting a bunch of frustrating cul-de-sacs. Finally tried Utica Drive. It was near Oakden but not off it. Nearly an hour into more doorknocking, a bright-coloured Kombi van cruised past, 'Earth's Eden' painted down the side by someone stoned, drunk or suffering vertigo.

By the time they made it back to their car to give chase, the van had disappeared. Ray gunned the Mustang. Empty tarmac for too long to make sense. Had to have turned off earlier. He threw a U-turn, returned to where they had spied the van.

'Down here somewhere.'

Parking on the ridge, walking down. Four driveways on, paydirt. The Kombi and a Beetle side-by-side in a parking bay beside a small gate leading to a stone pathway that morphed into steps. An unruly diverse garden of flowers, shrubs. At the bottom of the path, a brick-and-tile house, stretching wide across the block. The weathered wood door was open, music wafting out. So was a purple haze of marihuana.

They entered, walked down a narrow hallway past bedrooms, emerged into a sunken lounge. Lamps with bubble-glass bases, a round chair made out of black-and-white plastic strands tied around an iron frame. A lot more upmarket than the Tenderloin share house: stone feature-wall and fireplace. A guy, naked from the waist up asleep on a lounge. They climbed up the steps on the other side of the room. The music from that direction. The lounge room giving onto a kitchen. A petite young woman in a tie-dyed tee-shirt and shorts spreading peanut butter. She looked up and smiled.

Ray said, 'Jill?'

She pointed outside.

They stepped through sliding doors onto a high deck that ran the length of the house. A stereo was set up, speakers facing out to the garden below, terraces of vegetables and plants and flowers, the canyon beyond. Stilts beneath the deck. A tent pitched among the stones and flowers below. Seven or eight bods sunbaking or slumped on chairs and sofas all listening reverently to the music. Ray's impression: middle-class kids with monied homes to go back to. A tall raw-boned girl wearing a straw hat and a long coarse hippie-frock – Ray wasn't sure if it was cheesecloth but that's what he'd call it – stood back to the rail, face tilted up to the sky.

Smiled over at them.

'Jill?'

'Yes,' she said.

◆◆◆

They'd walked around the far side of the deck out of the sun. Here the music less dominant. Smoke from Jill's giant joint floating over the valley like the dreams that always featured in these songs. They'd got through the basics of why they were here.

'Pauline was my best friend.'

Ray picked her up straight away on the tense.

'You don't think she's still alive?'

'No. I feel it.' Touching her chest. 'She's gone. She liked adventure. Maybe she'd go for a day or two, but she would have stayed in touch.'

Offering the joint. Ray feeling it would be rude to decline, knowing Gordon would, accepted. Gordon asked how often she had met with Martin Davis.

'Twice. At the police station first. That's where we got talking about our missing friends. Then about four days later he called me up and we met up here and we had a long talk, almost all afternoon. He rang a few days after that and told me he was sure this guy Larry was responsible and asked if I'd remembered anything more, but I couldn't help.'

Ray became aware of grunting sounds under the deck, realised a couple was fucking blissfully beneath them. John Gordon on now to the Garden of Allah, Davis' notes mentioning Larry.

'It's a bar we like. Easter Saturday, Spike, one of the guys here scored a lot of acid and we all dropped tabs. Dennis Wilson was there, and he was really cool. We were all hyped about the love-in the next day at Elysian Park. Pauline went to the bathroom and didn't come back for a long time. I went to make sure she was okay. She was talking, well, flirting really, with this tall guy, long brown hair, cowboy boots. I let her be, didn't want to cramp her style.'

'This guy?' Gordon showing the McKnight snap.

'Is that Marty's?'

'Yes.'

'It was just a glimpse really, but I think that was him. Anyway, Pauline came back, and I think our trips had already started. She wasn't with him, but she said something about catching up with him at Elysian. That's what I remember, after that ...' Her hand moving like a swallow through the air.

Next day they had all gone to the love-in, painted flowers on their cheeks, danced. Spending time on and off with Pauline but hadn't spied her with the guy from the previous night. Pauline hadn't seemed hung-up about that, in fact hadn't even mentioned it.

Just before 4.00 p.m., the two friends had been jiving around to some protest songs.

'Pauline was really against the war, like she was the strongest of any of us on that. She was talking with anti-war people. Then they started playing sitars and that was more her thing than mine, and I went over to the carousel and smoked some weed. That was the last time I saw her. About five most of us wanted to come back. I looked for Pauline, but I couldn't find her anywhere.'

She had kept up the search for half an hour. Ray glad Gordon was being secretary. It really was peaceful out here. Or maybe that was the dope kicking in.

'In the end we thought, she'll come home when she's ready. Mort was still there but it turned out he never saw her.'

Gordon asked who Mort was. Apparently one of the housemates.

Ray said, 'She never called, never came back for her things?'

Nope. That was it. And that was why Jill had been so worried about her. She had gone to the police and reported her missing, rung around the hospitals. No sign of her.

'I had a real bad feeling. When that body turned up, I went to check with the cops.'

John Gordon asked if the family of Sherry Linden, the dead girl, had been there too.

'No. They weren't there at that time. But Jenny Wallace was supposed to be coming to stay with her brother and never showed up. He was there, the brother.' She searched for the name. 'Steve.'

John asked if she had a contact for him.

'No, I don't. I left that all to Marty. But I know the family lives in

Pasadena and Steve goes to UCLA.'

'Are Pauline's things still here?' Ray asked.

'I keep them in my room.'

More whiny, distorted guitar. Soundtrack of this American summer. Ray couldn't make out the lyrics but knew they'd be about dreams, and silver chariots and mushrooms.

♦♦♦

Taking their time going through Pauline's things. Clothes, good condition, a few records, a photo album showing a nice young kid with a typical American family, paperback novels. According to Jill, the Gerschaff family were from Arizona. They had been in touch regularly with Pauline but had not heard from her since Easter. They were shattered.

Gordon checked. 'When was the last time you spoke to them?'

She thought about three days ago.

Ray asked if Pauline had any enemies here at Eden, rubbed anybody up the wrong way.

Jill didn't believe so. There was a notebook that was a kind of diary, but she'd found nothing in there suspicious.

'I've been through it a half-a-dozen times,' said Jill.

Ray flipped through. No entry for the Easter Saturday when they had been at the Garden of Allah and Pauline had been seen with the guy who might have been McKnight. Nothing for the Sunday. John Gordon asked if they could meet Mort.

Mort had long dark hair and a thin beard. No more than twenty, reckoned Shearer. He wore a top hat and velvet flares with a singlet, and was stoned. He confirmed Jill's story. He'd been enjoying himself at the park and had dozed off. He got roused late and was one of the last to leave. He had not seen Pauline and had arrived home in the early hours of Monday morning. The others could vouch for that. He had spent the last few hours before coming home with a couple of girls from Miami. He didn't have their numbers or address.

Ray did not consider him a suspect in butchering Linden. None of the Eden people had been to San Francisco in months, so none of them had killed Judy Ikin either. They all recognised the photo of Spring, but only because Martin Davis had insisted on asking each of them, that day he'd called in. They thanked Jill, took their leave.

'You're welcome to stay.' Making eyes at John Gordon.

At the car, Ray said. 'I'm offended. All these young women throwing themselves at you. None of them asked me to stay.'

He was thinking about Janis. Now, she was all woman. Wondered if their paths might ever cross again. Wasn't sure if that would be a good thing for either of them.

But it damn well would be fun.

♦♦♦

The Marquis pool, a relaxing break. Beatles playing from every poolside transistor, Ray knowing lyrics already, sipping Coke with ice. Couldn't believe he was in fucking Hollywood. All good things come to an end though.

Back at their room, thick carpet under bare feet, telephone directories and pencils. A dozen calls and Ray had Jenny Wallace's mother, offered his condolence, explained he'd come here to find Martin Davis who had been in touch with her son, Steve. She confirmed it but said so far as she knew he hadn't discovered anything. Ray played dumb, asked how he might get in touch with Steve.

'He has a track meet Saturday so he's out of town, but he will back Sunday. He lives near the campus.'

She gave him the number, told him that Jenny had been planning to come to LA and stay with her brother for a few days but never made it.

'Jenny could be a free spirit but she would never let her brother down like that.'

She was convinced something terrible had happened. 'She used to hitchhike all over the place. Her father and I told her not to do that, but she wouldn't listen.'

Ray left his number.

'Steve Wallace back Sunday,' he explained to Gordon who must have caught nearly the whole thing. It was near 3.00 p.m.

'We should call Suffolk, see if he's done those photos.'

They did and he had.

♦♦♦

Suffolk handed them a photographic box.

'It actually worked out well. The contact sheets from my friends in San Francisco arrived so I've put those in there too. I've got no need of them. I've printed the seven eight-by-tens Marty wanted, three from the San Francisco be-in in January and four from Elysian Park, and I've put in my contact sheets too so you can look over them, see if there might be any more you want printed up. The other contact sheets are in the envelope marked *Saint Ignatius*. I was back down here then but those guys are good photographers and I've written their contact details on the back of the contact sheets.'

Suffolk gave them a discount. He told them to call him if they needed any help.

'What's your favourite track?' he asked as they were leaving.

Ray was confused.

'On *Sergeant Pepper's*. You have to have heard it.'

Ray said, 'I like the one about Lucy in the sky.'

The photographer grinning.

'Yeah, "Lucy in The Sky with Diamonds". LSD. Love that one.'

Ray felt stupid. At the car he asked John if he'd known that.

'No. Never thought about it, but it makes sense.'

Hungry now, they found a burger restaurant on Beverly. Red table-cloths, waitresses in red skirts and white blouses. The only place in LA without the Beatles on: Herb Alpert and Glen Campbell instead. Made him think of Kings Cross strongarming for Shaloub, parties afterwards in the Rainbow Room.

Discovering now he was partial to chilli with his meals. The beer growing on him too. John Gordon opened the photo box, three white paper bags. The first had *San Fran Be-In, Jan 67* written on it. Gordon slipped out the prints. Some they'd seen. McKnight large as life on the top one, talking bullshit with some freaks and bikers. More distant on the second but behind a cluster of anti-war banners: *Berkeley Against War, Vets Against War, Students Against War, Make Love Not War* ... There! You could just make McKnight out talking with two girls.

Gordon said, 'That could be Francine Leach.'

Ray peering close now, trying to recall the photo from the newspaper report pinned on the board in Davis' unit.

'Could be.'

They asked the waitress if she had a magnifying glass they could borrow. Wonder of wonders, she returned with one. You had to love America. With the magnifying glass, it was still hard to be sure.

The second parcel, Elysian Park, Easter Sunday, the same photos they had seen at the unit. Pauline Gerschaff blowing bubbles with the guy Mort they'd met today. Another photo showed Jill. Two photos of McKnight, one near the merry-go-round talking with girls, too hard to say if any of those were Gerschaff, one to the side of a small stage with the sitar guy, a long row of motorcycles behind, each tooled differently.

They moved on to the Saint Ignatius shoot. Five sheets. Gordon better eyesight, so Ray let him scan.

'We'll need time to go through these. Some are really clear but there's background detail too ... Holy shit!'

Swinging the sheet Ray's way, handing him the magnifying glass, and tapping a photo over to the right on one of the lower rows.

The little rectangles were about the size of a watch face. Ray put the glass above the black and white, zoomed—

McKnight in profile laughing. Right behind him facing the other way, Sherry Linden.

17 FROM THE UNDERWORLD

In another universe, the coastal cruise would have John feeling wild and free. This journey more like heading down into a crypt. Flashing on a vampire movie he'd seen: Van Helsing stakes in hand to drive through the vampire's heart.

Council of war, he and Ray after their meal last night. No half measure now. They were committed. This case theirs no matter what the protocol was, no matter they were thousands of miles adrift from where they had authority. One of them needed to be in San Francisco to work the case from that end – talk to people who knew Francine Leach, get photos and film of those early be-ins, find a connection between McKnight and the girls.

How did Judy Ikin fit in? They had a photo of McKnight and Sherry Linden in close proximity at St Ignatius. But did they know one another? Same with Jenny Wallace. If John could get evidence, he might pull the SFPD onside.

Not lost on him that he and Ray doing exactly what Martin Davis had. Perhaps if they hadn't pissed off LAPD, they might have been able to work from closer in. But in the end, you just had to do what you thought right. Didn't want to leave here shamed, defeated, humiliated. He needed to finish the thing, shut McKnight down.

If Ray was right and, stuff it, he usually was, McKnight was back in Frisco. Ray saying, he didn't mind one way or the other which city he took. John officially running the Australian end of the Martin Davis case whether the kid was dead or not, that making him the conduit to Spinetti and the SFPD. If McKnight was up there, they would need SFPD onside, so that argued for John travelling north. On the other hand, if it came to digging McKnight out of a rathole, they didn't come better than Shearer.

Ray had said, 'I'm a brutal cunt. I'll chop a hand off with a cleaver if I need to.'

And that was true, but some part of John – the part that had been cut out of him two years back – needed to finish this case himself. It was the same part that had felt impotent while a psycho readied to kill Denise. So, it was settled, and here he was driving north.

Before leaving, they'd driven to a car lot to get a car for Ray. It made sense for the Mustang to be going back to San Francisco. Ray settled for a '62 Pontiac Laurentian. A sparse goodbye, then John rolled, filled his tank an hour north of LA.

Around Monterey, stopping for a coffee, sandwich and petrol. Rain sheeting in, the wind off the ocean bracing, but the smell of the Pacific, and damp, old-style rain a pleasant change from the desert heat of LA. Monterey was dotted with posters for some big music festival coming a few weeks on. By then he'd be back in Sydney and in Denise's arms in weather probably a bit like this. He hit San Francisco by 6.00 p.m.

Saturday night, the Fillmore bill: Steve Miller and Big Brother. Two short weeks since his first time here, but John feeling like a veteran. Miller on first, rocking strong. John went to head backstage, figuring to ask Janis about McKnight. A tractor imitating a bouncer put his hand on his chest.

'Band only.'

'I'm a friend of Janis.'

'Everybody is a friend of Janis.'

John forced to bide his time, but it was easy. He liked the Miller band, bluesy but spacey too. Caught movement at the periphery of where he stood, the velvet curtains leading backstage parting, Nitro, Janis' roadie emerging. Nitro recognised him. John put in his request. Nitro whispered to the tractor, the curtains opened.

Janis was close by, leaning back, bare foot propped against the wall, swigging a bottle of spirts, talking to some longhairs.

'John!' Lighting up as she saw him. 'Ray here?' Excited at the prospect. John doused it, explained Ray was still in LA hunting leads and might be a few days yet.

'Thought your job was over.'

John explaining: things to tie off. 'Actually, you might be able to help.' Telling her quickly over a drum solo: a psycho, missing girls. 'Jenny Wallace was last seen at your Sunday concert here February nineteen, with Airplane.'

'That was a big night,' Janis sucking the life out of a roll-your-own.

John asked if she could recall a girl asking the band or crew for a ride to LA.

'Sorry, man. Too long ago, too many people.'

'Any of the guys here might have worked that show at St Ignatius high school where Sherry Linden was last seen?'

Janis grabbed him by the arm, led him to where a lean guy, bald pate on top, shoulder-length at the back, was soldering a lead on an amplifier.

'This is Moose. Anybody worked it, he did. Moose this is my friend John. He needs to ask you stuff.'

Background, the band climaxing, applause, cheers. Janis had to go.

'Give Ray my love,' she called.

John curious what exactly was going on with those two. Moose waiting. John quizzed him on the St Ignatius High School gig: Buffalo Springfield and Airplane.

'Yeah, I worked it.'

John out with a photo of Sherry Linden. 'Any chance you remember this girl?'

Moose shaking his head. 'Unless she came back and partied with us, I don't remember one from the other.'

John hit with McKnight's pic. 'How about him?'

'Larry, yeah. He's lugged for us quite a few times.'

'He works for one of those bands?'

Moose explaining these guys weren't employees.

'They just lug the gear on-stage, off-stage, pull it in and out of vans. They turn up on the day, they hang out by the stage, get paid ten bucks. Larry's a regular.'

'And he worked for you that concert?'

Moose thinking hard. 'I'd say ninety percent he did.'

'What about a show here, Big Brother and Airplane, Sunday February nineteenth?'

Moose knew for sure he was working that gig but couldn't recall if McKnight was too. John got some more names, fellow roadies he could ask. Feeling better already. No out-and-out proof yet to nail McKnight. But then nothing to clear him. Everything was heading where it ought to.

◆◆◆

Ray's headlights punching holes in the black. San Bernadino might be trouble if McKnight's biker pals spotted him, but he was in a different car now and had taken the precaution of filling up early. No need to stop in town. The Pontiac had more room than his kitchen. You could fit an army in the boot. He found a station that played country and western, and Elvis. Sang tuneless and loud to his heart's content about the girl with a ruby in her tummy. Didn't know what he might find in San Bernadino but the only plan he'd come up with. Too much time to kill before he could speak to Steve Wallace. Had to do something.

He hit town, taking it slow, the bikers clumped in the same place as last time. Ray following the road to McKnight's house, driving on past, checking for any tail, or sign of life in the house. It was in darkness.

Half a mile up the road, he swung around and cruised back, parking on the opposite side of the road to the house, fifty yards up, pointing back to town. Once bitten. He checked his snub nose, grabbed keys and torch, climbed out.

It was cool, a light wind blowing, the smell of dry earth in his nostrils. He walked quietly back to McKnight's stood and listened. It wasn't impossible that McKnight was back. Ray could make out no sound from the front, so he walked around the back like last time. The backyard was flat, weeds. A few fresh holes by the looks.

Maybe some half-hearted attempt by the cops to look for bodies. The patio was old chequered concrete slabs. Crossed those to the back door, took out his key, opened up.

The house smelled like it had been closed a while. Starting in the kitchen. Clicked on the torch. Cops had been through alright, cheap crockery pulled out of cheap cupboards; fridge, power cord yanked from the socket, door open. The bedroom had been tossed. Mattress up on the side, clothes pulled out of the wardrobe. Reminded him of Martin Davis' room above Hector's garage.

Ray exited, played the light over the walls and roof of the hallway. Checked the bathroom. Looked like dried blood on the floor. Landlord hadn't bothered to clean up. Or maybe McKnight owned it. Could explain why he lived way out here. Good place to bring girls though if you'd abducted them. Nobody would hear them scream. Vinyl records and album covers were strewn over the lounge-room floor, papers, old handbills mostly left where they'd been trampled and blown. A sofa, an armchair, both worn, springs ready to push through. A small desk stood by a phone plug. The phone was on the floor, cord yanked from the wall. A drawer from the desk had been pulled, the contents just dumped. Cops looking for a murder weapon and not much else. The torch played over ancient wallpaper, the dusty shade of a standard lamp. Overhead a lightbulb in a small, pretty glass fitting shaped like a tulip. A cheap stereo on the floor.

Ray collected the papers, sorted them patiently. Mostly various handbills for clubs and bands. Interesting because of the dates. Had to suppose McKnight collected these when he was in Los Angeles, so maybe they would aid Ray in plotting McKnight's whereabouts at any given time. Buffalo Springfield, Love, Jefferson Airplane. One in particular: The Doors, Cheetah, Santa Monica Pier, April 9. Linden's body was dumped in the Hills right around then.

Ray not wanting to be found hanging here. He started shoving the handbills into his bag, stopped. Handbill advertising The Doors and Country Joe & the Fish at the Earl Warren Showground, May 27.

Tonight.

Ray left quick, back in the car checked maps. A straight drive west. He could make it in about two hours.

♦♦♦

Summer night, ocean breeze, the smell of sea salt. Music seeping through tin walls of a showground shell. Ray making it. Late better than never. The whole trip wondering if he could bluff his way out of it if the highway patrol stopped him. Got lucky. Not a cop in sight.

He scrambled a park in close. The Doors must have already played. Different music, Country Joe, the band he'd almost caught that first night in San Francisco. Hells Angels hanging at the back gate by rows of cycles. Wondering if he'd recognise McKnight's, a white Triumph Bonneville, not too hard to miss but the lighting here grey flecked yellow, the shadows deep. Walking past casual like he was admiring the hardware. A Harley chopper, a black tank with a painted Marilyn Monroe naked vamp stretched across the tank, another chopper painted tiger stripes, a panhead showing shark's teeth like they used to put on the nose of fighter planes back in the war, another panhead with a swastika, a couple of tourers, confederate flags. A brace of Yamahas, forced out to the perimeter.

No sign of McKnight's ride. He walked in through the back gate, late now, self-appointed security bikers deciding it wasn't worth the trouble to strongarm an older cit. A guitarist, halo of curls playing some drifty music. The Doors singer that Ray had already marked down as a prize-wanker sipping a beer, arms draped around two sexy women. A guy with glasses, the keyboard player he remembered, supervising an organ being loaded into the truck.

'Excuse me,' Ray said, and the bloke turned without punching him. Ray pulled out the McKnight photo. 'I'm looking for a guy named Larry. Believe he helps sometimes with your gear. I'm a friend of Janis' and he stiffed her on a deal. Wondered if you'd seen him around?'

The bloke checked the photo. 'Not tonight. I remember him though.'

'You remember if he was working for you April ninth at Santa Monica?'

He didn't but he directed Ray to a guy who could have taken on Brute Bernard for a few rounds. He was lifting one of those big boxes with the spinning horns like it was a doll's house.

Ray asked. Janis' name the currency to buy respect.

'Yeah, Larry. He's not here tonight. He was helping a couple of shows that week at Santa Monica. Rides a Bonney.'

'That's him.'

Ray pushed his luck, pulled out a photo of Sherry Linden, wondered if she might have been with him.

Goliath said, 'Don't recall, but mostly these guys help out so's to pick up the chicks that hang around the bands. Wouldn't think he'd bring her. Like taking a ham sandwich to a picnic.'

The trip back to LA, Ray feeling like you do when you back a longshot that runs second, like you are smart but not smart enough.

18 CHILDREN OF THE FUTURE

Trying to draw a bead on Sherry Linden from her end was too hard. When she had picked up her things from the hostel after the St Ignatius concert, she had not told the witnesses who it was she planned to be travelling with, only that it looked like she was off to LA. Maybe cops could chase down the witnesses, girls who were by now in other parts of the country or city, but John did not have those resources.

Approaching Sherry Linden's disappearance from skewering McKnight's location at the time seemed more promising. But right now, the only confirmed homicide John could dangle for San Francisco PD was Judy Ikin. Could have called Spinetti right off, asked for juice to help put McKnight in the frame but his brains told him things would go better if he had some cold, hard links joining Ikin to McKnight.

Being a Sunday, he'd waited till 10.00 a.m. to call Malcom Broadbent, the BBC contact Shearer had uncovered while drinking at the Marquis. Broadbent affable. He was staying with friends, the Wilsons, while he shot his BBC pieces. John told him he was looking into the disappearance of young women. Broadbent intrigued. John more than welcome to head over and 'peruse' what Broadbent had. In fact, he had been planning to take another look at what he had shot so far, so John's visit fitted in perfectly. Was there anything in particular John wanted to see?

John said he was especially interested in the Human Be-In that happened in January, a concert in February, and the Saint Ignatius concert on April seventh. Broadbent hadn't got to San Francisco to begin filming till mid-March but as a matter of fact he had caught the Airplane, Springfield concert at St Ignatius on film. John had suggested 2.00 p.m. Broadbent said perfect.

◆◆◆

Right after Broadbent, John called Shearer. Sounded like he'd roused him from sleep.

They swapped notes.

John said, 'I saw Janis last night. She seemed really keen to see you. You didn't, did you?'

Ray said John had a vivid imagination.

John was thinking you'd be hard pressed to find a more unlikely pairing, then rolled again, maybe not. Ray spilled first on his Saturday night, and it all pointed in the same direction. McKnight had been in LA at least a couple of days before Sherry Linden's body turned up. They knew from the contact sheet Suffolk had supplied that McKnight and Sherry Linden had been at the same Frisco concert John was about to check footage of. John should have been surprised to hear Ray had driven out to San Bernadino but wasn't.

John running his account of his meeting with Moose.

'Ninety percent sure McKnight worked the Saint Ignatius concert where Linden was but couldn't recall her. Unfortunately, couldn't place McKnight at the Fillmore where Wallace was last seen. But that doesn't mean he wasn't there.'

Ray agreed. 'We just have to keep chipping away.'

John had explained that he was about to try the Tenderloin apartment building again, flash McKnight's photo. Shearer had wished him luck.

John looked back over Davis' original master sheet, made adjustments to it.

Francine Leach 19 – Jan 14 Human Be-In Golden Gate Park.

Jenny Wallace 18 – Feb 19 Airplane-Big Brother, Fillmore. Hitchhiking from San Fran to L.A. for concert.

(No confirmation McKnight worked Fillmore gig)

Pauline Gerschaff 21 – Mar 26 Elysian Park Love-In.
(confirm McKnight there, 95% met her night before)

Judy Ikin, April 2, Tenderloin.

(Spring – April 5, hitchhiking to L.A.)

Sherry Linden 20 – April 7 San Francisco Buffalo Springfield and Jefferson Airplane concert St Ignatius High School. Body found Hollywood Hills April 11.

(McKnight 95% worked the show, photo confirmation he was there. In L.A. 2 days before body turns up. Did she hitch a ride with him from SF?)

Mary Gannon 20 – April 11 Long Beach, Scherer Park. Local bands.
(turned up safe. False alarm)

~~Spring – April 5, hitchhiking to L.A.~~

The rain had cleared, the Sunday morning air pleasant, even in the Tenderloin. Jay Burnley was up and dressed and answered the knock on his door like an optimist.

'Hi, Mr Burnley, I don't know if you remember me …'

'Yes of course. Did you find her?'

Remembering Spring even though Martin Davis had been the focus of their previous interview.

'No, and we're worried for her. Just a quick question.' John pulled out the photo of McKnight.

'Ever see this guy hanging around the building? He rides a white-and-blue Triumph motorcycle.'

Burnley didn't think so. Said he would keep his eye out.

Strike one.

On the way back down, John took the corridor that led to Ikin's apartment, knocked on 6. The crone from last time still alive and kicking.

'Remember me?' John could hear a canary in the background. Smoke was choking it.

'You wanted to know about Judy, the dead girl next door.'

'Right. I have another photo for you to look at.'

She was eager, likely remembering payday last time. But she shook her head at McKnight.

'Don't ring no bells.'

Nor did a white-and-blue motorcycle. John about to call it a wipe-out. 'But her friend might. The one who organised the funeral. She asked me if I wanted to go. Left me a card.'

The crone disappearing inside. Minutes dragged. Gnarled knuckles, small business card reappeared. Name and number of a funeral home.

John thanked her, slipped her a dollar. She made that sound that mothers do when the hussy dating their darling son comes to the door. Then she retreated into the haze and shut the door. Funeral directors probably worked Sundays but better tomorrow with the Broadbent meeting now.

◆◆◆

Even way off, John divining that interior decor of the house: oil paintings on walls, Chesterfield sofas, crystal decanters, deep Persian runners. The dwelling you'd expect of a place in a suburb called Nob Hill.

The hill was steep, the houses painted fresh and even, stone-and-brick foundations with what looked like expensive wood turrets, those big bay windows. You could imagine sea captains fixing their caps before they headed off to clippers and new adventures while their wives shopped for bonnets and played whist.

Broadbent, a slim man around forty wearing slacks and turtle-neck answered and welcomed him in. It was right on 2.00 p.m.

'My friends are out at lunch, so we have the place to ourselves.

Well, along with Nebuchadnezzar.' Nodding to a fat, suspicious Persian cat.

The house three floors, Broadbent with the second to himself. He offered tea or coffee, John said he was fine. They climbed a narrow steep staircase, Broadbent explaining he'd originally come over to shoot some anti-war stuff.

'Britain is torn on Vietnam. Most are against it. We've never really recovered from World War Two. But some think we're deserting our ally. You're Australian? How's it being received there? We hear things, but only from other journalists.'

John told him probably much the same way as what he'd seen here. 'Young people don't want it. Older people think we're going to be overrun if we don't stop communism up there.'

Down a corridor, turned into a spacious room: ornate ceiling, armchairs, coffee table facing the end wall. Pretty much what John had pictured.

'I have my own sitting room,' said Broadbent, walked to the end wall and pulled down a professional screen. 'I've set up the reel with the April concert for you but it's easier to just go from the start in March if you don't mind.'

He drew blinds, killing sunlight, the room instantly dark. The projector ignited, a big professional one. John guessing it was the next size up from home movies at least.

'This is sixteen mil,' as if reading John's mind. 'Not edited yet. Like I said, I came here looking to cover the anti-war movement.'

Images on screen: Berkeley, student protests, banners and loudhailers, no soundtrack. Then what might have been Golden Gate Park. More protests. Two sides facing off, cops and pro-war one side – *Defend Our Freedom*, *Support Our Armed Forces*, *Traitors* – and a much larger group on the other. Longhairs, hippies; moms and dads, *Save Our Sons*, *Learn the Lesson*; Berkeley student leaders, *Students Against Warmongering*.

'I didn't realise it got this heated,' John surprised. The two sides swinging placards and fists.

The camera right in there now, bouncing around as the cameraman was jostled. Quick flashes: young guys in uniform pointing and gesturing at older, anti-war vets. John recognising the basement MC Murphy and his mates in the welter. Kansas Annie's hat, he was sure of it, blocked by two middle-class women spitting and swiping one another.

'Looks rough,' said John.

Broadbent said, 'I got a black eye out of that. Somebody banged the camera right back into my face. A lot of the local news here is censored. The newspapers are by and large pro-war, television too. In Australia, you'd likely be getting the US news footage. But the anti-war movement don't want this shown either. They're not stupid. This might play well in San Francisco and New York but in middle America and the south, they can't afford to be branded anarchists or communists. And quite frankly, it's only the independents and foreign press getting down and dirty and capturing this.'

John tracking more footage as Broadbent talked.

'What I noticed, however, that was really interesting: this has become more than just the war. That might have started it but now there are young people flooding into the city from all over America and the idea has expanded. It's not so much about what ought to be stopped now, but about what is possible.'

Now the shots were more benign: hippies dancing in the park, playing flutes. A line of people being given free food under a Diggers banner, poetry readings, sitar playing.

'There's a … spirit here, a zeitgeist the Germans call it. Do you know what I mean?'

John did.

'It's like a …' he couldn't find a better word, '… like you say, a spirit.'

Broadbent ran on. 'It's fascinating. This wouldn't be possible in a less affluent country. People have to work to put food on the table, they don't have the luxury of considered morality, but these young people are privileged. Like our romantic poets. They can afford to sit back and ponder, philosophise. And what's most fascinating of all to me, is how exactly it is going to play out.'

The vision now of bands. John recognising Big Brother, the

Grateful Dead, Country Joe & the Fish. The camera panning over a knot of hippies and bikers.

Broadbent said, 'Bikers are supposed to be the bad guys, aren't they? But it's like they have joined forces with the love generation. All the outlaws together.'

John straining to see McKnight. A few more minutes, different shows. The briefest glimpse of Kansas Annie, drug dealer Peggy. John felt a pang. Nothing good lasts forever.

Broadbent asked him about the missing women. John told him.

Broadbent said, 'I suppose that is the awful flipside of love and peace and all this chaotic movement. It provides the perfect cloak for a killer.'

Jefferson Airplane on screen.

'This is the St Ignatius concert,' said Broadbent to confirm. More music oriented than anti-war. The only sound the whir of the projector. Band shots, audience shots.

'There!'

John calling it. Unmistakable, Sherry Linden looking stoned in a clump of fans.

'I'm making a note,' said Broadbent.

More shots: crowd, band, side of stage … finally.

'And there.' John's heart pounding with excitement.

Larry McKnight standing in front of some amplifiers talking to a girl, her back facing the camera. It could be Sherry. Similar hair, build but hard to say if the top matched the earlier shot, the lighting made it so hard. Turn. Turn. If she just turns and it's her …

The shot cut away again.

'The film confirmed that photo we saw on the contact sheet. Sherry Linden was there. So was McKnight. One shot maybe put them together, but I couldn't swear on it.' The receiver seemed heavy against his ear. Back at the Clarence, Sunday night closing in.

Shearer's voice crackled down the line. 'I spoke to Carol again. She put me onto her friends who shot film at the Easter Sunday show. They said the best stuff was what they gave Davis.'

John said, 'That roadie Nitro is going to introduce me to the Dead tonight. If I can get confirmation on Jenny Wallace and McKnight, that's one more nail. I'm following up on Judy Ikin's friend, first thing tomorrow.'

Shearer said, 'You seen Kitty?'

'Not yet. Got in too late yesterday.'

'Give her my best. I better go. I'm meeting Steve Wallace near UCLA.'

John wished him luck, hung up and checked his gun. So much for love and peace.

◆◆◆

'I run track. Eight hundred is my best event. Jenny is a year older than me.'

Not much more than a kid, Steve Wallace still had zits. A fringe of light-brown hair, striped top, would fit right in with the Beach Boys. Ray toyed with his Coke. Some burger joint off campus: milkshakes, ponytails a jukebox playing something like the Monkees. Ray wished he was in San Francisco near Janis and Kitty instead of delivering bad news.

Steve Wallace taking the news of Martin Davis hard.

'I really liked Marty, and he was the only one seemed to care about Jenny. They've got the guy?'

'Not in custody. Larry McKnight. Did Marty mention him?'

Wallace alert like a retriever. '*That* Larry? He killed Marty?'

Ray told him that's the way it seemed. 'Looks like Marty was following him. Did he mention that to you?'

'He told me he had leads on this guy, Larry. He didn't know his second name but said he was a biker who was always hanging around the bands, loading their gear. He asked me to help, and I said I would after my track meet, the one I finished today.'

Wallace and Davis had first met at Hollywood police station. A body had been found in the Hills, and Wallace had been worried it was Jenny.

'She called me on Thursday, February sixteen to say she was going to come down to LA. There was a concert she wanted to see, Buffalo Springfield. The Doors were opening the bill, and she'd heard so much about them too. The concert was for the next Wednesday in Woodland Hills. She asked could she stay with me.'

Explaining she'd done that before, slept on the couch of his share house. 'Our family home is in Pasadena and Jenny always wanted to be part of the scene, so she prefers being with me than my folks.'

'How was she planning to get here?' Ray shaking the empty can.

'Hitch a ride. She did it pretty regularly.'

'You mean on the highway?' Ray sticking out his thumb to illustrate. Wallace waved that idea off.

'No, more like asking around for a friend who might be heading down, or a friend of a friend.'

Ray thinking, that would fit McKnight well. She's seen him around the traps, talked to him perhaps. He hears she wants a ride ...

'When was the last time that you know she was seen?'

'Her housemates last saw her Sunday the nineteenth. They all went to an Airplane–Big Brother concert in San Francisco at the Fillmore. She loved music. She lived for it. Her housemate said Jenny was asking around at that concert if anybody she knew was heading to LA for the next week. Her friend said, try the band.'

'Did you check with the bands?'

'I got onto the Airplane road manager. He swears he does not remember anybody asking.'

Ray said, 'Marty made a note of her visiting the Grateful Dead house?'

'Yes, on the Friday, a couple of days before. She told me about it. She was so excited she actually got to meet Jerry Garcia and Phil Lesh. She was over the moon. Marty had this theory that she might have met Larry there because apparently he was a regular, but we couldn't get any confirmation.'

Good theory: she might have met McKnight there, then seen him at the Fillmore. Felt she already knew him if he offered a ride. Ray asked Wallace if he feared for his sister.

'Jenny was wild and free and drove my folks nuts but she

loved us. There is no way she's living in some commune in the desert. Somebody killed her. I am sure.' Looking down, wiping his eyes. 'But I still hope. You know? I still pray.'

◆◆◆

Ray left. No breakthrough but at least Davis' notes confirmed. Kicking himself he hadn't been able to interview Wallace earlier. The Doors crew might have remembered McKnight at Woodland Hills. It wasn't the end of the world. He could find them again.

So far everything in Martin's theory panning out. McKnight had been at the be-in when Francine Leach had last been seen. He'd been at St Ignatius when Sherry Linden had last been seen. He'd turned up in LA and met up with Pauline Gerschaff and been at the same concert the day she disappeared.

Also telling but uncorroborated: Martin Davis' note Larry McKnight had been in LA on February 22. That would fit with Jenny Wallace going missing from San Francisco en route to LA.

Ray called Ian Suffolk and asked if he'd shot the Woodland Hills concert of February 22.

'Matter of fact I did. You want the contact sheets on that too?'

He sure did.

Suffolk told Ray to drop into the studio any time after today.

◆◆◆

The Dead doing a free show in the Panhandle. Nitro met John outside, waiting till the band finished their set. Gave them time to wind down. Chicks floating past, the crowd dispersing for mushrooms, junk, acid, soup.

Night was oiling its gun. Nitro prison handshaking one of the crew. Gesturing at John. They got the okay to talk. The only band member available, Pigpen. Moustache and eyes that played with fire. Sitting on a speaker box, flagon of wine. He knew 'Larry' and where he stayed in the Tenderloin, not exactly but he had the name of a housemate, 'Ron', and the block. Jenny Wallace he couldn't remember. A lot of girls came through there. No sooner said than a flock of them wandered over. John was about to go.

'That's Ron there.' Pigpen pointing to a six-foot guy in a red shirt and cords. John thanked him, eased away, waited. When Ron split, John followed, itching to front him, thinking better of it. Not all the way dark yet. They hit the block Pigpen had mentioned. Ron disappeared into a scarred apartment building. John took a post across the street.

Darkness got deeper. His legs got tired. Two hours crawled by before Ron swung out of the building and headed up the street. Foot traffic sporadic. John crossed, eased in behind his target. Up close. Felt the blood pumping in his ears. Waiting his chance. An alley mouth opening just up ahead to the left. Now!

He shoved Ron in there, whipped out the snub nose put its muzzle to the back of Ron's head, ushered him further into shadow. You learned things off Shearer they didn't teach you at the academy.

'Where's Larry McKnight?'

'No idea.'

John socked him in the kidney. Ron swore, sagged. John asked again. Cocked the trigger, prepared to put a bullet in his knee or spine. He'd had enough now. A big wave building in him, had to break.

'Try Bakersfield.'

John kept the gun on him. 'April seventh. Larry went to an Airplane and Buffalo Springfield concert at Saint Ignatius High School. You remember?'

Ron remembered.

'He come back after that?'

'Not for a couple of weeks. He went to LA.'

John hissed, 'You better pray he hasn't left Bakersfield.'

'Fuck y—'

All Ron managed before John hit him hard with fist and gun butt, knocking him down. Then John walked back up to the street feeling the best he had in ages.

19 I FEEL LIKE I'M FIXIN' TO DIE

James Perry shirt off, poolside with Ray, coffee and apple pie in front of him, Monday afternoon sun streaming. Ray had felt bad about not contacting him earlier but time, already tight then, now burning a hole in his pocket. John Gordon had called after bracing McKnight's pal Ron last night. The Bakersfield lead smelled good. Ray wasting no time: an anonymous call to LAPD.

Space in his schedule, he'd chased up Perry.

'You get your car back?'

Perry scoffed. 'Yeah, with the shit shot out of it. I thought I'd left that crap behind in Vietnam. At least for a few weeks.'

Ray asked if he'd heard anything of Spring. Perry hadn't.

'I stopped looking. I came back on leave thinking I could make a difference but ...'

Gesturing to streets beyond. 'Nothing I do is going to make any difference. Not over there. Not here. My brother is still going to be a fucking cripple whether Mary-Anne is alive or dead.'

Ray said, 'You're going to help get a killer off the street.' That's what he hoped anyway.

'Those cops gave me a good grilling, I can tell you. They wanted to know if I actually saw McKnight kill the kid. I told them I saw nothing. I walked out the bar and was waiting in my car. I heard the motorcycle fire up. It was McKnight. I followed him to San Berdoo. They got excited when I told them about the motorcycle following the kid from his house.'

Perry hadn't mentioned this before.

'When was that?'

'I forgot all about it till they started asking me about watching the joint over in Silver Lake. I remembered then, the first time that night when the kid went driving off, I went to follow but this cycle pulled out first. I tried to tail him, but another car got in between.'

'You're saying there was a motorcycle followed Davis when he left Silver Lake around seven?'

'That's right.'

'McKnight?'

'Couldn't see. He passed me too quick.'

'McKnight's got a white Triumph.'

'I know but I couldn't say for sure. There were other cars in between, like I said. And then when I thought about it hard, I couldn't be sure if I was mixing it up with McKnight's cycle when I followed that sucker all the way to San Bernadino. I know *that* was white. The cops wanted it to be McKnight following from Silver Lake, I know that.'

Ray thinking he would have pushed for that too. If McKnight was camped outside Davis' place it might help show intent.

'How far did the motorcycle follow Davis after you left Silver Lake?'

He couldn't say. There were other cars in front of him. The motorcycle had gone long before Pico.

Ray cursing. It could have just been a coincidence. But Lackowitz and Burns would read it this way: McKnight and Davis had a relationship, probably involving drugs. McKnight had staked out Davis, knew he would head to the bar. McKnight had probably gone there first, waited, biding his time to strike. And struck he had when Davis had left, in the wee hours.

Perry said, 'You think he did those girls?'

Shearer said, 'Yes I do.' Asked Perry was he going to stick around LA.

'Probably not. But if I go back to my town, well, it's home, you know? And I miss it a lot more when I'm back out there in Ho's jungle. A lot of the guys go to Hong Kong or Sydney because it's easier that way. I've already lost two good friends. You never know if you might be next. And you're living on the wire every day. Even if nothing's happening, you feel it. Then you come back here and kids are smoking weed and dressing up, like it's some play. You know, Vietnam, man, that is pretty unreal but here …' he waved his pie fork, '… here it's just as unreal. I don't know this world either.' He finished his pie.

Ray said, 'We're going to win though, right?'

Perry, a crooked smile. 'You ever see those things on the backs of comics you can send away for?'

Ray knowing exactly what he meant: five hundred plastic toy soldiers for some unbelievably cheap deal, X-ray specs where you could see through girls' clothes. Only trouble was you could never get any of the good stuff in Australia.

'My brother and me, we sent away for those things a few times. And they send them, you know? They actually send them, but they are never like you picture in your head. So, sure, we can win, but what we win I think is going to be like those comic things. Not what we picture. I better go.'

Shearer said, 'You ever get a furlough to Sydney, look me up. You can stay with me any time.'

Giving Perry his address. Perry copied it carefully into his little address book. They shook hands.

Perry said, 'If Mary-Anne turns up back at home, I'll let you know.'

◆◆◆

The Western Addition Library was new, all glass and brick. Out front, neat grass, inside quiet, a smattering of cardigans, twinsets and blue-rinse shades. Beverly Rennison waiting for him, raw-boned, archetypical librarian, glasses on a plain but lively face. Put John in mind of a girls' hockey captain.

The funeral home had been able to supply her phone number. Her mother had answered when John called, told him Beverly would be at work. He had called her there and she had agreed to meet him at lunchtime, on the late side, 1.45. Beverly with homemade sandwiches, asking if John minded her eating. They took a shaded park bench.

John kicking off: How long had Beverly been friends with Judy?

'We both started working here pretty much when the library

was opened around a year ago. I'm a librarian but Judy was an assistant doing night school to get to a place where she could get her qualifications.' A dainty eater, wiping the corner of her mouth. 'We got on well. We were both single. Most of the other women are married or engaged. I live with my parents still. Judy had her apartment. Then Judy met Michael and before long they were engaged but he was at sea a lot, so we still saw plenty of one another: movies, a meal in Chinatown, an art gallery. Unlike most of the young people in San Francisco these days, we are conservative. My parents are Republicans, Judy's were Democrats but conservative.'

John covered old ground. The police file said Judy had no enemies that Beverly could think of.

'That's right. May I ask why you are asking me this now? You mentioned some developments.'

John told her about the suspect Larry McKnight being sought in conjunctions with another homicide. Showed a photo.

'This guy, look familiar?'

Studying as she nibbled. Shaking her head. 'I don't remember ever being introduced to him by Judy. Larry, you say?'

'McKnight. He rides a Triumph motorcycle. Predominantly white.'

The make nothing to Beverly. She thought she would remember a white one.

This was heading nowhere. 'You said she had no enemies that you knew of. What about Michael, her fiancé? Did he have debts of any kind, a drug habit?'

Not that Beverly knew of. She'd met him twice: straightforward, a sailor who believed in God, Judy and the flag.

'Any confrontations Judy had that you can recall?'

Judy had told her about one.

'My mother was kind of responsible for Judy even hearing about it. My mom and a bunch of her friends – a few are Daughters of the American Revolution – decided to speak for the servicemen who they felt were being dishonoured by these student protests. Mom invited Judy. Judy thought she should go. They got placards and flags and stood on a street corner. A lot of retired people and old soldiers and workers joined them. And quite a few servicemen. Then the anti-war crowd appeared.'

John was wondering if this was the same demo Broadbent had filmed.

Beverly taking another neat bite. 'There was some abuse and some things; small rocks and cans, thrown at them, spitting, disgusting really, but nobody was hurt. Judy said people might have been injured, only the Vets Against War and some of the campus and Diggers leaders stepped in and calmed things down. I mean, Judy's Michael wasn't even involved in firing on people, just supply or mapping or something.'

Had Judy mentioned any of the violent protesters in particular?

'No. She said the women were the worst.'

John thinking on the crime-scene report. She had likely opened her door. Would she do that to somebody she recognised as being violent towards her?

Another thought. 'What about jilted suitors?'

'Michael was pretty much her first real boyfriend.'

John ran the list: Male work colleagues?

Not many in the library, all mild.

People in her apartment block?

She didn't interact much with them.

People from her hometown who might have turned up?

So far as Beverly knew, nobody had visited.

Had she ever mentioned anybody giving her a ride anywhere?

She walked or caught a trolley car.

Nearing the end now. John pulled photos of the other missing women. Did any of these faces ring a bell with Beverly as being in some way related to Judy?

No.

A washout.

Beverly despatched her last sandwich. John thanked her for her time and made sure she had his number.

'Just in case you remember anything.'

Ray a pool fixture. Getting the hang of this life of leisure, a steak residing in his stomach, a bourbon in his fist, the moon reflecting off blue water, the high laugh of a liquored woman a floating feather that had started the other end of the terrace. One of the hotel staff approached. Young man in a charcoal suit, white shirt, narrow tie.

'Mr Shearer, you have a call. Would you like to take it here or the lobby?'

Ray said, 'I'll take it in the lobby.'

The tiles were cool, the receiver warm.

'Shearer.'

'This is Ted Lackowitz.'

Bingo. The call he'd been hoping for.

'Hey, Ted, how's it going. You get my peace offering?'

Earlier in the day Ray delivering a bottle of the best scotch to Hollywood station with a note of contrition. He'd included the Marquis phone number, hopeful.

'We did. Apology accepted.'

'You guys are working late.'

'We always work late. You know that. Besides, it's been a big day.'

'Any news?'

'Matter of fact. Kern County Sheriff's Department picked up Larry McKnight about two hours ago.'

Yes! 'That's excellent. John will be very pleased. This has been kind of personal to him. Kern County ... that's Bakersfield, isn't it?'

Lackowitz laughing, 'You learn quick.'

'When in Rome,' said Ray, not sure if it fitted. Then, 'John's actually in San Francisco at the moment. Like I say, he has an affinity with Davis, if you know what I mean. He's half-convinced the kid was onto something with that chart of his.' Trawling.

'Well, we found no fingerprints matching Sherry Linden at McKnight's and without bodies, like we said, the rest is real tough.'

Ray spilling: Gordon finding more links between Linden and McKnight.

'Gordon has McKnight and Linden on film in close proximity at a concert in San Francisco the last night Linden was seen alive. McKnight left right after that concert for this fair city where Sherry Linden's body turns up a couple of days later.'

A thoughtful pause, then Lackowitz said, 'You guys have been busy too.'

'Well, we had time to kill, so to speak. I was thinking of dropping all of this in your lap before I headed back to Frisco, but I wouldn't want to stick my nose in where it's not wanted.'

Lackowitz grunting.

'We'd be happy to take whatever you got. Leave it at the front desk.'

'In that case,' said Ray, 'maybe we could organise a fair exchange. What are you doing with the stuff from Davis' unit?'

'Sitting in a box here.'

'You don't need it for the trial, do you?'

'Not much use for us apart from the notebooks. Those we'll keep. Everything has been itemised. Wouldn't want it out of our jurisdiction just in case but a loan could be arranged.'

'I'll swing by tomorrow, pick it up.'

'It will be waiting for you. Been a pleasure knowing you, Ray.'

'Same here.'

The detective said, 'Kern County, hey?' Ray imagined the ironic smile on his face before he rang off.

◆◆◆

Ray called Gordon at the Clarence. Clear as the ice in Ray's bourbon, he'd been waiting by the phone for news.

'Lackowitz just called. They picked McKnight up in Bakersfield.'

'You beauty!'

Mutual admiration ran its course.

Ray said, 'You going to celebrate?'

'Might stay in, finish the book I bought.'

Ray said, 'I'm staying in too. But the only thing I'm reading is the going to be the label on the bottle.'

'We still have work to do if we're going to tie McKnight to the girls.'

'I know, but it's good to have an excuse to celebrate with heavy drinking. Speak tomorrow.'

Ray taking the liberty of stocking up his own liquor stash while shopping for Lackowitz and Burns. He headed to his room. The night was young, and the bottle was full.

Around a third of the way through it, Ray's mind drifting back to Perry. The Yanks didn't have a draft just yet, but they were talking about it. Australia one step ahead there. National Servicemen being sent off overseas. Some to Vietnam.

Ray guessed had he been the age, he would have gone without thinking about it too much. But suppose Cassie was a boy, not sure he'd want her in some godforsaken jungle. The TV news making it all seem somehow unreal, melting in with *Combat!* and *Hogan's Heroes*.

These kids were real heroes, whether you believed they should be there in the first place or not.

Ray took another sip, lay his head on the pillow. It was cool in here. Things we take for granted: phone, teledex, newspaper, dunny paper … guessed Perry had dunny paper.

Drifting now. With Perry on a canoe down the everglades or whatever you called those … mangroves.

God protect you, James.

20 JANIS

The Elysian Park film recently in possession of LAPD now in Ray's boot. It was waiting for him at Hollywood Station, the projector and screen weren't. Likely now at the home of one of the station cops.

Carol's friends Greta and Rex who had shot the film lived close by and had fixed Ray up with a loaner. Ray thanked them, headed back to the Marquis. A message to call Desmond Campbell.

'The cops interviewed McKnight this morning. Of course, he's denying everything. Said he never knew Davis and didn't kill him, left the Dolphin that night and went straight home.'

Ray wondering who the attorney's source was. Obviously, somebody in close and personal.

'They ask about the other girls?'

'Mentioned it. McKnight wasn't paying too much attention till they began to lay out where he had been at the time each of them went missing. Apparently, he turned white as a freshly washed Klansman's sheet. Main thing for me is that the case against Patcher is looking weak, and they know it. Once I get charges dropped, that'll be it for me. I won't be able to help you much.'

'That's okay.'

'At least you know you helped free an innocent man.'

Only right, thought Ray but hardly balanced those along the way he'd burned.

Thanking the lawyer, who promised to call with any more news. Not enough throw in his room for the projector, wandering back to lobby. A brunette looking like Agent 99 told him she could arrange the conference room for him. Ray settled in for his movie show.

The footage was clear, well shot, but there was no shot of either McKnight or Pauline.

♦♦♦

The traffic an asthmatic rumble. The day grey and cool leaving John flat, a guest in a seaside resort in off-season. Night people just now getting out of bed, cracking their knuckles in anticipation of new adventures under the moon, blithely unaware it was smothered by a pillow of cloud. Certainly how it played at Jenny Wallace's old pad. John walking straight in the open door.

Similar to the other share houses: faded splendour, threadbare hallway runners but the rooms huge with fireplaces, ornate cornices, bay windows. The heavy smell of dope in the early hours had curled up on the old velvet sofa in the living room and not yet left. In the kitchen, a stoned hippie lifted hooded eyes from his bowl of cornflakes, said Shelley, Jenny's old roommate, didn't live there any more. Luckier with Olivia though. She was in the shower.

Had Dope-Man been residing here with Jenny Wallace?

'Before my time.'

Music seeping down from the floor above. Something bluesy. Olivia walked through after her shower, a happy coat over a slim body, hair wrapped in a towel, long facial features, twenty-three maybe. John said he was here about Jenny Wallace.

'Has she been found?' Fear and hope an uneasy blend.

'No, but maybe there has been some progress.'

She said she needed to dress. John prepared to wait.

'Come on.' Gesturing him to follow her through the kitchen to her room.

Another big room. The bed a double on a low base, unmade, the floor a jumble of clothes. Olivia walked to a clothes rack on the window side of the room, dropped her happy coat. Naked, she tossed up the day's outfit choices. Her breasts on the small side but suited her slim body. Her muff dark and bushy. Completely unconcerned about John's presence.

He told her what he could while she slipped on striped cotton slacks and a tee-shirt. No underwear. John got to the part about McKnight, pulled out the photo.

'Yes, I've seen him around. Jenny would have seen him too. You saying he's been arrested?'

'In Los Angeles for the murder of my client, this kid.' Another photo, Martin Davis.

She was not so sure that Jenny and Davis would have crossed paths. She didn't recall him.

'We believe McKnight was abducting girls, picking them up from be-ins, love-ins. Killing them.'

'That is so fucked up.'

Smelling her vulnerability. Flowers in your hair no protection from a psycho. Asking if she would mind telling him about the last time the friends had been together.

'A bunch of us went to the Fillmore to see Big Brother and Airplane. Jenny really wanted to get to LA to see her family and catch The Doors. Begged me to go, but LA is not my kind of town. She had this idea that she could ask around at the Fillmore and probably find somebody who was heading south in a day or two.'

'She wouldn't just hitch?'

'Maybe if she was desperate but there's always somebody heading north or south. You give them some bucks for gas, or lay some weed on them, everybody is happy.'

Around about 10.00 p.m., as far as Olivia could judge, she lost track of Jenny. She never saw her again. She couldn't recall specifically who she had been talking to, but Shelley had said earlier that Jenny thought she had scored a ride. No details on who with.

'We came back in dribs and drabs. Some of us went out to parties. Some stayed in, got stoned.'

She didn't see Jenny but didn't think anything of it. Jenny was a big girl, she could look after herself.

An ironic smile. 'We didn't worry about it till Tuesday.'

Two days after. All Monday, they just figured she was sleeping it off or still partying.

'Shelley and I checked her room Tuesday, about midday. She'd had a bag packed and ready in case a ride came up. The bag was gone. We guessed she'd scored a ride, had to leave then and there.'

'She wouldn't have left a note?'

'She might have but if she was in a hurry …' Olivia rolling a joint now.

So, she could have left as early as the Sunday night. Or spent the night somewhere Monday and come back in and got her stuff Tuesday. It was only when her brother had phoned days later that they had any concern.

John promised to keep her informed if he learned more, asked her to call if she remembered anything.

She blew a big smoke ring his way. 'Peace.'

◆◆◆

Ray should have gone over to Suffolk's studio and collected the photos the photographer had said he'd print up, but a mood had descended. Most days Ray could keep that hood off his shoulders. Those early years, the screams of his parents in that fire had shaped it.

Before, when it got bad, he could always go see his brother Patrick the priest and Catholic powerbroker. One of the few things in common: hearing your parents being burned alive.

That had always bonded them, but two years back that changed forever.

They hadn't shared a word since Patrick had betrayed him.

So, nights like this when the darkness closed in, there was little you could do but shut your eyes. John Gordon had done what he knew he must if justice was to be served. They would find the killer, hold him accountable. Ray didn't enjoy killing but he wouldn't resile from it. Still, nothing was bringing the kid back.

Last night, Ray burying a whole bottle of Grandad. Now starting on a second. No. Screwing the cap back on. He wouldn't drink alone. Not two nights in a row. That was too pathetic.

Barney's. He found a stool, started slow, brooding. He didn't deserve Marie or Cassie. He should be the one being sent off to the jungle to die, not James Perry. You're supposed to leave this world better for having been in it. Ray couldn't imagine that would be the case when he checked out. Trying not to think on Janis because he saw in her all the tragic mistakes of his own life. And yet he came here to drink and pretend she hadn't been the real reason he'd picked Barney's.

And then after he'd been nursing a whiskey for the best part of an hour, there she was.

He could not fucking believe it. Like magic.

'You're in San Francisco.'

She was already several sheets to the wind.

'Ray, baby!' She hugged him like he was the most important thing in the world. She never smelled fresh. Not like other girls, soap and shampoo. Ray didn't care.

'John said he saw your show last night.'

'Uh huh. He told me about these girls. You getting anywhere?'

'Hard to say.'

Steve Wallace had given him a photo of Jenny Wallace. Ray pulled it out, asked Janis if she recognised the girl from the Fillmore concert with the Airplane. She studied it.

'I'm sorry, Ray. I hate to say it, but they all look alike in a way. All these girls. All prettier than me.'

Ray folded the photo away, asked if she'd like a Southern Comfort.

'I'll have a whole bottle.'

Ray signalled just a single shot. 'How did you get—'

'On the back of a Harley. The whole fucking way. Can you believe it? I'm supposed to be doing a HALO show tonight with the Dead and a bunch of other bands and I just thought, I'm always doing all this stuff for other people and how many of them do anything for me. Then I thought of that first night we met and how you stood up to that asshole in the liquor store ...'

Her drink arrived, she downed it, pointed for another. Ray nodded for Kostas to oblige.

She gazed into Ray's eyes like a love-struck teenager, and it made him feel warm inside like whiskey did, and he loved it.

'I just knew you'd be here,' she said and kissed him hard. He tried not to respond.

'What are you scared of Ray?'

He liked to think, nothing. That wasn't true. He was scared of losing what they'd had. Even if it was a memory, or an illusion.

Janis rubbed his thigh, said, 'We could find a rooftop like last time.'

The second drink gone in a flash.

Ray said, 'You know better than that. You can capture magic in a bottle. But only once. The next time you try that, it escapes.'

'Not if you're quick.' Getting in close, staring into his eyes, kissing him again. 'I have to be back in San Francisco for Saturday, but we could stay down here together a few days.'

Ray dodged, asked what was Saturday, a concert?

She laughed, 'I love how you call it a concert.' Mimicking a conductor.

'I'm out of touch.'

'That's why I like you. I'm out of time.'

And he wasn't quite sure what way she meant but his chest was tight, and he knew she was fragile.

'Saturday is this whole trip, the Fantasy Fair. I'm not playing but it's going to be amazing. All my friends are on the bill.'

Ray said, 'I have to tidy up this case first.'

'We never have to do anything, Scamp, you know that. We choose it. We choose our path to glory and perdition.'

And then over her shoulder like an apparition, walking in off the street on another hot LA night, a face he recognised, a young beauty with high cheekbones and a deluxe smile.

Spring.

21 NOT SO SWEET MARTHA LORRAINE

Ray blinked. Not a mirage. Then he was next to her.

'I've been looking everywhere for you, Mary-Anne.'

Certainty fleeing her smile. This guy knows my real name. Ray absorbed that in an instant.

'And who are you?' The moxie still there.

'My name is Ray. Martin Davis' parents sent us from Australia to find him.'

'Oh,' relaxing now.

Ray shooting a glance Janis' way. She was already in a throng with a cigarette in her fingers and a cackle.

'Could we sit and talk? What would you like to drink?'

She didn't seem to be with anybody.

'Sure. Tequila. But don't call me Mary-Anne.' She saluted him with the tequila, 'I've been in Mexico.' Took a sip. 'So how is Martin?'

'Martin's dead.'

Lowering the glass slow. 'When?'

'A week or so back.'

On a level of shattered where ten has the pieces all over the floor, she was a three.

'How did he …' Ray expecting 'die' but she said, '… do it.'

She thought he'd killed himself over her.

'He didn't. He was stabbed to death trying to find out who killed you.'

That blast stripping paint.

'What?' Shaking her head. Ray couldn't tell if it was because she thought that was stupid, or tragic.

Ray said, 'So you've been in Mexico?'

◆◆◆

Spring had hitched a ride to San Diego with some surfers. She had an aunt down there. But the surfers were going on to Mexico, so she went straight through with them.

'It was fabulous. Blue skies and ocean and everything so fucking cheap.'

Yeah, like life. At least so far, she hadn't been defensive.

'I met James Perry. That's why you got out of Frisco.'

Anxiety sparking in her eyes.

'Don't worry. He's left town now. He told me why he was after you ...'

Her head dropped. Shame or sham?

This time when she spoke, it was flat as a decal.

'I loved Phil. We were going to get married, get the hell out of that shitty town. That accident, it could have just as easy been me.' Meeting Ray's gaze. 'I didn't leave because he was in a wheelchair. I left because if I stayed, I was never getting out.'

'Perry said you took Phil's money.'

'He wanted me to have it.' Taking a big gulp of liquor. 'You think I'm some little bitch, judge me all you want.'

'You broke Martin's heart.'

'You got a cigarette?'

Ray didn't. She leant around to the booth behind. The guys there had no trouble finding her a cigarette and a light. She took a deep drag.

'Things were over between Martin and me only he didn't understand. Or wouldn't. It would have dragged out another week or two before he got the message. Then I heard James had come looking for me and that wasn't healthy for me or for Martin. So, I got out of Berkeley.'

'You could have sent a message.'

Shaking her head. 'Martin didn't want to hear that message. I loved Phil. I never loved Martin, but he was cute, and I wanted to ... give him a taste of some ... fucking life. But he was dependent. Like a kid. If I had got back in touch, it would only have hurt him more.'

Janis spun his way through smoke. Spring's mouth dropped open. 'Janis! I love you.'

'Thanks, honey.' She fixed Ray with a look. 'Eric Burdon's throwing a party. Come when you're free.' She pulled a biro from her bra and wrote an address down Ray's arm.

'I have to do this first.' Ray's eyes sliding to Spring. 'Then I'll come.'

Janis kissed him on the forehead and exited, one of a swirl.

'You know Janis.'

At least Spring in awe of him for something.

'Yeah.' Life is weird. You go looking for one thing, find something else entirely. 'So back to you and Martin. You decided it wasn't working out. You started looking elsewhere, like a guy named Jay in an apartment in the Tenderloin.'

She seemed impressed he knew.

'Yeah. I liked Jay. He loaned me some records for the weekend, and I thought it was like a come-on … maybe. Cause, you know you have to take them back.'

Spring taking another drag. 'I spent the Friday with Martin. He was tripping the whole time. Annie and a bunch of others were heading out of town, and I wanted to go too but I thought I better stay with Martin. And I was fucking miserable. Saturday was April Fool's Day. I'm thinking, Spring you're the fool. So, come the Monday I grabbed Jay's albums and went back to his apartment, thinking maybe we could ball. But he wasn't there. Though I did find a little jewellery for my best pal Annie on the stairs on the way out. I'm guessing you met Annie?'

'I did. Nice girl. She OD'd a couple of weeks back.'

Spring's face crumbled. Real tears. She wiped. 'She said she was off that shit.'

It might seem like a beautiful peaceful world but it's just a thin curtain. One click, and that set becomes the clinical tiles of a morgue. Ray too many hours behind the stage to be fooled.

Spring was still crying. She seemed to care about Annie a whole lot more than Martin. But at least she cared.

Ray let time crawl, said, 'You ever run into Francine Leach in San Fran?'

Spring still thinking on Annie, distracted.

'I know a Francine from back home but she's Francine Weston. Why?'

Ray ignored her. 'When did you get to San Francisco?'

'Beginning of last December.'

'You go to the first be-in?'

'No. I went to some marches in Berkeley, but I missed the be-in.'

'How about Jenny Wallace?' Ray showed the photo.

'Might have seen her around. I think so.'

'How about this girl?' Laying out the photo of Sherry Linden.

'No. Why are you asking me about these girls?'

'They are missing. Martin thought they were dead,' Ray scooping the photos back up. 'Martin thought there was a pattern and you fitted.'

Spring not one to surprise easy but her mouth gaped. Ray pressing.

'Sherry Linden disappeared after an Airplane concert at a San Francisco high school gymnasium. Her body turned up in the Hollywood Hills. That's what gave Martin the idea. And then he started investigating, I suppose you could say, and he came up with a suspect. Larry McKnight.'

'Larry? He's a sweet guy. He wouldn't harm a fly.'

'Larry McKnight is sitting in a cell for murdering Martin.'

'No.' Her body rigid as concrete.

'I'm afraid so.'

'I don't believe it. It's bullshit. The pigs are making shit up.'

'Larry seems to know all or most of these missing women.'

'So? Everybody in that scene kind of knows everybody. Martin thought he killed me, right? And here I am.'

Ray conceded.

'Let me tell you about Larry.' Spring done with her cigarette and edgy for another. 'When James turned up looking to blow my fucking head off, Larry protected me.'

'How did you learn about James?'

A shrug. 'People. They told me this guy was asking around. I knew who it was. I had to get out, but I needed to get my shit together. I went looking for Annie 'cause she knows everybody. And this was the Tuesday after that weekend with Jay's records.'

Ray in his head, April 4.

'Larry was one of the crew who had been away with Annie, and he heard that I needed to get stashed away till I could get to LA. He kind of bodyguarded me while Annie organised that place in the Tenderloin. I had to go back to Berkeley, get some things. Larry dropped me back, waited while I grabbed my stuff. Then he took me to the other house.'

'What happened when you got to Martin's? Was Martin there? Did you tell him about Perry?'

'Martin was off tripping. I didn't tell him. The less he knew, the better for him.'

'It wasn't because you'd have to tell him why James was after you?'

'Maybe that too. I'm not proud but you don't understand … that small town, if I'd have stayed, every day for the rest of my life they would have been whispering and pointing at me as the one who put Phil in that wheelchair. I packed up a few things. I stayed in the Tenderloin for a night and then I got my ass out of there.'

Ray needed a long moment to get all the stuff she'd told him straight in his head.

'You said that Annie and Larry McKnight and a bunch of other people were away for that weekend?'

'Yeah, they camped somewhere near Big Sur. I would love to have gone.'

'When did they get back?'

'Late Monday. I remember because it was after I had been to Jay's.' Boom.

If McKnight was away, then he couldn't have killed Judy Ikin on Sunday.

Ray said, 'Can you remember who else went camping on that weekend?'

Spring blew smoke, contemplated. 'I'm pretty sure a girl named Josephine – she's a silversmith, she made the necklace for Annie – and her guy Redbeard, on account of he has a red beard.'

'Where would I find them?'

'Haight-Ashbury.'

Ray said, 'Did you know a girl named Judy Ikin, lived in Jay's apartment block?'

'No.'

'She was killed in her flat. Body would have been there while you were trying to return Jay's records.'

'That's horrible. So much fucking death.'

Ray took a deep breath said, 'You need to go see Detective Lackowitz at Hollywood station.'

'Never. I want nothing to do with pigs.'

'Then you had better find out who the lawyer is for your friend Larry. He's going to need to talk to you.'

Ray asked if she had a number that he could reach her at.

'Why would you need to speak to me?'

'Girls are dead. So is Martin. You have valuable information.'

She gave him an address in the Palisades.

'I don't know the phone number. Anyway, I think I'll head back to San Francisco. There's a big music festival coming up. You're sure James has gone?'

'Yeah. Life here was too dirty for him. He's going back to the jungle of Vietnam.'

Ray checked the address Janis had written on his arm. Spring saw him.

'You going to the party? Can I come? I love Eric Burdon.'

◆◆◆

Ray parked, got out and walked to the front lawn of the house, the night losing heat the way a mother loses belief in her child, suddenly aware not knowing when it actually happened. Music from inside. Glimpses between open drapes: chicks with bangles, beads, dancing like Egyptian priestesses – well, how Ray imagined they might have been – guys with beards, different shades of skin, bongos and even from out here the smell of hooch.

Leaving Spring back at Barney's, lying he had stuff to do. He was good at lying. Especially to himself. Just a glimpse of mussed hair, Janis he was sure, spinning past like a dust storm the other side of a long window. What did he think would ever come of this? He'd never leave Marie and his child. Not ever. He could live here, he guessed. If he had them with him. What was there in Sydney for him except revenge? And once that was done what would there be left? Slippers and a pipe, Cassie on his lap, tearing open carefully wrapped Christmas presents. That felt like somebody else's dream. He hadn't earned that life so he couldn't believe in it, couldn't believe that might be reserved for him.

Why he was here, standing outside this house, no real puzzle. Tragics fit together like a detonator to TNT, can't resist the explosion. At the end of the day, if you believed in God – and somehow Ray did though he couldn't explain why – then he was heading for hell in the next life. That left only this time, these pulsing hours under a bright moon with a cool wind battering your face. This was the hand you're dealt. You knew you shouldn't be in the game dammit, but you were. You were at the table with four kings, and no, it wasn't perfect, but it was as good as you were ever likely to get. His feet started towards the house.

No one challenged him. The pad expensive, a stereogram playing some jazzy music he didn't know. Guys and chicks against walls, gesticulating, smoking. Red wine in china mugs, tumblers of tea-coloured liquor, beer bottles. Ray drifting through like thought in an asylum, stepping over, propping, squeezing past down a dark hallway. She was in the third room he passed, tying off readying for a hit, a guy with an afro and a skinny white shirtless bloke for company. He blew her a kiss from his heart.

Goodbye, baby.

22 SAN FRANCISCAN NIGHTS

The most relaxing sleep John had scored in a long while. Earned. The best part of the night chasing down anyone who could put McKnight with Sherry Linden. Tougher to crack the Airplane's inner sanctum than Big Brother.

The word: Janis doing a HALO show. John thinking she could help, but Big Brother and the Dead no-shows. John one of a hundred solemn to the sounds of those Quicksilver guitars. Drifting with them still when the barking phone roused him. A quick time check: only 7.15. Shit.

Surely not Shearer at this hour. But it was.

'Did I wake you?'

'Yes you fucking woke me.'

'Sorry.' John imagining Ray's stubble on the receiver, a sticky tumbler from the night before beside the phone. 'I met with Spring last night.'

John snapping up. 'She's alive?'

'One hundred percent. Been hanging in Mexico with surfers. And listen, from what she says, Larry McKnight could not have killed Judy Ikin.'

Ray's words slipping through John's fingers, smashing. Sweeping them back up quickly, piecing what Ray was saying: Kansas Annie, McKnight, Redbeard and his woman off camping the entire weekend when Ikin was killed. McKnight bodyguarding Spring.

John's brain working better already. Wouldn't have been hard for Martin Davis to get wind of McKnight hanging with Spring. Put two and two together, getting five.

Ray's calculation: LAPD would not follow up at all. They might only pursue a murder charge against McKnight for Martin Davis, nothing else.

John said, 'What about Martin Davis? McKnight killed him, right?'

'Spring is adamant he didn't. But what I'm thinking: he did, but it was unrelated. Davis is following him, McKnight fronts, asks him what he's doing. They fight. Davis winds up dead.'

'What about the motorcycle that James Perry saw following Martin?'

'Maybe it was just a coincidence.'

John took the hit. Figured his next move. 'I need to find Redbeard and Josephine, confirm Spring's story.'

Shearer said, 'Exactly what I was thinking.'

◆◆◆

John showering, Johnson and Johnson talcum powder, a fresh shirt. According to Spring, Haight-Ashbury the best place to shed leather looking for Josephine and Redbeard.

John scouring: coffee shops, psychedelic dungeons. A quick breakfast fix: pretzel and coffee. The coffee still burning, back on the street and a hit on Redbeard. A guy selling fringed leather jackets. Redbeard likely at the flea market two blocks over. Trawling past fob watches, Harold Robbins paperbacks, kitchen chairs, old brass.

Fifteen minutes in, spying a guy with a red beard playing a flute. John waited till the end of the long, undulating tune.

'Are you Redbeard of Josephine and Redbeard?'

'I am he.' Stagey voice.

John said, 'I thought so. You were a friend of my friend Kansas Annie. Did you know Annie was dead?'

'I heard. Real bummer.'

John playing it like it had been told to him. Saying he was real surprised she had overdosed. 'I thought she was over that.'

'Me too.'

'I was trying to find a guy she said she went away with on that trip ... Larry. He was there, right?'

'Yeah, Larry. Hangs with the Dead guys sometimes.'

'You seen him around today?'

Redbeard hadn't.

'But I've got the right guy? Biker sort. I was thinking of getting a motorcycle. I don't know any bikers. Annie, wow. She told me that it was the best weekend she had.'

Redbeard said how beautiful it was around the Big Sur. He knew a ranch where they could camp, would go about once per month. John slowly teasing it out of him. Redbeard had a van. They would all pile in, leave on the Friday and get back Monday morning as Josephine had a straight job.

John leaving with a God bless and may the fair winds blow. And the solid belief that Spring had not been lying. That was a problem.

Larry McKnight had not killed Judy Ikin.

The strength fleeing John's legs, shuffling not walking. Fuck. It had to be McKnight. Everything aligned. Only it didn't. So, maybe he was wrong about Ikin? A separate murder, nothing to do with Martin Davis.

Spring wasn't dead, she was fucking alive. So was that other girl who'd gone missing out of Santa Barbara. Maybe Francine Leach had joined the Weathermen and Jenny Wallace was on a bad acid trip in Mexico with some itinerant surfers in the Spring tradition.

John wandered into a coffee shop, ordered a cup of tea. Sick of the coffee here. Sick of the whole box and dice. He should have kicked back and enjoyed these days instead of tilting at windmills. What the fuck was the matter with him? There was a hole right through his head and heart, but it had been stupid thinking finding some nameless killer would make him whole again. There was no coming back.

The tea arrived.

Empty now, John's head no more than a beach, thoughts breaking waves, rolling in and out. Looking around at the posters, handbills stuck up in the shop. Meditation, group therapy, Buffalo Springfield, Peanut Butter Conspiracy. Swirls and flowers on pink and blue and caramel paper. His eyes drifting through plate glass to the sidewalk as the Americans called it. Bearded Angel waving his hands in some story to a Van Dyke bearded freak in a floppy hat.

What was real, what was fake? Done with plasticity. Our desires lead our thoughts down dangerous alleys.

Without permission, John's thoughts wending and bending through a crowded bazaar. Redbeard, McKnight, Janis, protests, musicians, cops, Diggers, bikers … different tribes gathering over and over in the same spaces … sometimes it was just the music. High school gymnasiums, Golden Gate …

Wham! The idea smacked into him like a blind bird.

◆◆◆

'Say again?' Ray had picked up the phone to be hit by a Sherman tank at high speed. Gordon slowing a fraction. 'I'm saying what if Martin Davis was right? He just got the main player wrong.'

Ray digesting it slow. Gordon still gabbing.

'Like we said before. Davis wanted it to be McKnight. It even makes sense: he knows McKnight is hanging around with Spring and then she goes missing. But that still leaves Leach, Linden, Wallace and Gerschaff. Four girls vanishing after these events. There must have been others who were at all those same events. We could go back over the photos, the film, anything else the fuck we can find and see if there is somebody else with the same opportunity as Larry McKnight.'

Ray testing it, no hollow sound. Be-ins, love-ins, concerts. A lot of those people were the same crowd. What Spring had said, everybody knows one another. Travel between LA and San Francisco easy. Maybe there were two or three hundred regulars. But how many had been at all those shows where the girls disappeared?

They already had a bunch of photos, some reels of film … but was this wishful thinking?

'You saw the bodies of Sherry Linden and Judy Ikin. You sure it's the same killer?'

Gordon took his time. 'I want to say no, I'm not sure. But—'

Ray finished it for him. 'Something in your gut says it's the same person as killed Linden. Me too. But I bet you LAPD won't see it that way.'

Gordon said, 'Are we being stupid?'

Ray thought probably, but the thing had its hooks in him too. He said, 'Let's go through every piece of film, photo or interview we have, see if we can find an alternative to McKnight.'

❖❖❖

Ray's first heading: McKnight / Friends, Known Associates. Gordon could follow up the San Francisco friends, but the best source would be McKnight himself. Quickest way to McKnight was Spring. The address she'd given Ray was in the Palisades. No time to waste.

He drove west to Santa Monica, cut north. Surf shacks, stilt homes, dunes and ocean. Reminded him of the northern beaches in Sydney, money blending with family beach shacks, Ray guessing Spring's new surfer pals were her hosts.

He found the place in a cul-de-sac. Spring moving up in the world. Not too fancy though, a tin water tank, parked around it a VW Kombi and Beetle. A low-level house on some grass at the foot of a cliff, a hammock strung between posts of a concrete verandah, a ping-pong set-up, the thwock of bat on ball mingling with what was left of the ocean's roar after battling this way through coast-road mufflers.

Two Murray Rose types playing, barely glancing at him.

'I'm looking for Spring.'

'Inside,' before Murray One smashed a backhand and the ball skidded off.

Over cushions on the floor, Spring in a bikini spread-eagled on her back reading a magazine.

'How was the party?' Not missing a beat, just a sideways glance from those big eyes.

'Didn't go. We need to talk.'

'I don't need to do anything.'

'You want to help your friend Larry or see him end his days in a gas chamber?' Ray sitting though he hadn't been invited. He said, 'I believe you that Larry didn't kill those girls. But somebody did. Maybe somebody close to Larry. San Francisco PD and LAPD are both gunning for him. I want you to get me in to see him.'

Spring putting the magazine down, rolling to face him. 'How am I supposed to do that?'

'Call his lawyer. I have the name here.' Tapping his pocket.

One call to a grateful Desmond Campbell had got the name, a Mr Johnson Scarsdan.

'What do I say?'

'You say you know LAPD and SFPD are gunning for Larry, and you and your friend might be able to help.'

First two attempts strike outs. Spring making Ray a cordial between flicking glossy pages. Ray drifting, ping-pong punctuating silences. Third attempt raised Scarsdan. Spring doing her bit. The lawyer said he would run it by McKnight.

Ray took the phone, told Scarsdan to call him at the Marquis.

Spring announced she was going for a swim. Good to be so young. Ray'd missed out on those slack teenage years: comics and sunbathing.

The McKnight angle underway, Ray headed back east to Suffolk's studio. Chowed down a hotdog he acquired en route.

◆◆◆

True to his word, Suffolk had the contact sheets of the Woodland Hills concert ready. He had also printed a number of photos he previously supplied the music magazines. Mainly band shots. Ray poring. No Jenny Wallace, nor for that matter, McKnight. He tried committing faces to memory anyway, especially those side of stage and backstage. He was looking for a common point, San Fran and LA. Maybe it was remote, but there had to be some chance that Jenny Wallace had scored a lift with her killer, told him about the show she was heading to LA for. Maybe her killer went to it? Could have dumped her body somewhere in between the cities, decided to go to the Woodland Hills show anyway, check out fresh kills.

Could have been working there even. Maybe Jenny made it all the way to the show and had a great time and the guy who'd given her the lift had promised to drop her at her brother's after: 'No don't tell him, keep it a surprise.'

And then she'd been slaughtered.

A lot of maybe. There was nothing Ray could see in these snaps. John Gordon had asked for a copy of the Elysian Park photos and contact sheets. Suffolk said he would send them on to the Clarence.

◆◆◆

Post his call to Shearer, John thinking his first move needed to be on Francine Leach. He had no close contacts for her, but she'd gone missing after the January Human Be-In in Golden Gate Park. The Diggers and free press should have photos of that event. Recalling when they were chasing Kansas Annie, Jay Burnley making mention of a guy at some church. John had grabbed his notebook, flicked back through pages, found it: Theo at the Glide church somewhere near Union Square.

Even from the outside, the church building was impressive. Could have been the headquarters of Mexican soldiers in one of those westerns where a bunch of American misfits extract some hot woman from the clutches of the moustachioed bad guys.

Out the back of the church itself was a big room like they use in jumble sales. All kinds of art and sculpture going on. One guy using a cut-down garden rake to smear paint over canvas – not art canvas, just canvas. A chick on a stepladder with a stiffy-inducing mini screwing lightbulbs into the mouth of a sculpture, a fish with, like, five human heads coming out of it. Maybe Country Joe? One of the heads looked a bit like him. Denise would have dug the place.

People coming and going, all looking like they had some purpose. A lot of black men and women with afros. John headed to a trestle table. A student type, glasses and pullover, hunched studying an album cover.

'Where would I find Theo?'

The guy pointing down a corridor. John passed one door, might have been some sort of prayer group. Big coloured bloke in a striped poncho with his arms out, a semicircle of bowed heads. Following the smell of ink and the mechanical repeat sound of a lever pulled over and over. Doorway two. John stuck his head in. Floor to ceiling handbills and paper, a tall blond guy, long hair and moustache, sleeves rolled up working a gestetner, another slimmer guy in a cardigan collating.

'Theo?'

The big guy said, 'Yep,' not stopping.

John said, 'I'm looking into the disappearance of some women.'

'You police?' Still pulling.

'In Sydney I am. Here I am just a stickybeak.'

Got the guy's attention. 'Go on.'

'Girl named Francine Leach, disappeared after the first be-in.'

The younger, skinnier bloke evened up a pile of bills, 'I remember Francine. She's missing?'

'Since that day. The cops never asked you about her?'

Theo said, 'They don't like coming here. What do you want to know?'

John told them: Who was at the be-in? What photos, if any, did they have? Would anybody remember Francine from that day?

Theo didn't know Francine but said they had lots of photos. 'The day was well chronicled.'

The other guy, whose name was Judd, said he was pretty sure he remembered Francine being there.

Theo stopped pulling and began to help Judd with the collating.

'You mind?' Theo pointing to a sloppy pile, John evening it up as they kept talking. Ink over his hands but fuck it. Judd couldn't remember who might have been there with Francine. 'She was very against the war in Vietnam. That was her prime focus. Some people are writers, poets, some go more for art, but she was political. Your best chance would be asking Students Against War, or Berkeley Student Action.'

Theo said, 'I can handle this, show him the magazines and photos.'

John following Judd out, waving a thank you but Theo was too focused on getting the pile square.

Judd led him past two more doorways before they turned into what was like a small library or reading room, shelves of books, stained coffee table, sofa, stray hairs.

A big corkboard with photos pinned.

'This section is all the be-in. There's a photo album somewhere.'

Rummaging through a pile of stuff. His hand triumphant with a stiff cardboard album.

'And check out these magazines.' Using the term loosely. Half of them just gestetner pages stapled, the photos more dark blobs than anything. 'I better go back. If you need help, you know where to find us.'

There wasn't much different to what he had seen already. Golden Gate Park, crazies dancing, people with flowers in their hair, a lot of glasses, turtlenecks, earnest student types. A few shots of the bands. Pigpen, Airplane … McKnight. Looking hard now for faces in the crowd. Was that Redbeard? Pretty sure it was, on the flute, and a roadie he'd seen with Nitro, at the back. Bent over the sitar on another shot, the Kraut. Studying the faces of the crowd close but John could not spy Francine. A hat that might have been Annie's but maybe not. A lot of damn hats. Students Against War. Looking very close: a couple of faces rang bells.

This was going to be near fucking impossible.

Back to Jenny Wallace's old address. The former housemate Olivia was in when he called around. Not really a surprise. Very few of this crowd seemed to work. Later in the day, bodies rolling through the hallway. In her bedroom, John a little disappointed this time she was dressed. He apologised, said he hoped he wasn't bothering her.

'No bother.'

'Can you cast your mind back to the Fillmore that last night, think if you saw Jenny with any of the people you'd normally see at those events.'

She sighed at the impossibility. The trouble was, Olivia explained, about half the people seemed to be the same ones at every event. John thinking, 'Exactly.' Asking if Olivia had any photos he could check out. She pulled open her dresser drawer, a big bunch of photos, black-and-whites and colour. No order. Going through them would take forever.

'I just shove them in there. You want you could take them, bring them back.'

'You sure?'

'Yeah.'

John thanked her. Olivia scooped handfuls into a paper bag.

Ray back poolside at the Marquis when John Gordon's call found him courtesy of a nicely packaged brunette. The news was not encouraging. Nothing so far. Ray confirmed he was in the same boat. He explained he thought McKnight was the quickest route to any alternate killer.

'Until I hear from the attorney whether McKnight will see me, it's drinking by the pool.'

Gordon trying to crack through to Jefferson Airplane.

'I was hoping Janis would help me, but I haven't been able to find her.'

'She was here in LA.' Ray fessing up. 'I saw her just before Spring showed up. Forgot to mention it. She might be back in San Francisco by now.'

Gordon said, 'I'm going to try the Winterland tonight. Byrds and Moby Grape. If we can just get one strong lead on somebody from the scene talking to one of the missing girls, it could change everything.'

Sounded like it was grinding him down. Ray knew the feeling.

'Hey. Don't quit. The fat lady has plenty of showtime left.'

About ten minutes after Gordon had called, the brunette was back with the telephone. It was the lawyer Scarsdan. McKnight would see him tomorrow. Ray smiled, the fat lady had some breath in her lungs yet.

23 PRIDE OF MAN

When the first time you interact with somebody is at ten paces of gunfire, your first impression isn't always a good one. Maybe it was the prison overalls, the bare meeting room in the LA county jail, and Scarsdan and Spring being there, but McKnight seemed a whole lot milder this time.

After McKnight and Spring had their goo-goo, you-poor-thing moments, McKnight spearing Ray.

'You trust this guy?' Asking Spring.

'I think so. But he thinks you killed Marty.'

Ray said, 'I'm willing to be convinced otherwise.'

McKnight said, 'Why do I give a fuck what you think?'

'Because LAPD and SFPD have you in the frame for a series of murders of young women and I might be able to help. I know your attorney explained this.'

A moment, then McKnight said, 'Okay. Ask me.'

'Tell me what happened with Martin Davis.'

'Nothing happened. I didn't kill the guy.'

'You didn't know he was following you?'

'He turned up a couple of times.'

'And bought drugs off you. Uppers.'

McKnight went silent. Ray looking to Scarsdan who said, 'It's okay, you can tell him.'

'Yes,' said McKnight.

'So what happened that night he wound up dead?'

'How the fuck would I know?'

Spring chimed in, 'I told you, Larry didn't kill Marty.'

Ray said, 'Do you know who did?'

McKnight shook his head. 'I came out of the bar, got on my cycle and rode to San Berdoo.'

'No weapon, no bloodstains,' put in Scarsdan.

Ray said, 'You think it's coincidence? Martin Davis is following you and he gets killed.'

'I guess,' McKnight shrugging his shoulders.

Ray asked if McKnight could tell him about San Francisco, 'When Spring asked for help.'

Would have preferred she wasn't in the room but couldn't risk McKnight clamming up. He'd already cautioned Spring on the way she was to say nothing. He reminded her now. Prompted McKnight. 'Larry?'

McKnight told pretty much the same story Spring had.

'Some psycho was trying to kill her. I wanted to help.'

Ray's radar was good. He believed him. But Ray knew his radar wasn't perfect.

Ray producing photos. First Francine Leach. 'You know this girl?'

McKnight studying. 'She looks a bit familiar but ... no. I don't know her.'

'Her name is Francine Leach. She was at the first be-in.'

'I was there but, no.'

Next photo Jenny Wallace.

'Yeah, I've seen her around, concerts and things in San Fran.'

'The Dead house?'

'Could be. I don't know her name.'

'Jenny Wallace. She was looking for a ride to Los Angeles. Last seen at the Fillmore concert on Sunday February nineteenth, Airplane and Big Brother. She wanted to come to LA for a concert at Woodland Hills.'

McKnight nodding, 'Oh yeah, Doors and Buffalo Springfield. I rode down for that.'

'How about the Airplane–Big Brother show on the Sunday, were you there for that?'

McKnight scanning his memory. 'Yes, I was.'

'And you don't remember her asking you for a ride to LA?'

'No.'

'Now think carefully here, Larry. Was there anybody at the Fillmore show who was down here a few days later. Maybe at the Woodland Hills show? Any road crew or musicians? Bikers? Have a look at these photos.'

McKnight obliged, picked out a couple of side of stage bikers.

'They are definitely in San Francisco sometimes. I'm not sure if they were at the Airplane–Big Brother gig.'

Ray noting names 'Don' and 'Sanchez'. Next photo, Pauline Gerschaff.

McKnight shaking his head. 'I don't think so.'

'Were you ever in the Garden of Allah?'

Recognition. 'Oh yeah, I got her now. Sorry, I was thinking San Fran, not LA. We got talking there. That's right. She was in some commune I think.'

'She told her friends she was going to catch up with you the next day at Elysian Park.'

'That's right. She did. We talked for a while, smoked a little reefer but I was working, helping out. Polly, right?'

Pauline, yes, likely called herself Polly.

'She disappeared after that show. Hasn't been seen since. You remember seeing her with anybody in particular?'

The lawyer paying attention now. Spring urging McKnight to remember.

'It's a while ago.'

'How about those guys you mentioned, Don and Sanchez, were they there?'

'I don't think so.'

Ray urged him to check the photos. McKnight couldn't see them there.

Ray said, 'You were at a concert in San Francisco at the Saint Ignatius High School in April. Jefferson Airplane.'

McKnight nodding, 'Yeah.'

'Did you see this girl there?' Dropping the photo of Sherry Linden.

'If I did, I didn't speak to her, I'm pretty sure.'

'You rode down to LA not long after.'

'The next day. I got some work at Santa Monica, a Doors show.'

'See anybody there you recognised from San Francisco?'

A couple of guys who'd worked the Fillmore with him. Ray got more names but not Sanchez or Don.

'What about your pal Ron? Ray thinking that it might be somebody real close to McKnight.

'Ron never leaves San Fran.'

Scrub Ron.

◆◆◆

John had been sitting there slowly sifting the photos he'd picked up from Olivia, hoping to find a face he recognised hanging with Jenny Wallace. The phone rang. It seemed early for Ray who had called first thing to say he was meeting with McKnight. John only going half-throttle on this stuff until he heard what Ray had learned. John answered the phone.

'Mr Gordon, this is Detective Will Young. Captain Spinetti said it was okay to give you a call. I caught the death of Millicent Smith who you likely know as Kansas Annie. I'm writing up the report for the coroner and you were one of the last people to speak with her. It's just a formality but if you could drop down to HQ for a statement.'

John lying, said he would be happy to.

Young said he had a mountain of stuff on today but wondered if 2.00 p.m. tomorrow suited.

John said he would see Young then. Off the phone, empty yet again. Too many young people dead.

Martin Davis, Kansas Annie, Judy Ikin.

Telling himself, 'You're a homicide detective, what do expect?' His mind drifting to his own situation then, Denise. Already pressure to start a family. Her old man would look after them financially if they wanted to go that way. Big step. And maybe then Homicide would be all wrong for him.

Back to the photos, sifting, the radio tuned to an underground station. Sometimes a thought grows in your brain without you even realising. If you work at it hard enough, you can probably trace how it got there. Like what happened to John right then, primed to be thinking of Annie because of Young's call. Some kind of Indian music jangling in his ear. That playing back to where he met Annie that first time … and the next thing you know you are looking out over a vast expanse of possibility, like those Spaniards landing in South America. Only the expansive space is just a photo. But your imagination and memories all mix in an instant and germinate an idea. And the idea, an embryo a millisecond ago, becomes real. Living, pulsing.

Flicking back through Olivia's photos, not too excited yet, still measured. After all it was just an—

And there it was. A photo of a campus lawn, or a park, and in the foreground smiling to the camera Olivia and Jenny Wallace, and there, not so far in the background, sitting cross-legged on a mat, the sitar player from the cellar. The one with the German name.

John's head ablaze. Tearing back through his notebook. Something Jill had said when they interviewed her at Earth's Eden. Found his abbreviated notes.

Pauline against the war … strongest of any of us on that … Then they started playing sitars …

Another image flashed: Martin Davis' butcher's paper. The Human Be-In in January, the first disappearance, Francine Leach. He was certain there had been a photo of that pinned on Martin Davis' butcher's paper that showed the sitar player. Rifling through his memory from the church yesterday. There were photos of musos, Redbeard, he was sure, and he was pretty certain that the sitar player … trawling for the name … Ernst somebody. Setting the solid blocks down: Ernst was on the spot for Wallace, Leach and Gerschaff. He could easily have come in touch with Judy Ikin at one of those war demos that went south. That only left Sherry Linden.

◆◆◆

The cellar closed: a sign, *Open 4 p.m.* Still more than an hour off but figure some staff would be here. John banged on the long wood panels. Gave it ten seconds, pounded again. Heard bolts drawn. A Troy Donahue haircut wearing a neckerchief stood there waiting for a good reason.

'Sorry man. The sitar player Ernst ...'

'Deiger.'

'Yeah. I need to find him quick.'

'Why?'

John spinning, 'The pigs grabbed a chick he knows. She asked me to get him to the station.'

Troy understanding gave John an address that meant nothing to him.

'On the border of Chinatown,' Troy explaining.

John effusive, flashing a peace sign.

John drove, finding a park tough. The hydrant might be pushing it. Found an alley with other vehicles passing illegal time, joined the queue. Checking his Smith & Wesson, slipping it behind his waistband, shirt covering. No plan yet.

He strode down the street, found the building. Took a deep breath. He should ring Shearer. He found a payphone but couldn't get it to work, told himself he'd tried.

◆◆◆

The building was old and the entrance dark. Deiger third floor of a walk-up, narrow staircase and low-watt bulb. It was the closest flat to the landing. No bell, John knocked, still calculating the chances of Deiger being in when the door opened. Maybe six-one, flared, light cotton trousers, drawstring not buttons, tie-dyed tee-shirt, a wispy Scandinavian beard and moustache that was either new or so light John hadn't noticed it before.

'Hi, my name is John. You're Ernst?'

'Last time I checked,' a smile, German accent but not so heavy. From the flat, Indian music on low.

'I'm a huge fan and I just ... wanted to know more about the sitar, and you. I'm sorry turning up at your door.'

'Hey, John, we are all neighbours of the universe, all brothers in love. Come in.'

Stepping back. John entered a mid-sized, one-room flat with bathroom-toilet right there at the entrance. Deiger closed the door lightly behind. It was clean, reasonably neat. No bed visible, just a thick exercise mat like they used to have at the school gym, a colourful blanket over it. There was a small kitchen table and two chairs against one wall. A tape was rolling on a flat Grundig tape-recorder on the table. Deiger said he was having a juice.

'Would you like one?'

'Please.'

The fridge also sparse but neat. Eggs, some vegetables. Deiger pulled out a carton and poured what looked like apple juice. John scanned the room quickly; posters, an African mask or two, a wardrobe and small bureau. Either of those could hide shit.

'I like to sit on the floor,' said Deiger and gestured.

John faked a smile, sat on some kind of beaded mat, the gun poking into his spine, bloody uncomfortable.

'So?' Deiger with that enlightened smile that was a cross between smug, stoned and salesman.

John offered, 'First time I saw you was I think the Human Be-In.'

Deiger nodding.

'And then, maybe it was at an Airplane–Big Brother show at the Fillmore. Weekend after Valentine's Day. I mean, you weren't playing but I was there with some friends, and I think they know you, so I recognised you.'

'Who are they?'

'Some chicks. Shelley, Olivia and Jenny.' Studying Deiger's face, his brow wrinkling.

'Maybe I know them by sight.'

Or maybe you're being coy, checking me out.

'But I couldn't believe it, I went to LA for the Easter love-in and you were there too.'

'That was beautiful, wasn't it? The energy was so uplifting.'

'Mind-blowing.'

Deiger looked John right in the eye. 'Do you play guitar?'

'I wish. I'm no good ... I mean, I've never tried ... triangle in primary school, that was about it. But I thought I'd like to learn guitar and then I see you with the sitar and it just blows my mind. It's so ...'

'Free,' suggested Deiger.

John's turn to nod, 'Unencumbered.'

Deiger smiling, 'I like that. That's San Francisco, right, the energy?'

'Absolutely.'

They both smiled.

Deiger sipped, said, 'Well, John, the sitar is a complex instrument. In all humility, I say it is far harder to play than guitar or even violin. It is not something you can learn by yourself. You would need a teacher.'

'Have you ever taught anyone?'

'No, but it is an intriguing thought.'

John asked where Deiger had learned. He replied he had spent three years in India.

'I went there for meditation initially. I am from Bavaria and there they are mainly interested in soccer and beer. Are you a Christian?'

'Raised as one.'

'Me too. Christianity is wonderful. It's just the Christians who are a worry.' Laughing at his own joke, John joining in.

Ernst serious. 'But it is a fine foundation and philosophy. It helps embrace many other philosophies and this ... fluid nature ... is important I think if you want to learn sitar. The musician does not play the sitar, the soul does, the deepest innermost person. If you have shit in your body, you won't be able to play.'

'No drugs?'

'Natural drugs, yes.'

'Sex?'

'It makes it more difficult. Abstention is preferable.'

'You're kidding me. Man, I see you, you have chicks hanging off you.'

Hoping he wasn't laying it on too thick. Deiger with an indulgent smile.

'You want to learn the sitar to get the chicks, John?'

'Well, one or two I wouldn't say no to. There's this chick I knew, I haven't seen her around lately, Sherry. You must remember her. She doted on you, man.'

Deiger shaking his head. 'I'm not sure.'

'Yes, you were talking with her. She was about to go to LA. It was at an Airplane and Springfield concert at a high school here. Early April.'

'I think you smoke a little too much reefer my friend.'

John pushing it. 'No, I'm certain. It was, hang on … the day of my brother's birthday, April seventh.'

Deiger said, 'Sorry to disappoint you. That whole week I was in Oregon and Seattle.'

'I swear you were here.'

Deiger getting up, heading to the bureau behind John. John spinning on his arse, his hand back under his shirt, resting on the butt of the gun. The bureau had a pull-down wooden lid that could act as a writing desk. John couldn't see what was there. Deiger reached in.

'I think you will take this as proof …'

The droning music seemed suddenly louder, John's forehead swollen, his finger curling around the trigger. If Deiger turned quick, John would draw and fire. But Deiger stayed facing away and his right hand shot up waving a handbill.

'Here.'

He turned with a grin on his face. John did not relax his hand. Yet. Deiger slapped the handbill in John's lap. It proclaimed *Ernst Deiger at the University of Oregon April 5–7*.

'This is a sign you smoke too much hooch, friend.'

◆◆◆

The meeting with McKnight had not cleared Ray's confusion. The guy's insistence he hadn't knifed Martin Davis was understandable. Ray had seen a hundred such similar denials by arseholes guilty as sin. But McKnight readily admitted he had been at concerts with the missing girls.

Maybe he knew Ray had him dead to rights on Pauline Gerschaff, but he certainly hadn't dodged having met her at the Garden of Allah. Nor had he taken the easy way out: 'remembered' alternative suspects at events that would spread suspicion away from him.

So now Ray was even wondering if it were possible that McKnight hadn't murdered Martin Davis. The attorney had told him that the police had found no murder weapon or bloodied clothes in the house. Okay, the murder weapon he could have tossed, but James Perry had followed McKnight all the way to San Bernadino and had not mentioned him stopping anywhere. Perhaps he got no blood on him, it was as simple as that? An efficient killer. Or maybe Davis was in the wrong place at the wrong time? Somebody killed him for his money and his camera, and McKnight was the patsy?

Back at the hotel, Ray tried John Gordon. He wasn't in, Kitty was.

'So when are you coming back my way?' she purred.

'I'm hoping in a day or two. Don't worry we've got plenty of time to catch up after that. When did John go out?'

'This morning. I'll leave a message under the door that you called.'

'You're an angel.'

'You better believe it.'

Ray wishing he had Kitty there right now. What he had was a whiteboard with stuff over it. He went back to Martin Davis' notes. Some he could now embellish with what he and Gordon had discovered, some he was still behind where Davis got to.

Ray stared hard, poured himself a bourbon, stared some more.

He took the dead and missing women one per time. He sought them in other photos, other concerts. He looked for strangers' faces common to more than one concert. He drew a timeline as to where his killer had to be if he was responsible for all those dead and missing women. He made notes on what the murder weapon might be, started thinking about how you would transport it. The blade seemed deep, a stretch to hide it under your jacket if you were riding a cycle. Options: The killer had another location where he killed. Then he dumped the body. Could you do that on a motorcycle? Tough, a car would make it easier. But then Judy Ikin had been killed in situ, killer needed nothing but a blade for that.

He tied himself in knots. Tried to untangle them with more booze. He lay down on the bed. He'd always dreamed of a Viking funeral. Somehow this mattress was now his boat carried on the river's rhythm. He was dead. The funeral pyre built beneath him. He didn't care, through the flames, Valhalla.

Then he heard them just faintly, the screams. Sweat broke out on his forehead. He thought he had buried those screams. But they were phantoms. You rid them no more by firing a bullet through their heart than you did by sticking a needle in your arm. But we are what we are.

The hippies were dancing around him in the park. Young women, whose faces he knew as if they were his sisters. Francine, Judy, Sherry, Jenny and Polly. Martin Davis smiling at him, still young enough to have angry skin. They were hushing him, but his heart was jabbering into his ribs. The screams.

'It's okay, Ray, they are dead. They are with us. Don't fight it.'

Ray smiled up at Davis, in on the joke. Right on, baby, light my fire.

24 NIGHTS IN WHITE SATIN

Deiger a complete wash. An hour sitting on the fucking uncomfortable mat only to be kicked in the face by your own expectations. It hadn't been just the Linden murder that didn't play. Deiger had been in Philadelphia when Judy Ikin had been murdered. John should have called Shearer right away, confessed he was having doubts they were anywhere near to being on the right track. Nothing had panned out. Maybe the whole idea was dumb and all they would achieve was to get McKnight to walk.

He drove towards the water, parked. Night fell as he brooded. He got out, started walking, strangers passed in a blur. He was an alien in this city. The wharf came and went, fishing boats rising on a small swell. He cut back.

Years ago, as a kid he'd bought a cheap comic, Gordon and Gotch, one of those that cost a shilling. Weird tales. The one that got him was *Fisher's Ghost*. The ghost of a dead man sitting on a railing pointing to a paddock where his body was then uncovered, and his killer exposed and charged. With each approaching stranger, now John expected Judy Ikin, Sherry Linden or Martin Davis, and in their eyes, disappointment, contempt. He had failed them.

Even when they passed, not phantoms after all but flesh and blood people, it did not scrub away the residue of guilt. John found himself climbing into the Mustang, cruising slowly to the hippie kingdom.

Nothing on at the Fillmore. He found a park around Haight-Ashbury, started walking. Coffee shops and bars still open. The smell of incense and weed powerful. His feet dragged him back towards the cellar. As he passed a coffee shop, folky music punching out, he caught a glimpse: Nitro sitting back with some girls and musician types.

'Hey!' Nitro shared a prison-style shake.

John pulled up a chair, started thinking about Nitro. Has he been at most of the concerts? Kind of person with the opportunity. Somebody poured red wine from a flagon.

John said, 'Were you in LA for the love-in down there at Easter?'

'No man.'

He could be lying. 'How about the be-in here in January?'

'Back then I was still in Texas. Monica was though, right?'

The chick to Nitro's right nodded, said, 'It was happening. You could taste the love.'

John shrank. Fuck, was he going to suspect every person in San Francisco now? His brain kicked in, remembering something.

'Monica. You wouldn't be Kansas Annie's friend?'

'Yea, that was a bummer with Annie.'

John said, 'Am I right you met up with Martin Davis, Spring's guy, in Los Angeles?'

'Yea. I ran into him at the Bowl. He was on this whole dark trip about Spring being kidnapped or something.'

John buzzing. 'He mention anybody he suspected?'

'No. Just rambling. We were going to get together. He was over in Silver Lake. But he was laying this heavy shit. I steered clear. I didn't need that vibe.'

'But you spoke to Annie about it. I was looking for Davis. She told me her friend was going to ring back. I'm guessing that was you.'

'When I got back here, I told Annie I'd seen him in LA. She asked if I had his address. He'd given it to me, but I couldn't find it. I rang her the night she died. I was probably the last person spoke to her. Sad.'

Guilt kicking in, John wondering if Annie had decided to celebrate the news before heading out.

'At least she lived in style,' said Nitro.

But she didn't die in style, thought John. A flash of the apartment, her body. John's mood plunging south. The other girl with Nitro, freckly with long strawberry-blonde hair reached across resting her hand on his thigh, maybe reading that.

'Wanna trip?' she said, opening her mouth to show a pill on her tongue.

The music, the waft of reefer, the soft moonglow on the streets of San Francisco.

What harm could it do?

◆◆◆

Ray woke cold and stiff. A marble, sculpture, two roaming eyes. The room was dark. A clock clanked. He turned to it, one of those black rectangular ones with red and white hands and no numbers, just longer lines for three and nine. Fuck that. Give him the old-fashioned alarm sort where the bell hops up and down and you slam your palm down to shut it up. Took him time to focus, then do the geometry on the clock face and work out it was around a quarter to four in the morning.

What woke him wasn't the cold but an idea, must have been hiding back there behind the drapes in his mind, wormed out by alcohol and those Suffolk pics. The idea had tried to wriggle away with the distraction of consciousness, but Ray had it by its tail and would not let go. Laying it on its back, turned a spotlight on its face.

What if McKnight didn't kill Martin Davis? What if it wasn't just bad luck either. What if it was deliberate, the killer stalking Davis because Davis was a threat?

Playing with that: say somehow the killer learns Davis is chasing this thing down. Sure, right now he has the wrong target, McKnight, but sooner or later Davis may see the error of his ways. And he may start to look wider.

And he may start to look at me, thinks the killer.

It plays.

How does the killer find out that Davis is on to something?

Well, simplest way would be Davis fronts the real killer and says, 'I think there is somebody out there abducting girls and killing them. I think it's Larry McKnight.' Or word just filters back somehow. Face it, Davis is asking everyone in sight. Steve Wallace is talking, Jill and the Eden crowd too. Any of them might drop it in conversation. Then if I'm the killer, what do I do when I hear this?

What if I know he's surveilling McKnight? Then I get an idea: I could kill him, let McKnight take the blame. Or simpler: I'm just watching Davis, waiting for my opportunity to strike. What if I follow him to the biker bar? I kill him, McKnight's arrest is a happy bonus.

A bell shrieked in Ray's head. James Perry had mentioned a motorcycle that had moved off after Davis. Ray's focus up until now had been whether that was McKnight, but what if it was the killer? It put the killer on a motorcycle. Well, that wasn't such a long shot. McKnight mingled with bikers. They were everywhere: at the Fillmore, Golden Gate Park, even Berkeley. Certainly LA. Martin Davis might have approached one of those bikers and asked them about McKnight. Did they see him with a girl from San Francisco? Maybe it was stupid. But then again—

The attorney that Martin Davis had turned up, Des Campbell, had been going to see if his client John Patcher had heard a motorcycle the night before he found Sherry Linden's bracelet up in the Hollywood Hills. Ray hadn't followed up. Patcher had mentioned a van. Of course, they didn't have to be exclusive. Easier to dump a body from a van. Killer could own both, bike and a van.

Ray went to the bathroom, took a piss, still inspecting his new idea. He showered, redressed in slacks and a polo shirt. Too early for the calls he needed to make. He slipped out of the hotel, started walking the streets, the air clearer than it would be in an hour or two. Nobody much about, maids, Latino mostly, hustling off to wealthy employers in Beverly Hills. That hunched look people get when they work as a servant. He shook his new idea again, listened carefully.

Martin Davis is wrong about Spring. She's not dead. He's wrong about McKnight. He didn't kill anybody. But he's right that young women who have been at these gatherings in San Francisco or LA are being preyed upon. Davis is going to ask everybody in those circles. The killer hears about it, kills him. Removes his diary and camera. Did that mean the killer had to be LA-based? Not necessarily.

By the time Ray was back in the room, it was near 7.00 a.m. He didn't want to call and maybe wake Gordon, wondered if it was too early for Hector. Nah, Hector was a tough old bird who'd worked hard his whole life. He wouldn't be indulging in sleep. Ray dug through his wallet for the number. The phone was answered on the second ring.

'Hector Jiminez speaking.'

'Hey Hector, it's your Sydney mate, Ray.'

'Hey Ray, how you doing?'

'Doing a lot of scotch my friend.'

Hector laughed. Ray apologised if he woke him. Hector said he'd been up since 5.00 a.m.

'My bones don't need a lot of rest.'

Ray got down to it. 'Hector, the night Martin was killed, we had a witness who said there was a motorcycle seemed to start up and go right after him. You mentioned you noticed a strange motorcycle hanging about in your street.'

'Yes, a motorcycle. I did. Maybe even the day before, cruising up and down the street, slowing near my house. I am thinking maybe one of Martin's friends. I am coming back from my neighbour's.'

This was good. Ray reined himself in though.

'It wasn't white, was it?'

'No. Not white, black.'

'Do you know the make of the motorcycle?'

'No, Ray, I don't remember it that well.'

Strike one.

'Did you see the rider's face?'

'No, he is wearing a helmet.'

Strike two.

And just as Ray was getting ready for the umpire's call …

'But I remember one thing. The rider's helmet. It is like an American airplane.'

He'd lost Ray. Ray had to ask what he meant.

'That picture they paint on the planes, a star with red, white and blue wings.'

Now Ray knew what he was talking about. The air force symbol.

'That picture was on the helmet.'

They talked a little longer. Ray asked if Hector would mind canvassing his street to see if any neighbours remembered the motorcycle. Hector was happy to oblige. Ray buried the receiver in its cradle. He had the feeling he had seen something recently … What was it? He began replaying his recent days in reverse. Nothing at the Palisades, or Barney's, before that. McKnight's? No. Later.

It was the smell that started to lead him, like he was blindfolded. Pine needles and salt air. Coast. But not the heat of Venice … cool … dusk … Gotcha! The Earl Warren Showground in Santa Barbara. A Harley in a row of bikes, the tank painted like in those old war-photos they did with fighter planes, shark's teeth. A helmet hooked on the bar. With the air-force logo? Ray thought so. A new idea. Find the cycle, find the rider. Ray almost frenzied now. Shortest distance between two points, a straight line. Look for the McKnight photos.

Flicking through with card sharp speed, discarding misses with a backhand flick, photos raining over the room. There. Side of stage, rows of motorcycles. Elysian Park. The same Harley panhead with the helmet sitting on the pillion.

◆◆◆

Ray surprised that Suffolk the night owl would be up this early.

'What's up?'

'There is a photo of a motorcycle you took at Elysian Park. I can't read the number plate even with a magnifying glass and I need to. Can you blow it up enough so I can?'

Suffolk said he could try.

'You can't be sure how clear it will come up, but I've got equipment at my studio.'

'I need it yesterday.'

'After eleven.'

Ray thanked him, an eager virgin after a girl let him get to first base.

'So you're not finished,' said the photographer.

'You're never finished,' said Ray. He hung up, thought about calling Scarsdan, McKnight's attorney, but realised he wouldn't be in at the office yet. If McKnight knew that cycle, it could be all they needed.

Ray dialled the Clarence. Gordon wasn't answering. Ray studied the hard-to-read clock till it was almost 9.00 a.m. He called and got Scarsdan, said he needed to know if McKnight knew the owner of a particular motorcycle and described it. Scarsdan said he'd try and get an answer by noon. Too early to go to Suffolk's studio yet. Time on his hands. The cycle had been at Elysian Park. He decided to try Earth's Eden again.

◆◆◆

Jill was stewing apples on the stove. Otherwise, nothing seemed to have changed: a guy slumped in the lounge room, the stereo playing Beatles. Ray surmising the couple were still humping under the deck. Jill wore a green-and-orange sari. Sun streaming through the window revealed she wore no underwear, arousing Ray. This surprised him but he felt no guilt.

'I don't remember seeing that motorcycle. Maybe Mort?'

Ray tried everybody else in the place who was compos. Nobody could remember the bike or the helmet. Jill made him an instant coffee and they sat in the garden among flowers matching her sari, and bees. Ray felt he owed her. 'They have Larry McKnight, but my partner and I aren't convinced he is the killer.' He gave his reasons.

She took his left hand and held it between her palms.

'I'm feeling your energy,' she explained.

Ray tried not to ogle her breasts beneath the thin material. She closed her eyes. The sun beat down on her face.

'There is a darkness in you. But the light is trying to force its way in.' She opened her eyes. 'You have to give it a chance, Ray.'

Only, Ray was thinking: I let the darkness out, I become a sitting duck for everybody in the world who wants to get me.

'Why won't you let go?' she asked, earnest.

'I need its strength,' said Ray.

'Light gives strength too.'

'Not for the kind of work I need to do.'

'Be careful, Ray. The darkness I saw is like a storm and if you are not careful it will claim you too.'

◆◆◆

Ray hunched over the table at Suffolk's studio. The photographer had an album playing, more distorted guitar. Tambourines.

Ray said, 'You think that's a zero or a six?'

Suffolk had been right. Even though it was blown up, the registration plate was tough to read. A magnifying glass didn't make it that much easier.

'Hard to tell. I think a six. Maybe. Shit, I don't know. The trouble is the Folsom Prison inmates make these plates. They're not space age.'

Ray could check for both a zero and a six, he supposed. Though how, he hadn't quite worked out. He scooped the large print. 'What do I owe you?'

'On the house.'

Ray thanked Suffolk, said hopefully he wouldn't need to call on him again.

'No problem. It's kind of … I want to help.' Off Ray's look he said, 'I feel like we have a special opportunity here to change the world. And I'm part of that, recording it. I think someday somebody might look back on these photos and say, wow, they're like the new Founding Fathers. Idealist, huh?'

'Nothing wrong with that.' Even if Ray couldn't subscribe.

'If there is some asshole out there killing these women. That goes against everything this movement has been about. I hope you get him.'

◆◆◆

No word from Gordon all yesterday, nor so far today. Ray rang Kitty, shot the shit. She hadn't seen him since yesterday morning. Ray telling himself no need to worry. Probably out late, tired, or off early hunting. He asked if she could poke another message under his door.

'Consider it done.'

Turning his attention to how to get a trace on that cycle numberplate without involving LAPD. Once they knew what he knew, his options would be limited. He was about to call his old pal Desmond Campbell, see if he had a contact in whatever motor registry they had in California. Then he remembered. Pulling the card from his wallet, looking at the work number that had been scribbled down, calling.

Answered on the first ring. 'Garage.'

'I'm looking for Ross, the Australian kid.'

The phone thumped into some hard surface. Whoever had answered yelled 'Ross!'

A moment later an Australian accent. 'Hello?'

'Ross, it's Ray from Barney's.'

Ross was pleased to hear from him. Ray got to it. He needed to trace a licence plate, could he help?

As a matter of fact, he could. The cops would come in and were always checking up about some plate or other. He'd got to know a few of them.

'Don't tell them it's for me. If they ask, say you saw a hot chick riding this motorcycle.'

Ross said he understood. Ray explained he wasn't that sure of one of the digits so he'd be grateful if he could get the two options.

'Do my best, mate. Call me back around four this arvo. I reckon

I'll have something by then. Might even be able to get the driving record.'

Ray said that would be magic.

The hours passed slowly. Out to the pool, another check of his case notes to see what he might be missing. Around 3.00 p.m., Scarsdan called to say McKnight thought he'd seen a motorcycle like Ray had described, painted like a fighter jet, but he couldn't be sure when or where.

'It's not anybody he hangs with.'

Damn.

◆◆◆

Four p.m. on the dot Ray champing at the bit, dialling Ross back.

'You got a biro? Here you go,' said Ross.

The two names meant nothing to Ray. One address was in Simi Valley, the other Santa Barbara. Click. The Earl Warren Showgrounds, the fighter-jet cycle in a row at Santa Barbara. The owner of the motorcycle was a Leslie Purcell, born 1922.

'Bonzer,' said Ray. 'Beers on me.'

But even as he spoke, he was thinking about his gun.

25 I HAD TOO MUCH TO DREAM LAST NIGHT

John's head had been put in a cement mixer then reattached. Shit. Last night was there, yet not. He remembered his body being in geographical spaces: the beaded curtain, half-naked women writhing to music in some basement party. Nitro through a fish-eye lens. Later, the park, bongos at a zillion miles an hour, kaftan twirling, flagon wine. He'd driven back here, the lights a rainbow. Buzzing till God knew what time. Exploring some theory in his head that everything was related if you could just trace it through. What had happened back in Australia to Denise and him was to prepare him for the task at hand. What that task was though was elusive. He had jotted something in pencil on his notepad, in the dark, the letters skewiff: *The cycle will be complete*. Whatever the hell meant.

A note under his door. He staggered up and slit open the envelope. *Ray called. Chasing something. Call him a.s.a.p.* Guilty, yesterday's message to do the same ignored on the night table. He buzzed reception, his tongue spastic. Lucky it was the young guy, not Kitty. Didn't want her to know his state. He called the Marquis, Ray wasn't in. John didn't bother to leave another message. He looked at the time. 1.33 p.m. Remembered with a jolt he was supposed to be meeting Detective Young downtown.

Making it going on twelve minutes late, overly careful on the drive, praying he had no flashback. Some guy named Owsley had been the magician last night. They all bowed to him, begged for the magic under his cape. John wanting more. Nitro or someone putting a hand on his arm, shaking their head, 'Not this time.'

Just as well.

No accidents on the way, a bonus. He dragged himself out of the car, let the sun roast him. The big building familiar now. Young had told him to take the stairs to the third floor. John knowing the Yanks counted the ground as one. Familiar territory; the ring of phones, curses. A fat D pointed him towards Young, a solid-built young redhead, Celtic skin, strong handshake. Light streamed in through a tall, dirty window. He waved off John's apology for being late, led him to a cheap desk.

'Thanks again for coming in. We get thirty of these overdoses a week and they all have to be logged, especially when there's no one else around. Coroner needs it official.'

John sat on a plastic chair with steel legs. The sort with a scooped seat. Young's chair didn't look any better. There was an old typewriter in front of him.

'The report if you're interested.' The cop shovelling over a bound report.

John half read it, flipped through the black and white photos. The scene as he remembered it. Annie lying on the floor, stone cold dead. Checked the close-ups. Lying on her side, her sloping neck, the line of her arms, she could have been sleeping. Wished he could will her back to life. But you never can. I hope it was worth it, Annie.

Young said, 'Let's get this shit done.'

John gave his name, date of birth. Young supplied the relevant dates and time, asked when John had last spoken with Annie. John related how Annie had called him at the Clarence, told him she would see him at the Fillmore that evening.

'How did she sound?'

'At that time she sounded unimpaired. Of course, she never showed up at the Fillmore.'

And I never called in and found her body and made an anonymous call.

Young typed, showed John where to sign.

'Family claim the body?' John signed with a vicious stroke. Angry at Annie.

'They were from Kansas. They drove to pick her up from the morgue and take her back. Kids never think of that. It's all about the buzz. Poor parents left to clean up the mess.'

◆◆◆

Ray hit Santa Barbara in the hour when light softens, and flowers start to smell. Purcell's neighbourhood reminded him of a dozen back home, California bungalows feeling their age, good size blocks. A suburb past its prime but no invalid: young families with second-hand bicycles, older originals who'd never moved.

A couple of more recent ranch homes in patches, but in Purcell's neck of the woods it was a cluster of like-minded bungalows. A few with freshly painted concrete paths, new woodies in a carport, more with browning lawns and a tangle of side foliage. Purcell's one of these, two thirds along, a couple of big willow-style trees shading the verandah, making the place darker than most. There was no sign of a motorcycle out the front. Ray drove slowly, he'd take one look then park a block away. At the end of the street, he turned right, wondering if there was a lane for garages at the back of the property, but it seemed the houses just bordered those behind with picket fences or hedges. Assume then that Purcell wasn't home.

Fifty yards up the street, just after the next intersection, he parked. Plenty of space in drowsy suburbia. If he had to get out of Purcell's in a hurry, he could scale the back fence, run left and be at his car pronto. He left the car and walked back to Purcell's street, Hacienda. What he was looking for was an old person. Two houses in, an elderly gent wearing a cap kneeling in his front garden with a can of bug spray.

'Giving it to them suckers?'

The old fellow looking up, flaky skin, sunburned nose. 'Doing my darndest.'

Ray said, 'Don't know if you can help me but I'm looking for a motorcycle, painted like they used to paint those fighter planes in the war. I saw it and my friend said it was around here somewhere.'

'Two doors up.' The old boy pointing.

'Don't suppose you know the fella's name?'

'Purcell. Trying to think of his first name but I struggle a bit nowadays. There were two boys. One was killed in the war. The older boy. John Purcell was their father. They bought into this street when I did, back around thirty-two.'

'The parents are no longer with us?'

'No siree. John died about the time President Kennedy was killed. He and the boy with the motorcycle both used to work at the Air Force base, Camp Cooke. The boy still does, though it's called Vandenberg now.'

Ray thinking, that's why he has the motorcycle and helmet like that.

'Valerie, John's wife, she died around two years back.' Blasting a bug with a sharp hard pump.

Ray thanked the man for his time, sauntered towards the Purcell house, turned up the path. By the time he reached the porch, the trees afforded cover.

The door was on the left-hand side of the house with a little portico, so from the street he was hidden as he knocked. He tensed. The revolver was in his pocket, ready in case. Silence within. He knocked again, louder this time. If Purcell was in, Ray would make out like he had the wrong house.

Still no response.

The door lock looked standard. Ray drew his master keys, slid one in, jiggled. The door gave.

◆◆◆

He took a step inside and closed the door ever so softly. Stood in the small entranceway, ears straining. Only the hum of a fridge somewhere. Cooler and dark here. He moved, a quick glance at the lounge room on his right, the blinds pulled almost the whole way down but his eyes growing accustomed. First rule, establish an exit.

Ray walked down the short hallway. The first room to the left a bathroom. The window the old narrow casement type with a vertical arm when shut. No easy escape. A bedroom to the right, probably used to be the parents'. Next on the left, another large bedroom, would have been the boys' room. To the right another bedroom, smaller, a guestroom doubling as a sewing room maybe. There was still a machine on top of a dresser.

The hallway ended in a good-size kitchen. Dirty. Pans and plates left in the sink. A few others forlorn in a plastic dishrack, empty beer bottles on the formica table, scummy tumblers, an ashtray full of butts. The fridge the shuddery kind. A doorway and step led through to a laundry and general storage area, easy access to the backyard through a wooden door, long key sitting this side in the lock. Ray opened the door, his escape route. The backyard wasn't quite as big as most Australian ones. There was a concrete apron and a shed to the left before a tangle of shrubs and unruly weeds hid most of a back wooden fence.

Moving quickly now, Ray headed back inside past a cheap print hung on the hallway wall, some beach scene. The main bedroom first. No idea when Purcell might be back. The bed was made, but even beyond the impregnated tobacco odour, the room smelled, needed airing. A stack of *Playboy* magazines on the floor by a night table, another ashtray and more butts. Boots, and socks sprawled on the floor. The wardrobe was walnut, good quality once. Ray flipped it open. Shirts, jeans, a worn suit. He sifted pockets for handbills or stubs, got gum and coins. He pulled out drawers. Underwear, a few ties. Searching the drawers closely for something, anything that could point to the girls, Purcell a killer. Cufflinks, a watch that had died, nail-clippers, an old cigar box. He gave up, checked under the mattress for money or weapon. Clear. No diary, a generic calendar on the back of the door. He checked the dates. Easter marked loud and clear. Pauline Gerschaff taken Easter Saturday.

Tingling all over now as he moved next to the lounge room, the big front room that faced the street. A nice old dining table that looked rarely used. A phonogram. Ray flicked through records, Sinatra, none of the hippie stuff. Not even Beatles. Sepia-tinted photos all over a mantlepiece. Going back a way, family shots. Dad with thirties hair swept back, Californian Poppy basted, a wide tie. Mum looking like a million other mums, two boys, here about twelve and ten. A war photo, bare-chested soldiers somewhere in a Pacific hellhole, dog tags on gaunt chests. Ray picking out both boys, a sergeant with an open shirt, arms around their shoulders, a samurai sword in his fist, another soldier with a Jap's hat, desert flap at the back, pretending he was bayoneting something, face screwed in a scream – maybe '*Banzai!*'. A portrait shot of mum just south of forty. Ray scanned for a phone. Not in this room.

He went back to the hallway. There it was near the front door. Intent on establishing an exit he'd walked straight past. The phone perched on a phone book. No teledex, but there was a pad and biro, just fitting on the table beside the phone. He tried to read the notes, but the hallway was too dim, so he took the pad and headed back to the kitchen where there were open venetians. Scribbles, doodles of planes and motorbikes, on the front of the pad. He flipped a couple of pages of numbers, names of bars. Wondering should he take it with him? Checked the back cardboard base where he himself habitually jotted down stuff in a panic.

Motherload.

In biro, *31 Carmino*. Hector's address. The rumble of a motorcycle broke that thought into a thousand pieces. Ready to step straight out the back, torn. The pad missing might alert Purcell. Valuable time wasted. Ray moved quickly up the hallway. From here could hear the bike-stand kicked out. He put the pad down, turned to go. It fell. Picked it up, replaced it. Boots on their way now. Ray's hand closing over the butt of the revolver as he moved swiftly down the hall. In the kitchen when he heard the front door give. Through to the laundry. The boots following, aiming straight for the kitchen, odds on. Ray out the back door, easing it shut, hoping Purcell would think he hadn't locked it.

He sprinted, his foot snagged, pitched him onto thin grass. A hose and sprinkler. Shit. Righting himself. If Purcell opened the door, he'd spy him before he made the fence. A woodpile, a chopping block, too low for concealment.

The shed.

Ray headed for it. A bolt, padlocked. Fuck. Hands full, a choice, gun or keys? Ray slipped the revolver back, pulled out keys. One shot at it. He guessed right. The padlock sprang, Ray slid the bolt, eased the door open and stepped in, closing the door again.

Darkness, no windows here. Junk and household wares from the forties, a Bakelite radio. Ray edged his way around boxes, a side wall of tools hung neat. A torch, or flashlight as the Yanks liked to call it, on a wooden work bench. Ray kept retreating, eyes adjusting but it was too dark to be certain of anything and he had to pull up before he hit an old-fashioned push lawnmower. He slid the gun from his pocket, waited, ears straining. Quiet. Holding his breath a long while. Still quiet. A good place to hide stuff here.

Ray thinking of the torch back there with the tools. Did he risk it? Ray edged back, grabbed the torch. In for a penny.

He clicked it on, held it low behind boxes. Most weren't taped, just had the flaps turned in but it was dry in here, no smell of mould, more dirt, and dead bugs. He started on the boxes. The first one, kitchenware: a flip toaster, spice cannisters, pots. Next one, crockery and cutlery. The third box had a rectangle drawn on the side. Once Ray opened it, he understood the symbol: framed photos and cheap prints, twenty years old or more. One showed the old man standing with a group of young soldiers at what looked like army barracks, Camp Cooke on a background sign. The Purcell boys not in the photo from what Ray could see.

Ray stopped and listened again, switched off the torch just in case. Still no sound. His guess, Purcell boozing. Torch back on. The next box had OB written on its side. It was taped. Using his keys to slit it open. Soldier stuff: a helmet, uniform, canteen bottles, webbing, a pair of boots. Ray pulled the clothes out.

Beneath them, three shoeboxes side by side. Ray lifting the lid of the first. Small black and white photos with serrated edges. War stuff. Faces hard to make out. Young men, laughing, shirtless or wearing singlets. Well fed. Training camp maybe, a bunch of close-ups, faces Ray didn't recognise except for one picture, one of the Purcell brothers. Maybe these were the effects of the brother KIA? Deeper down in the pile as the war progressed, the photos changing. War horror.

Tension and strain in the few soldier close-ups but mainly long distance, palms and jungle. Bodies piled high. A Jap with his throat cut. No GI corpses in these shots, maybe out of respect for the dead on your own side. And there would be plenty of dead, you could see. The party was well and truly over by now.

Ray expecting more of the same, but the second box was different. Young women, loads of them. Likely 1940s from the fashion. Some posed, some just innocent snaps. A lot of swimsuit stuff. More juicy ones now, topless shots, varying degrees of innocence in the poses and faces. Some looked like girls fresh out of high school others had the hardness of whores. Must have been about twenty different women all up, blondes and brunettes equally distributed. Ray thinking of those *Playboy* magazines in the bedroom. Deeper down skewing pornographic. Nude girls shot from the back, then above, like Purcell had been standing on a chair. A blonde girl with an eagle tattoo above her breast, a brunette a rose tattoo on her thigh.

Last box, Ray's head pounding now, trying to listen out for Purcell but juiced on this. This could be the proof they needed. More modern shots: fifties and sixties, still a mix of innocent shots, but the nudes were more blatant stuff, legs apart. Ray barely dared breathe, rolls of negatives, a metal box, lid taped. Ray eased the tape up with his fingernails, lifted the lid.

Wham.

Looking up at him a face he'd seen a hundred times this last week, Francine Leach. She was clothed, sitting maybe on a car seat, not even looking at the camera. But in the next photo she was sprawled somewhere in sparse scrub naked: unconscious or dead. Ray tearing through more photos. A girl not on their list, naked, definitely dead. Then another face he recognised too well. Pauline Gerschaff. She was smiling but not at the camera, at other hippies.

Not even aware she was being photographed. Looked like Elysian Park. His blood chilled as he flipped the next.

Pauline, lifeless on the floor of this shed, propped against the bench, her head askew from where the muscles and tendons in her throat had been severed. And there, just visible, on the bench above, a samurai sword. No doubt what had been used on Sherry Linden.

Ray slipped the snap in his pocket. One was all he needed. Then, suddenly alert, noise close. He killed the torch, reached for his gun, held his breath. The sound was near the shed. Then he heard the whump of an axe splitting a log on the woodblock. A pause, Ray picturing the swing. Then, *Whump!* Imagining the sword slicing Sherry Linden in two. One more thump. Wood for the heater, Ray's guess. If Purcell glanced at the shed on the way past, he had to notice the padlock. Ray cocked and aimed at the door. He would shoot first, worry about the charges later. Already thinking he could say Purcell came at him with an axe. The tramp of feet right past him … continuing. Ray did not relax. Purcell could be foxing. Ray kept the weapon pointed at the door. A minute ticked by. Another. Ray exhaled.

Carefully putting the lid back on the metal box, no tape though. Replacing everything in the box and folding it over, trying to reuse the old tape on the top of the cardboard box. Hard in the dark, not daring to flare the torch. He eased towards the door, put his ear right at the jamb. No ugly sound. He opened the door quick so he could fire if he had to. Clear. Then pushing the door to, the padlock clipped, retreating to the jungle at the back and over the fence.

26 ARE YOU EXPERIENCED?

The Deiger dead-end weighing on John. A message from Ray that he might be onto something killing the last gleam. Why wade through more photos? Ray's hot lead made John an even bigger loser. But it would likely peter out, even more depressing. The TV set in the room warming for the first time since they'd been in San Francisco. John lying on the bed, steak and fries slowly digesting. John zoning out on *Gomer Pyle*, thinking that he was to Gomer what Shearer was to Sergeant Vince Carter. Rain lashed the windows. The phone rang.

'Gordon.'

'Mate, we've got him. We've fucking got him.'

Shearer's words Cassius Clay punches into his noggin. Trying to focus, his brain still scrambling with an onscreen Gomerism.

He said, 'Tell me.'

Ray giving him the whole run-down. Didn't know how Purcell managed to con the girls but it was him.

'John, I was in there. In his shed he has photos of the girls. Could be others going back years too. I took one of Pauline for proof.'

'LAPD?'

'Just got out of there this minute. I was going to stop and ring you but thought, better to hit Lackowitz first.'

The right move.

'How'd he react?'

'He loved me telling him he had the wrong guy in lockup. Especially since we were the ones pointed him in that direction. Then I showed him the photo and his mood changed.'

'You told him you broke in?'

'I told him a door was open and he didn't believe me. His notes will show he got an anonymous tip off to check out Purcell in relation to Martin Davis.'

'When are they going in?'

'There was talk maybe tonight but I think the DA wants it airtight with warrants and shit. Likely first thing tomorrow. Burns said I could come and take a deep back seat.'

Least they could do. They hadn't wanted to know about the girls before.

Ray said, 'Everything okay? I thought you would be over the moon.'

John said, 'I thought I cracked the case, but it was all chalk.' Spilling then on Deiger. 'At least you came through.'

Ray trying to pump him up. 'I got lucky on the motorcycle thing. All of this is down to you. You had the belief.'

But John knew it was more than that. It had been a heck of detecting by Ray to sift anything from the pile of ashes they had been staring at.

Ray said, 'Listen, they won't go in till dawn. Why don't you drive down? No traffic. You don't want to miss this.'

Shearer was right. He didn't.

♦♦♦

Lackowitz had said it was okay they drive themselves but not to park in Purcell's street.

'And for Chrissake, stay out of the way.'

Ray drove though John could have managed no problem. Too buzzed. The night drive from Frisco fast and easy despite dumping rain on the early stretch, only the occasional lorry to slow the Mustang. Hendrix, Burdon and Airplane keeping him company along with images of Davis and dead girls.

Ray waiting at the Marquis. Twenty minutes killed with coffee, revisiting the case. Just after 4.00 a.m. they headed to Santa Barbara in the Pontiac, Shearer choosing a station big on both Sinatras, Nancy and Frank, and The King. John didn't care. Ray's car, Ray's turf.

Santa Barbara gun-duel western movie quiet. Unlit and dark grey. A black-and-white already in position at the east end of the street where Purcell lived. Ray threw a left up a hill then a right and one block on another right, came back down the next street at right angles to Purcell's street.

'Street I parked last time,' said Ray.

A big advantage Ray having scoped the area already. The first wink of sun catching the windscreen, Ray pulling to the curb two thirds of the way down the hill just before a street that ran to the left. He pointed along it.

'Four houses in, see that fibro place?' Ray indicating a house on the right hand, lower side of the street. Probably built as a holiday place, years back, a Chevy parked in the driveway.

'That house's backyard backs onto Purcell's backyard. When I left Purcell's, I came up the side of the house there on to the street here. I'm guessing that Chevy is LAPD.'

Though they were looking down towards the house there was no line of sight to its backyard, the roofline of the neighbouring California bungalow this side blocked it.

'Come on.'

A bird tweeted overhead. They edged down to the street and walked one house in, staying on the higher, left side of the road, the opposite side to the fibro. The elevation and angle gave them a clear but partial view of the fibro's back lawn. Large trees blocked the back fence. John checked his watch, wondered had the cops already gone in. A sudden loud bang.

'Rammed the door,' spat Shearer.

Then: clap, clap. Gunshots, handgun.

John strung tight, waiting. The door of the fibro opened with a shudder. Two broad plainclothes cops striding out with purpose, not running.

'It wasn't a cop got shot,' said Shearer, reading the body language. The cops walked right past them on the lower side of the road, cut down the verge and around the corner at Hacienda. An ambulance siren drowned out the bird.

'He didn't answer the knock. We used a ram on the door. Joe went in first, I was right behind him. Purcell came straight out of the bed-room with a revolver, swung it our way. Joe took him down, double tap.' Lackowitz standing on the public side of the black-and-white, out front of the place of the old boy Ray had collared yesterday.

'Dead?' The ambo guys, unhurried, Ray reading that as fatal. The arrival of the coroner's wagon, confirmation.

'It was close range. I'm letting the science boys go through it first but there was a smell of ash and gasoline coming from the back. There's a forty-four-gallon drum near the shed half full of paper ash. My guess, he burned the photos. You sure he didn't see you yesterday?'

Ray was positive. 'But I couldn't lock the back door, and I couldn't reseal those boxes perfectly. He could have noticed the door, gone straight to his stash in the shed.'

Ray thinking, a good thing that the photo he removed identified the inside of the shed. Otherwise, somebody might claim the photo of Pauline Gerschaff was a plant. If the other photos were gone though, they might never know now who those other women were. Shit.

'How's Burns?'

'Joe's okay. He's sitting in the car having a brandy.' Lackowitz glanced over at the forensic team exiting the house. 'I'd like you to stick around. Probably take an hour or so then you can walk me through the shed.'

Ray said it was no trouble. Lackowitz left.

'If they'd have gone in last night, they'd have those photos. There must have been twenty girls. Maybe he killed most of them.'

John Gordon said, 'It's not your fault.'

But it was damned well how Ray felt.

The sun threw off its jacket. Gordon said he was thirsty.

'I'll go get us a Coke.'

Ray didn't argue. The crowd building, neighbours rubbernecking from their front lawns, others banking up around the intersection.

The body came out strapped on a stretcher, covered in a sheet. A tall, fair-headed man wearing a dog collar had a word to the bearers. They paused in the loading and the minister said a prayer over the body. Then they slid in the stretcher and the wagon doors slammed shut, Ray catching the back of the head, straggly strawberry blond strands. The minister grave, heading to Ray. Ray wondering why he wanted to speak with him but the minister going straight past to the old-timer Ray had chatted with the day before.

'Reverend Harrison,' said the old-timer.

'George.'

They started talking softly. Ray moved their way for the shade of a tree on the front lawn of the house.

'They say what happened?' asked George.

Ray couldn't make out all the words the reverend spoke, caught a few, '... serious crime ... thought I was making progress with him ... never recovered ... brother ...'

If the reverend thought the brother's death had broken Purcell, Ray had no sympathy.

Gordon arrived with the Cokes, said, 'TV vans are coming.'

They retreated to the street where they had parked, sat in the car, thankfully shaded, slugged the sweet, carbonated syrup.

'It's over,' said Ray, thinking an awful lot of people were going to get slammed with an awful lot of hurt.

◆◆◆

Somewhere north of an hour and a half before Lackowitz and Burns trudged up to them back at the car on the incline. Ray asked Burns how he was doing, knowing he wouldn't tell him anyway.

'I'm okay.'

Lackowitz said the press was out front, suggested they go in via the fibro's backyard. A local cop had been stationed at the end of that street now to block press and non-residents. Lackowitz badged him and the four crossed to the fibro and down the narrow side path, reversing the route Ray had taken yesterday. This backyard bare and weedy. A craggy, lined face, Ray thought a woman's, watched through louvres. A milk crate got them over the fence.

The drum had been upended on a big white sheet. Techs sifting ash.

One said, 'About ninety-five percent lost but still some partial photos.'

Ray catching a glimpse of bare thigh in a small black and white photo. They entered the shed. It didn't look too different at all except some of the boxes had been turned at an angle.

'This is where I was crouched down hiding when I found the box.' Ray pointed to the same box he'd slit open and attempted to reseal. Empty now.

'Figured that would be it. That's how we found it.'

Ray explained there had been shoeboxes inside and a shallow metal box that had been taped.

'That was the one I couldn't reseal.'

Burns said they found a box like that by the drum. Nothing else seemed to have been disturbed.

An excited shout from near the back of the house brought them all out.

A tech, white lab jacket over a long-sleeved shirt, climbing out from under the stone foundations wearing a huge grin. In gloved hands he held a bayonet.

'Hidden in an old pipe.'

'Holy shit,' said Lackowitz. 'I think you just found the weapon that killed Davis.'

Ray had to agree. He said to the tech, 'You find a samurai sword?'

'Not yet.'

Ray turned to Lackowitz. 'You spy it?'

'Yeah, in the photo you gave me lying on the bench in there,' jerking his head to the shed.

Lackowitz a pro.

Ray said, 'Well, keep looking. I think that's what he used on Judy Ikin and Sherry Linden.'

Another tech walked out from the weeds near the back fence carrying a long metal probe.

'Lieutenant, I'm going to have to ask you to go out the front way.'

Lackowitz said, 'Why's that, Edgar?'

Edgar said, 'I've done a lot of crime scenes with bodies buried in soil just like this. My guess is you're going to need some careful spadework back there.'

27 GOOD VIBRATIONS

Continuous pale blue sky. The occasional ice cream-blob cloud. Clear ocean, hot bright sand. Beers that chilled fingertips, unbelievably cheap brought to your wicker chair in the shallow shade of a low roof.

Shearer had said, 'Why not Mexico?'

The best idea. Three days of heaven. For the first time since the devil incarnate had invaded his life, two years back, John healing, writing a daily postcard for Denise. The American guy with the beard the only other whitey in the little village advising him that he should post from San Diego on the run back.

'May never reach home otherwise.'

◆◆◆

They had returned the Pontiac and cruised south in the Mustang. Tourists in Tijuana, thinning out down the coast. John didn't even know the name of this little place. They had stopped at a couple of other spots but there were too many heads and bikers tuning in and dropping out of LBJ's world.

The bus didn't run here, the road not much more than crushed rock. The bearded American who favoured cigars drove a jeep. A simple regime: Shearer and John rose late, swam in the mild ocean, breakfasted on whatever was the daily fare from the village house where a large lady cooked in a big old oven. Day spent with cards, drinking. Afternoon siesta. Night mosquitos loitering in the corners of their bare shared room. A plug-in low-speed fan reminded John of Hector's.

They'd hauled out of LA on the Sunday. Lackowitz told them that three bodies had so far been found buried in the backyard. One was likely to be Pauline Gerschaff. They weren't sure on the other two yet but Ray said he was hoping one was Jenny Wallace so the family could put an end to that chapter. LAPD had a rough picture of Purcell. He'd grown up in the house with his older brother, mom and dad. The father had worked at the army training camp that had become Camp Cooke. Thomas, the older brother, surrounded by military his whole life, had signed up for duty in the Pacific. Younger brother Leslie had followed suit but according to neighbours and other locals he'd never really achieved anything much, unlike his brother who had been a quality track athlete.

Thomas never came back from the war, and in a way neither had Les. Heavy drinker, bar room fights, drifting job to job. When his old man died, the mother pre-deceasing her husband, Les drifted further out to sea, started smoking dope, trying to hang with the hippies but didn't fit, and he knew it. John imagined the man's resentment. You lose your brother, put your life on the line but you're still not cool enough. The motorcycle gave him a way in. Bikers suddenly hip. He could at least hang on the fringes. Leslie Purcell lived by himself. He'd occasionally go off the rails. Old army buddies and a school mate or two he hadn't burned, stepping in. The local minister slogged away.

The techs hadn't found the sword, presumed he had dumped it, but were convinced the bayonet had done the job on Martin Davis.

Down here by the sigh of the ocean, John becoming as frugal with words as Shearer. It wasn't till the last day, the Wednesday, when they acknowledged that the holiday was over that they talked about the case.

'You can see why Spring would have loved Mexico,' said Shearer.

John said, 'We need to tell Jill about Pauline.'

Shearer squinted, the setting sun still throwing off enough rays, sucked on his beer.

'Yes we do.'

Lackowitz had embargoed talk until LAPD had completed their backyard body search but promised he would contact SFPD on the quiet. Officially though, LAPD weren't putting Judy Ikin's murder in the pool of Purcell's crimes. John understood it, didn't like it though.

Long after the sun had sunk, still drinking tequila. John believed he had never known tranquillity until this moment. Thought about coming here with Denise one day. Would make a wonderful anniversary destination but he'd not be able to afford that for a very long time.

'Here's to us,' said Shearer. They clinked glasses a final time.

John a prayer to Martin Davis, Pauline, Jenny, Francine and Sherry: Here's to you.

'Fuck!' said Shearer.

'What's up?'

'Is it June seventh today?'

John had to check his brain. 'Yes, it is.'

'The Epsom Derby. I forgot about the tip Granite gave me. George Moore.'

'Would it make this any better?'

Shearer looked around him, laughed.

'No. I reckon this is as good as it gets.'

28 FOR WHAT IT'S WORTH

Jill's tears warm into Ray's shoulder. They were standing in the tiered garden out the back, overlooking the valley. Gordon and he had driven from Mexico, just one stop in Tijuana to load up with sombreros and scarves for the girls back home. One last night back at their old motel planned, then a slow Friday drive to San Francisco, flying out Saturday. A few of the others at Earth's Eden had caught on why they were here. Ray noting how their shoulders sagged. Gordon and he ticked off as harbingers of doom.

'Thank you,' Jill said, wiping her eyes with her fingers. She kissed them.

'I'm so sorry we didn't have better news,' said Gordon.

Ray could tell his mate had taken more than a few punches in the gut this trip. Felt the same.

'She will be at peace,' said Jill.

Ray hoped so, couldn't get that photo out of his mind: Pauline dead in the back shed. He would never know the Pauline that Jill had in her brain, that living breathing young woman. The image of Pauline that he would be forced to carry with him forever was no more than a slumped body in an old shed.

Spared the same visit with Steve Wallace. When Ray rang, the kid said Lackowitz had already been in touch with his parents to say they believed his sister's body had been recovered. There had been some jewellery in the grave that matched the missing person's report. Lackowitz had briefly interviewed Steve about Leslie Purcell. Neither he nor any of the family had ever heard of him.

'How did she wind up there? You got any idea?' he asked.

Ray said he did not, thinking Jenny could have hitched down with somebody and Purcell found her in LA or equally Purcell was up in

San Francisco at the Airplane–Big Brother concert, or thereabouts when their paths crossed. The boy thanked Ray for his efforts. Ray feeling like a fraud. Sure, Purcell most likely would have kept on killing but Ray couldn't bank much credit for anything.

The same clerk with bad skin tending reception at the Paradise Motel showing zero excitement at his returning customers. They wound up with a room on the same floor as last time but a different wing. John Gordon said he wanted to buy a pair of earrings for Denise. Ray wanted to get something to eat.

◆◆◆

There was a steak place Shearer had grown fond of near the Marquis. John dropped him, said he'd pick him up in an hour. When they'd been staying at the Marquis, John had asked one of the girls where he should shop for jewellery for his wife. She had said Beverly Hills. Denise wasn't a glamour kind of girl, but John knew her. And he knew if he bought her earrings, even though they might stay in the box, she would always know that he had gone out there into a world of which he had no understanding, to get something that said 'I love you now and forever'.

He cruised till he found a jeweller's in a strip of shops. Clean glass, mirrors, silence of a church. The store empty apart from a dark-haired male customer bent over a display case of rings. John scanned about for earrings with single small stones, no illusion about how much this stuff would cost. He guessed the jeweller must have a mirror by which he could watch the shop. You wouldn't leave it unattended. The guy next to him raised his head, shook it like he couldn't find a solution.

'How the heck do you know what one they're going to like?'

And then he smiled at John. John nearly went through the fucking floor. He could barely speak but he managed to say, 'They'll like that we took the trouble. I hope.'

The jeweller, bow tie, grey hair, glasses, black suit appeared from behind a black curtain balancing a tray of rings.

'Mr Presley, I believe any of this range will please your wife immensely.'

◆◆◆

Ray did not fucking believe this. For the third time he said, 'You're bullshitting me.'

'I am not. He was as close as you are to me right now.'

Ray did not want to believe it. '*You* saw Elvis Presley?' Not meaning to hit the first word like John Gordon didn't fucking deserve that but he didn't.

'I didn't just see him. He actually spoke to me.'

That was so far-fetched it had to be true. Ray knew Elvis was in LA to do a movie with Nancy Sinatra. How could he have fucking missed this? Elvis' biggest fan, by what cruel twist of—

'What did he say again? Word for word.'

'Um … "How the heck do you know what they like." Think that was it.'

'What did you say?'

Gordon said he couldn't remember exactly.

Fuck! How could you not remember?

'As I was leaving, I said, "Congratulations to you and Priscilla".'

'What did he say?'

'He saw my wedding band and said, "You too?" And I said, "Yeah." Actually, I think I just nodded. And he said, "Kids?" I said, "Not yet." Then he winked at me and nodded at the ring.'

That had to mean Priscilla was pregnant. That's why he was getting the ring. And you, you fucking-idiot Shearer, weren't even there! You could have suggested a celebratory drink. Instead, you were overpaying for a T-bone. Ray swearing to himself he would never eat steak again. He knew what it was of course, judgement from the almighty. His dalliances with Kitty and Janis had not gone unnoticed on high. This was payback.

The hurt burned until well into their second beer at Barney's.

'Hey, Ray!' Turning to see a tangle of hair: the Aussies, Ross and Mick.

'I believe I owe you a beer,' said Ray.

''ken oath, you do.'

They moved to a booth. Ross slapped a manila envelope in his hands.

'What you asked for.'

Ray remembering now Ross had said he would try for Purcell's driving record. He dropped it on the table, said, 'Ross, forget I ever asked about this.' Purcell's identity would be going public tomorrow.

'About what?' The kid giving a cheeky grin to show he got it.

The night passed easily, drinks, talk of Mexico and the Rabbitohs. For a while Ray could almost believe the world was normal. The lads ate up Gordon's Elvis story.

Ross said, 'This is LA. You never know who you'll meet.'

Mick said he would have been excited to meet Nancy Sinatra. Ray thought back on his last time at Barney's: Janis writing the party address on his arm. Wondered if she forgave him. Wondered if she even remembered. He looked around him, the laughter, the bikes revving outside in the hot night air. For all the possibilities that the USA offered, he was pleased his kid would be growing up in Sydney. You didn't have monsters like Leslie Purcell roaming the streets.

♦♦♦

They left Los Angeles 9.30 a.m. next day, John letting Ray drive. Pleased to relax instead of having his eyes locked on blacktop. They went the coast road via Santa Barbara. No desire to stop. At San Luis Obispo they found a featureless bar serving men in overalls, slugged a beer before continuing, roof down. The air cooler, cleaner than Los Angeles now. Time rolled. John's lids grew heavy. Something poking into John's arse. A manila envelope. A vague memory now of Barney's.

'What's this?'

Ray explaining that when he'd rung Ross chasing the ID on Purcell's motorcycle plate, Ross had offered to try and pull his driving record. 'Bad people drive badly. Traffic violation might be the tip of the iceberg. You should always check out their history.'

Likely no photo of Purcell, but John was curious. Still had no idea exactly what the man who had killed Martin Davis looked like. He slit open the envelope and pulled out a xerox. Typed sheet only.

Charges going way back. Drunk-driving twice. Speeding at

least seven times. You could blame it on the war, sure, but lots of soldiers didn't come back as psycho killers. He shoved it in the glove box, shut his eyes, Ray allowing him a pop station for now, Monkees and Rascals.

When John woke, they were in a lay by on a clifftop near Big Sur. The wind was up, whitecaps flecked the Pacific, Ray standing outside.

John got out and joined him. 'Did I miss much?'

'Nothing as good as this. The world is a strange place, mate. How can you get Purcell's backyard and this in the same universe?'

Knowing Shearer didn't expect an answer, and he didn't anticipate giving one, but it came to him. 'This didn't have anything to do with man.'

◆◆◆

It was around 6.00 p.m. when they got in. They had to be at the airport at 2.00 p.m. the next day so they would have time to breakfast and drop the car back before checking out. Kitty had left for the day. John got the feeling Ray wasn't too disappointed. They found an Italian restaurant and celebrated. John suggested one last night at the Fillmore, Ray shrugged, he could do that. The Fillmore was dark though. John slowed past some heads on the street and asked what was up.

'Everyone's heading to Marin County for the Fantasy Fair. Lot of people already lit out. Was supposed to be on last week but got washed out.'

Shearer said, 'Looks like we have some drinking time then.'

A quiet bar, polished wood, brass rails. They took it slow and easy. Some way through his first bourbon, Shearer said, 'I need to thank you. I came here thinking I wanted to see America, Disneyland, all that. I never expected what I found, and I don't reckon I'll experience the likes of it again.'

'Ray Shearer, a fan of Frank Zappa and the Mothers of Invention.' John shaking his head, laugh lines sprouting, wished Denise was there, she'd get it.

'True. But I still prefer Elvis.'

John venturing, 'You and Janis seem to hit it off.'

Shearer drank, thoughtful. 'Janis and me, share the same human quality: extremely poor judgement. What about you? What voyages of self-discovery for John Gordon?'

John had thought about that, maybe not so head-on, but he'd skirted around it. Especially on those long solo drives.

'I feel privileged that I have been here. These times. This whole scene. There's a spirit here, you feel that? Like people can change things for the better. I don't know if they will. But I'd like to peer twenty years into the future. Martin Davis died too young, but he made a difference, didn't he?'

'Yes, he did.'

They drank to Martin Davis. Then they drank to James Perry, wherever he might be in Vietnam. Then they just drank.

◆◆◆

John woke, checked his watch, close to 3.30 in the morning. Shearer breathing evenly the other side of the room. John found it hard to sleep the night before a big trip. He lay in bed drifting from space to space over what he needed to prepare for – Denise, Geary, the parents of Martin Davis. Checklisting the morning next: car, check out, taxi …

Passport! Did he have his passport handy?

A glance at the clock. Near 4.30 a.m. now. He wasn't going back to sleep. He got out of bed and clicked on the table lamp, rummaged around his suitcase. Mild panic till he recalled he'd left his passport in his briefcase. The passport had wedged itself midway in the leaves of his notebook. Pulled it out, placed it in his jacket pocket with the plane tickets. Went to replace the notebook. It had flipped open on notes on Judy Ikin. *Killed early hours April 2.*

Like a spotlight had flared. April 2. The date echoed.

Fuck!

◆◆◆

Ray was romping with some babe. A big motor yacht. Elvis in a daggy skipper's cap at the helm, looking back over his shoulder.

The girl Ray was humping naked apart from long white boots. Nancy?

The boat was rocking suddenly, a violent storm …

'Ray! Wake up.'

And just like that, Nancy and Elvis gone. A low glow in darkness, John Gordon's face eager.

'Did we sleep in?' Ray thinking a dash to the airport.

'No. Listen, that envelope—'

'What time is it?'

'Five. That envelope …'

'What envelope?'

'The manila envelope. Where is it?' Gordon was already dressed in slacks and a shirt.

Ray's brain easing into a slow jog. 'Um … the glove box, I think. Or still on the car floor. Why?'

But he was speaking to air.

He was sitting up, fully awake when John Gordon returned ten minutes later brandishing the document.

'That driving record Ross ran for you. Have a look.'

Ray blinked, checked. Speeding citations aplenty, a couple of DD too. 'And?'

'Look at the date on the second DD.'

Ray did, April 2, 1967. Time of offence was given as 2.15 a.m.

Local Santa Barbara police had stopped him. Ray feeling the heavy thud of doom in his chest.

John said, 'You get picked up for DD here, what do you think happens?'

'Same as home I reckon. Charge you, throw you in the tank.'

He knew where this was going. Alice down the fucking rabbit hole again.

'You know what that means,' said Gordon.

He could not believe this. Could not believe he was going to speak the words.

'If this is right, Leslie Purcell did not kill Judy Ikin.'

29 PSYCHOTIC REACTION

Ray said, 'It could be a mistake.' Knew how lame that sounded.

'On a DD?'

'We got it wrong then. Purcell never killed Ikin. It was unrelated.'

'No. You saw Ikin's body … Sherry Linden's.'

That samurai sword cutting deep in his memory, thinking: Who the fuck are you kidding, Shearer?

Ray said, 'Our plane goes in a few hours.'

'Who cares about that, Ray? You reckon I could return home and just go, "Oh well, did our best, ran out of time." Could you?'

No. 'What do you propose?'

'Suppose …' Gordon tentative like he was walking barefoot in the dark, every thought broken glass '… suppose Purcell wasn't in this alone.'

Ray nodding slowly, thinking it through. An image flashed: a notebook by the telephone stand at Purcell's. Explaining to Gordon. 'It had Hector's address where Martin Davis was staying.'

Gordon methodical. 'Like somebody else had called that through to him.'

Ray nodding, exactly what he was thinking. 'Somebody might have called Purcell, said, "This kid is onto us. He needs to be removed."'

'Only whoever is on the phone can't do it, because he's in San Francisco.' The words coming out of Gordon like a spiritualist at a séance.

'Possibly. Now Purcell has the address for Martin. He re-cons the house, waits for and follows Martin. Maybe a day or two. By Friday night he's ready to act. He follows him, guesses Martin is going back to the biker bar in Venice. He cuts in front of James Perry when Perry is trying to tail Davis. He gets to Venice, waits his chance. When Davis walks out, Purcell bayonets him.'

Gordon was onside with that.

Ray spitballing: 'Purcell and his accomplice find out Davis has this theory about the missing girls. Spells danger to them. They need to find him. Whoever made that call, from here in San Francisco or wherever, how did they get that information? I mean, we were looking. Spring didn't know where he was.'

Gordon turning pale as an Irish nun.

'What?'

Gordon said, 'Kansas Annie. A girl, Monica, called her with the address the night she died. But I looked, there was nothing written down, nothing by the phone. What if the killer was there when that call came through? Everybody I spoke with couldn't believe Annie was back on the gear. Maybe she wasn't? What if Annie was murdered too? The killer took the pad.'

Ray thinking: we're grabbing too much now, toddlers at a birthday party.

'Why kill her? Even if she learns later Martin has been killed, would she get the connection that she supplied the address? It's a long shot, she mulls it over and goes, "Gee, I got Martin's address, then I talked to X and Martin gets stabbed down in LA."'

John nodding but troubled. There was something he should be seeing. 'At the crime scene. I missed something, I feel it.'

Ray suggested the missing pad.

'No. Something else. I felt it when I looked over the photos with the cop.' Taking himself back to the scene, that night, talking himself through it.

'The door was locked. Means nothing either way, all the killer had to do was pull the door to when he left.'

'Bruising?'

John recalling, kneeling over the body, feeling for a pulse ...

'There might have been some that I put down to her falling off the bed.' … feeling for a pulse, yes, he's bending over her – something there …

Bang! 'That dog-tag necklace she loved. I swear she wasn't wearing it.'

'Maybe she took it off? Could have been by the side of her bed.'

John grabbed his wallet. 'Young, the detective, gave me his card.'

'It's Saturday morning.'

'You think he would call Spinetti this hour?'

Shearer a time check: 8.40. He said he did not.

John said, 'Good,' dialled off the card. A quick answer the other end.

'Detective Young, this is John Gordon. I'm so sorry to call you, but Captain Spinetti said it would be okay … thanks. It's about Millicent Smith, Kansas Annie. I need to ask you about a necklace.'

Young no memory of any dog-tag necklace either on the body or in the apartment. He asked them to hang up while he called somebody in the evidence section to check the list of personal effects. He promised he would call straight back.

Somewhere more than ten but less than fifteen minutes later, the phone ringing. John answered, holding the receiver out so Ray could listen in.

'No, there was no necklace. Can I ask what this is about?'

John said, 'It might be pertinent to a homicide investigation. I have to go. Thanks for your help.'

Shearer said, 'I'm not sure it's a good thing, mate, but you're starting to act a lot like me.'

John managing a smirk. 'I think our killer took Annie out of the picture. The killer could have punched her in the back of the head and rigged her for an overdose. It looked like she'd fallen off the bed. Nobody is going to question that too much. When she was dead, he took the pad and the necklace.'

'Why?'

'Remember what Lackowitz and Burns said: sometimes the murderer takes a souvenir.'

Ray remembered them saying that, but it didn't feel right to him. 'Apart from photos, I don't remember the cops finding things from the victims at Purcell's house. In fact, he buried Pauline Gerschaff with her jewellery.'

'But Purcell might not be the leader here. Maybe all he did was get rid of Davis and the bodies.'

Ray conceding his partner might be right, pointing out though, even if he was, they had a plane to catch.

Gordon said, 'I'm not getting on that plane till I know what happened to Annie.'

'You might be here a long time.'

'Fuck that shit, Ray, come on. You feel it too. I know you do.'

Ray no stomach to disagree, said, 'What do we tell Geary?'

'Fuck Geary. You got rushed to hospital with appendicitis ...'

'Me?'

'Alright, *I* did.'

Ray laughing, picking up the phone, dialling the operator, asking to be put through to a funeral director in Santa Barbara.

'Which funeral director, sir?'

'Doesn't matter.' Explaining aside to Gordon, 'Saves having to call the police, and you know these guys will be working weekends.' He got the 'Connecting you now'.

A man's voice answered, 'Eternity Funeral Home, Wilbur Richards.'

Ray said, 'I'm hoping you can help me, Mr Richards. My father is very sick and has asked for a Reverend Harrison.' Ray remembering the name from the street exchange back in Santa Barbara.

Richards found the number for the church, an after-hours too, just in case. Ray thanked him, tried the after-hours number first. Harrison answered. So far so good.

'Reverend,' said Ray, 'my name is Raymond Shearer and I have been employed by the family of a young man allegedly killed by Leslie Purcell.'

Harrison expressed his sorrow over the whole mess.

Ray said, 'I believe Purcell was one of your parishioners.'

'Yes, he was. I really thought we had been making progress with him. How can I help you, Raymond?'

'My clients would very much like to know as much as they can about the circumstances of Martin's murder. The police are certain that Leslie Purcell is Martin's killer. I wonder, does Leslie have any close friends we might be able to talk with?'

'Leslie was very much a lone wolf. Rarely socialised with anybody. Though, I really thought we had connected. Last Easter he was part of a special three-day spiritual retreat. But with alcoholics—'

Ray alert as bird dog in bulrushes. 'You say he went on a retreat this Easter?'

'Yes, we have a camp about an hour north of here.'

Ray thinking of the marked calendar hanging off the bedroom door. Maybe those Easter dates weren't marked for the love-in?

Ray said, 'This retreat was what, Friday to Sunday?'

'Monday. We came back late Monday. I picked him up and delivered him home myself.'

Click: It wasn't Purcell riding his motorcycle to Elysian Park, but photos proved the cycle was there. Somebody else had taken Pauline Gerschaff. Maybe she'd been held prisoner till Purcell returned and they'd killed her together. Ray's brain leaping. The samurai sword, unrecovered.

'Reverend, do you know if Leslie ever travelled to San Francisco, or had a close friend in San Francisco?'

'Like I say, he didn't have friends really, but when he was in trouble with alcohol or the law, he had some old army buddies who would bail him out. One in particular, he wasn't from Santa Barbara. From what Leslie said, he would sometimes stay a day or two to get him back on his feet.'

'You wouldn't know this man's name?'

'No, I'm sorry.'

'His vehicle?'

'I did see a van parked there at one time when I was making a call to a neighbour.'

He couldn't recall colour or plates. Ray thanked him for his help.

'Please pass on the condolence of the whole community to the boy's family.'

Ray said he would. Blasted Gordon with the news.

John hyped. Ray dialling LAPD, hoping to get Lackowitz, info on Purcell's army unit, a name. John life-and-death alert, driving to the core of it now. His brain agile, processing fast: Kansas Annie among others likely murdered by this guy. An army connection. His brain swerving on smoking tyres towards Judy Ikin. Samurai sword. Sherry Linden: Patcher, the vagrant said he had seen a van near the body dump site.

Ray listening as the phone rang out, but John's focus now on something so close he could smell it. He almost had something …

'No answer.'

Shearer slammed the phone down. 'Now what?'

Whatever had been in John's fingers had turned to smoke. 'The tattoo place where Annie lived. Maybe they can help?'

◆◆

Under a half hour and they were there. Not long open but even so the smell of ink, antiseptic and motor oil a heavy canopy. The tattoo guy bald with a beard and prison-nursed biceps. He talked while he traced an eagle on a biker's neck. He remembered John from their phone calls.

'That Saturday when Annie likely died. What time did you work till?'

'Didn't stop. Saturday is always a big night.'

'If anybody went up there to her flat, you'd see, wouldn't you?'

The steps started right outside his door and there was a window. Covered in pigeon shit and exhaust grime but you could see okay.

'Might, might not. This takes concentration.'

Shearer stepped in. 'You ever see any vehicle around that time near Annie's. Any motorcycle?'

'Man, check it out.' Gesturing with his head to a line of five cycles outside. Right, dumb question.

John said, 'How about a van?'

'We did see a van there some time. Well, not me, but Zipper.

He'll be in later. I remember he said, looks like Annie has a visitor.'

John asked when Zipper would be in.

'About an hour.'

'He on the phone?'

'Nope.'

◆◆◆

They retreated to the car. Ray said, 'Let's grab a coffee.' Starting towards a greasy spoon down the same strip. Passing a gun shop, tough wire behind plate glass. An American flag. Brain is a weird thing. It jumps from stone to stone over the hissing stream of the subconscious. John's leapt from the flag to James Perry. To Vietnam. To Judy Ikin. Army connection. Judy Ikin and Sherry Linden sliced and diced. Annie passing on messages that sealed Martin Davis' fate. Somebody there when Annie got Monica's call with Martin's LA address.

Annie … Judy Ikin.

Something Ray had said before: Why kill Annie if she had unwittingly passed on the information about Martin Davis? She was murdered. But not like a psycho killing, different, camouflage for the killer. They turned into the diner. Worn stools. Ray ordering, John only part hearing.

Judy Ikin, Annie. There's a connection.

'The dog tags,' whispering it.

Shearer read him. 'Go on.'

John drilling down. 'You said, why would he kill Annie? He didn't cut her up like the others. He wanted to hide it. Why?'

Shearer waiting patiently for John to trace it through. John had it all now.

'Chronology: Judy Ikin was murdered on the Sunday. Now Spring told you—'

'That she went to Jay Burnley's apartment on the Monday morning to return the albums.'

'And Kansas Annie told us that Spring found the dog tags that day, with the chain broken, and gave them to her. What if she found them in the apartment building or just outside?'

Shearer nodding, the memory there now. 'She did. She told

me that night at Barney's.' His excitement infectious. 'Judy Ikin puts up a struggle, snaps the chain. The killer pockets his tags but heading down the steps, he loses them.'

John said, 'If the killer learned Annie had his dog tags, then he had to kill her. The tags could prove he killed Ikin.'

Ray's mouth bunched. 'I wonder if Spring remembers the name on the back?'

The coffees hit the counter. Ray and John were already gone.

'Spring already left for the Fantasy Fair. I'm going myself soon as Josephine packs up. Which won't be all that long. Nobody here today, they're all heading up the mountain.'

John locating Redbeard at his usual spot in the flea market. 'Where's Josephine?'

'Right there.' Redbeard pointing down the line of stalls to a tall woman in a prairie dress and boots. Homemade jewellery spread out on a card table. John approached said they were friends of Spring and Kansas Annie.

Shearer said, 'You fixed up a necklace for Annie, didn't you? Dog tags.'

'That's right. It was really groovy.'

Any chance she remembered the name on the tags? John shuffling, on a knife edge.

'Gee, I did read it. I remember that. Wait on, it reminded me of a classical composer because I studied classical piano and violin. Purcell!'

John punctured: they had blown it. Purcell *was* here. He had killed Judy Ikin.

Shearer asked Josephine if she remembered the name or initial.

'No. But I recall Purcell.'

Shearer thanked her. They started off.

John said, 'I fucked up. Purcell was here himself.'

'Maybe not. He had a brother Thomas Purcell. They were in the same unit.' Shearer striding purposefully. John an effort to catch up. 'Thomas was killed in the war but maybe somebody close to him kept his tags.'

Ray stopped at a payphone, pulled out the tattoo parlour number, pumped coins. John listened to the burr of the ringing phone. Then, answered.

Shearer, no delay. 'Zipper in yet?' Nodding to John, waiting. Then: 'Mate, you noticed a van at Kansas Annie's ... yes, right. When was that, you remember? Did you see the driver? ... what about the licence plate, decals ...?'

The response broke a smile on Ray's face. 'Thank you.' Shearer hung up, smug. 'The van had lettering on it, he remembered: "Vet".'

John grasping, 'We're looking for a vet?'

'Yeah, but not the kind fixes dogs. I'm thinking Vets Against War.'

The Glide Church almost deserted too, everybody decamping to 'the mountain' for the festival. But Theo was still pulling sheets through the gestetner.

'Vets Against War? They've been in this since the beginning.'

'The Human Be-In?' Shearer.

'Yes, they were there.'

John said, 'We're looking for whoever drives a van with the word "Vet" on it.'

'That would be Dermott O'Brien, formerly Sergeant Dermott O'Brien.'

'You know where we could find him?' John trying to keep the excitement from his voice.

'I delivered some pamphlets to him once at a rooming house. Not far from here, Clementina near Gallagher Lane.'

'Thank you,' John turned to go.

Theo called out after them, 'Only they won't know him by that name. Everyone calls him Murph.'

◆◆◆

Ray working it all through in his head as he drove: should have recognised him in the photo of the sergeant, his arms draped around the Purcell brothers while he held a samurai sword. Like sons to him. Or maybe it was more than that. Ray had known lots of homos who hid their true nature from themselves, not just others. Either way, the sarge had lost somebody he loved. Wearing the dead kid's dog tags had to testify to that.

Maybe he'd been normal before the war, maybe he'd been psycho from the start. Right under their noses. John Gordon had made the wrong call on Ernst Deiger but the real killer had been sitting just feet away. And that first night they'd met him, hadn't he leant over Annie and lit up her cigarette? He would have seen the dog tags. He'd known back then. Ray working it: Murph goes to kill Annie, when, or just after she gets the call with Martin's address. Ray remembering now, the box in Purcell's shed, the initials OB. For O'Brien. The mementos had been his not Leslie Purcell's.

Purcell might have killed Martin Davis for him, carrying out his order. But the girls, Ray was guessing even if it wasn't all O'Brien's work, he was the driving force. He killed Ikin, then he knew he had to kill Annie.

They found a space to park, spied a couple of likely buildings. The usual three floors, fifteen rooms give or take. No sign of the van. Ray checked his Smith & Wesson. Gordon the same.

Ray said, 'Maybe you don't want to be part of this. I don't want to involve the cops. I'm going to tell him he has one chance. Come clean and we take him in. He denies anything, I will threaten to put a bullet in his head. He still dicks me around, I will carry out the threat. Then get out of there.'

Gordon said, 'I'm with you one hundred percent.'

Out and moving towards the first building. The blood pumping to Ray's head. Been here before. No slack on this line. You hesitated, they'd be throwing dirt on your coffin.

A black guy out front enjoying a cigarette.

'This the rooming house?'

He pointed to the neighbouring building. They crossed quickly, stepped inside. Dark in the entrance way, a smell of last week's rain lingering. The overhead bulb was out but enough light through the door fell on the letterboxes: O'Brien apartment 12.

Climbing the stairs. Wide, once splendid, now a characteristic of buildings with pigeons roosting in the eaves. At the first floor, a dim bulb spread low cheer. A door banged up above somewhere, a woman's voice called out. Footsteps headed their way quick. Ray pulled his gun just in case, hid his hand under his jacket. A kid about fourteen in a baseball uniform flashed onto the landing and skittered past.

Silent all the way to the top floor after that. A bulb on the landing, then a corridor in darkness. The smell of boiled cabbage and mould. The lino flooring chipped. Number 12 was the first on the right. Ray nodded to Gordon, making sure he had his gun drawn. Then he knocked.

Ray thinking, they should have checked the side of the building for fire escapes first. Knocked again. Nothing.

Too dark to see clearly and Ray hadn't brought a torch, so he read the lock with his fingers. Stood to the side in case a shotgun blast came streaming through the door. Tried his master keys. First choice wrong. The second slid in. Held his breath to hear the click. Gordon and he on either side of the door, ready for the worst. Ray pushed the door in hard.

Light streamed out, no gunfire. Ray ducked in, Gordon covering. They were looking at a small sitting room combo kitchen. Empty of everything but cheap furniture and light tinted by a grime-stained window. Gordon closed the door behind them. Ray stepped down the narrow and short corridor. Bedroom next.

Ray clicked the light on. A camp stretcher, bedclothes tucked. A wardrobe its door part open. No window. A smell of old sweat. A long metal footlocker by the bed. Ray signalled he would check the bathroom. Tiny. Old tiles, some chipped, all worn. A bath and washbasin. A toilet jammed in the corner. They went back to the bedroom.

'You see any keys?' asked Ray.

Gordon shuffled detritus on a bedside table. Some coins. 'Nope.'

'My guess, he's taken the van.'

Ray rumbled the wardrobe: a few clothes and shoes, no weapons. The footlocker had a small padlock, but that hadn't been snapped shut. Gordon flipped open the lid. A folded American flag, some framed photos. War years. A portrait of Thomas Purcell in uniform, a photo of the brothers with O'Brien between them. Deeper down a few older pictures, likely O'Brien's mother and father. The look of the poor dressed for a special occasion. A bible: the inscription, *To Mary on her first communion.* A few souvenirs, cheap mugs, a hula girl made from elastic and plastic. No sword. Army boots.

Shearer brandished the photo of Thomas Purcell. 'This is the older brother. You think O'Brien was queer for him?'

Gordon shrugged. 'Obviously meant a lot to him.'

They moved back into the small sitting room.

John Gordon's voice turned him. 'I think I know where he is.'

Holding a flyer that had been left in the pages of a newspaper.

KFRC Fantasy Fair and Magic Mountain Music Festival.

Ray had one thought: If O'Brien knows Spring found those dog tags, he will kill her.

30 FIRE

It should have taken half an hour, but concertgoers choked roads. Sunshine, roof down, Shearer cursing the whole way to Mill Valley. The crowd biblical, a shambling tsunami of headbands, sandals, bedrolls. Hells Angels cruising on chrome through the low tide. The pilgrims not all heads. Straights in glasses, turtlenecks, humming 'Windy'. John in his passenger seat gleaning intel from pedestrians. The highway to the amphitheatre on the south side of the mountain where the concert was being held was closed. No private vehicles allowed. School buses were running crowds to the venue from parking stations. The civic centre was the best but further on from here.

Ray looked for space among the chaos, jammed the Mustang between brush and a Beetle. They got out and scanned. Ray in slacks, Hawaiian shirt, and jacket to cover his gun. John in jeans, revolver stashed beneath his tee. Finding the Vets Against War van a needle and haystack thing. One guy had a clipboard, as official as it got in this world.

John asked if he'd seen the Vets Against War van.

'Yeah, we let it up go up the mountain. We figure those guys deserve a bit of consideration.'

Shearer cursed, told John, 'We need to get up there as soon as.'

Noting people were being ferried on the backs of Harleys, Hells Angels for chauffeurs.

'That's the artists,' explained Clipboard.

Ray started towards a general staging post: a few bikes, guitar cases, beers, joints. John followed, looked over to see Janis talking with the chick from the Airplane. Saw her eyes shift to Ray.

Ray saw Janis tracking him even though her lips were still moving as she talked to the other singer.

'Hi, Janis,' he said.

'Surprised you're here. Thought you might still be lost.'

Guessed it was a crack about Los Angeles. He wanted to tell her he did front. But then it would get even more complicated. Instead, he said, 'I had to work.'

A bitter laugh from Janis, a smoke between her lips. 'Oh yeah, you were working hard.'

The other chick knowing stuff was going down. Janis turned to John, greeted him, introduced him to 'Grace'. Gordon started saying how much he loved her music, playing his part, giving Ray a chance to hive off Janis.

Ray said, 'Listen. Nothing went down like you think—'

'Not my business if it did.'

'Even so, you and I have been honest with one another, haven't we?'

'What's it matter, Ray? Truth and bullshit are two sides of the same coin.'

'That young girl I was with. I think her life might be in danger right now. And she's up there on the mountain with the guy I've been tracking. Only I didn't know it till now. John and I need a ride up. You think you can arrange it?'

She finished her cigarette, watching him through narrow eyes, dropped the butt and squished it. 'Not the kind of ride I thought you'd ask me for. Weren't you heading back home today?'

'I was. But I have to finish this thing.'

Janis whistled like a wharfie. 'Cal!'

One of the Angels turned. He was older, with a long beard split grey and black.

'My friends here need a ride up the mountain.'

◆◆◆

The road narrow, twisting. As their cycles overtook one bus, other buses coming back down squeezed them. If John had put out his elbows, they would have been skinned. The heads on the bus were hollering out the windows, whooping, high as California homegrown could get them. John's rider squat, with a handlebar mo. He'd taken a huge slug of mescal before tossing the empty bottle and climbing on the bike. But despite the near-death experience, John felt no fear. His mind was stuffed with a single idea: find O'Brien and take him down.

By the time they reached the site, the area was clogged again. Buses disgorging concert goers, Angels taking a quick break. John thanked his rider and waited for Ray to fall in beside him. Sun was filtering through treetop leaves, a boogie blues wafting their way, powerful harmonica, a riff that hit your gut: 'Rollin' and Tumblin''.

Ray whispered, 'Look for the van.'

Surreal now, the music pounding, the clumsy metal of the gun poking into his back, freaks spinning past doing that court-jester thing with their arms and toes. Ray jabbed him in the ribs nodded over to where a familiar face held court with three girls and a freak. McKnight. John followed Ray. Caught McKnight's look, wary.

Ray said, 'You seen Spring?'

'Yeah, a while back. Why?'

Ray didn't answer direct. 'You see her, don't let her leave your side.'

McKnight asked what was going on. 'Is solider boy back?'

Ray said, 'Not that one. Where was she, last you saw?'

McKnight said, 'Near the small stage,' pointed.

Ray motioned John follow. The crowd thick now up the back of the main amphitheatre, chances of recognising anybody Rizla slim. They scanned a few minutes, heading across clay soil and tree roots. Then, at the back of the smaller stage, a clump of vehicles: probably trucks for sound and lights gear, a fire truck, and one other vehicle backing on the bush, a van with big letters across it – *Vets Against War*.

As Ray approached the van, the PA voice barked, 'Kaleidoscope.' The air erupting with drums and what sounded like electrified fiddle. John's heart pounding in time. The van's sole window the front windscreen. John cupping his hand, peering. A man's voice from behind.

'What y'all doing?'

John turned, recognised one of the older vets who had been with O'Brien at the cellar.

Ray said, 'Looking for Murph? He here?'

The guy smiled. 'Well, he's here, but not *here*. I think I saw him heading into the woods for a little bit of discrete conversation with a young lady.'

Ray smiled like he was in on the joke. 'Right. How long ago?'

'Ten minutes or so.'

Ray saluted and made like he was leaving.

Once they passed the fire truck, they ducked back up its other flank and broke into the bush. Frantic banjo at their heels. Shearer was running fast as he could, but this was not a trail, it was thick vegetation. He yelled back over the music, thinning at this distance.

'He won't make it too close. He'll walk her in deep.'

John running too now, branches swiping, spikes spearing. No exact fix on the killer, just heading out in a straight line from the van. Hoping. Shearer obviously thinking the same as John, gesturing a V-shape with his arms. He'd go right, John left.

The foliage varied, tall trees and thick undergrowth, strips of sparser shrubs, grasses. John thinking: if he's going to kill her in broad daylight, he'll want the densest cover. Hurdling low bushes, tall spikey knobs catching him like maces in battle. He could just hear Shearer crashing away. Flashing back to that day in the church with Denise. The madman had made a pit of knives …

Wait – did he hear something? Or was it some instinct that breached reason. He found himself quietening his stride, angling a shade to the left.

Not more than twenty yards away, he caught movement, colour. John drew his gun, stepping forward, cautious. Difficult, the bushes his height here, tall trees shouldering them. Twelve yards, he could see a man. Ten yards, O'Brien a.k.a 'Murphy', naked from the waist up staring down at something. John felt his balls tighten as he pushed forward.

◆◆◆

In a small grassy patch about wide enough for three people to stand, Spring, naked on the ground, bound, gagged, whimpering. Murphy holding forth.

'Shame about Annie. I liked her.'

John trying to get a clear shot, but a trunk five yards ahead blocking. Had to step sideways.

'That other silly bitch with the sailor boyfriend … Wanting to send more boys to be bayonet practice for a bunch of Chinks.' Touching the dog tags on his bare chest. 'Annie told me you found these.'

John saw O'Brien reach for something. By the time he cleared the obstructing branch, steel gleamed in O'Brien's fist.

'You'll be with my brave boy. The Japs cut him in two. Strung the top half of him between two trees, one arm tied to each tree like a Christmas decoration.' O'Brien came out of his reverie. He held a samurai sword, double-handed, swished it like a slugger coming up to bat. 'They cut his mouth into a smile. Mocking us.'

John almost clear now, losing a few words before picking up O'Brien again.

'… granted an honour your frivolous life of drugs and sex would otherwise not deserve. To leave this world as he did.'

O'Brien swept his hands high.

'Drop, the sword. Now.'

O'Brien looked at him, the revolver in John's hand.

'No.'

'I won't ask again.'

'Then you had better shoot. By the time I'm hit she'll be in two pieces.'

John doubted that but—

'You loved him. I get it.' Needing to draw O'Brien. 'Never married, right? You two used to soap one another in the shower. Tug away when the lights went down—'

O'Brien hissing. 'Shut the fuck up. There was nothing like that!'

'Maybe not on his part. Let's face it, good-looking guy, that. Pulling all the girls, was he? Isn't that why you really kill them? Because they have what he wanted. Not your tired old homo—'

O'Brien screamed, 'Liar!' charged.

John fired point-blank into his chest, stepped sideways. Steel and humanity slid to the forest floor. O'Brien on his knees as if in prayer. John raised the gun to fire again. O'Brien pitched forward.

John numb, head ringing. O'Brien hadn't moved by the time Shearer reached him, knelt and felt for a pulse. None. Shearer pulled a knife and cut the girl free. She was sobbing, but John felt nothing.

Ray rested a hand on his shoulder said, 'You alright?'

John resurrected, nodding, smelling the earth, the blood.

◆◆◆

For Gordon's sake, Ray wished he'd been the one to take out the fucking psycho. But fate makes its own choice. The girl had been lying in a puddle of her own urine. Ray soothed her as she clung to him weeping.

'It's okay,' he said over and over. Of course it wasn't, would maybe never be. But she was alive. O'Brien though was well and truly dead. Ray handed Spring her clothes, helped her to dress, she was still shaking.

When she was done, Ray said, 'You can never tell anybody what happened here. Understand?'

She nodded slowly.

John Gordon still had the gun in his hand. Ray took it from him said, 'Help me get him back up.' They pulled O'Brien back to kneeling position. 'How many times did you fire?'

'Just one shot.'

'Good.'

Ray told John to hold O'Brien's body like that. Then he wiped the gun clean, reversed it so it was pointing at the hole in O'Brien's chest and pressed O'Brien's right hand around it, trigger finger in position.

'Let go.'

John did. O'Brien's corpse hit the dirt.

Ray took out his handkerchief, picked up the samurai sword, slid it into its scabbard and placed it in front of the body like he figured a suicidal veteran might have done before the final act. O'Brien had brought with him a long kitbag that held the rope he'd used on Spring, and a shovel. No question what that was to be for. Ray put them back in the bag. He reckoned it was better to leave it looking like a suicide than try to bury the body.

'Come on.' Ray wrapped his arm around Spring, and they started to walk out. John Gordon joining silently.

As they drew closer, he could make out the music again. The song was 'It's All Over Now, Baby Blue'. Ray hoped it was for John Gordon and Spring. But it wasn't for him.

Not quite.

31 A WHITER SHADE OF PALE

Across the Pacific, John under one dark cloud: Would it be possible to pick up with Denise? Had the killings ground him into dust. Instead, back in her arms, like he'd been plugged into the mains again. She was the source of John Gordon, simple as that. Shearer, Spring and he had agreed to never discuss with anyone what had happened up there on the mountain, but that didn't include Denise. Melded in the molten heat of imminent death, there could be no secrets between them. Telling her second day back about how he had screwed up, nearly sent the wrong man to jail for life. He hoped he had atoned for that mistake now.

'I'd have been there. I would have pulled the trigger. That poor girl.'

John looking deep into her eyes, grateful for small mercies. Denise naked and beautiful.

She reached over and placed the huge sombrero on her head. 'Tell me about the bands.' John knew the pain and horror was over then, all of it. When your wife is nude beside you in a sombrero asking you to tell her about the music half-a-world away, the sirocco cannot reach.

John tried to do it justice. 'There is a big concert this weekend. A lot of the same bands that played at the Fantasy Fair are playing in Monterey, a bit south of San Francisco. Jimi Hendrix is playing.' He dropped the needle on the track.

They kissed then as the wind cried Mary.

◆◆◆

Granite had done a good job, and Ray's plan had worked perfectly. The letter sent to the target claiming he was potentially an heir and that he should consult his solicitor to make a formal application sparked action just like a jigger under a horse's saddle. The target bolting to his advisor quick smart. Dempsey, Ray's personal choice to shadow the target, confirming the target had gone just where Ray had suspected: the same solicitor who had acted for him years back when he'd found himself in hot water.

From then on, simple. All Ray had to do was present to the solicitor as a new client with sensitive documents he needed to preserve in the 'right hands' in case some misfortune befell him. The solicitor discrete: he had performed similar functions for others in that situation.

'No offence, but this office doesn't seem exactly secure,' Ray frowning, looking around.

'I assure you it is very secure, but I also have a safe at another location.'

The other location, the solicitor's house in Rose Bay, the one Ray was standing right out front of at 2.30 a.m. on a Tuesday morning. The hedge cover from a little-used road. Granite's intel from his safecracker mate he'd had do the groundwork: the family slept on the second floor of the ersatz Georgian house. Ground floor where the study was boasted a kitchen, dining room, lounge room, laundry and bathroom.

The study was out the back, so Ray skirted the house quietly and used his keys on the simple Lockwood of the back door. A labrador slept in the lounge room, more soundly than normal tonight – a sedative in the meatballs it had found earlier on the back lawn. The study was not locked. The safe itself easy to find behind a door in the lowest level of a large wall cabinet. Not a combination safe even, only a lock. Ray was prepared with a master key, but apparently these locks were harder to trick than your average door's, so the original was best. Fortunately, Granite's expert had located it on his earlier foray. Ray now devoting himself to the study desk, locating the hidden drawer, second on the right. Popping it out, an old watch case, the key inside that.

He removed the key and opened the safe. Jewellery cases, some coins, stamps. Ray ignored those, focused on the valise that had compartments assigned by alphabet. There were only a dozen manila envelopes in all and only one under M. Ray opened it. He allowed himself a smile.

There was nothing like the satisfaction of a job well done.

Replacing everything in order, leaving. Smoke.

◆◆◆

Police HQ. As always. The slow clack of typewriters, cigarette smoke, unattended ringing telephones. He climbed the stairs to Vice, nodded to a number of former colleagues. McDermott was right at the back with the form guide open.

'G'day, Ray. How was Disneyland?'

'Kings Cross with clothes on.'

McDermott and his mates chuckling.

Ray said, 'Have a word?' Heading down the far end of the corridor by the window where blokes would stand and smoke. looking out over the park across the way.

'What's up?'

'Need a favour.'

McDermott a shark. Best way to attract him, blood. A favour meant you were wounded.

'I'm listening.'

'Before I went to the States, there was a house fire in a big place at Cammeray on the water. During the investigation into arson, I happened to find some very nice ice under the floorboards. I'd like to dispose of these diamonds as soon as possible. I believe you may have better contacts than me.'

McDermott grinned, pulled out a packet of Craven A, tapped one out and lit up.

'What's in it for me?'

'Twenty percent.'

McDermott blowing a ring. 'Get serious. Forty.'

'Thirty.'

'You got the merchandise?'

'I hid it on a boat down at the marina. I was going to pick it up, but then I got hauled off to the States so it's still there.'

'Maybe the boat isn't?'

'I checked. It's there. But I didn't want to grab it yet. If I'm holding the stuff and then something goes wrong there's a straight line to me. We could get it tonight.'

'Time?'

'One thirty?'

McDermott nodded. 'One thirty, Cammeray Marina.'

◆◆◆

Ray's guess: McDermott gets there early, scopes. He was nothing if not cautious. But lulled. He had a lot of stuff on Ray, a lot of leverage. But someone takes away your crowbar, all you're left with is a damn big rock.

Ray driving through deserted Sydney. On the radio, a woman singing a haunting country ballad about a farm boy suiciding. Not Nancy Sinatra, but just as good. Something mysterious going down between the boy who kills himself and the girl who is telling the story. Tossing something off the Tallahassee Bridge. There were always undercurrents, always something lurking. Like McDermott.

If he was a dog, you wouldn't approach unless he was muzzled.

It was 1.25 a.m. when Ray arrived, the place desolate. As expected, McDermott already there. Ray recognised the immaculate HD, olive with a white top. He was alone.

Ray parked. The light clink of rigging carried on a strong wind. It was cold. Ray signalled McDermott follow him and started up the jetty to where boats were moored. There was a locked gate topped with barbed wire, but it was easily negotiated by pulling in a dinghy moored on the shore side, climbing in, then letting it drift around the gate from where they were able to haul themselves up onto the jetty the harbour side of the gate.

The launch was a beauty, wooden, stately close on forty feet. Ray eased himself aboard and McDermott followed. Ray headed into the cabin, fiddled around under an inbuilt locker, came out with Tupperware. He opened a lunchbox, removed a small felt bag. Tossed it to McDermott. He peered in.

When McDermott looked up, confused from what turned out to be nothing but kids' marbles, he was staring into the barrel of Ray's revolver.

'What the fuck's going on, Ray?'

'You and me have unfinished business, Mac. You nearly cost John Gordon and his girl their lives. And remember Michael Foley? We killed him because of you.'

McDermott said evenly. 'We've been over this, Ray. I have a document that details you, your brother, all the dirty linen.'

'What if I don't give a fuck? What if I'm dying of cancer?'

'You look fucking healthy as a sinner to me, Ray.'

'What if I found out that your document was in the safe of a solicitor in Rose Bay?'

Ray saw the instant shock in Mac's face, saw him trace the line and arrive at home.

And, just as he expected, Mac went straight for his gun.

Ray punched two into his chest. Mac looked shocked before he crumpled onto the canvas drop sheet Ray had placed earlier in the day when he planted the marbles. He had promised Granite that his horse-trainer mate, whose boat it was, would not find a thing out of place. McDermott breathing. Just. Ray staring down at him.

'You didn't have to do what you did, Mac. You were just plain greedy. I will ask my brother to say a prayer for you.'

McDermott's face contorted from rage and pain.

'... uck you.'

Ray would have put one in Mac's head but did not want to risk a hole in the boat so let him bleed out while he cast off and headed off through the heads and to open sea. The canvas was weighted, and sharks were attracted to blood, big bad blood. Now Ray could finally wash his hands of it, finally breathe easy.

That chapter was closed.

32 THE END

Weeks on. The bookies' Caulfield and Melbourne Cup doubles arriving in the post. Radiators and Simpson electric blankets stored, Electrolux three-speeds out of hibernation. Still generating heat: gossip on the baffling case of Inspector McDermott, vanished off the face of the earth. Whispers between the dunny partitions of HQ: his past had caught up with him. Others pointing to his beloved car being abandoned at Bankstown Airport where light planes could depart without scrutiny. Ray had started both rumours. It was easy.

'Say, did you hear that Mac had double-crossed a certain night-club owner up in the Cross? I heard he took a downpayment to guarantee a licence, but it got knocked back.'

And: 'I heard on the grapevine he had bought a beachside block in Thailand.' Someone sold the rumours to the Telegraph. Once in print, practically gospel.

By Christmas week though, the only thing anybody cared about was turkey, roast chicken and gifts for the kids. Ray springing for lunch for his Arson boys: steak sandwich and beer. The summer air making everybody lazy. One of his sergeants had been reading a cheap paper magazine, *Terrible Crimes*. The sort of pulp you shelled out for along with the crosswords and *Witchetty's Tribe*. Ray's Pelaco getting whiffy under the arms as he put his feet up, smirked at his brown shoes, remembering what Frank Zappa had to say about brown shoes. Ray began browsing the magazine, the litany of horror crimes: *The Pyjama Girl, Hindley and Brady*.

Stopped cold. *The Black Dahlia*.

Peering up at him the face of Elizabeth Short a.k.a. the Black

Dahlia. It wasn't the first time he'd read about the case but whatever memory remained had been almost buried. Almost.

Now he knew why the photo of the girl he'd found in Purcell's shed had pricked him.

◆◆◆

'You sure?' With John Gordon now at the Bricklayers, Gordon studying the photo.

'Yeah. I must have read this story sometime. You don't forget those eyes. Those eyes were on a photo in that shed. And there was another shot, her thigh with a rose tattoo. There must have been another three women at least from that era.'

Gordon reading aloud. 'The body was found on a lot in Los Angeles in nineteen forty-seven by a mother pushing her pram. Severed in two, the body was posed oddly. Gashes roughly three inches long had been carved across her face from the edges of her mouth ...'

He put the magazine down, took a long slug of beer.

'What O'Brien said the Japs did to Thomas Purcell.'

Ray said, 'In September nineteen forty-three, Elizabeth Short was arrested for drinking at the El Paseo Restaurant in Santa Barbara. She used to work at the mail exchange general store at the Camp Cooke base. Where old man Purcell worked. I saw a photo of him standing out front of what I reckon was that very building. I'm thinking the boys could have been back home on a furlough, could have known Elizabeth. Maybe O'Brien was with them. Maybe Thomas Purcell and Elizabeth got on, and O'Brien didn't like that. Or maybe he wasn't even there but in nineteen forty-seven O'Brien is in LA with Les Purcell when they run into Short. Something sets him off ...'

'He tries to fuck her and can't manage it. Or she says he's nowhere near as good as Thomas was.'

'Yeah. She mocks him or Purcell and then he justifies his rage by telling himself her murder is a monument to Thomas Purcell.'

'And he keeps doing it over the years.' Gordon a bitter half-smile, absorbing it. 'We scrubbed the murderer of the Black Dhalia, mate.'

Ray drained his beer said, 'Shame we can't tell anybody.'

EPILOGUE: PIECE OF MY HEART

October 1968. The Healing TV pulsing black-and-white glory. Ralph Doubell coming from nowhere to take Olympic gold in the men's 800. Ray on his feet cheering. Cassie laughing at him. Not used to her father getting so excited. Mexico City. Ray had been to Mexico, could you ever believe that!

Yet another postcard written to Hector, just waiting for a stamp. So far, he'd sent about seven and Hector had replied, apologising for his English. Ray's Spanish stopped at *cerveza* and *gracias, señor*.

He hadn't forgotten his Disneyland promise to the girls. Granite had told him that Rain Lover was a certainty in the Melbourne Cup. Ray's plan, whack a hundred on. If it won, Disneyland for all.

Later, after tea, Ray watering the small back garden, watching the mist from the hose. Sensing somebody there. Turned to find John Gordon. They hadn't seen much of one another lately. They never needed to. Ray turning off the tap, pleased.

'Hey, stranger, you want a beer?'

'I wish. Got a homicide in Pyrmont. But I've been meaning to give you this.'

He held out the twelve-inch square LP. The artwork was incredible, like a giant cartoon.

John said, 'I didn't know if you realised it had come out.'

◆◆◆

Marie had long gone to bed. It was warm and there was a frog or something croaking outside. Ray sat in the armchair and put the album on the phonogram, waiting till now, some solo pleasure. The only illumination, moonlight through the window. He listened to her smoky voice and his mind drifted back to a hot night on a studio roof under barely any moon. She'd been recording this then, hadn't she? Or working on these songs at least.

Funny how life turned out. Martin Davis looking for the wrong guy, thinking his girl was dead. If he hadn't been so obsessed, she would have died too. He actually saved the life of the girl who wanted to be rid of him. Judy Ikin was murdered by an ex-serviceman because she wanted to support servicemen. John Gordon who didn't give a toss about Elvis got to gab on with him while Ray who worshipped Elvis got indigestion.

Nothing made sense.

Least of all him and Janis. You couldn't get two more fucking opposites. The music stirred the smell of Barney's Beanery, leather vests stained in motor oil, sweat and too-fast living coming off Janis' skin. His loneliness and guilt. But he remembered that night with her so clear. And he wondered if she'd been thinking of him when she sang this. He wondered if they could ever meet again. He wanted to believe that. Ray closed his eyes.

He desperately wanted to believe.

AUTHOR'S NOTE AND ACKNOWLEDGMENTS

Could there have been any place further removed from the hippie-psychedelic maw of Haight-Ashbury in the northern summer of '67 than the cold concrete corridors of my Christian Brothers school situated in Perth, the most isolated city in the world? I doubt it.

Okay, it wasn't a gulag, but it wasn't that far removed. You risked a beating if any of the three buses you needed to catch to get to school broke down and you were late. You would definitely cop the cuts from the Latin teacher if you got more than one out of ten wrong in your vocab. You could be expelled for hair that reached below your collar, and I'm not sure that those caught talking during general assembly were ever seen again after the sound of their indoor thrashing reverberated around our quadrangle.

And yet because of this repressive atmosphere, anything that represented freedom of thought and expression detonated among we students like an atomic bomb. I suppose it was a bit like being a young Czech at the same time, living under totalitarian rule.

When the summer of love bloomed, I was midway between my thirteenth and fourteenth birthday and like my closest friends my world revolved around football, cricket, Marvel comics, and most of all music.

The Beatles had driven us all euphoric just a few years before but then along came 1967. Long before we could actually hear these exotic bands, we discovered them by teen publications like *Hullabaloo*. In those days it could take months before a US or UK release made its way to Perth. So, our eyes boggled as we read about The Mothers of Invention, The Doors, Country Joe & the

Fish, Peanut Butter Conspiracy, Buffalo Springfield and so on. We even collected names of obscure bands in notebooks and waited impatiently to hear what the artists sounded like.

Finally, 'underground' music arrived on the actual vinyl. We saved our pennies, begged for birthday gifts from our parents, pooled our collections, and 'blew our minds' listening to the array of amazing bands. Some were nothing like we imagined. Sopwith Camel for instance wasn't a crazed guitar band at all. Hendrix defied gravity. The Doors were every bit as menacing as their press indicated. In Perth at that time the radio stations didn't play underground music, apart from some cross over singles that were kind of psychedelic pop: Green Tambourine, Sandcastles, Run Run Run, Psychotic Reaction.

However, Peter Holland on the ABC (6WF back then) did. Holland was our champion. He had a late-night show (well, for us it was late night) and we would sleep with the transistor under our pillow. Sometimes he'd get bumped by live cricket from South Africa. That was okay, we all played cricket anyway. But other times he would play Vanilla Fudge, or Climax Chicago Blues Band or Grateful Dead. Brilliant.

I can't overstate the influence these artists had on us. Favourites of mine were Country Joe & the Fish, the Doors and Vanilla Fudge. I loved the electronic organ sound.

A year or so on when my friend Michael O'Rourke got an import copy of a Mothers album where Frank Zappa had listed his influences, we found ourselves investigating Pinter, Ionesco, Grappelli, Kafka, Segovia and other hitherto unknown artists. Music, art, drama was all new and wonderful and we experienced it thanks to Zappa.

On radio David Ellery joined the Holland charge and we started to get more great music. Even though we were too young to go to licensed gigs, Michael, Al Howard and I would hit youth dances where local musicians like Dennis James, Al Kash, Rex Bullen and Steve Tallis had us gaping in awe.

We started forming garage bands. Al on guitar (left-handed),

Michael bass, Phil Riseborough or Mark Rodoreda on drums. I played organ, natch. We tried to write songs, made up album covers and posters. With another good friend David Hodgekiss, I would do the record shop rounds, pose for 'groovy' psychedelic photos and just try and be hip.

Therefore, I want to acknowledge all those bands who made our lives exciting, whether they were from San Francisco or Perth. Foremost, I must pay tribute to those who make it into the book, most especially Janis Joplin. I hope she's not offended at her portrayal.

To Peter Holland and David Ellery for bringing us the music via the radio, and in more recent times, Cool Bill McGinnis who has been super helpful, bless you and all those who shared the experience of being thousands of miles from the action in sleepy Perth.

Of course, this is a fictional story. I have tried to use as many real concerts and dates as possible in telling this story. I think there was only one show I made up to fit. Some of the streets are real, some not. I might have got plenty of stuff wrong. I wasn't around in LA or San Francisco in 1967 so maybe the bars aren't how I described them, or the neighbourhoods were a little different, but I hope the emotional veracity connects nonetheless.

In relation to *Summer of Blood* the book, I must pour out love and vibes to my editor Georgia Richter who jumped on board *Summer of Blood* like it was a roaring Harley. Georgia is not just a great editor, she is always supportive and fun. The Fremantle Press promotion team led by Claire Miller also can take a piece of my heart for the great work I am sure they are about to embark upon. Jane Fraser, CEO at the time the book was commissioned, has since headed out on the highway looking for adventure and whatever might come her way, but I thank her for the belief in the book. Also, all those on the distribution end from Fremantle and Penguin. Apart from Cathy Szabo, we don't meet but I know you're out there working hard on my behalf. I must, too, thank Jane Palfreyman, who way back in 1999 published *Big Bad Blood*, the book that first brought Ray Shearer and John Gordon into the fictional world. It wasn't till 2017 that I found what I thought was an idea worthy to bring them back. My agent, Wanda Bergin, will also, I know, be doing all she can to spread the love, thanks Wanda.

Without my wife, Nicole, I simply would not be able to fashion these stories. I owe her more than can be expressed here for the positivity and support in every way. She is one in a trillion.

I will, however, withhold any praise from those music publishers who, for quoting lyrics, wanted fees that would have been more than what I will get for writing the whole book. It's a shame because those artists deserve every chance to reach out and touch even one new fan. In the original draft, the song lyrics fitted deeply with the action and psychological space of the characters but that's life. Thanks though, to Robert Griffin at Hal Leonard for his assistance and professionalism.

Last, I want to thank whoever you are right now reading this book. I hope I did well. I hope you enjoy it, for I loved every minute of its creation.

For those who would like to enjoy the soundtrack to the book, listen to this Spotify playlist:

open.spotify.com/playlist/1TpvX33jsEaB2XhMsJtibm

Dave Warner

ABOUT THE AUTHOR

Dave Warner is an author, musician and screenwriter. *Summer of Blood* is his twelfth adult novel, with previous novels winning the Western Australian Premier's Book Award for Fiction and the Ned Kelly Award for best Australian crime fiction. Set in 1967, *Summer of Blood* is the second novel to feature detectives Ray Shearer and John Gordon, following on from *Big Bad Blood*, set in 1965.

Dave first came to national prominence in 1978 with his gold album *Mug's Game* and his band Dave Warner's from the Suburbs. *Summer of Blood* pays tribute to many of Dave's musical heroes of his youth. Dave continues to write and record music, has been named a Western Australian State Living Treasure and has been inducted into the WAMi Rock'n'Roll of Renown. Connect with Dave here:

davewarner.com.au
Instagram @davew.author
X @SuburbanWarner
facebook.com/Dave-Warner-370719336278939
Youtube @mrmugsgame

First published 2023 by
FREMANTLE PRESS

Fremantle Press Inc. trading as Fremantle Press
PO Box 158, North Fremantle, Western Australia 6159
fremantlepress.com.au

Cover image by Jesse Ballantyne / unsplash.com
Cover design by Nada Backovic, nadabackovic.com
Printed and bound by IPG

 A catalogue record for this
book is available from the
National Library of Australia

ISBN 9781760992200 (paperback)
ISBN 9781760992217 (ebook)

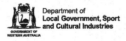

Fremantle Press is supported by the State Government through the
Department of Local Government, Sport and Cultural Industries.

Fremantle Press respectfully acknowledges the Whadjuk people of the
Noongar nation as the traditional owners and custodians of the land where
we work in Walyalup.